HIDDEN
IN
SHADOWS

ALSO BY VIVECA STEN

Hidden in Snow

Still Waters

Closed Circles

Guiltless

Tonight You're Dead

In the Heat of the Moment

In Harm's Way

In the Shadow of Power

In the Name of Truth

In Bad Company

Buried in Secret

HIDDEN
IN
SHADOWS

TRANSLATED BY
MARLAINE DELARGY

VIVECA STEN

AMAZON **CROSSING**

Previously published as *Dalskuggan* by Forum in Sweden in 2021. Translated from Swedish by Marlaine Delargy. First published in English by Amazon Crossing in 2023.

Published by Amazon Crossing, Seattle

www.apub.com

Amazon, the Amazon logo, and Amazon Crossing are trademarks of Amazon.com, Inc., or its affiliates.

ISBN-13: 9781542037518 (paperback)
ISBN-13: 9781542037525 (digital)

Cover design by Ploy Siripant
Cover image: © Szabo Ervin / Alamy Stock Photo; © Dudarev Mikhail,
  © nblx / Shutterstock

Printed in the United States of America

To my father
Tord Bergstedt
1933–2020

SATURDAY, FEBRUARY 22, 2020

1

It is minus twelve degrees Celsius as Anna Larsson drives along Tångbölevägen, which is a very narrow road. Seven-year-old Hugo is in the back seat in his skiing clothes. They are on their way to Duved for slalom training, which begins at eight o'clock on Saturdays.

Dawn is creeping across the sky, but it is still only half-light.

A movement up ahead causes Anna to slow down. The other day, there was a reindeer standing on the bend—you have to keep your eyes open. Then she realizes it is only a little hare scampering across the frozen ground. It stops, turns around, and continues in among the trees.

"Mommy," Hugo pipes up. "I need to pee."

"Can't you wait, sweetheart?" Anna says over her shoulder. "We'll be there soon."

"I need to pee *now*."

Anna sighs. They are only fifteen minutes away from Duved, and it is bitterly cold outside. However, Hugo tends to wet himself if the situation becomes too urgent.

The road widens, and she pulls over to the side.

"Hurry up," she says to her son, who has already begun to unfasten his seat belt.

He clambers out and trudges over to some bushes a few yards away. After a very short time, he is back, yanking the door open and looking agitated.

"There's a man lying on the ground!"

"What do you mean?"

"Over there—he's hurt himself!" Hugo insists.

It's probably nothing, Anna thinks. She doesn't have time to go and look; they must get going. In thirty minutes, Hugo needs to be standing by the lift at Duved, ready for action. It takes him a while to get his gear on, and she dislikes pressuring him.

On the other hand, Hugo doesn't usually tell lies.

What if there is someone lying there?

She can see in the rearview mirror that her son is not himself. He is wide eyed and seems upset. The feeling that she ought to go and check, just to be on the safe side, grows stronger.

"Okay. You wait here and I'll be right back."

As soon as she opens the door, the cold sinks its teeth into her. She can feel it on the skin around her nostrils, and her breath immediately forms a white cloud. The birch trees look like statues made of rime frost.

Anna plods through the snow, following the same route as Hugo. As she slips and grabs hold of a branch, she suddenly realizes what is in front of her.

Hidden among the bushes, there is a man lying on the ground. His hands are bound behind his back. His face is bloody.

She stares at the body.

The snow covers the dead man like a powdery blanket, but there is no hiding the deep wound in the back of his head.

The white surroundings absorb every sound.

A wave of nausea rises from her stomach, and she has to swallow hard to stop herself from throwing up. She stumbles back to the car to call for help.

2

A shrill signal wakes Detective Inspector Hanna Ahlander on Saturday morning.

She gropes for her phone, still half-asleep. The bedsheets are sweaty thanks to a nightmare about the assault she suffered in Barcelona. It still haunts her, despite the years that have passed and the expertise she has developed investigating violence against vulnerable women.

Who is calling this early on the weekend? It's barely eight. She had been looking forward to sleeping in after a night out with friends. Tomorrow her sister, Lydia, will be arriving with her family to spend the winter sports break in Åre, and the house will be anything but quiet—Lydia's children will make sure of that.

What if something has gone wrong at the last minute?

Anxiety about her sister makes her take the call, holding her breath.

"Are you awake?" Daniel Lindskog says in her ear.

Daniel is her closest colleague. They know each other well, but don't socialize outside work. Technically they are both attached to the Serious Crimes Unit based in Östersund, but Daniel is a few years older than Hanna and holds a more senior position. He is also the person who arranged her current post in Åre/Östersund.

"Mmm," Hanna mumbles sleepily. She forces her eyes open and rolls over onto her back. As usual she hasn't pulled down the blind; she doesn't want to shut out the glorious view of the lake.

Not that it makes much difference today. The sun is on its way up, but the mountain known as Renfjället is swathed in thick, gray fog.

Heavy snowflakes are falling from the sky, and the fir tree outside the window is now clothed in a white shroud.

Hanna blinks, failing to focus her gaze or marshal her thoughts.

"We've found a body," Daniel says; she can hear the tension in his voice. "Suspected homicide."

"What?"

Hanna is wide awake now. She sits up, pushes her tousled brown hair off her face. Homicide? It's been only two months since their last major investigation.

"The call came in a little while ago," Daniel continues. "A man's body has been found near Tångböle, between here and the Norwegian border."

Hanna tries to process the information. She hasn't lived in Åre for very long and isn't yet familiar with all the place-names.

"What do we know so far?"

Her voice sounds hoarse, unused. Yesterday she had dinner at the wine bar with her new friend Karro. It wasn't a late night, but right now she wishes she had said no to that last drink. She's not sure she should get behind the wheel of her car this morning, but she doesn't want to share that with Daniel.

"It seems the body is in a pretty bad state," he says. "It looks like an execution. Not good."

They have worked together for only a few months, but she can tell how stressed he is. A door slams, the rushing of the wind forms a background to his voice.

"Can you be ready in fifteen minutes? I'll pick you up."

No time off this weekend, then. At least she won't have to drive, thank goodness.

She reaches for her jeans and sweater, on the floor by the bed. "No problem. See you shortly."

She quickly washes her face, ties her hair back in a ponytail, and gets dressed. Then she goes up to the kitchen on the ground floor. Lydia

4

and her husband own this luxury mountain home; Hanna has been living here since she left Stockholm in December.

Her head is spinning. Another serious crime in Åre. A shudder runs down her spine.

She switches on the coffee machine, presses the button for extra strong. Through the kitchen window she sees Daniel's car arrive. He sounds the horn a couple of times, and with one last look at the mess in the sink—she really must clean up before Lydia gets here—she grabs her jacket and steps outside.

The cold air takes her breath away. It is absolutely freezing. She should have put on an extra sweater but doesn't want to run back inside when Daniel is already waiting.

He leans over and opens the passenger door. His expression is grim.

Despite the gravity of the situation, she is pleased to see him.

She is always pleased to see him.

3

The flashing lights of the emergency vehicles color the winter landscape alternately white and blue as Daniel and Hanna approach the scene. Several police cars are parked along the road, and the area has already been cordoned off.

The information received from the regional dispatch in Umeå had been disturbing. The woman who called in had talked about a badly mutilated body; from her description, it sounded horrific.

What's going on? Daniel couldn't help thinking back to the case last December; it had hit him very hard. At any moment he can conjure up the image of the pallid corpse in the snow by the VM6 ski lift.

He takes a deep breath, gets out of the car. The cold immediately strikes his face. At times like these he is grateful for his dark-brown beard, which offers at least some protection for his chin.

He and Hanna make their way to the spot where the snow-covered body is lying among the bushes. They try to keep their distance to avoid contaminating the scene. The CSIs haven't arrived yet, and the one who lives closest, Carina Grankvist, is in Mattmar. They can only dream of a local pathologist up here; resources are heavily centralized in the northern police district. The forensic pathology lab is in Umeå, where the body will be sent once the CSIs have finished.

It is light enough to see properly now. Daniel immediately understands why the regional dispatch referred to a serious crime. The man on the ground has a gaping wound in the back of his head. His hands are secured behind his back with cable ties; his fingers look as if they have frozen together.

The platinum wedding ring is barely visible against the bluish-white skin.

"Seems as if someone smashed his skull," Hanna says. His dark-brown hair is smeared with dried blood, and despite the snow, fragments of bone can be seen among the sludgy mess.

"Someone who was really angry," she adds quietly.

The wind has picked up, and a sudden gust moves the tops of the tall firs. A little snow tumbles down from a thick branch and is whirled along the road.

The body is lying on its side, one cheek turned toward the forest. Daniel can see clear signs of violence. The nose is damaged, presumably broken. Blood has poured down over the lips and chin, onto the collar of his jacket.

He notices a faint shadow of stubble, which could mean that the guy was attacked in the evening or at night, several hours after his last shave.

"I'd put him at around thirty-five," Hanna says. "A little over medium height, at least six feet. Weight approximately one hundred and ninety pounds."

The victim looks like a typical Swede, with winter-pale skin and short, dark-brown hair. *Not so different from me,* Daniel thinks. They must be about the same age.

That's how quickly life can end.

He studies the clothing from a distance. The man is wearing jeans and a sweater, but no jacket, boots, or gloves, which suggests that he was indoors when he was attacked. If he had been killed outdoors, he should have been warmly dressed.

How did he get here? They are quite a ways from the nearest populated area; plus if the assault had happened here, there would be more blood, more footprints, other signs of a struggle. On the other hand, the overnight snowfall has laid a soft blanket over the forest landscape. The world is hidden in white.

All he can see are fresh paw prints from a small hare.

Hanna looks up; her face is pale.

"Looks as if we have a new homicide case on our hands," she says quietly.

Daniel meets his colleague's gaze. He knows what she is thinking. They only just got through the previous investigation; now they must gather their strength again.

Hanna points to something under one of the trees, half-concealed by the snow.

"What's that?"

She moves forward cautiously, drops down on one knee, and picks up the object. It is a shabby black leather wallet.

"So not a mugging," Daniel says automatically. If it were, the wallet would have been missing.

Hanna checks the contents and holds up a pink driver's license.

"Johan Lars Andersson, born 1985. Do you know if he's local?"

Daniel thinks for a moment. It sounds familiar, but both the first name and the surname are among the most common in Sweden. The face is so badly beaten that it is impossible to recognize the man.

"No idea," he admits.

Hanna stands up, brushes the snow off her legs. A few flakes drift through the air and land on the ground.

"I wonder what he's done to make the perpetrator attack him with such violence," Daniel muses, almost to himself. "It really is brutal."

REBECKA

2012

Rebecka Ekvall is curled up on the wide window seat. She doesn't care about the draft; this is her favorite place in her bedroom. It has been ever since she was a little girl with blond braids. She has always loved sitting here in the blue hour, when the sun has dipped below the horizon and the evening light is at its softest.

A car is approaching along the main road. Two headlights turn into the yard and illuminate the last of the asters in the flower beds. It has been a cold summer, and soon it will be winter. The snow usually begins to fall in October this far north.

Rebecka leans forward to see better.

Two men get out of the car. One is Pastor Jan-Peter Jonsäter; she has been listening to him all her life. The other makes her catch her breath. He is Ole Nordhammar, the assistant pastor who works with youth projects. On Tuesdays he runs Bible evenings for older teenagers. Rebecka has never missed a single one.

What is he doing here?

A faint tingle passes through her body. Ole is the kind of person that the boys admire and the girls swoon over. He is good looking and charismatic. He has a way of talking that makes you feel special— chosen, in fact. Rebecka has had a secret crush on him for a while but has never uttered more than a few words in his presence. She is much too shy; she gets tongue-tied and blushes as soon as he looks at her.

Ole strides toward the front door. He is wearing a handsome dark-blue tweed jacket that fits his broad shoulders perfectly. Rebecka's father, Stefan, steps out onto the porch and warmly shakes the two men's hands.

Rebecka narrows her eyes; her curiosity is aroused. They rarely have visitors here at Storvallen. It is close to the Norwegian border, and isolated. The nearest neighbor lives quite a distance away. Since she finished high school in June and began to help with the sheep and the small dairy, she has spent most of her time at home. She sees people only when she attends church or her Bible studies in Snasadalen.

It doesn't really matter. Her parents have always been strict about who she is allowed to hang out with; it was important that she stuck with the other children in the church community when she was growing up. By the time she began the childcare and leisure program at the high school in Järpen, she was already used to avoiding contact with *the others*.

"The lost," as her father refers to them. The ungodly.

Rebecka mainly feels sorry for them. They have lost their way here on Earth. They have not understood that God's love is their salvation.

She herself is deeply grateful that she has been fortunate enough to grow up within the church. Mother and Father were already members of the Light of Life before she was born—as were their parents before them.

They have all had the privilege of walking through the valley of the Lord.

She hears the murmur of voices from downstairs. She goes over to the door, tries to listen. Father says something, but she can't make it out. Then it seems as if they move into the main room; the voices fade.

Rebecka lies down on the bed and wonders if she ought to do some reading from the Holy Scripture in preparation for next Tuesday's Bible evening with Ole, but after only a few minutes, Father calls to her from the bottom of the stairs.

"Rebecka, could you come down?"

She doesn't know how to react. He doesn't usually want her or Mother around when Pastor Jonsäter comes by. It is the men who take the lead within the church, while the women are responsible for home and family. It is a natural division of labor—that's what it says in the Bible.

"Rebecka?" her father says again.

She looks around the bedroom with its yellow-striped wallpaper. She doesn't have a mirror—that would encourage vanity. However, she smooths down her braided hair and tucks her blouse into her skirt.

The three men are seated in the living room, drinking coffee and eating cookies. Her mother, Ann-Sofie, is busy in the kitchen and gives Rebecka a cautious smile as she passes by.

"Good evening," Rebecka says; should she curtsy, or step forward and hold out her hand?

Her father nods encouragingly.

"Come and sit down," he says, pointing to the space on the sofa beside Ole.

Her body is tingling with nerves; they are only inches apart, she has never been this close to him. She can smell his aftershave, a manly aroma of something exciting and worldly. Ole's dark hair ends in a neat line at the nape of his neck, which is broad and firm.

It is hard to believe that he is almost thirty-three. He really is attractive, even though he's so old.

Ole favors her with his smile. Rebecka blushes, she can't help it, and has to look away.

Her mother pokes her head around the door, the coffeepot in her hand.

"Anyone for a refill?" she asks tentatively.

Father frowns. "Not now. Can't you see we're busy?"

Mother blinks. The apology is instant. "Sorry. I won't disturb you." She disappears back into the kitchen.

Rebecka wonders why her mother doesn't realize that the men want to be left in peace. She herself would never dream of bothering them in that way; she knows better and sits quietly on the sofa. She has seen Father's stony expression when they have had guests and Mother has failed to behave properly, heard the sobs when he has chastised her after the visitors have gone.

The three men continue to chat. Rebecka keeps her hands folded in her lap; there is no coffee cup set out for her. Occasionally Ole bestows another warm smile on her, and every time, her cheeks flush red. Once he even winks at her, but mostly he talks to Father and Pastor Jonsäter.

It's fine; Rebecka is perfectly happy to be so close to him. Just wait until she tells Lisen, her best friend, that Ole has been to their house!

Eventually the pastor gets to his feet.

"It's good that the young people have had the chance to get to know each other," he announces contentedly.

Rebecka is confused; she and Ole haven't exactly conversed. But he smiles again, and she goes weak at the knees.

"I've noticed you at our Bible evenings," he says. "You're such an eager participant in our study of the Holy Scripture."

Rebecka turns even redder. Questions are burning on her tongue as they say goodbye in the hallway, but she dare not open her mouth. Instead, she goes up to her room.

What was this meeting about?

An inner voice whispers an answer that she can hardly bring herself to acknowledge. God has a plan for her. Ole might think she is suitable to be a pastor's wife.

She will turn nineteen in November—high time to find a husband. Her mother married at the age of eighteen, just like most of the girls in the community. If Rebecka hadn't gone to high school, she would probably have been engaged already.

She doesn't know what to think. It seems presumptuous to entertain such an idea. The thought that a man like Ole could be interested in her, timid little Rebecka, so young and insignificant.

But the warmth in his expression when he looked at her this evening . . .

She drops to her knees, closes her eyes, and clasps her hands in prayer. She pictures Ole's blue-gray eyes, his well-formed features, his firm chin.

Her body tingles with excitement.

She is certain that God will show her the way.

Daniel is thinking about the dead man as he drives away from the scene. Hanna is sitting beside him in silence.

They are on the way to Staa, a place so small that it is barely visible on the map; its main claim to fame is that it houses one of the community's recycling centers. The victim, Johan Andersson, lived there with his wife, Marion Weiss Andersson. It seems likely that she doesn't yet know what has happened to her husband.

He is gone, brutally murdered with a cruelty that reminds Daniel of the years he served in the suburbs of Gothenburg. Serious violence was ever present in the city. Here in Åre, crime tends not to be quite so shocking and ruthless.

That's why he moved here three years ago, but it will be a long time before he forgets the sight of Johan. The battered face, the deep wound in his head . . . and he'd been left on the ground with his hands tied behind his back like a piece of dead meat.

It seems like revenge of almost biblical proportions.

What had the poor guy done to be subjected to something so vicious?

"How are you doing?" Hanna asks, glancing up from her phone. She is busy checking various databases in order to find a picture of the victim.

Daniel shivers and zips up his jacket. "This wasn't exactly how I was planning to spend the weekend."

"I know." Hanna manages a wan smile. "I can't believe we're facing another homicide case so soon after . . ."

She doesn't need to go on.

"Johan was a plumber," she says instead. "He owned his own business, together with a colleague named Linus Sundin. The firm is called Andersson and Sundin Plumbing, and Johan's wife takes care of the bookkeeping."

Daniel appreciates that Hanna has started looking into Johan's background right away.

She keeps scrolling. "Wow," she says quietly.

"What?"

"There's quite an age difference between Johan and Marion. She's forty-four, he was thirty-four."

Ten years. Same gap as between Daniel and his partner, Ida—he's thirty-six, she's twenty-six. They met at a nightclub eighteen months ago, were attracted to each other like magnets, and he fell madly, passionately in love. However, he has realized that society is more forgiving when the man is older rather than vice versa.

"It seems as if Marion and Johan married when she was thirty-four and he was twenty-four," Hanna continues. "That's pretty young for a Swedish guy, especially given that they probably dated for a while before the wedding."

"True. Any children?"

"No—in spite of a long marriage." Hanna smiles again. "Not quite the same as for you and Ida."

They know each other well by this stage. Daniel has told her that Ida's pregnancy early in their relationship was unplanned; they had been together for just over a year when little Alice came into the world. He sees his daughter in his mind's eye, five months old now. She was born in September, fulfilling a dream Daniel had held for many years to start a family one day. Right now, she is probably gurgling in her highchair while Ida eats breakfast. He still has the same strong feelings for his girlfriend, but he must admit that having a baby has been much harder than he ever could have imagined.

A sign displaying the word STAA appears, and Daniel turns left onto a narrow road that reminds him of the one where Johan Andersson was found just a few hours ago. There is little indication that the snowplow has passed through. Daniel is grateful for the car's four-wheel drive; up here it's essential.

The Anderssons live on Dalövägen.

Hanna pushes back a few strands of dark-brown hair with her right hand. She is also finding the situation difficult. There are tense lines around her mouth, and her shoulders are slightly hunched.

"I hate conversations like this," she confides. "I wish it was over."

Daniel nods. Informing someone of a death is one of the worst aspects of police work. "I know, but it has to be done."

Hanna chews on a cuticle and looks out the window. "It's still hard."

Even though Hanna only joined the team in December, Daniel feels closer to her than any of his other colleagues. They both live in Åre but often travel together to Östersund, usually two or three times a week. This has enabled them to get to know each other better. They often just chat, but sometimes the conversation goes deeper. Daniel has heard a great deal about Christian, Hanna's former partner, and the ongoing dispute about their shared apartment—Christian is refusing to pay her any money on the property.

Daniel hasn't been quite so open about the problems between him and Ida, especially when work takes precedence. He does talk about her and Alice a lot, though. And Hanna probably suspects that everything isn't necessarily rosy at home; it's rarely easy to be married to a police officer.

She focuses on her screen once more.

"Now I get it," she says suddenly. "Johan's wife is from Germany—she was born in Ramsau—that's a ski resort in Bavaria, isn't it?"

16

Daniel hasn't a clue. He's not particularly familiar with German geography.

"That explains her name—I thought it sounded Germanic."

"What about Johan?"

"He was born and grew up in Duved and attended the ski academy in Järpen. Apparently, he was a very good skier as a teenager, and competed for several years. Maybe that's how they met—in the Alps?"

Daniel realizes that he knows exactly who the victim is. He's *that* Johan Andersson, the skier from Duved who was a member of the national team. It didn't click at first, because both the first name and the surname are so common.

Now he understands, and somehow that makes the situation worse. This murder is going to grab the headlines.

"Why would someone kill an ordinary guy, a plumber?" Hanna wonders gloomily. "What could the motive possibly be?"

"It's too early to say."

"Money? Some kind of revenge? I'm guessing the perpetrator was known to him—that's usually the case." She sighs. "Women are murdered by men, and men are murdered by other men."

Daniel knows that from a statistical point of view, she is right. She also has an impressive level of expertise after seven years with the City Police in Stockholm, working mainly on domestic violence.

Hanna is passionate about helping vulnerable women, and her skills were invaluable when they solved the case in December.

Before long they arrive at Johan Andersson's home—a dark-brown house with a garage in the same color. The yard has been cleared of snow, and a Volkswagen Passat is parked on the drive.

Daniel feels a sense of dread.

This is the worst kind of conversation.

Telling someone that a loved one has died.

5

The door opens almost as soon as Daniel knocks. A woman in jeans and a black polo-neck sweater is standing there. Her brown hair is streaked with gray at the temples, and she has dark circles beneath her eyes.

This must be Marion, Johan's wife.

Poor woman.

Daniel tries to explain who they are without frightening her, but Marion's hand flies to her mouth as soon as she hears the word *police*.

"Has something happened?" she gasps. Her German accent is noticeable.

"Can we come in and sit down?" Hanna asks gently. Daniel gives her a grateful look; she's good in situations like this.

Marion's face is ashen.

"We can go into the kitchen," she says, leading the way into a white-painted room where both the cupboard doors and countertops are pretty shabby. Beyond the kitchen they can see the living room, a few steps down in an extension.

"I'm afraid we have some bad news," Daniel says as soon as they are seated at the oval dining table. He takes a deep breath as Marion's eyes fill with tears. Naturally she realizes that something bad has happened; Daniel feels so sorry for her, but she must be informed.

"Unfortunately, your husband is dead. I'm very sorry."

Marion stares at him; then a whimpering sound comes from her throat. She presses her hand to her mouth, but it doesn't stop the agonizing cry.

Daniel glances at Hanna, who is closest to the sink.

"Would you like a glass of water?" she says, filling a glass and placing it on the table. Marion gazes at it for a few seconds, then raises it to her lips with trembling fingers.

"Johan can't be dead." It's as if she hasn't taken in what Daniel has told her. "We're going skiing in Trillevallen today."

She is in shock—hardly surprising. Daniel tries to find the right words, although deep down he knows there aren't any. He won't be able to ease her pain, whatever he says.

"Your husband's body was found by a passing driver just off Tångbölevägen this morning." It's hard to mitigate the truth. "He'd been badly beaten. His nose was broken, and he'd suffered a severe blow to the back of his head."

Marion's face crumples and tears pour down her cheeks.

"Are you saying he was beaten to death?" she stammers.

"I really am sorry," Hanna says. "That does seem to be the case."

"I realize this is hard," Daniel adds. "But we have a few questions, if you can manage to tell us what you know?"

Marion swallows and bows her head, which Daniel takes as a yes.

"When did you last see Johan?"

"Yesterday evening, about seven. He went out and didn't come back, and the van is gone. I've been calling his cell phone all night. I was so worried." Marion lets out a sob and buries her face in her hands. "Then I thought maybe it got too late and he couldn't drive . . . I was sure he'd be back soon."

Daniel exchanges a glance with Hanna; it's not going to be easy to get anything useful out of Marion, but they have to try.

After a brief pause, he says, "Do you know where Johan was going when he left the house?"

"He . . . he was going for a few beers with his friends. They often meet up on Fridays."

"Where do they usually go?"

Marion is crying now; Daniel has the feeling that she's barely holding it together.

"I don't really know . . . Pigo, maybe? Or Jemten?"

Two restaurants in Duved.

"Can you give us the names of his friends? We'll need to speak to them."

"Calle would have been there," Marion mumbles, clasping her hands on her lap. "Carl Willner, he's one of Johan's oldest friends."

Hanna makes a note.

"Can you tell us about your husband?" Daniel asks. "Do you know if he had any enemies, someone who wished him harm?"

Marion sits there motionless, as if she were paralyzed.

"Why would he have any enemies?" she says eventually.

"It's just a routine question," Hanna reassures her.

Marion shakes her head, clearly at a loss. "Everyone liked Johan. He was so kind . . . one of the good guys, through and through." She smiles weakly in spite of her tears. "Johan was always cheerful—as soon as he opened his eyes in the morning, the laughter was there. That was the first thing that struck me when we met—his positive attitude to everything. He loved life."

She stands up and goes into the living room. She returns with a framed photograph of Johan in his skiing clothes. He is standing on a podium, holding up a bronze medal.

There is no mistaking the happiness on his face.

Marion runs her fingertips over the picture.

"This is my favorite photo of Johan," she says, with heartrending grief in her voice. "It was when he came third in the super-G in Val d'Isère. The world championship in 2009. It was a fantastic day. We'd gotten together the previous year, and I was so proud of him."

She takes a shuddering breath.

"How long did he compete for?" Daniel asks. He doesn't remember how things went for Johan. Back then the main focus was on women's skiing; Anja Pärson was the big star.

Marion shakes her head sadly.

"He broke his leg at a training camp before the 2010 Olympics, just after we married. The injury never really healed properly, and we moved here in 2011 when he was forced to end his career."

She looks at the photograph again, clutching the frame tightly. Her tears drip onto the glass, forming tiny transparent pools.

"He hadn't fallen out with anyone?" Hanna ventures.

Marion barely registers the question.

"I'm sorry," she whispers. "I can't do this."

Daniel realizes that they will have to come back another day. There's no point in talking to the poor woman right now.

Marion turns away from them. "I need to be alone."

REBECKA

2012

December

Everyone is looking at Rebecka, seated at the top table with Ole. The guests cannot stop applauding. Ole has just given a riveting speech about their shared future within the church, how they will walk hand in hand through the valley of the Lord.

He has vividly described his love for God, how blessed his union with Rebecka is, and he has spoken with deep sincerity about their future children, whom he longs to raise in the name of Jesus.

It is not only Rebecka who has tears in her eyes.

Ole accepts the guests' appreciation with a disarming "Amen." Rebecka smiles in embarrassment, her cheeks flushed red. She isn't used to being the center of attention; she finds it difficult to cope. For Ole it comes naturally. He is accustomed to recognition; he is powerful in a way that draws everyone's eyes.

As his new wife, she will have to learn to live with it.

Rebecka senses that more than one female guest is casting envious glances in her direction.

The fact that she is a married woman still feels unreal. God has chosen her to be Ole's bride. It is a great honor; she only hopes she will be able to live up to her husband's expectations. She also hopes that he is as happy as she is, that he is glad they have just become man and wife.

That she is good enough.

He has selected her and her alone, she tries to tell herself. Which means she must be worthy, even if she herself has never dreamed of such good fortune.

Mother and Father are incredibly proud. Lisen, her best friend, is also thrilled. Imagine—Rebecka has married such an important man. Ole, the assistant pastor who studied at the University of Umeå and now has an excellent job with an accounting firm.

People are chatting and laughing. Their meaningful smiles make Rebecka blush even more as various dishes are carried in and out.

Ole says something to the person sitting next to him. Rebecka looks at his well-shaped lips, wonders how it will feel when they brush against hers tonight. Will they be warm or cold? Dry, or moist with saliva?

All at once the thought makes her feel both expectant and a little frightened at the same time. Tonight, they will be together for the first time. He will touch the most private parts of her body, they will be united as man and wife.

Rebecka is finding it difficult to tear her eyes away from her new husband. The charismatic smile that he bestows with such generosity. He is so handsome, and so tall—almost a head taller than Rebecka. He also has a promising future—Father has said so on many occasions. He might well succeed Pastor Jonsäter one day, in which case her husband will be the leader of the church.

The room is filled with the hum of voices.

Around eighty people have gathered in the hall next to the church. A wedding is a big occasion. Mother and Father have not stinted on anything.

A trickle of sweat finds its way down her back. Rebecka sits up a little straighter. It is warm, despite the December cold that has Jämtland in its iron grip.

Everything has happened with such dizzying speed. She feels drunk, even though she has barely sipped her wine.

Father spoke to her the day after that first meeting. His expression was serious as he told her that Ole was interested in taking Rebecka as his bride. Pastor Jonsäter had blessed their union, and it was God's will that a young woman should find a husband.

"Be fruitful and increase in number; fill the earth . . ."

Rebecka listened carefully, as she always does when Father explains something.

That evening her mother came into her room for once and sat down on the edge of the bed.

"Imagine—Ole is going to be your husband," she whispered, stroking Rebecka's cheek. "What an honor. I remember the day your father and I got married as if it were yesterday."

"Have you been happy, Mother?" Rebecka dared to ask, although the words stuck in her throat.

"We had you, didn't we?" her mother went on. "Nothing has given me more happiness."

Rebecka knows that her mother is sad that no siblings came along, not least because the church values those women who bear many children. However, Rebecka's birth was difficult, and there were no more.

It is God's will, her mother would answer when Rebecka was a little girl and asked why she didn't have any brothers or sisters.

After that evening there were no delays. She and Ole became engaged, and the time whizzed by. In less than three months, she has gone from being unmarried to sitting here as his wife.

She glances admiringly at her husband once again.

He is still deep in conversation. The other man is paying close attention to every word. No one interrupts Ole. There is a self-evident air of authority about him.

Rebecka wants to shine, to make him understand how happy she is going to make him. He will never have cause to regret his choice.

Ole is so impressive. He is the one who planned the entire wedding; no detail was too small. He even picked out her dress, decided on her hairstyle. And their wedding rings, of course.

It is wonderful to be taken care of like this.

She has promised to serve and obey him before God. From this moment on, she belongs to him.

For the rest of her life.

6

A couple of hours after the visit to Marion, Hanna is seated in the conference room at Åre police station. Her stomach is rumbling; she has eaten nothing but a pitiful banana all morning.

The white walls blend in with the heavy snow falling outside the windows. The only splash of color is the red chairs around the table. Two are occupied by her colleagues Anton Lundgren and Rafael Herrera. Both are local detectives who have been called in because of the homicide. Daniel is there too, of course.

Carina Grankvist, the CSI from Mattmar who examined the scene where the body was found, is also in attendance.

Rafael, or Raffe as he is known, is in the process of setting up the video call with Östersund, where the Serious Crimes Unit is based. His dark ponytail bobs as he reaches for the mouse and enters the code.

"Johan Andersson." He shakes his head. "Wow."

"Did you know him?" Hanna asks.

"Mm. He was in the year above me at the ski academy. Such a nice guy. He was really unlucky to be injured so early in his career. He wasn't bitter, though—you never heard him complain."

Raffe is a dedicated snowboarder and lives in Kall with his girlfriend. He can still pull off a few tricks on the slopes that make teenagers look on, openmouthed and envious.

"Who would have thought Johan would die like that?" he says with a sigh as the screen comes to life and Birgitta Grip, the head of the unit, appears. Several other team members are with her, as is the on-duty prosecutor. Grip will act as leader of the preliminary investigation until the case is allocated to a permanent prosecutor.

She looks troubled as she runs her fingers through her short, steel-gray hair.

"Where are we?" she begins. "Do we have confirmation that the victim is Johan Andersson, the skier?"

Daniel nods.

Grip is familiar with Johan's career, as most residents of Åre probably are. It was only Hanna who didn't realize who he was, although to be fair Daniel hadn't immediately made the connection earlier when they were at the scene.

"Has the family been informed?" Grip continues.

Daniel confirms that he and Hanna have been to see Marion. Johan's parents, Tarja and Torsten, have been told by colleagues in Östersund, and his brother, Pär, who lives in Strömsund, has also been contacted.

"There is going to be considerable interest from the media," Grip says. "We need to be particularly careful when it comes to confidentiality." She gives her team a challenging look from the screen. "What do we know about how he died?"

Daniel flicks through his notebook.

"As far as we can tell, Johan died as a result of repeated blows to the back of his head. His skiing career ended in 2011, and he now runs a plumbing firm with a partner. No known enemies, according to his wife."

"It's hard to believe he's dead," Raffe says. "He was such a good guy."

Hanna pictures the snow-covered body, the blood on the pale cheek.

"His hands were tied behind his back," Daniel goes on, "so there's no doubt we're dealing with a serious crime here. He was more or less executed."

His description is dry, bordering on clinical, but that's the way it has to be. He is not trying to diminish the deceased, but it is difficult when a living human being, a person who was crying and laughing not so long ago, becomes a homicide statistic.

Even the police are reminded of the fragility of life.

Grip turns to the CSI. "Carina—what can you tell us?"

Carina Grankvist still looks frozen, in spite of two sweaters and a thick scarf wrapped around her neck. She is a few years younger than Grip, who will turn sixty in the summer. Unlike Grip she has not let her hair go gray; instead, it is colored dark blond, and is cut in a soft pageboy style that frames her face. Combined with her curves, it gives her an almost motherly air. Hanna finds it easier to imagine Carina surrounded by grandchildren rather than bending over a mutilated body.

"I wish I had more to give you," she begins, "but the heavy overnight snow complicates the situation."

"Do you think Johan Andersson was murdered in the place where he was found?" Grip asks.

"Doubtful." Carina adjusts her scarf. "I believe he was killed elsewhere. There were no signs of a struggle, no broken branches or any other indication that violence had occurred in that location. However, there had been a lot of people moving around in the snow near the body before I arrived, so it was impossible to secure any footprints."

Hanna thinks back to the scene. Before the police got there, Anna Larsson had walked back and forth near the body. She herself and Daniel had also left their own prints—it was unavoidable.

"In which case he was presumably transported there by car," Hanna says. "There were no snow scooter tracks, were there?"

Carina shakes her head.

"Could the perpetrator have used the victim's own vehicle?" Anton speculates. "It seems to be missing."

Anton has a point. According to Marion, Johan set off in his van on Friday evening to meet his friends for a beer in Duved. All police in the area have been asked to look out for a white van with the company name on the side.

"Not impossible," Grip says before addressing Carina once more. "Any chance of useful tire tracks from the scene?"

Carina turns over a piece of paper.

"I'm afraid not. As I said, it had snowed heavily overnight. We ought to check with whoever was out in the snowplow though, find out what time they passed that particular spot. Just in case they noticed anything."

"I can do that," Anton offers. He lives in Duved, and his local knowledge is good. As far as Hanna knows, he is the only member of the team who was born and raised in Åre. No one can find their way around the mountains like him. And no one is as fit either. He is obsessive about training and a regular at the gym.

"Okay, let's see," Grip continues. "What conclusions can we reach about the perpetrator at this stage?"

Hanna puts down her pen. "Either it was one person who was strong enough to move Johan Andersson's dead body, or two people helping each other."

"If it was one person, then it's likely to be a man," Daniel says. "A woman on her own is unlikely to be able to carry that weight."

Hanna gives him a meaningful look. Sometimes she gets so tired of all those preconceptions.

Daniel smiles and holds up his hands as if to ward her off.

"What can you tell us about the murder weapon?" Raffe asks Carina.

"That's a matter for the forensic pathologist."

"But you must have some idea?"

He gives her a big smile, half-encouraging, half-challenging. Hanna can really see how he switches on the charm, a skill he uses to great effect.

Raffe's family background is Chilean, although he was born in Sweden. His parents fled to the country in the seventies, during

Pinochet's dictatorship. He has the good fortune to always look slightly tanned, even though they live so far north.

"There was a large wound in the back of the victim's head," Carina replies. "It could have come from a sledgehammer or some other kind of heavy hammer."

Hanna wonders what this tells them about the killer. Most families in the area would own tools like that—standard equipment for a household in northern Jämtland. From a statistical point of view, the most common murder weapon is a kitchen knife. Several powerful blows with a sledgehammer indicate something else. That the person in question really meant it.

Who would want to do that to him? What had he done to provoke that level of rage? She remembers the photograph Marion showed them of Johan on the podium. The joy in his moment of triumph, the glow of happiness surrounding him.

One of the good guys, through and through—that was what Marion had said about her husband.

So what had happened?

"Daniel, you can lead the team," Grip says. "It worked well in December."

A special group is formed in investigations of this kind. Apart from Daniel and Hanna, two colleagues from Östersund are also included. Anton and Raffe, while covering minor crimes in Åre, will also help when needed.

Hanna has a distinct feeling of déjà vu. This is exactly the same combination as back in December, when Amanda Halvorssen disappeared. That was when Hanna started working in Åre after her humiliating departure from Stockholm.

She still carries with her the tragic events that took place before Christmas.

Grip allocates the various tasks. They need to analyze every detail of Johan Andersson's life. Go through his finances, check out his company, his circle of friends and acquaintances, his most recent personal and professional contacts. His phone is missing, so they will have to ask his provider for a list of calls.

"Try to stick to normal working hours," Grip says. "We don't want to hit the overtime ceiling before we've even gotten through the first quarter of the year."

Hanna chews her lower lip. She would have preferred a few words of encouragement, but then again it isn't Grip's fault that she has to remind them of budget concerns. No doubt she is under pressure from her superiors.

She glances at Daniel, who is frowning. He is already struggling to make things work with Ida and little Alice. Hanna is pretty sure that a new homicide case won't go down well at home.

As if he has read her mind, Daniel glances up and meets her gaze.

"Okay, let's do this," he says, getting to his feet.

7

Daniel can hear Alice gurgling happily as soon as he opens the door of the apartment on Granlidsvägen.

It is almost five o'clock. He has spent the whole afternoon putting together a plan for the investigation and discussing which resources can be deployed.

A number of uniformed officers have been brought in and are currently conducting door-to-door inquiries in Tångböle, the area where Johan was found. The authority responsible for clearing the snow has been contacted, and Johan's body is on the way to Umeå for the autopsy. Hanna is busy identifying the victim's friends and acquaintances.

Daniel is pleased that everything has gotten underway so quickly. He can't devote every waking hour to a new case—Ida wouldn't like that.

They will meet first thing in the morning at the station to continue. Despite Grip's comments, overtime cannot be avoided right now.

"Hi, sweetheart," he says as he walks into the kitchen, where Ida is trying to interest Alice in a spoonful of puréed carrots. Ida's dark-blond braid is anything but smooth, and there's something orange stuck to her hairline. Daniel gives Alice a kiss on the forehead. "How are my girls?"

Ida sighs and turns up her face for a kiss on her cheek. "She's not a fan of this," she says. Alice has enthusiastically spat out most of her carrot all over the white-glazed hardwood floor. Daniel tears off some sheets of paper towel and begins to clear up the mess.

"Shall I take over?" he offers. Ida shakes her head.

Daniel pours himself a glass of water and sits down at the table as Ida gives up trying to interest their daughter in her meal.

"I heard on the radio that a man has been murdered in Tångböle," she says over her shoulder.

Only eight hours have passed since the call came in, but the case is already in the press. Daniel hopes they haven't gotten hold of all the details yet. Thank goodness he and Hanna managed to inform Marion, giving her a little time to absorb the tragic news. She is clearly devastated, and when the media find out who the victim is, they will hound her.

"I'm afraid that's true. That's why I had to leave so early this morning."

Both Alice and Ida were asleep when the regional dispatch contacted him.

"You saw my note?" he adds, to be on the safe side. They'd talked about driving over to Edsäsdalen, having lunch at a mountain restaurant called the White Reindeer.

Another time.

Ida puts down the teaspoon. "Was it someone from Åre?"

"I can't answer that."

Ida often wants Daniel to tell her about work when he comes home in the evenings. She claims it makes her feel less isolated; it can be lonely, spending all day at home with Alice, particularly since Daniel tends to shut down when he is tired or stressed—a habit that doesn't exactly help the situation.

However, he can't ignore the rules on confidentiality.

"I'm sorry, but I can't," he reiterates. "We haven't released the name of the victim yet."

He nods toward the stove, tries to change the subject.

"How about spaghetti vongole for dinner? With a glass of red wine—it is Saturday, after all. I think we've still got a bottle of that Barolo you like."

Cooking is one of his favorite activities—after all, his mother grew up in northeastern Italy. He often starts planning dinner as soon as he wakes up in the morning.

"I'm sure it will be delicious."

Ida sounds exhausted, and Daniel feels a pang of guilt. It's not easy, looking after a five-month-old baby by herself, especially when their plans for a day out have been canceled at the last minute. He gets up and lifts Alice out of her highchair. He loves the weight of his little daughter, the soft skin, the chubby neck resting on his chest.

"I can take care of Alice," he says. "You've had her all day."

"In that case I'll go and shower."

"You do that." He blows on the back of Alice's neck so that it tickles and makes her laugh. "I'll tidy up in here and get started on dinner."

Ida blows him a grateful kiss and heads for the bathroom.

Life feels good. Over the last month things have gone better, both with Alice and their relationship. He really wants to make this work.

If only the new investigation doesn't cause problems between them. Just like the one in December did.

REBECKA

2013

November

Behind the white bathroom door, Rebecka is weeping silently.

She and Ole had just sat down to breakfast when she felt a trickle between her legs. She mumbled an apology and hurried to the toilet.

Now her bloodstained panties are lying on the floor, proof that she has failed to get pregnant yet again. She winces at the cramps in her belly. She felt the pains as soon as she woke up but didn't dare say anything. Instead, she tried to ignore them, hoped it was merely her imagination.

She rubs the area below her navel with one hand in an attempt to drive out the evil.

They have been man and wife for almost a year, but still there is no child on the way. Lisen, who married Isak just before Ole and Rebecka's wedding, is due to give birth any day now.

It is only Rebecka's stomach that remains flat.

She desperately longs to be a mother. She loves small children, which was why she begged to be allowed to enter the childcare and leisure program in high school. She also knows how disappointed Ole will be.

He is so fond of children, so attentive to all the pregnant women in the church. He often talks about the joy of being a parent. Sometimes he praises Lisen and Isak, and the other day he said that Lisen was a real woman. That she was blessed by God and a joy to her husband.

Rebecka wishes he would speak so affectionately about her.

She buries her face in her hands. She had been so optimistic this time, counted the days on her fingers, hoped that their latest night together would produce the right result.

She can't stop crying. She tears off a piece of toilet paper, wipes her nose. She stares at the dark-red stains.

If only she could become pregnant, if only they could have a little baby together. Ole would be so proud and happy. It breaks Rebecka's heart when she sees the disappointed expression that he can't quite hide. It hollows her out from the inside. She understands how much he suffers, how much it hurts him.

Her barrenness.

Every night she prays to God, begs him to let it happen, to let life grow within her.

She wants it so much.

"Rebecka?" Ole calls out from the kitchen. He doesn't like eating alone, always needs her to be seated opposite him. Lisen thinks it's romantic, and Rebecka has to agree. It's an advantage to have a husband who longs for her as soon as she is out of his sight.

"Coming," she replies quickly so that he won't wonder what she is up to in the bathroom.

She rinses her flushed face. Ole doesn't like her to wear makeup. She rarely uses mascara or even moisturizer these days. He says that such vanity is sinful. However, she finds an old powder compact and dabs a little under her eyes to hide the evidence of her tears.

There is no point in telling him what has happened; it would simply make Ole as sad as she is. He has more important things to think about—tomorrow he is preaching at their sister church in Trondheim. She doesn't want her failure to distract him.

Rebecka takes a deep breath and unlocks the door. She forces the corners of her mouth up into a smile and heads for the kitchen.

God cannot be so cruel as to deny her and Ole a child. For the sake of their marriage, she must get pregnant, so that they become a proper family.

It's the only way she will be able to prove to Ole that she is a real woman, one who is worthy of his love and respect.

8

The police station is quiet and empty on Saturday evening, but Hanna appreciates the peace after the intense discussions of the past few hours. The fact that another brutal murder has taken place in Åre still feels unreal.

She sees Johan Andersson's dead body in her mind's eye. The defenseless position on the ground, the crushed skull. His arms tied behind him, wrists blue where the cable ties had cut into the flesh.

Who does that to another human being?

Hanna shudders. She has worked as a police officer for nine years, since she was twenty-five, but some sights are harder to deal with than others.

Is she going to be able to step up and track down the killer?

In December she herself came close to death, and she has needed the last couple of months to recover. She has slept a lot, worked at a steady pace. Her focus has been on barfights and a fraud operation in Krokom.

To have any chance of securing a permanent post, she is going to have to show what she is made of. Right now, she is on a temporary placement. She is very happy here, and there is nothing to go back to in Stockholm—not after the dispute with Manfred Lidwall, her former boss in the Domestic Violence Unit. When he shut down a serious assault case against a woman because a colleague was involved, Hanna was so mad that she accused him of incompetence and corruption. That led to Manfred pointing out her faults at some length and telling her to get the hell out of the City Police.

She was finished.

If her sister, Lydia, hadn't stepped in as her legal representative and forced him to give Hanna a good reference, she would never have gotten the job in Åre/Östersund. She owes a huge debt of gratitude to both Lydia and Daniel, who organized the post just when she needed it the most.

Hanna fled to Lydia's house in Åre because she had nowhere else to go.

It was the worst twenty-four hours of her life when Christian, her partner, finished with her on the same day Manfred informed her that her presence was no longer required in the unit. She had no money, and Christian owned the apartment they shared.

With a sigh Hanna turns her attention back to the search through various databases to see if Johan shows up. She has also attempted to contact Carl Willner, the childhood friend Johan met yesterday evening, but he isn't answering his phone.

At six fifteen her phone beeps—a text from Karro.

Feel like meeting up at Bygget?

Bygget is Åre's most popular nightclub. It will be packed because it's the Saturday before Week Nine, the winter sports break in Stockholm. Hanna can't face it. It is impossible to leave the events of today behind her. Her head is too full of images of the dead man and his devastated wife.

Plus, she needs to go home and clean the house—Lydia, Richard, and the children are arriving tomorrow.

She shuts down her computer and texts Karro:

Thanks for asking, but I can't tonight. Next time! ☺

She hopes Karro won't be offended. She's really nice and has become a good friend here in Åre. She's also Anton's younger sister—maybe he's going too?

39

Hanna is about to put her phone in her purse when it rings. It's her mother, who lives in southern Spain. For a moment she considers not answering; Ulla rarely calls, and never to ask how Hanna is. The last time they spoke, the conversation was mostly about how disappointed Ulla was that Hanna and Christian had broken up.

Can she pretend she hasn't heard the signal?

Duty takes over, and she accepts the call.

"Hi, Hanna—it seems like forever since you called me."

Maybe that's because you always make me feel worse. Hanna bites her tongue, and simply says, "Work has been very busy."

"I don't see how that's possible—Åre is such a lovely, peaceful place. It was absolutely idyllic when you and Lydia were little and we used to spend the school vacations there."

Hanna thinks about Johan again. There is no point in saying anything; her mother would never understand how Hanna feels after a day like this.

"Times change."

"Aren't you going to ask how your father is?"

No one can evoke feelings of guilt as quickly and effectively as Hanna's mother.

"How's Dad?" Hanna says obediently.

"He's good, but of course he's getting old."

Olof will turn eighty-seven in the summer. He is quite a lot older than Ulla and has never been particularly talkative. These days he is retreating into himself more and more.

But he is the one who has always cared the most about Hanna.

"Did you want something special?" she says, even though they've only been talking for a minute or two. She doesn't have the energy to deal with her mother today, or to let her underline the fact that Hanna is a bad daughter who doesn't keep in touch.

"Actually . . . there was something I wanted to mention, now I've finally gotten hold of you."

She sounds . . . troubled. This is unusual, and Hanna is immediately suspicious.

"The thing is . . . Christian and his new girlfriend, Valérie, are coming over for dinner tomorrow. I presume you have no objections?"

Hanna almost drops the phone. She can hardly believe her ears. Is her mother seriously intending to carry on seeing Christian? After the way he behaved?

"He's down here in Nerja for the sports break, and he called us," Ulla goes on. "You know how fond we are of Christian—I just had to invite them."

"You can't be serious!" Hanna's voice is shrill, but she can't help it. "You do know what he did to me?"

Ulla sighs.

"Darling Hanna, I realize that you see some terrible things because of your job, but not all men are bad. It was such a shame the two of you broke up, but your father and I will always regard Christian as a member of the family. He can't be the only one to blame for the failure of your relationship."

He was unfaithful, Hanna wants to yell. *He lied and went behind my back. We didn't break up—he left me.*

"He would have been a wonderful father if you'd had children," Ulla says, sounding melancholy. "I don't suppose we'll be blessed with any more grandchildren . . . ?"

Not this too. The constant nagging about her age, the fact that it's high time she got pregnant. Hanna has heard this way too often. Enough—she can't listen to one more word.

Especially not tonight.

"I'll speak to you some other time," she says, and ends the call.

She shouldn't be upset; she knows what her mother is like. And yet there is a lump in her throat that is impossible to swallow as she pulls on her down jacket to drive home to Sadeln.

41

9

The line to get into Bygget, the nightclub below the VM8 ski lift, snakes its way across the snow-covered parking lot when Anton arrives at about nine o'clock.

One of Sweden's best-known hip-hop artists is playing tonight, a guy who also happens to live in Åre. The place is bound to be packed—and with the sports break just beginning, Åre is full of young people from Stockholm, ready to party.

Anton doesn't go out very often, particularly since so many people recognize him and know he's a police officer. It doesn't look good if he's staggering around with a beer in his hand. Not that he's in the habit of getting drunk; he's far too meticulous about his fitness regime. He goes to the gym at least five times a week and follows a strict lean-protein diet.

Tonight, he is finding it especially difficult to relax. The murder of Johan Andersson weighs heavily on his mind. Just a few years older than Anton, he was a real local hero who won the Åre Cup several years in a row. Even though his career never recovered after his leg injury, Johan will always be a part of skiing history.

The local boy who won a medal in the world championship.

It's hard to believe that he's dead. There's going to be one hell of a storm when his name is released. Anton's parents know Johan's—Duved is even smaller than Åre.

Poor Tarja and Torsten.

Anton was on the point of texting Karro to tell her that he'd decided to stay home. He's not in the party mood, but she persuaded him to come along. For once, as she put it.

He hears a familiar voice from the middle of the line.

"Anton—over here!"

His sister is waving to him, and Anton goes over to join the group of girls.

"Hi," he says, giving Karro a hug. She's only a year or so younger than him. Unlike Anton, who is single, she has a partner and two children. The older girl is already at junior high; Karro was only twenty when she became pregnant for the first time. Not that it stops her from enjoying herself—she's a real party animal, much more than Anton ever was. Tonight, she has curled her blond hair and applied her makeup with care; she looks very pretty.

Anton nods to her friends—he knows them all.

He tries to push the murder of Johan to one side. It's Saturday, and he can't tell his companions what has happened. Not that he wants to.

He forces himself to smile.

"Time to have some fun!"

An hour later the whole place is bouncing in time with the music. The area in front of the stage is crowded, and sweat is pouring down the well-known artist's face as he raps one of his most popular tracks.

Anton sticks to the edge of the dance floor; he doesn't like to be in the middle of a crush. On the news they were talking about some kind of Chinese flu virus that might be on its way to Europe. He looks out across the mass of people and hopes that none of them has been in Asia recently.

"He's fantastic!" a voice shouts in his ear.

Anton gives a start. "What?"

The guy standing next to him has to yell to make himself heard above the loud music. There are a lot more Stockholm accents than Norrland here tonight, but this person sounds as if he's from Jämtland.

"I said he's good!"

"Yes." Anton smiles without taking his eyes off the band.

Hip-hop isn't exactly his thing, he plays sax in a local jazz ensemble in his spare time, but there's something about the rapper's words that find their way right into his heart. He manages to touch a sore point, how painful it can be to find yourself at the bottom, not to fit in with everyone else.

Anton is all too familiar with that feeling. Neither Duved nor Åre are big places—here everyone knows everything about one another.

It's not easy if you stand out in a small town, and he has never been a person who likes to attract attention.

"Do you come here often?" the stranger says with a laugh. "Sorry, that's one of the worst lines that's ever come out of my mouth."

Anton turns his head.

His new acquaintance seems to be in his early thirties, just like Anton. His blond hair is so short that it almost looks like a buzz cut. The sleeves of his pale-blue shirt are neatly rolled up.

When he smiles, he has a dimple in one cheek.

Before Anton can answer, the guy holds out his hand.

"Live for today," the rapper says.

"Want to come outside for a smoke?"

Anton doesn't smoke. It's not compatible with his training, and he's never really liked the taste. However, he'd like a breath of fresh air. It's sweltering in here, with hundreds of enthusiastic clubbers swaying in time to the music and singing as loud as they can.

He contemplates the stranger and likes what he sees.

"Sure," Anton says, setting off toward the door.

10

She knows it's pointless, but Marion can't help picturing Johan's dead face.

She is lying under the covers in their double bed, the description the police gave her echoing through her head. The words run on a loop, even though it's pure torture. *Beaten, broken nose, severe injuries to the back of the head. May have suffered for a long period. A great deal of blood.*

She can't bear it.

She has spent the entire day walking around the house like a zombie, with an iron lump of anguish in her chest. She squeezes her eyes shut in order to get rid of the horrific images, but it doesn't help. Nothing helps.

He is gone, and the pain is unbearable.

Never again will she hear Johan's carefree laughter. Life hadn't been kind to him, but still he loved it. Even the broken leg that destroyed his career didn't make him bitter. Instead, he trained to be a plumber, and started over.

What is she going to do now?

They had been together for twelve years, married for ten. With him, it didn't matter that she was shy and reserved; he made her open and positive, happier somehow. In Johan's company she became her best self. He had a way of bringing out the finest qualities of everyone he met.

And now he is gone. Forever.

Marion presses her face against the pillow until she can hardly breathe. Then she sits up, pushes her spine against the headboard. With her arms tightly wrapped around her body, she rocks back and forth.

How can she possibly live without him?

After a while she reaches for her robe and makes her way down to the kitchen, barefoot. All the lights are still on; she didn't dare switch them off when she went to bed. To tell the truth, she is afraid of the dark. If Johan was out, she often waited up until he came home; it was hard to get to sleep otherwise.

She picks up the photograph she showed to the police. Gazes at Johan's face radiating happiness.

Time slips by as she sits there with the photo in her hand.

Eventually she puts it down and goes over to the pantry. They don't usually have much alcohol in the house, but she thinks there might be a bottle of German brandy that her brother, Florian, brought with him the last time he came to Sweden.

Asbach Uralt, his favorite.

She ought to call Florian, tell him what's happened, but she can't bring herself to say the words out loud.

Johan is dead.

As long as she doesn't talk about it, she can pretend he's coming back, as if the last twenty-four hours never happened.

Clutching the brandy, she heads for the guest room. She can't go back to their bedroom, where everything reminds her of Johan.

The first swig is so strong that she almost chokes, but Marion puts the bottle to her lips and carries on drinking.

REBECKA

2015

DECEMBER

The sound of Ole's car on the drive makes Rebecka hurry.

She is standing at the stove, stirring his favorite stew—moose meat with parsnips and carrots. It is Friday, and she has made a special effort.

The front door opens, and she hears him taking off his outdoor clothes and hanging them up. Ole is very particular about that—there is a proper way of doing things.

He is speaking on the phone, and his tone is warm; no doubt he is supporting a member of the congregation. Ole is so wise; many people seek his advice in difficult situations.

She gives him an inviting smile when he appears in the doorway after finishing his call.

"Dinner will be ready soon," she says. "It's moose stew—your favorite."

Ole nods and sits down at the table. Picks up the newspaper and begins to read, running his fingers through his thick hair. He is frowning slightly, concentrating. Rebecka hopes he will say something. She has been at home all day, and longs for company. His silence also makes her feel unsure of herself. It's hard to work out what he is thinking when he is closed like this.

Only once did she try to bring it up. Told him she wished they could talk more. Be more affectionate. His icy stare made the words dry up in her mouth. She understood that she had made a huge mistake. If she were a better wife, she would know what he wanted. Without any need for explanations.

Rebecka drains the potatoes. She must earn his love. She often thinks about that. Everyone loves Ole, especially her parents.

It's just that she's so lonely. During the day he is at work, and he devotes many evenings to the church, not getting home until after eleven o'clock.

They have been married for three years, and she is still not pregnant. He is disappointed in her, of course he is. Ole had a choice of countless women before they married; why has he had the misfortune to acquire a wife who is infertile?

Rebecka tries to fill her time with cleaning and cooking. The freezer is full of casseroles and stews, the shelves in the pantry are packed with jars of homemade jelly and marmalade. She does a lot of baking.

The longing to have a job of her own is growing within her. She would love to work in a preschool, to follow the career she trained for. She feels very strongly that God meant for her to take care of little children.

If not her own children, then she will find another way.

However, Ole won't hear of it. He doesn't like the idea of her having to mix with *the others* every day, those outside the church. He says it's bad enough that he has to do it because of his job with the accounting firm; he doesn't want Rebecka exposed to the same thing.

Plus, she needs to take it easy. He doesn't want her under any kind of stress, because that might ruin her chances of getting pregnant. Her role is to stay at home, create a happy and God-fearing environment.

The work Ole carries out in the name of the Lord is so much more important than anything Rebecka does.

And yet he takes the time to call her frequently during the day, to ask her how she is feeling, what she is doing. If she pursued a career, she wouldn't be available in the same way.

Rebecka places the stew on the table and serves her husband first. Then she begins to serve herself but stops when she sees the look on Ole's face. The look that says she mustn't take too much, she mustn't get fat.

He has strong views about weight; he detests fat people and their lack of self-discipline, as he sees it. He himself practices moderation when it comes to both sugar and alcohol.

Rebecka smiles apologetically and puts down the ladle. In comparison with his portion, hers is minute. But that's fine—Ole really does care about her appearance.

How many married men do the same?

As soon as they have said grace, he picks up his fork. Rebecka puts a piece of meat in her mouth and chews slowly to make it last longer.

And thanks God that she has such a concerned and dedicated husband.

SUNDAY, FEBRUARY 23

11

The sun is struggling to break through the clouds as Hanna gets into the unmarked police car at nine o'clock in the morning. She is cold and tired; she slept badly. She sighs so heavily that Daniel can't help but react.

"Didn't you sleep well?"

Hanna shakes her head.

"Yesterday was tough," he says, patting her shoulder. "I had weird dreams too—Johan's body had disappeared, and we were searching the forest in the middle of the night."

They have just held a brief meeting at the station. The atmosphere was subdued. There is increasing speculation online about the identity of the victim; a lot of people are beginning to suspect that it is Johan Andersson. Raffe had seen various posts on social media.

They are on the way to visit Linus Sundin, Johan's business partner. Daniel merges onto the E14 and heads west. The Sundins live just over half a mile outside Duved.

Hanna yawns. It took her a long time to clean the house yesterday; she didn't finish until midnight, but now everything is spotless. Even Lydia ought to be satisfied with the result.

A tingle of stress passes through her body. She has been looking forward to the visit, and is very fond of her nephew and niece, but no doubt Mom has called Lydia and told her about the latest phone call, confided that Hanna more or less hung up on her.

Should she explain what happened before Lydia brings it up? They have very different perceptions of their mother, and Lydia has always been the favorite.

The timing of their visit couldn't be worse, given that Hanna has just started a new homicide investigation. How are they going to spend time together if she has to work around the clock?

Hanna straightens her shoulders.

No doubt it would have been better if she'd found a place of her own before the sports break; she could have met up with Lydia's family over dinner, then gone back home. Avoided confronting all those difficult emotions. But it seems silly to look for an apartment until she knows whether her post will be made permanent—not to mention the issue of tying herself into a lengthy lease in her precarious financial position.

Anyway, it's too late to move now. She needs to focus on the case and the day's tasks.

"Do you think Linus Sundin knows what's happened?"

Daniel keeps his eyes on the road. "I guess so—I expect Marion will have contacted him."

"Depends on their relationship. Then again, Marion did the bookkeeping for the business, so they must know each other pretty well."

Hanna leans back in her seat. She hopes they're not going to have to deliver another death message. Marion's grief yesterday still weighs on her.

"What does Ida think about your new case?" she says in an effort to divert her mind. It's meant as a casual question, but Daniel's expression grows serious.

"We haven't talked about it much, but I hope she understands that it's going to take up a lot of my time."

Something in his posture suggests that he is far from confident of Ida's response.

They are approaching Duved and have to slow down. There is a line of cars outside the entrance to the ski resort, all waiting to turn right. Hanna can see that the long, narrow parking lot is already full, and there are plenty of people waiting for the lifts even though it's still early in the morning.

It feels as if half the population of Stockholm has traveled to Jämtland this week.

"No mistaking the fact that it's the sports break," she says.

"Mm."

Everywhere will be packed over the next eight days, especially the slopes and the restaurants. The après-ski celebrations will continue into the small hours, which usually means the police have their hands full dealing with all the drunken tourists weaving their way home.

It is probably the worst week in the entire year to conduct a homicide investigation.

12

Daniel has just told Linus Sundin that his friend and partner is dead.

They are sitting in the family's gray-painted kitchen. He did his best to break the news gently, but it's obvious that it came as a huge shock.

"You're telling me that Johan's been murdered?" Linus stammers. "Is this some kind of bad joke?"

"Marion hasn't contacted you?" Hanna says.

"No."

Linus slumps on the white chair. He seems dazed, sitting there in a blue bathrobe straining over his belly.

"I heard they'd found a body in Tångböle," he says, taking a deep breath. "But I could never have imagined it would be . . . Johan."

Daniel gives him a minute to gather his thoughts.

"What . . . what happened?" Linus asks eventually.

They tell him about yesterday's discovery. Daniel avoids the worst elements just like they did for Marion; a detailed description of what Johan looked like isn't going to help anybody. It would be macabre to talk about the frozen body lying in the snow, the hands tied behind his back, the blood, eyes like glass marbles . . .

"It . . . it doesn't make sense," Linus says, clasping his hands in his lap. "Why would anyone murder Johan?"

"That's exactly what we're trying to find out," Hanna replies. "We have one or two questions, if that's okay?"

Linus nods. His dark hair is tousled, the sleep creases from his pillow haven't yet faded from his slightly puffy face. Daniel wonders if he was out partying last night; the shaky hands and bloodshot eyes suggest quite a hangover.

"Everyone's talking about the murder, because it just happened," Linus mumbles. "But to think that it's Johan, that he's gone . . ."

His voice dies away, and he swallows audibly.

"How well did you know him?" Daniel asks.

"We've been friends for years. We went to school together here in Duved. Then he was away for a few years while he was competing in Europe, but we hooked up again when he came back. I guess you know that an injury ended his career?"

Daniel nods. Having read about Johan's success as a skier, he has a better understanding of what a blow the broken leg must have been. Johan sustained the injury at the final training camp before the Winter Olympics in Vancouver.

When he was in the best form of his entire life.

The Olympic dream was shattered there and then.

Linus pushes his chair back, the legs scraping loudly across the floor. He sways, as if he is about to lose his balance, and his hand shoots out to grab the edge of the table for support.

Daniel's suspicions about Linus's condition are growing stronger. The guy is still drunk.

"Johan was a good person," Linus says sadly. "A true optimist, always cheerful and generous."

He is echoing Marion's words about Johan's fine character.

"How long have you been business partners?" Hanna asks.

"Let me think . . . We must have set up the company about five years ago. We were both employed elsewhere, but neither of us liked the owner. We started talking about doing something together, and one thing led to another."

"Can you tell us about your professional relationship? How was the company doing?"

"Okay, I guess. We had plenty of clients, and Marion took care of the admin."

"Did you socialize outside work?"

"Not exactly."

Something in Linus's expression makes Daniel react, and he can see that Hanna has picked up on it too. *What's going on?*

"Why not?"

Linus shuffles uncomfortably. "I thought the world of Johan, but I haven't got much in common with his wife."

"But you work together, don't you?"

"Yes."

Silence. Daniel doesn't speak either. Sometimes it's better to keep quiet until the other person becomes so stressed that they start talking.

Which is exactly what Linus does.

"Marion's not what you'd call easygoing. She's from Germany and she can be quite difficult. It's her way or the highway, if you know what I mean? Johan and I have always gotten along very well, but there were often problems with Marion. She insisted on getting involved in how we ran the business, and she had opinions on most things."

"I understand," Daniel says. "We were actually thinking of going to see Marion again when we're done here. She was so shocked yesterday that it was hard to get a clear viewpoint from her."

"That's got to be a first."

The comment is so sarcastic that Daniel looks up.

"I don't want to speak ill of Marion in a situation like this," Linus goes on, "but she really isn't easy to deal with."

He sighs heavily, and the smell of his stale breath reaches Daniel's nostrils. He is beginning to wonder if Linus's drinking habits affect his credibility. He certainly doesn't like Marion.

"So, what can you tell us about Johan's marriage?" Hanna wonders. "Any idea why they don't have children?"

Linus hesitates before answering. "I don't think that was what they wanted, but I've never discussed it with Johan. He was very good with kids—my son adored him. Sometimes he would take Lukas out on the snowmobile."

He falls silent, and the only sound is the faucet dripping into the sink. It seems a worn gasket has not been replaced, even though Linus is a plumber.

The atmosphere is more than uncomfortable. Time to change the subject. Daniel is thinking about the way Johan was killed. It was neither an accident nor a spur-of-the-moment act. The brutal violence, the bound wrists indicate that the perpetrator was extremely angry.

Someone has been deeply offended and has taken out their rage in the worst way imaginable.

"Do you know if Johan had any enemies, Linus? If he'd fallen out with anyone?"

"Could he have gotten into a dispute with a client?" Hanna adds.

"You're the cops, but it sounds crazy to me. Surely you don't kill because of a shoddy plumbing job?" Linus turns away, suppressing an inappropriate yawn. "Everyone liked Johan," he says firmly. "I know that's what people always say, but he was the kind of guy you instinctively warmed to. A genuinely good person, kind and considerate. The only downside, if I can speak frankly, is that he let Marion tell him what to do far too often."

Daniel notices that Linus's tone changes as soon as he speaks about Marion. Could she have been a source of conflict between the two business partners?

The statistics for homicide are crystal clear: the perpetrator is almost always someone close to the victim.

"Was there any friction between you and Johan? Were you in agreement about how the firm should be run?"

Linus glances toward the window. Daniel does the same. Snow crystals have stuck to the glass, and a long icicle is hanging from the roof. There are traces of small fingers on the inside; presumably his son has pressed his hand against the pane.

"Everything was fine between me and Johan. I can't comment on what Marion thought."

The answer is brief, the tone curt. Linus suddenly seems more sober, as if he is trying to pull himself together.

Daniel can see that Hanna is thinking. Her instincts are usually good—that's one of the things he appreciates most about her.

"Johan was found in Tångböle," she says. "But he lives in Staa, just over six miles away."

"Yes."

"Do you know if he had any connection to Tångböle?"

"Not that I'm aware of."

Daniel realizes where Hanna is going.

"We need a list of your clients, together with their contact details," he says. "Everywhere Johan has been recently. As soon as possible, please."

"No problem. I'll get that to you today."

The door opens, and a boy in pale-green pajamas peers in, his hair ruffled. He can't be more than five or six years old. Daniel finds it hard to imagine Alice at that age—a little girl who can walk and talk.

"Daddy, I'm hungry!"

Linus looks at Daniel. "This is Lukas. I need to fix his breakfast." He pulls the boy close and gives him a hug. Daniel notices that the child also reacts to the smell of booze. No kid likes to see their parents under the influence.

Time to finish up. Just a few more questions.

"When did you last see Johan?" he asks, even though Lukas is tugging at his father's hand.

"He came by on Friday evening, at about eight o'clock."

Daniel checks his notes; that must have been after the visit to Pigo.

"Any particular reason?"

"We hadn't arranged anything. Sandra and I were still at the kitchen table when he showed up; then he told us he was going to be away for a week."

This is fresh information. Hanna frowns.

"Did he say where he was going?" she asks.

"No. He hadn't said a word about a vacation, and we had a lot of work booked. We're always busy when the Stockholm crowd arrives for the sports break. You know what it's like—there isn't a cottage to be had anywhere in Åre or Duved."

"How did you react?"

Linus picks up his son and settles him on his knee.

"It feels stupid now, but I was pretty angry. It was so unexpected, and it was going to cause real problems for the business."

"And you have no idea why Johan was planning to go away?"

Linus shakes his head. Daniel glances at Hanna. He senses that she is thinking the same as him. Had something happened to Johan Andersson that made it necessary for him to disappear quickly?

Had he been threatened?

REBECKA

2017

AUGUST

"You're so good with the children," Maria says to Rebecka as she emerges from the kitchen at the preschool. "They really like you."

Rebecka finds her new colleague's praise embarrassing. Maria is a few years older and has worked at the Little Snowdrops preschool in Ånn for a long time. Rebecka has been here for only a few days. She's not used to positive comments or associating with *the others*. Most things are still unfamiliar and different.

She has been married for almost five years now, and this is her first job. It feels unreal, but they had no choice when Ole was made redundant from the accounting firm. As soon as he secures a new post, she will go back to her normal life, but right now they need the money. And he does so much within the church. Ole has never been so busy, despite not getting paid.

That doesn't matter, the important thing is to carry out God's work.

"I love being with the little ones," she says, nodding in the direction of the hall where most of the children are having their afternoon nap.

"You're going to be a wonderful mom one of these days," Maria says with a smile.

Rebecka gets a lump in her throat. By this stage she knows it's not going to happen. She is worthless as a woman. If the church didn't have such strict views on divorce, no doubt Ole would already have left her.

Maria pushes back a strand of blond hair. "By the way, a few of us are going out this weekend—would you like to come along?"

Rebecka is confused. Is Maria asking if she wants to go out and enjoy herself? Without her husband? The inappropriate suggestion is bewildering. Women don't do that kind of thing—not on their own.

"I can't," she whispers, feeling embarrassed.

"Is it because your husband wouldn't like it?" Maria winks at her. "I live with my partner too, but you can't spend all your time together, can you?"

Rebecka tries to smile, even though Maria's words are . . . offensive. Men and women have different roles to play in life—surely she ought to know that. At the same time, Rebecka doesn't want to criticize her new colleague. She has always been aware that other rules apply outside the church. People associate with one another differently from the way in which Rebecka has been brought up.

As a pastor's wife she must be perfect. She would never dream of going out alone or drinking alcohol in public. Not that Ole would allow it. He understands what is and is not suitable behavior, and he advises on her choice of clothes and colors.

He knows best, and that makes her feel secure—she can rely on him.

She has a driver's license, but Ole insists on taking her to work every morning and picking her up at the end of the day.

His consideration knows no bounds.

Rebecka gives Maria a sympathetic look. If only the older woman realized how wrong she was. Maybe Maria would be able to welcome God if she opened her heart? However, she would have to make radical changes to her lifestyle, distance herself from bad habits and practices.

Elsa, one of the three-year-olds, comes running with tears in her eyes. Rebecka immediately scoops her up.

"Another time, maybe," Maria says, leaving her to it.

13

The sound of her phone vibrating on the kitchen counter brings Marion back to the present moment. She is sitting at the table with an untouched cup of coffee in front of her. It has gone cold, but she doesn't remember when she poured it.

Time has lost its meaning.

She picks up the phone and sees *Linus* on the display, which makes her feel uncomfortable. She has hardly spoken to him since the huge argument at the office a few weeks ago; she's stayed away as much as possible.

At that moment a car pulls up in front of the house. Through the window she sees two people get out—the detectives who were here yesterday, a man and a woman.

Marion rejects Linus's call and puts the phone in her pocket. She can't cope with talking to him right now. Everything is still so awful; she is listening for Johan's footsteps the whole time. Waiting for that irresistible laugh.

The house is unbearably empty.

She makes a huge effort, stands up, and opens the front door.

"Hi," says the female officer, who introduced herself as Hanna. "May we come in? We have a few more questions, if that's okay?" Her expression is warm as she adds, "If you can manage?"

Marion nods and turns away. She has just seen herself in the hall mirror. Her face is sallow, with dark circles beneath her eyes. The

German brandy has left its mark. It did make her forget the horror for a few hours, but as soon as she woke, reality caught up with her.

They go into the kitchen, and Marion sinks down onto a chair.

"How are you feeling?" Hanna asks. Her tone is gentle and empathetic, even though they don't know each other. No doubt it's part of her job—what does she know about losing the person you love most in the whole world?

"Not so good," Marion mumbles.

"Is there no one who can come over for the next few days? You shouldn't be alone right now."

Marion clasps her hands tightly, she doesn't want to lose control and break down in front of the two officers. The truth is that she doesn't have any close friends in Sweden. She didn't have many in Germany either; she's always been a lone wolf.

Plus, it's not easy to get to know people here in Åre. The Swedes keep to themselves; they are reluctant to admit anyone new into the community. Sure, she knows the neighbors, they've had dinner occasionally, but Johan was more than her husband. He was her best friend.

Her soulmate.

"My family live in Germany." Her voice is flat, distant.

"Is there anyone we can call? A close relative, maybe?"

Marion waves a dismissive hand. "My parents are dead. I have a brother, Florian, who lives in Stuttgart. I'll speak to him later today."

"How about Johan's mom and dad?"

Marion doesn't have the energy to explain that unfortunately she's never really gotten along with her in-laws. Tarja and Torsten didn't like the fact that Johan was with a woman who was so much older than him. Or that they married in Germany without telling anyone in advance, and with only two witnesses.

Marion blinks back the tears.

In the bedroom is their wedding photo from Ramsau, the ski resort where she grew up. It was taken on the slopes, immediately after the outdoor ceremony. The sun is sparkling on the winter snow; the sky is clear blue. She is holding a bouquet of dark-red roses, which stand out beautifully against the white surroundings.

It was the happiest day of her life.

But Tarja and Torsten have never welcomed her. These days they meet up two or three times a year, usually around Christmas and Easter. It has become the norm for Johan to see his parents alone, without Marion.

Tarja called her more than once yesterday, but Marion couldn't bring herself to answer.

She hasn't even considered asking them to come over.

"Do they know . . ." Her voice breaks. She takes a deep breath, tries again. "Do they know that Johan is dead?"

The officer who introduced himself as Daniel says, "They were informed yesterday. We've also contacted his brother, Pär."

"Johan was godfather to Pär's eldest son."

It's almost impossible to get the words out. Johan loved hanging out with ten-year-old Robin. He was like the son Johan never had.

The thought is as painful as ever. She'd hoped and longed to become pregnant for many years. Now it's too late. She is forty-four, and Johan is dead.

She will never be a mother, never have a child of her own.

Never see Johan as a father.

He would have been a fantastic dad.

Daniel clears his throat, and Marion realizes that she was lost in her own dark thoughts.

"There are certain indications that your husband might have been threatened," Hanna says. "Do you know anything about that?"

"What do you mean?"

"We've just been to see your husband's business partner, Linus Sundin," Daniel explains. "He said that Johan came by on Friday, said he was going away the following day."

The very mention of Linus's name makes that dreadful feeling return. What has he said now?

She tries to process this new information.

"Going away?"

"According to Linus, Johan was planning to be away for at least a week, even though they had a lot of work booked," Hanna says.

"But it's the sports break," Marion says, totally confused. "We're always really busy then."

"So, you had no idea about the trip?" Daniel says.

What kind of threat are they talking about? She tries to concentrate, but it's hard to focus.

"We're wondering if the reason behind it was some kind of concrete threat," Daniel continues, making a note.

"Had he received any strange letters or worrying phone calls?" Hanna asks. "Had anyone approached him at work, said something unpleasant?"

Marion doesn't know what to say. The only person she can think of in that context is Linus.

"In that case let's move on," Daniel says. "We found your husband's wallet, but not his phone. Do you happen to know where it might be?"

Marion shakes her head. Johan always answered as soon as she called, with a cheery *Hi, sweetheart!*

She will never hear those words again.

Daniel's voice brings her back to reality.

"Okay. Regarding his friends, we've been trying to get a hold of Carl Willner, whom you mentioned, but no luck so far. Could he have left town?"

"I don't think so. Johan was meeting him at Pigo on Friday."

They've been best friends ever since high school, even though they chose different paths in life. While Johan was competing, Calle studied economics at the University of Gävle. He stayed there for a few years and moved back to Duved comparatively recently.

Marion has always liked him.

"And what was Johan's relationship with Linus Sundin like?" Hanna wants to know. "Was everything okay between them?"

"I believe you're responsible for the bookkeeping," Daniel adds.

Marion hesitates. This is probably the right moment to tell them about Linus, but she doesn't know if she has the courage.

Her phone buzzes again. She takes it out of her pocket and sees that Linus has called four times. Her pulse is racing. She can't bring herself to speak to him. He's bound to be furious—God knows what he might do in that state.

And Johan isn't here to protect her anymore.

Before Marion can say anything, Hanna reassures her: "We're grateful for any information you can give us. The most important thing right now is to find your husband's murderer."

Those words make Marion realize what she must do. She is going to tell them about Linus, however difficult it might be.

She has to do this.

"Were Johan and Linus on the same page when it came to finances, for example?"

Marion doesn't answer at first. The last discussions between the two men were horrendous. Linus accused her of stirring up trouble, but she'd had to tell Johan what was going on.

And make it clear that she was on his side.

"They quarreled," she says eventually. "And Johan hated quarreling."

She remembers his frustration, his aversion to conflict. He saw the best in everyone, and Linus exploited that. Johan desperately wanted to believe in his partner, but it became increasingly obvious that Linus put his own self-interest first.

"What was the quarrel about?"

"It was about . . . money."

"Can you explain?" Daniel presses her.

Marion licks her lips. She doesn't want to say the wrong thing, or provoke Linus even more, but there is no alternative. She has to give this information to the police.

It could be the key to the entire case.

"Linus wasn't doing his job properly. At the same time, he wanted to take more money out of the business, more than it could stand, though both Johan and I were against it."

The reluctance can be heard in her voice as she continues: "I took care of the books. I knew what resources were available, and how our liquidity was looking."

"Tell us about this quarrel," Hanna says. "Was it a physical confrontation?"

"The last time was very upsetting. We were at the office in Duved three weeks ago, toward the end of January. Linus frightened me—I honestly thought he might become violent. His demands were totally unreasonable, given that he was the cause of the downturn in our finances."

"In what way?"

Marion wishes she didn't have to say any more. Linus will be furious if he finds out, and what will she do then?

"He . . . he drinks. He's always drunk a lot, but it's gotten worse over the past twelve months. He used to only drink at the weekends, but now it's during the week as well."

She looks away, out of the window at the snow-covered drive where Johan's white van should be.

Her heart contracts.

Darling Johan.

"When Linus drinks, he can't work. He started missing various jobs, and this winter the situation has escalated. Johan tried to cover for him, but he couldn't cope with doing the work of two people. Our income was dropping too—we couldn't invoice a client when Linus didn't show up. Our profits last year were much lower than the previous year."

"Why did Linus need the money?" Hanna asks.

Marion's mouth is so dry that she can hardly speak, but Hanna's eyes are fixed on her. She is waiting for a response.

Her phone buzzes yet again in her pocket, as if Linus senses that she is talking to the police about him. She rejects the call, her fingers trembling as she touches the phone.

Please don't let him find out what I'm telling them.

"I . . . I suspect that he has some kind of gambling addiction. I've seen him on the computer in the office a few times when he didn't know I was there; he was using an online casino."

She stares at her glass of water, pictures the scene. If Linus had been allowed to continue, the whole business could have gone under. In the end Marion told Johan that he had to confront his partner.

She had never seen Linus as aggressive as when Johan demanded the truth. Linus had said terrible things about her too, accused her of destroying the friendship between him and Johan. He more or less spat out her name.

Hanna listens with her head tilted to one side. "What happens to the company now Johan is dead? Do you inherit?"

"No. I inherit fifty percent of Johan's share, and Linus gets the other half. They agreed on that right at the start when they didn't know how things would go. The one left behind would always own the majority."

Daniel looks at his colleague, then at Marion.

"So now there's nothing to stop Linus taking out more money?"

"No," Marion admits, seeing his angry face in her mind's eye. "Nothing at all."

REBECKA

2018

APRIL

Ole is waiting in the parking lot as usual when Rebecka emerges from the preschool. She gets in and fastens her seatbelt as quickly as possible. He doesn't like waiting.

Maria is standing in the doorway. Ole raises his hand and gives her a charming smile. He has never been inside, but occasionally he has chatted pleasantly with Maria when she and Rebecka have finished work at the same time.

Something about his tense jawline makes the warning bells start to ring.

"Is everything all right?" she asks.

Ole doesn't answer; he just increases his speed even though it's raining. The car skids on the wet asphalt, and Rebecka has to grab the edge of her seat to steady herself.

She feels a lump forming in her stomach. She goes over the past twenty-four hours in her mind. Everything was perfectly normal this morning. She had prepared his breakfast before it was time to leave for work, and they had chatted about this and that on the way.

She looks down at her clothes—is she wearing something unsuitable? She has worn the pale-blue sweater many times with his approval, and her pants aren't too tight.

Then it strikes her.

The other day she went to a little café nearby with Maria during their lunch break. It's happened only a few times. Maria keeps asking, and Rebecka doesn't want to appear rude. Her colleague is always so kind and considerate; they have become friends, even though Maria is not a member of the Light of Life. Rebecka can't keep saying no.

Someone from the church must have seen them and told Ole.

Feverishly she tries to work out what can be used against her. They were there for no more than half an hour. Maria is so funny it's hard not to laugh at her stories. Maybe someone noticed that Rebecka was drawing attention to herself through inappropriately loud laughter.

They are going to her parents' for dinner, but Ole turns onto a narrow forest road. The car stops abruptly.

Rebecka sits perfectly still.

Ole turns to face her.

"You are required to show me respect." His voice is quiet, his tone ice cold. "God has said that a wife must obey her husband."

"I know," Rebecka whispers.

"You may not run around the town without me."

It is as she feared; a member of the church must have seen her. How could she have been so careless?

"It will never happen again," she promises. "Please forgive me."

She realizes that he is upset; she should have known better. Ole wants everything to be perfect—God is always watching them.

He grabs her hand and squeezes it; it hurts, but not as much as the shame burning inside her.

"If you do it again, that will be the last time you go to work."

Would God really stop her from spending time with the children? Would he punish her so harshly?

She loves her job. It was never her intention to stay at Little Snowdrops for so long, but Ole hasn't managed to find another accounting position. Instead, he devotes himself wholeheartedly to the Light of Life. Pastor Jonsäter gives him more and more to do—sometimes he has to stay up late into the night to write his sermons.

He has never been so stressed.

The last thing he needs is a wife who fails to show him respect or to support his important work in the name of Jesus.

"I promise," Rebecka reiterates. "I'll never do it again."

14

Thick mist covers Lake Åre like a lid as Daniel drives back from Staa. One minute visibility is good; then he hits a wall of gray, impenetrable fog. He is still thinking about the conversation in Linus's kitchen. It didn't sound as if he was the person behind any threat to Johan, but maybe he is a good enough actor to hide it?

Daniel is beginning to wonder whether there are other matters Linus is keeping quiet about.

"What do you think about Linus's financial problems?" he asks Hanna.

"That came as a real surprise. Both the issue itself and the fact that there was conflict between him and Johan. He didn't say a word about any of that to us."

Daniel agrees—there was no hint of the tension that had clearly existed. Marion's information has given the case a completely new direction.

She also said Linus had acted aggressively.

"The question is—how desperate was Linus?" he says, slowing behind a truck.

Hanna drums her fingers on her thigh as she thinks.

"We need to double-check the shared ownership agreement between Linus and Johan," she says. "And take a close look at Linus's personal finances. If what Marion says is true, then Linus could have a motive for wanting to see Johan dead."

She takes out her phone. "I'm going to try Carl Willner again—he might know more about their relationship."

There is no answer, but just as she ends the call, the phone rings. From the conversation, Daniel gathers that it's the regional dispatch in Umeå.

"Good news—a patrol has found Johan's van on a minor road between Tångböle and Staa. Up by Lake Gev, if that's any help?"

Daniel knows roughly where it is.

"Carina is already on her way there with a colleague," Hanna adds.

Daniel glances at the clock—almost twelve. He has promised Ida that he won't be out all day; they are going to visit her mother, Elisabeth, in Järpen this afternoon for coffee and cake.

He pulls into the next road and turns the car around.

This has to come first—it can't be helped.

Fifteen minutes later they have reached Lake Gev; the blue-and-white police tape shows them where to go. An area of several hundred square yards has been cordoned off, and just like yesterday there is a police car parked in the middle of the road.

Daniel can see a white van next to a ramshackle house with broken windows and a few planks missing from the facade. Only the rear part of the vehicle is visible by the corner of the dwelling.

The two of them go over to join Carina, who got there first this time. She opens one of the back doors, and an acrid smell immediately reaches their nostrils.

"Shit," Daniel says, recoiling.

Carina flings both doors wide open to reduce the impact of the stench, but it is still almost unbearable.

The muted daylight reveals the interior of the van. This was Johan's mobile place of work. There are shelves along the sides, with various items of plumbing equipment in untidy heaps. Black cables hang from hooks on the roof, and there is a suction device in one corner.

However, what catches Daniel's attention are the large, dark stains on the rubber mat. They both look and smell like dried blood; he doesn't need a trained police dog or a CSI to confirm it.

"I think we've found the answer to how Johan Andersson's body reached the place where it was discovered," Hanna says in a subdued tone. "It can hardly be anyone else who was lying in here."

"Do you think he was killed inside the van?" Daniel says.

"Looks that way."

Daniel glances around, hoping to spot a potential murder weapon, but nothing catches his eye.

"How's this for a theory," Hanna says. "The perpetrator dumped Johan on Tångbölevägen; then he drove the van here and hid it as best he could. Then he was picked up by an accomplice."

Daniel nods slowly. "Which means two people must have been involved, as we suspected. One to drive the van, one to drive the other vehicle."

Hanna realizes that she is almost up to her knees in snow. With a grunt she bends down to brush off the worst of it around the tops of her boots.

"We don't know if the murder was planned, or whether it happened on the spur of the moment," Daniel points out. "The method is certainly cold blooded, but that doesn't necessarily mean it was meticulously prepared. Something might have gone wrong on Friday evening before Johan could get away."

"So the person or persons who were threatening him might have found him before he left. That led to the killing, which meant that the van had to be hidden."

Daniel is inclined to agree. The fact that they have the van is a positive. It was a lucky break, just like the discovery of Johan's body. If that little boy hadn't persuaded his mom to stop the car so that he could pee, then Johan could well have remained where he was, hidden by snow until spring.

They've had more good fortune than they could have expected—but they still don't know who the killer is.

15

It is two o'clock before Daniel and Hanna arrive back at the station. Daniel has sent an apologetic text to Ida, telling her that he is delayed but on his way home.

They have gathered in the conference room with Anton and Raffe. Hanna has just made another attempt to contact Carl Willner. They all look tired, apart from Anton, who is bursting with energy.

Daniel summarizes the conversations with Linus and Marion.

Raffe leans back, arms folded. Today the black ponytail has been replaced by a smooth man bun, shining in the glow of the overhead light.

"The question is—who's the most credible, Linus or Marion?" he says. "I don't like the fact that the two people who were closest to Johan are telling such different stories."

"That's the problem," Hanna agrees. "Linus doesn't have anything good to say about Marion. He claims that she is so difficult at work that any socializing between families is impossible. While she says that Linus drinks too much, is aggressive, and doesn't do his job properly."

"Both of those assertions could be true," Anton chips in with a smile.

Daniel glances at his colleague. Why is he in such a good mood? The contrast with Raffe's grim expression is striking. Anton almost seems elated, even though they are investigating a tragic homicide.

"So Linus said that Johan was intending to go away," Raffe says. "What's that all about?"

"Marion insisted that Johan hadn't mentioned his plans to her," Daniel replies. "But why would Linus make up something like that, if he's the one behind the murder?"

Hanna thinks for a moment. "If we assume that Linus is the perpetrator, then he had presumably already made up the tale about Johan's sudden trip. When the body was discovered so quickly, he decided to stick to his story. I'm sure Johan wasn't meant to be found the day after the murder. If he had *only* been missing"—she draws quotation marks in the air and goes on—"and Linus had told us that Johan was planning to go away, then we would have been searching for a missing person, not a killer. The investigation would have had a completely different starting point."

Daniel rubs his chin, his short beard scratching his palm. He is pretty sure that Linus was surprised to see them yesterday. He was noticeably shocked when they were sitting in the kitchen—but maybe that wasn't because of the news about Johan's death, but because his body had been found so soon?

Linus had had no time to prepare himself. If he'd already come up with an explanation for Johan's absence, it's entirely possible that he would have stuck to it, even though the circumstances had changed.

Just as Hanna has suggested.

Daniel is itching to search Linus's house, but they don't have enough evidence to warrant that. They still need to verify Marion's allegations about his finances, and the forensic examination of the van is ongoing. Carina is a thorough and highly competent CSI. If there are any telltale fingerprints, DNA, or anything else that might strengthen their hypothesis, she will find it.

He turns to Raffe. "We need to take a close look at Linus's financial situation as soon as possible. Can you contact the tax office and the banks?"

"No problem."

"Hanna—what are we going to do about Johan's best friend, who isn't answering his phone?"

Hanna puts her elbows on the table and rests her chin on her hands.

"I thought I'd go to his place when we're done here. He lives in Duved, on Karolinervägen. Anyone want to come along?"

Daniel looks at his watch. Five to three. He ought to bring the meeting to a close and go home to Ida. She hasn't replied to his text, and she's not going to be happy that he's so late for coffee and cake at her mother's.

But they really do need to talk to Willner.

"I'll come," Anton offers, raising his hand. "I live in Duved."

"Perfect."

Daniel is about to say that he will come too, even though he doesn't have time, but Raffe takes the discussion in a different direction.

"What about Johan Andersson being the victim—there's a lot of activity on social media right now. Do we know when his identity will be made public?"

"I think Grip is holding a press conference at five o'clock," Daniel says. He hates that kind of public appearance. When Grip asked him to lead the special unit, his only stipulation was that he wouldn't have to sit on a podium answering idiotic questions from journalists.

Raffe nods. "That's just as well. The internet is boiling over with speculation."

The meeting is over. Daniel gets to his feet. He hears Hanna and Anton exchanging a few words about Carl Willner, deciding which car to take to Duved.

He feels a pang of guilt. He ought to be speaking to Johan's best friend himself. Willner is a key witness, and Daniel is leading the investigation. However, he has to prioritize Ida; she has been alone with Alice almost all weekend. He wants to be a father who is present in Alice's life, a good partner to Ida, a man who is there for his family.

And yet . . . going to see Carl Willner feels much more important than sipping coffee with his mother-in-law.

Although he has no idea how he is going to explain that to Ida.

16

Carl lives in an apartment to the east of the center of Duved. He is the same age as Johan, single, and he works as a business development officer for Åre Council.

Hanna is following Anton. Because he lives in Duved, it made sense to take two cars, so that he doesn't have to drive back to Åre afterward. When she turns onto Karolinervägen, she sees Duved's impressive nineteenth-century wooden cathedral, dominating the area with its three spires and room for nine hundred people.

The sun has come out, and its light is reflected in the leaded windows. The ice-blue sky provides a beautiful background.

Hanna remembers attending the service there on Christmas morning when she was a little girl. She recalls a colorful nativity scene and tall candles flickering along the chancel. Round-cheeked children singing "Silent Night." How old would she have been then? No more than six or seven. The family always spent the February sports break in Åre, but on that occasion they had come up for Christmas too.

Someone was holding her hand—probably her father. Her mother rarely touched her; she was never one for kisses or tender gestures. Lydia was sitting beside her; she had brought candy and gave one to Hanna when she wouldn't sit still.

It was a different time, before she learned about all the terrible things in the world.

The memory vanishes as quickly as it came into her mind.

She glances at the dashboard clock. Lydia and her family are taking the afternoon flight from Stockholm. They are due to land at Östersund Airport at about four o'clock, which means they should be in Sadeln by five thirty.

She is really looking forward to seeing her sister. Not only has Lydia supported Hanna in the dispute with her former boss, she has also been a great help in dealing with Christian and the issue of the apartment they shared. Its value has increased significantly since they moved in five years ago. Lydia has been trying to persuade Christian to give Hanna a share of the profit when he sells and buys a new place, even if he is technically the owner.

As usual, the thought of her ex puts Hanna in a bad mood.

Over two months have passed since he dumped her. She had no idea that he was seeing someone else behind her back. He is now living with Valérie, posting one fantastic picture after another on social media. They go to restaurants, spend lovely weekends at castles, enjoy amazing walks in beautiful parks.

Hanna knows perfectly well that she shouldn't look at the photos on his Facebook page, but sometimes, especially late at night, that's exactly what she does.

Not that she wants him back—she has passed that stage. But the anger hasn't gone away; she still feels cheated and let down. The fact that her mother has invited Christian and Valérie to dinner on top of everything else is just too much.

If she could at least get some money from the apartment, that would be a form of redress—particularly as she helped to pay both the interest and monthly fees during the years they lived there.

Hanna grimaces at her own naivety. She walked straight into the classic woman's trap—sharing the expenses without any formal ownership agreement. She has only herself to blame if she ends up with nothing.

How stupid was she?

Up ahead Anton is signaling. He pulls into a parking lot outside a red apartment block. Hanna follows him and turns off the engine. She doesn't have time to brood over Christian; she has a job to do.

She hopes Carl Willner is home, and that he can help them get closer to solving the murder of Johan Andersson.

REBECKA

2018

AUGUST

Sunday dinner at Ole and Rebecka's, with their guests Pastor Jonsäter and his wife, Karin, is coming to an end. Rebecka says goodbye in the hallway as Karin thanks her one last time. The men have already gone outside and are chatting on the porch.

Jonsäter puts a fatherly arm around Ole's shoulders and says something. Rebecka smiles; she knows how much his approval means to her husband.

As the car disappears Ole comes back into the house. The smile he wore for their guests has disappeared; his face is closed and grim. Rebecka glances anxiously at him. His silence makes her nervous.

"That was nice, wasn't it?" she says to lighten the mood.

"You think?"

Her stomach flips and she thinks hard, trying to work out exactly what she has done wrong.

She allowed Ole to dictate her hairstyle and her dress, as it was an important occasion. Not many people can invite the leader of the church to an intimate dinner. She tried to support Ole throughout the meal, laughing at his jokes with extra enthusiasm. She was careful not to take up too much space, so to speak.

Clearly, she has failed.

The sun is slipping down behind the treetops, and she shivers as a chilly breeze sweeps in through the open window. She steals a glance at Ole, attempts to read his expression, without success.

Her charming husband, the man who was chatting easily to the pastor a moment ago, is long gone. She is about to say that she will get started cleaning up in the kitchen when Ole grasps her arm.

"Don't ever do that to me again."

His tone is vicious. He raises a threatening index finger.

Rebecka makes a huge effort to understand.

"What have I done?"

"Don't play the innocent with me!" His grip on her arm tightens. "Did you think I'd stand for you interrupting me time and time again in front of Jan-Peter?"

His eyes are filled with contempt. He shoves her in front of him toward the living room. "Where does this sick need to be the center of attention come from? It's as if you think everyone wants to listen to your inane babbling."

Rebecka doesn't think she talked a great deal, but no doubt he is right. She should have watched her tongue.

"I'm sorry," she whispers. "I didn't mean to do it."

"Do you really believe you're that interesting?" Ole pushes her again, she almost loses her balance.

"I'm not trying to make myself interesting."

"You're a vain and deluded woman," he yells. "Do you know what Isaiah has to say about that?"

Rebecka shrinks into herself. She is not permitted to argue with her husband. It is wrong, she knows that—but she didn't do what he is accusing her of. She didn't interrupt him, that's not what happened. Quite the reverse—she was careful to keep a low profile.

She can't understand why he's so angry.

Could it be his disappointment over their failure to have a child that is talking? Or stress because he has yet to find a new job? Ole always wants everything to be perfect.

The injustice makes her open her mouth. She is on the verge of tears.

"Please, Ole—why do you always have to misunderstand?"

Ole stares at her as if she has said something utterly unbelievable.

"Are you blaming me, your husband, for this situation? After what you've done?" At first he sounds stunned; then his voice takes on a new sharpness. "Is there nothing inside that stupid head of yours?"

Rebecka realizes she has gone too far. "That's not what I meant," she stammers. "I'm not blaming you."

Ole takes a step closer. It comes with no warning. He simply clenches his fist and punches her hard in the stomach.

The blow is so powerful that Rebecka falls to the floor. She curls up in pain, she can't breathe. Fear makes the tears flow, she can't help it.

The look in Ole's eyes is terrifying.

"Look what you made me do!" he bellows.

She hears rather than sees him grab his jacket and leave the house. The door slams shut. Rebecka remains where she is, lying on the carpet. The shock is almost worse than the pain. She has offended against both God and her husband.

She has made Ole hit her.

How could she do something so terrible?

17

The apartment is in the middle of the second floor. The nameplate says WILLNER, and Anton rings the bell.

"Let's hope he's home," he says to Hanna, who is waiting on the stairs. When nothing happens, he presses the bell again. Finally, he leaves his finger on the button for an extra-long time to make sure that if anyone is in there, they will hear.

The door is yanked open by a well-built man in his thirties, with a white towel wrapped around his hips. He is drying his hair with another towel.

"What the hell?" he snaps before the door is fully open. "Take it easy!"

Then he freezes, stares at Anton.

Who stares back.

"Oh!" Carl exclaims.

It takes Anton a few seconds to gather his thoughts. Hanna can see that something isn't quite right; she looks from one man to the other, and back again.

"Do you two know each other?" she asks.

Anton comes to his senses. He pretends he hasn't heard Hanna's question, and holds up his police ID.

"Carl Willner?"

He tries to sound perfectly normal, with limited success. Hardly surprising, given that he and Carl were lying together in Anton's bed just a few hours ago.

"Er . . . yes?"

Carl is clearly taken aback. The strained silence seems to go on and on. Hanna looks as if she would like to give Anton a push and tell him to pull it together.

He is trying but doesn't know how to behave. He can't possibly explain to Hanna that he and Carl met at Bygget yesterday evening and have spent the whole night together.

His palms are sweating. He has to find a way to get through the next hour.

Hanna moves forward to stand beside him.

"We need to speak to you," she says to Carl. "Can we come in?"

"What's this about?"

"It's probably best if you get dressed first."

Carl nods and disappears into the bedroom, while Hanna and Anton sit down in the living room. The sofa and armchairs are in pale leather, and there are fitness magazines on the round glass coffee table. Anton recognizes them; he has several of the same publications at home.

Hanna gives him an inquiring look. "Are you okay?"

Anton manages a smile. "Absolutely. Just tired, I guess—I was at Bygget last night with Karro."

She doesn't ask any more questions. *Thank God.*

After a few minutes Carl reappears. He is barefoot, wearing jeans and a white T-shirt. His biceps are as impressive in daylight as they were the last time Anton saw them. He knows he must be professional, but the situation is making him extremely uncomfortable. He very rarely picks up a guy at a club. Åre is too small, and he prefers to keep his personal life private. Sexual preferences might not matter in the big city, but up here it's different. In spite of the tourists, Åre has a typical small-town mentality. The police station is an old-fashioned workplace, and the ethos of the force is conservative.

That's the reason why he hasn't yet come out at work. He can't even count how many so-called gay jokes he has heard during the ten years since he started at the police academy.

"We've been trying to get a hold of you," Hanna begins in a slightly accusatory tone of voice. "Why haven't you been answering your phone?"

Carl looks perplexed, then spreads his hands wide. "Oh—is it you who's been calling from a withheld number?"

"Yes."

"Sorry, but I never answer calls like that."

"Haven't you listened to your messages?"

Carl shrugs. "I was out last night—it was a late one."

He gives Anton a meaningful look, which Anton ignores.

"I've only just got up," Carl says, without the least sign of embarrassment. "I haven't had time to check my voicemail yet."

Anton remembers the kisses before Carl left his apartment; his earlobes are burning. He also has a terrible feeling that Carl doesn't know what has happened to his best friend.

Hanna softens her tone.

"We need to speak to you about your friend Johan Andersson."

Carl looks bewildered. "Johan?"

Hanna hesitates; she too has realized that Carl has no idea about Johan's death.

"He was found murdered yesterday morning."

The room falls silent. The seconds stretch out unbearably as Anton sees Carl's face change.

"What do you mean? Are you telling me that Johan is dead?"

Hanna's expression is sympathetic.

"It can't be true!"

"I'm afraid it is. I'm so sorry to bring such terrible news. That's why we've been trying to reach you."

Carl closes his eyes. Anton wants to place a hand on his arm, stroke his back, console him, but it's impossible with Hanna here. Under normal circumstances he would show warmth and empathy, but right now he's sitting here as stiff as a board. He still can't process the fact that he'd spent the night with Johan's best friend, an important witness.

"Oh my God," Carl says after a long silence. "I don't know what to say." He takes a deep breath. "Murdered, you said? He wasn't the person who was found in Tångböle yesterday?"

"He was. Once again, I'm sorry."

Carl clasps his hands in his lap.

"I know this isn't easy," Hanna continues gently, "but we do need to ask you a few questions."

Carl's eyes are shining with unshed tears.

"Could you start by telling us how the two of you knew each other?"

Anton is grateful that Hanna is taking the lead. He still can't get his head around the predicament in which he finds himself.

"We've been friends since childhood. We went to school together. I also competed in downhill skiing, but I was never anywhere near Johan's level. We remained good friends, and as soon as he came back to Sweden, it felt as if he'd never been away."

Anton can hardly bring himself to look at Carl. He must get a grip; he can't let Hanna carry the whole load. He is here to do his job.

"When did you last see Johan?"

He attempts to sound professional, but the words are somehow stilted.

"On Friday. At Pigo."

Anton is familiar with Pigo. It is one of the nicest restaurants in Duved, with rustic decor and a big open fire. He has eaten countless pizzas there over the years.

"Could you tell us about your evening?" Hanna prompts Carl. "The more details the better."

Carl swallows several times. "We'd arranged to meet at seven. Johan was a little late."

"Did he say why?"

"Just that he had a lot going on at the moment."

"Did he seem the same as usual? What kind of mood was he in?"

Carl searches for the right words. "Johan was almost always in a good mood, but he was unusually . . . wired, if you know what I mean. He couldn't sit still, it was as if his thoughts were shooting off in all directions."

"Did you talk about anything in particular?"

"No, we just chatted, same old same old. Hockey, how Modo are likely to do in their next match . . ."

His face crumples. Anton has to make a huge effort to stop himself from reaching out a consoling hand.

"Sorry," Carl mumbles, wiping away a tear. "I just can't take it in."

"No problem," Hanna reassures him. "We're not in a hurry."

"Did Johan say why he was so wired?" Anton says in an attempt to contribute.

"No. But he was always such a calm person—that's why it struck me. It wasn't like him to be so restless. And he left after only twenty minutes, even though we'd arranged to have a pizza together."

"Did he explain why?"

"Again, he just said he had a lot going on. Apparently, he was going away the following day and still had to pack."

Hanna looks at Anton. Carl has just confirmed what Linus told them about Johan's plans, which means Linus wasn't lying. And yet Johan's wife claimed that she didn't know anything about the trip. That might mean that Johan didn't have time to get back to her before he was attacked.

"Do you know where he was going when he left the restaurant?" Anton asks.

"Home, I presume."

"You have no idea about his travel plans?" Hanna says. "Whether he was staying in Sweden or going abroad?"

"I don't know."

Silence. Carl bites his lip, as if his feelings are catching up with him.

"I could tell he was happy about going away," he adds. "Although he really did have ants in his pants. As if he had too much to think about."

Something isn't right here. Anton can see that Hanna is equally taken aback. Their current hypothesis is based on the assumption that Johan had been forced to leave because of some kind of threat.

In which case he would hardly have been looking forward to the trip.

"What time did he leave the restaurant?"

"Let me think . . . Just before seven thirty. The rest of the gang were due then, but he'd gone before they showed up."

"Did he have his van with him?"

"I think so. He only had a low-alcohol beer because he was driving."

Anton tries to summarize the conversation in his head. Just over twelve hours passed between the visit to the restaurant and the time when Johan's body was found.

Where was he during those hours?

"Are we nearly done?" Carl says, his voice strained.

"Very nearly," Hanna replies.

Carl sinks back in his chair. Dusk is falling even though it's still afternoon. Dark clouds have chased away the sun, and the light outside the window is gray. Carl looks pale and drawn, far from the charming guy Anton met at Bygget yesterday evening. Anton wants to reach out and take his hand. Or preferably give him a big hug.

"You said that you and Johan were childhood friends," Hanna goes on. "So I'm assuming you also know Linus Sundin, Johan's business partner?"

"We went to school together as well."

"What can you tell us about the relationship between Johan and Linus?"

"It wasn't . . . too bad."

"What exactly does that mean?"

"Johan and Linus had . . . very different views on the business."

Hanna says nothing. She waits for Carl to continue, even though he is clearly troubled. Anton is impressed. She's a good cop, with an excellent interviewing technique. The slightest opening and she's in there.

"Linus drinks too much," Carl confides reluctantly. "He always has done, but recently it's gotten worse. Everyone's aware of it, but you know how things are . . . It's not easy to tell someone they need to cut back on the booze."

"Do you know if Johan tried?" Anton asks.

"No, but I do know that Johan was worried. Marion took care of the books, and she was concerned. The company had to pay the price in more ways than one when Linus was hungover and didn't show up to work. Johan prefers moderation, he doesn't drink very much at all."

Carl falls silent as he realizes what he has said. "I mean he *didn't* drink very much . . ." The ensuing pause is painful.

"Anyway . . . neither Johan nor I like to get drunk, but Linus doesn't have those . . . boundaries." He looks down and interlaces his fingers. Despite his best efforts, Anton can't help remembering what they did last night, their bodies intertwined in his bed.

"Linus has always put away a lot of booze. We used to joke that he had to drink more than anybody else, but now he seems to have lost control."

"Do you know if he has any other problems?"

Carl looks up. "In what way?"

"Does he use drugs?" Hanna clarifies. "Is he addicted to gambling?"

"Not that I'm aware of."

"Does Linus have a tendency to become violent or aggressive when he's drunk?" Anton asks.

"Sometimes." Carl inhales sharply. Anton can see the wheels turning as the import of the question hits home. "Do you think Linus killed Johan?"

REBECKA

2019

MAY

Rebecka's movements are slow and heavy when she arrives at the preschool in the morning. It is a glorious spring day; the air is mild even though it's not yet eight o'clock, but every bone in her body is aching.

Yesterday Ole hit her again.

She's not really sure how long it's been going on, she can't remember how things were between them before it began. This time she couldn't even work out why. He came home in a bad mood, and whatever she said or did was wrong. When he discovered that one of his socks had gone missing in the wash, that was enough of an excuse.

It is like walking on eggshells when he is in that mood, just waiting for a reason to explode. At the same time, the fear before it happens is almost as bad. It can be a kind of relief when the blows come, because at least then she knows it will be a few days until the next occasion.

Ole never apologizes afterward. Usually, he acts as if nothing has occurred, or he might say that she forces him to punish her. She is too mouthy, a bad wife. He is only the instrument of the Lord.

She must learn to fear God.

Last night as she lay in bed, weeping silently, Ole slipped beneath the covers. In the darkness he ran his hands over her body, pushed up her nightdress, and rolled on top of her.

It hurt everywhere when he thrust into her, but she was too frightened to protest. It would only make him angry again. Make him hit her again.

Rebecka didn't think she would be able to go to work today. When she saw her puffy eyes and tearstained face in the bathroom mirror, she wanted nothing more than to call in sick, but Ole was already preparing to drive her to Little Snowdrops. She didn't dare say anything about staying home.

And they need the money she earns.

Ole hasn't managed to find a new post, almost two years after he had to leave the accounting firm. She's not actually sure if he's still looking, because the church takes up all his time.

Rebecka has frequently heard both her father and Pastor Jonsäter praising Ole's assiduousness and sense of duty. She wonders if they have any idea of how he treats his wife when no one is looking.

Do they know and choose to close their eyes to the truth? What would God say about that?

It doesn't matter—God doesn't care about her tears. If he did, he wouldn't allow Ole to carry on like this.

Rebecka hangs up her jacket and sees Maria heading toward her with a cup of coffee, smiling as usual. Maria has become one of her best friends, even though she is not a believer.

The preschool is a beacon of light in Rebecka's life, the only place where she feels safe.

Maria's smile vanishes as she reaches Rebecka. "What's wrong? Are you sick?"

Rebecka realizes that she must look awful. She tries to pretend that everything is fine. She thinks she has cracked ribs, one of them might be broken, but she dares not go and see a doctor. What would she say if someone asked how it had happened?

Would God punish her if she revealed that it was her husband who had hurt her?

"You look terrible," Maria goes on. "Do you really think you should be here today?"

Rebecka manages a wan smile. "I just didn't sleep well. I'm sure I'll feel better once I've had a coffee."

Maria gives her an odd look.

Over the past year, when Ole has become increasingly unpredictable, Maria has asked several times how things are at home. Rebecka has answered evasively. It's obvious that Maria is trying to reach out to her, but the shame is too great to allow Rebecka to confide in her colleague.

She can't tell her about Ole, about how frightened she is of her own husband.

She has only herself to blame for the situation in which she finds herself. If she could be more loving, do the right thing more often, then Ole wouldn't treat her like this.

It is her own fault.

She also fears the consequences. If she took courage and told Maria the truth, then Maria would say she ought to leave him. That would mean abandoning everything that makes up her life—the church, her friends, her cousins. Father and Mother would break off all contact with her—she would be a pariah. Not even Lisen would be on her side.

Ole's future as a pastor would be in jeopardy.

How could she possibly do that to him?

18

Ida notices that Daniel is on pins and needles. They have only been at her mother's for twenty-five minutes, but already he is restless.

A wave of disappointment washes over her.

Surely, he can spare a few hours for the sake of his family? He's been gone all weekend, and she has longed for his company.

They are sitting in the yellow-painted kitchen in Elisabeth's apartment in Järpen, where she has lived since the divorce. Ida and her sister, Sara, were only three and five back then. They have very little contact with their father.

Elisabeth has set out coffee, cinnamon buns, and a selection of cookies. Alice is sitting on Ida's knee and in a good mood. She is half sucking, half playing with a piece of bun.

Sara walks in and reaches for her niece.

"What a little sweetheart," she clucks, giving Alice a hug. "Can you say hi to Auntie Sara?"

Now Daniel is fingering the phone in his back pocket. Ida pretends not to notice. They arrived an hour late because he stayed at the station for so long; surely, he can switch off now? It's obvious he needs to rest.

"How are things at work?" Elisabeth asks, smiling warmly at Daniel.

He doesn't respond; he seems to be completely absorbed in his own thoughts.

"Daniel—Mom is speaking to you."

"Sorry, what did you say?"

"I was just wondering how things are at work."

"This new homicide investigation has given us a lot to do."

"You mean that poor guy who was found in Tångböle yesterday?" Sara says.

Daniel nods, and Ida shuffles uncomfortably. It's a dreadful story, and she feels very sorry for the family. However, she wishes that someone other than Daniel were on the case.

"Who would have thought something like that could happen here?" Sara adds. Alice is now happily tugging at her aunt's hair with her chubby little fingers.

"I heard it was Johan Andersson," Elisabeth says. "The skier from Duved who was so successful for a while. It's terrible if that's true." She looks at Daniel. "Was it him?"

"We haven't released the name yet. I'm sorry, but I can't talk about it."

Ida doesn't understand why he has to be so secretive. She's seen several posts on Facebook naming Johan Andersson as the victim; people have commented with the heart and crying emojis. Someone uploaded the photo of Johan on the podium when he won his medal at the world championship. Lots of questions, lots of speculation—the usual stuff you find online.

She places a hand on Daniel's arm. "Do you really have to behave as if you're dealing with state secrets?"

It sounds more critical than she'd intended, but everything was so difficult before they left home. Just when she had put the snowsuit on Alice, she messed herself. The sweet little dress she was wearing had to go straight in the wash, the snowsuit too. If Daniel had been back in time, they would have arrived at her mom's before disaster struck.

"I have a duty of confidentiality, Ida. I didn't invent it, but I am bound by it." Daniel reaches for a cinnamon bun. "These are delicious, Elisabeth—did you bake them yourself?"

Ida can see straight through his attempt to change the subject, but her mother seems pleased.

"I did. The trick is to spread the dough with plenty of butter and sugar, and leave them to rise for a long time."

"Daniel has been working nonstop all weekend." Ida can't help herself. "Yesterday he went to work at seven thirty and didn't get back until dinner. Same again today, that's why we were late."

Daniel looks confused, as if he's not sure why she's brought this up. Is she mad at him, or is she joking?

"Oh dear," Elisabeth says. "That sounds exhausting. Can you take tomorrow off to make up for it?"

"That's not exactly how it works."

Daniel smiles bravely. Ida knows exactly how it works. She learned that in December when that poor girl went missing. He'll be back at the station by seven o'clock tomorrow morning. They usually have a briefing at seven thirty, and before that he has to update himself and go through any reports that have come in over the past twenty-four hours.

His eyes are fixed on a distant point now, as if he is drifting away again.

"You need to think about your family," Elisabeth admonishes him. "It's not easy to be home alone with a baby. Believe me—I've done it twice."

Her mother's words instantly make Ida feel better. She has put Ida's own feelings into words; it is a form of the validation she has longed for. She doesn't want to nag when she tells Daniel that she wishes he would spend more time at home. She loves her daughter very much, but it can drive her crazy when she's home alone with a baby who just cries and cries.

She loves Daniel too—she's never been so much in love.

Elisabeth runs a hand over her beautifully styled hair. She is a hairdresser, just like Sara, and takes pride in her appearance. Ida has always been proud that her mother looks so good.

"I remember how hard it was when the girls were little," Elisabeth goes on. "Thank goodness times have changed and fathers take their share of the responsibility these days."

Daniel is still smiling, but Ida can see the tension in his jawline. Suddenly he stands up and takes Alice from Sara.

"I'll go and change her," he says, heading for the bathroom. Ida feels guilty; she didn't mean to create a bad atmosphere.

She just wants him to understand how she feels, without her having to put it into words every single time.

19

The house in Sadeln is in darkness when Hanna gets home after visiting Carl Willner. She has done some shopping in preparation for Lydia's arrival; it is ten past five.

The invasion will soon be here, she thinks with a smile.

She kicks off her boots, hangs up her jacket, then goes around switching on the lights. She begins with the living room, continues into the library, and finishes up in the huge kitchen.

This is no ordinary weekend cabin—it's more like a Swiss chalet. Her sister and brother-in-law live a completely different life from Hanna.

She starts unpacking the groceries. Lydia sent her an extensive list of "bare essentials," and Hanna fills the refrigerator with cheese, sausage, and what seems like gallons of milk and orange juice.

The supermarket was incredibly busy; there was no mistaking the fact that the sports break had begun. Every checkout was open, but there was still a long line at each one.

Her mind wanders as she puts things away. Mentally she checks off one point after another from the day's tasks.

She is glad they managed to get a hold of Carl Willner eventually, but there are still plenty of question marks around Johan Andersson's death. At least it was good that Carl was able to confirm Linus's alcohol problem, and the fact that he didn't do his job properly.

What was going on with Anton? He didn't seem to be engaged at all, and hardly said a word. Then he left as soon as they were done, which definitely isn't like him.

Hanna closes the refrigerator and folds up the two grocery bags. Just to be on the safe side, she wipes down the counters as well.

Marion's information about Linus's need for money is interesting. They haven't yet looked into the state of the Sundin family's finances, but it seems he could well have had a motive for murdering his partner.

Both Linus and Carl claimed that Johan was planning on going away at short notice. Hanna can't get her head around it. Why would Johan do that if he wasn't under threat? But if he was, then who was behind it? Not Linus—he knew about the trip and was still in Duved. And Carl had said that Johan seemed happy, as if he was looking forward to getting away. Which doesn't sound like a person trying to escape from a death threat.

Something isn't right.

Johan's name has now been released. When Hanna drove home, Grip had just held her press conference, and there was a discussion on the radio about the murder of the well-known skier. Needless to say, this increases the pressure to solve the case.

Hanna glances at the clock: five thirty. Lydia and Richard should be here at any minute. Everything looks good; the house is ready. She has even bought some brightly colored tulips. As a final touch she lights the candles in the numerous glass lanterns.

The sound of a car pulling onto the drive breaks the silence. Hanna sees a large black SUV, and she can just make out the children in the back. She smiles and heads for the front door.

"Auntie Hanna!" shouts a cheerful voice, and in no time ten-year-old Linnéa is in her arms. Fabian, who is twelve, is close behind. He too hurls himself at Hanna, even though he's almost a teenager. They are followed by their parents, laden with bags and suitcases.

Lydia looks excited, while Richard rolls his eyes at the tumult.

Hanna hugs her niece and nephew, buries her face in their hair. It doesn't seem long since they were little, and now they are growing up. They are both hugging her back, and all the stress lingering in her mind disappears in an instant.

She straightens up and grins at her big sister.

"Welcome home!"

Lydia steps forward, wraps her arms around Hanna, and pulls her close. For a moment it feels like it did when Hanna was a child.

When Lydia is here, everything is fine.

20

Anton is sitting in his favorite armchair in the dimly lit living room. He has opened a bottle of beer but has taken only a couple of sips.

It is past ten o'clock, he ought to go to bed, given how little sleep he had last night. There is a briefing tomorrow morning shortly after seven, which means getting up at six fifteen to fit in his shower and have some porridge for breakfast.

The TV is on, the news has just started, and they are talking about a severe form of flu that has spread to Northern Italy. He isn't really listening. His thoughts are whirling around the afternoon's encounter with Carl Willner. The sense of unreality as he sat there on the sofa with Hanna, trying to play his part in the interview.

The shock when Carl opened the front door.

It might have been one of the most stressful moments of his life. Carl was the last person he'd expected to see. Hanna must have realized something was wrong.

Or is it his imagination? Did he manage to keep up the facade?

Anton has no idea.

He must stop thinking about Carl, but he can't help it. The memories of their night together keep creeping in. The chemistry between them was incredibly strong, everything felt right. That was why he let Carl come home with him, even though it was against his usual principles. It seemed completely natural to suggest that they leave the nightclub together.

The impulse came as the words left his mouth. When Carl's face lit up, a warm glow filled Anton's body.

Carl has awoken something within him that he hasn't experienced for a very long time. He glances toward the bedroom. Less than twenty-four hours have passed since they lay in there together. Should he call Carl, explain? Say that he was just as surprised as Carl when they saw each other this afternoon?

No, that would simply confuse things even more. Carl is a witness in a homicide investigation. They can't have any personal contact until the case is over, or at least approaching a conclusion.

Anything else would be unethical.

Hanna gave him an odd look when they parted company, but Anton pretended not to notice, said he had to leave right away. Hopefully she will have forgotten all about it by tomorrow.

As long as he doesn't let himself be unduly influenced so that he misses something. Should he put his cards on the table, inform Daniel?

But then he would have to come out.

Anton doesn't know if he's ready for that.

He has asked himself the same question over and over again: Is it time? He feels as if he just keeps on brooding about it. He's not ashamed of his sexual orientation, he doesn't really want to creep around, but something is holding him back. It's easier to let people believe that he hasn't found the right person yet.

Digs about being the eternal bachelor are better than thoughtless gay jokes behind his back.

He knows it's stupid, but the stress is there.

It took time for him to acknowledge the truth. He even had girlfriends when he was in school. He's always looked pretty good and been the type to play sports. It was less complicated to be like everyone else and make out with the girls at parties rather than admit that he was interested in the boys.

He longs to talk about it, but always comes to the same conclusion. It's too difficult to tell his parents, especially his father, who had a career in the military.

How would Karro take it? No doubt she would accept it with equanimity, but what if she let something slip? He loves his little sister, but she's impulsive and has a pretty big mouth.

Carl's face comes into his mind. Anton would really like to see him again, but it's out of the question. He can't risk his career for Carl's sake. He's not there yet.

He reaches for the beer bottle and tightens his grip.

Why does life have to be so goddamn complicated?

REBECKA

2019

SEPTEMBER

The door to Little Snowdrops opens as Rebecka is on her knees cleaning up the remains of lunch, which three-year-old Emmy has just thrown up all over the hall floor. The little girl's forehead was burning; they've contacted her mom, who is on her way to pick Emmy up.

However, the brown-haired man in the doorway doesn't seem to have anything to do with Emmy. He is wearing blue dungarees and carrying a large toolbox. He must be a tradesman—a plumber, judging by the logo on his jacket.

Rebecka gets to her feet. She grimaces at the revolting rag and puts it aside.

"Hi," says the man. He is smiling warmly at Rebecka, his eyes sparkling. His mouth is generous, his body fit and lithe, like a sportsman's. *Athletic,* she thinks automatically, although she shouldn't be paying any attention to the way he looks.

"I've come to fix the toilet."

"Of course—come with me, and I'll show you where it is."

The staff toilet has been out of action for a week. It will be nice to get it fixed.

The man follows her down the corridor. She opens the door and points. "There you go."

"I'm sure we can sort this out," he says, pressing the flush button without anything happening. "How urgent is it? Are people standing in line?" He gives Rebecka a teasing wink. It takes a few seconds for her to realize that he's joking.

"It's not very urgent," she says with a nervous laugh.

"That's lucky." His smile grows even wider. He lifts the lid of the cistern and inspects the float. "Okay, I think I know what the problem is."

There is something about that intense blue gaze, the joy that seems to be lurking behind it. His eyes are surrounded by a network of fine laugh lines, the kind you get from squinting at the sun outdoors.

It feels as if they've met before, although Rebecka is sure they haven't.

"How long will it take?" she asks.

His laugh is spontaneous and heartfelt. It doesn't sound scornful or supercilious like Ole's, just irresistibly inviting. As if life is too short not to be happy.

It does something to her, that carefree laugh. It arouses a longing deep inside her. Rebecka can hardly remember what it feels like not to be frightened and sad.

"How long is a piece of string?" he says.

At first, she doesn't get it; then she realizes that he is teasing her again.

"I understand," she says, her cheeks flushing bright red. He must think she's a complete idiot.

"I just need to check if I've got the right parts with me," he says. "You did say it wasn't urgent?"

He smiles again; Rebecka's face must be bright red by now. In order to hide her confusion, she takes a step back. She ought to go, but she is finding it hard to tear herself away. The kindness and humor in his eyes are drawing her to him, as if he is a sun that can warm her. She is always, always cold.

"Sorry," he says, placing a hand on her arm. "I'm only joking. I didn't mean to embarrass you."

Rebecka feels a shock run right through her body when he touches her.

What is happening?

She becomes aware of how close to each other they are, how soft his brown hair looks. He has a tiny scar at one corner of his mouth, which makes him appear slightly amused all the time. Almost expectant, as if an exciting surprise is waiting just around the corner.

His hand is still on her arm. When she looks down at his fingers, she sees a platinum wedding ring.

He is married.

So is she.

"I feel as if I know you," he says.

His voice speaks to her heart, as if the words are meant for her and her alone, even though they don't mean anything special.

"I have to go," she mumbles, and hurries away.

21

It is past eleven o'clock. Ida is in bed, knowing that she needs to sleep.
Alice usually wakes twice during the night wanting to be fed. Last night
was particularly difficult; Ida didn't get much rest at all.

They try to share the burden, but Ida is often woken by Alice's
crying.

This new homicide investigation is playing on her mind. She has
had several text messages from friends who have heard that the victim
is Johan Andersson. They are wondering if she knows anything about
the case, given that Daniel is a police officer.

There is wild speculation about the motive behind the murder of
the local skiing hero. The fact that it is the sports break and the place is
full of tourists doesn't exactly help.

The anxiety comes creeping in, despite her best efforts to resist it.

She turns her head in Daniel's direction. He is in a deep sleep,
stretched out on his side. Alice is snuffling happily in her crib.

Ida would be prepared to die for her daughter, but she was
completely unprepared for how much hard work a baby could be. Or
how much her relationship with Daniel would be affected.

She had pictured herself sitting on the sofa with a sweet little girl.
Nobody had warned her about leaky breasts, sudden hormone surges,
or endless sleepless nights with a colicky baby.

She has never been as much in love as she is with Daniel, but still
she sometimes feels abandoned. He was altogether somewhere else this

afternoon when they were at her mother's. He hardly contributed to the conversation at all.

It can't be like the last time, when he couldn't think about anything except the Amanda Halvorssen case. All at once, she and Alice meant nothing to him.

That made her feel insecure. She had never expected to come second.

When the situation was at its worst, he was gone around the clock for several days. One evening he came home late when she was still awake. She knew he was exhausted, but so was she. Alice's colic was driving her crazy. Nothing helped—she was the worst mother in the world.

Daniel sat down at the kitchen table to eat, but she couldn't leave him in peace, she had to talk to him. She wanted to make him understand that he was neglecting her and his daughter.

It ended in disaster. Daniel had had a huge outburst of rage. He had picked up his plate and hurled it at the wall, then stormed out of the apartment, leaving Ida surrounded by shards of crockery.

The incident had terrified her.

Who does that to their partner and baby? Ida has asked herself that question many times.

Could he do it again?

She doesn't understand how a person can get so angry that they lose control like that. Even if she got mad, she would never allow her temper to run away with her.

He's a grown man, and they have shared responsibility for their daughter—Daniel knew that when they decided to go through with the pregnancy. In fact, he was the one who wanted it most at the time, although Ida would never admit it out loud now.

When Daniel eventually came home, he apologized over and over again. He did everything to persuade her to forgive him. He is still deeply ashamed; Ida has seen the pain in his eyes when they have talked about what happened.

Gradually she began to understand the background. Daniel told her about the hot temper he has struggled with throughout his life. It comes from his maternal grandfather in Italy, who frightened Daniel's mother so much that she never went back there, even when Daniel's Swedish father abandoned them.

Ida breathes out through her nose. She reaches for her phone, resists the temptation to check Instagram, see what they are saying about Johan's murder. She wants to support Daniel in his work, but he has to understand how hard it is for her to be alone with Alice all day. Particularly at this time of year, when it is almost impossible to go out with the stroller because of the snow. She is an active person and worked as a ski instructor for several seasons. In a normal year she would have had her hands full this week.

Being trapped inside the apartment is driving her insane.

Daniel turns over, his breathing deep and regular.

She will not allow him to disappear like that again. Nor will she stand for another display of temper. It's just a job, for God's sake.

The fact that he is a police officer cannot rule their lives.

22

The cuticle on Marion's thumb is bleeding. She is sitting at the kitchen table and notices it only when a drop of blood trickles down the back of her hand. She doesn't remember chewing the skin; she has no idea where the hours have gone since she sank down on this chair.

She licks off the blood, unable to muster the energy to fetch a piece of paper towel.

She is exhausted but finds it impossible to rest. Every time she lies down, her heart starts racing. She has lived here for almost eight years, but everything in the bedroom feels weird and unfamiliar.

Marion picks up her phone and scrolls through the camera app, tries to lose herself in old photos of Johan to find peace for a little while.

The room is dark; the only light comes from her screen. The sudden ringtone makes her jump.

It is Linus again.

Her whole body goes ice cold. She had been rejecting his calls all day, until they stopped. She had hoped that meant he'd decided to leave her alone.

Clearly not.

With a trembling finger, she touches the icon to decline the call. No doubt it's about the visit he had from the police—he's afraid she'll tell them what he's really like.

She still finds thinking about the big argument in the office back in January deeply unpleasant. It was horrible, especially when Linus came right up close and yelled at her, told her not to interfere in the company.

Neither she nor Johan could have imagined that Linus would change like that, become so aggressive. Johan quickly stepped between them, but Marion was shaken for several days afterward. She would prefer never to see Linus again; he scares her.

She knows he blames her for the conflict, although, in fact, he has only himself to blame. Marion had done her best to handle the situation professionally, keep her personal opinions to herself, but when Linus started failing to do his job properly, she had no choice but to tell Johan.

Particularly when there were problems with the tax authorities—she simply had to speak out.

All of this is Linus's fault, no one else's.

She has never really understood why Johan put such trust in his partner. She was never completely comfortable with Linus, but at the beginning she had no idea how bad it was going to get.

Johan was a fine, honest person, while Linus is rude and hard to understand.

He is also out for revenge.

The screen goes dark, and Marion lets out a sob of relief. But he calls again. And again. There is no end to it, the shrill signal makes her feel as if her head is about to explode.

She fumbles with the phone, almost drops it trying to switch it to silent. Finally, she succeeds.

The only sound in the darkness is her own frightened, shallow breathing.

The screen lights up again. Linus has sent a message.

Fuck you if you badmouth me to the cops.

MONDAY, FEBRUARY 24

23

It is exactly seven thirty in the morning when Daniel kicks off the digital briefing with Östersund.

He has been at the station for almost an hour, reading through material from the previous day, reports from the door-to-door inquiries, and information from members of the public who have called in. Raffe is sitting beside him, across the table from Anton and Hanna.

CSI Carina Grankvist is also present via the link. She is wearing round spectacles today, which give her a slightly owlish appearance.

"Good morning," Birgitta Grip says. She looks exhausted. Her eyes are narrow slits below heavy lids, and there are deep lines between her nose and mouth. She has had her hands full too, not least because of the pressure from the media. None of them have had enough rest over the weekend, and Daniel slept for less than five hours last night. He took the late shift with Alice in order to appease Ida.

Just as well—he's unlikely to get home at a reasonable time today either.

The tiredness sits deep in his bones.

Anton doesn't look too bright either, even though he has neither a partner nor children. He'd seemed so upbeat yesterday.

Grip taps her pen on the table. Beside her are the investigators based in Östersund, and Jenny Ullenius, the prosecutor. She is wearing a black polo sweater and is about forty years old. She's new—Daniel hasn't worked with her before. She seems happy to let Grip lead the meeting.

"There's a great deal of speculation about the cause of Johan Andersson's death," Grip begins. "I don't know how many questions I was asked at yesterday's press conference."

Daniel isn't surprised. His mother-in-law and sister-in-law had already worked out who the victim was.

"The tabloids are reveling in the news," Grip continues, "and the internet is going crazy. There are all kinds of theories out there, from the involvement of a criminal gang to debt collection. Even suicide."

"Johan deserves better than that," Raffe growls.

Daniel remembers Johan's hands, bound behind his back. Anyone who had seen the body would never use the word *suicide*.

"Have we heard anything from forensics?" Grip says. "What's happening with the autopsy?"

"I've emailed Ylva Labba and asked her to prioritize the case," Daniel replies, "but it might take a while."

Ylva is the forensic pathologist who was involved in last December's case. She is both conscientious and efficient, but the pathology unit in Umeå is responsible for the whole of Norrland. They carry out something in the region of five thousand autopsies per year.

This is a serious homicide, but Daniel doesn't have high hopes of jumping to the front of the line.

"Keep pushing," Grip says, turning her attention to Carina. "How about the victim's van?"

Carina's face comes into focus on the screen.

"We've begun, but remember that less than twenty-four hours have passed since it was found. I'm going through the contents, but so far we haven't come across anything that could be the murder weapon."

Daniel had hoped for the opposite, but few killers leave the weapon at the scene, even if they act out of sheer panic. This perpetrator had had the presence of mind to move the body and hide the van.

"However, we can confirm that the blood on the floor of the van is the same type as Johan Andersson's: B positive," Carina adds.

"Any trace of other individuals?" Hanna asks. She is leaning back in her chair, her gaze sharp and focused.

"Yes. We have a number of hairs that don't match the victim's. The problem is, of course, that we can't say for certain if they got there when the crime was committed or on another occasion."

This is a dilemma. If they find Linus's DNA in the van, it will be easy to explain away. He worked with Johan, so of course he has been in the van. Any decent defense lawyer would quickly cast doubt on such "evidence."

"We've sent everything to the National Forensic Center in Umeå," Carina concludes. "We'll see what they have to say when they're done."

"In a hundred years," Hanna says in a theatrical whisper.

Raffe grins, but Grip is clearly not amused. Daniel understands why, but sometimes a joke is just what you need to get through the day.

"How about Linus Sundin's finances?" she snaps.

Raffe takes over. "It wasn't easy to track down the information, given that it was Sunday. However, we have found out one or two things."

He flicks through a pile of papers on the table; they look like forms from the tax authorities.

"We've looked at Linus's declarations for the past few years. He's had an annual income of just over four hundred thousand, roughly thirty-five thousand a month, which is normal for a plumber. He's also had significant residual taxes of about fifty thousand, three years in a row. Always paid at the last minute."

"Do we know where this residual tax comes from?" Jenny Ullenius wonders. "Is it based on secondary income, or did he pay too little tax in the first place?"

Daniel understands why she is asking. If Linus paid too little preliminary tax, that suggests he had an ongoing need for a greater disposable income. However, if it's based on secondary income, then where did that money come from?

Why would he work elsewhere when he had his own business?

"No other employer has registered his details," Raffe replies.

"So we must be looking at too little preliminary tax," Jenny says. "Interesting."

"Marion Andersson ought to know," Hanna points out. "She does the books." She makes a quick note and signals to Daniel: *We need to check that out.*

"I wonder if Linus and Johan quarreled about that too," she says in passing.

"I also took a look at Sundin's house," Raffe continues. "It's worth a couple of million but mortgaged up to the chimney tops."

"Do you know if he has any other loans?" Daniel says. "Credit card debts? Payday loans?"

"I'll check it out today."

"What about door-to-door inquiries?" Grip asks.

Daniel has gone through the reports from the officers who canvased the villagers in Tångböle—or whatever they're called when their houses are so spread out.

"Nothing. No one seems to have seen or heard anything during the early hours of Saturday morning. The weather was pretty bad, of course, with heavy snow."

"Have you spoken to whoever cleared the snow?" Grip says.

Anton nods. "I spoke to the guy who was responsible for the Tångböle area. He was there just before six on Saturday morning. He followed his route with the plow, doesn't remember anything in particular."

Just as Daniel had expected; the likelihood of the snowplow driver having noticed anything wasn't great.

"Judging by the snow on top of the body, Andersson had been lying out there for a number of hours," Carina explains. "Just over four inches came down during the night, so I would think that the body was placed there at around midnight. My conclusion, bearing in mind the amount of blood in the van, is that he was dead when he was dumped."

Hanna sits up a little straighter. "According to Carl Willner, Johan left the restaurant at about seven thirty on Friday evening. He allegedly left Linus's house just after eight. That gives us an interval of four hours between the time he was last seen alive and his death."

Daniel feels a pang of irritation at the mention of Willner. He is still disappointed that he couldn't attend the interview.

"So the big question is where did Johan go next?" Hanna wonders out loud.

"Is there an electronic logbook in the van?" Raffe says. "If so, we'll be able to see where he went when he left the restaurant. A lot of people with company vehicles use electronic devices so they don't have to keep a written record of all their business trips."

"Good point—I'll take a look," Carina says.

"Did Willner have anything else of interest to offer?" Daniel asks.

Hanna fills everyone in on Willner's information about the dispute between Linus and Johan; then she turns to Anton. "Anything you want to add?"

He shakes his head; he has hardly said a word.

"What about the list of clients Sundin was supposed to email to you?" Grip says.

Raffe makes a note. "It hasn't arrived yet—I'll follow up."

Daniel leans forward. "As far as I'm concerned, another big question is the trip Johan was planning. Or rather—the assertion that he was looking forward to it."

This information is confusing because it contradicts the theory that Johan was under serious threat. They need to speak to other people who knew him well to try and get to the truth. Maybe his parents can help? They weren't up to answering any questions on Saturday when they were informed of Johan's death, but Daniel wants to try again today.

The screen goes blank, and Grip disappears from view for a few seconds. Her voice can still be heard, although it's a bit scratchy.

"Are we nearly done? Anything else?"

How about more officers? Daniel thinks. They need considerably more investigators if they are going to get everything done, especially bearing in mind Grip's instructions to avoid overtime. Which they completely failed to do over the weekend. He raises his hand, unable to hide his displeasure. His body is tense with frustration and a lack of sleep.

"What's the situation regarding additional resources? The current team is too small."

Grip frowns. "I can't spare anyone else at the moment."

"Can't we draft people from elsewhere in the county?"

"You'll just have to manage as best you can."

"So, no overtime, no more staff. How do you expect us to solve the case under those circumstances?"

"Daniel," Hanna says with a note of warning in her voice. "We'll be fine."

He folds. "Okay," he says, gathering up his papers. They quickly divide the tasks between them; there are still a lot of people to speak to, with Johan's family at the top of the list. He looks at Hanna.

"How about we start with Johan's parents and brother, then call on Linus again?"

"Right now?"

"Yes."

Daniel points to the blank screen and allows himself an ironic smile.

"Best we make a move straightaway. I wouldn't want to crash the overtime ceiling."

REBECKA

2019

September

Rebecka has just finished her lunch break when a white van pulls into the parking lot. The door opens, and the man who came the other day climbs out with a toolbox in his hand.

Her whole body starts trembling.

She hasn't been able to stop thinking about him, although it is total insanity. What would Ole do if he knew she was thinking about someone else? What would the church say?

She doesn't even know his name.

Over the past couple of days, she has tried to convince herself that the brief encounter meant nothing. That what she felt was pure imagination. You can't fall head over heels in love with a complete stranger in minutes.

And yet the image of his lovely smile has stayed in her mind. That inviting laugh, so natural and spontaneous. The carefree air that made her feel like her old self just for a moment, the Rebecka who was happy and loved life.

She goes hot and then cold when she hears his voice in the hall. She has to go and catch a glimpse of him.

She can't resist.

"Hello again!" he says. His face lights up in a way that makes her hold her breath. He looks so excited to see her. So . . . pleased.

Ole has never looked at her like that. Not even when they first got married.

"I was hoping I'd see you again," he goes on.

Rebecka swallows. She has no words; she simply stands there, mute.

He hasn't shaved today. A faint dark shadow covers his chin, making him look unreasonably attractive.

She wants to reach out and touch his cheek.

"Sorry—I shouldn't have said that. I didn't mean to embarrass you again." His laugh is loud and heartfelt, just like last time. "Making you blush seems to be my specialty."

"It's fine," Rebecka stammers. What on earth is wrong with her?

"Maybe I should introduce myself—my name is Johan."

His eyes draw her in. He holds out his hand, and when Rebecka shakes it, she feels as if she has had an electric shock. Nothing like this has ever happened to her before.

"Rebecka," she croaks, regaining the power of speech.

"Nice to meet you, Rebecka."

He gives the impression that he has been looking forward to this meeting all day.

While Rebecka tries to think of what to say, two-year-old Frasse comes barreling toward her with tears in his eyes. Johan crouches down so that he is on the same level as the little boy.

"So, what's happened here?" he says, picking up the child. "Has somebody been mean to you?"

He whirls Frasse around until the boy has forgotten his troubles and is almost choking with laughter. Gently he puts him down, then watches as he toddles back to the playroom.

"They're so sweet at that age," Johan says, with longing in his voice. Suddenly the silence is palpable. "I realize we don't know each other. But I was wondering . . ." He breaks off, as if he's embarrassed.

Rebecka hardly dares look at him.

"I was wondering if you'd like to have a cup of coffee with me?"

Rebecka hesitates. He is married, she has seen his wedding ring. He must have noticed that she is too.

Ole would kill her if she said yes. She still remembers how angry he was when she went for coffee with Maria eighteen months ago. Seeing Johan on a one-to-one basis totally goes against her upbringing; it is at odds with every rule in the church.

She must not do it.

And yet she hears her own voice say, "That would be nice."

24

Daniel almost dozes off in the passenger seat on the way to Östersund, where Torsten and Tarja Andersson have lived for several years. When Hanna called to inform them of the visit, Johan's mother told them that his brother, Pär, would be there too.

"Is everything okay?" Hanna asks as they reach Mörsil. "You haven't said a word in half an hour. Are you still mad at Grip?"

Daniel gives a start. "Alice was awake a lot during the night," he says, stretching to get his circulation going.

"I understand."

She doesn't, but Daniel doesn't bother explaining that it's more than the lack of sleep that is weighing him down. The atmosphere between him and Ida was frosty on the way home from Järpen yesterday. No matter what he said or promised, Ida was short with him for the rest of the evening and went to bed early.

He doesn't know what is going on. A week ago, everything was fine, but now things have changed completely. It's been only two days since Johan's body was found. Daniel can understand Ida's anxiety, but he has repeatedly assured her that he will do his best.

He glances at Hanna, wonders if she would have reacted the same way in a similar situation. Probably not. Not only is she a skilled police officer, she is also intuitive and empathetic. And nowhere near as insecure as Ida.

Hanna has both hands on the steering wheel in the correct position, ten and two. A few strands of brown hair have escaped from her loose ponytail. Daniel likes the fact that he never has to choose his words carefully when he is with her. Sometimes she almost seems to know what he is about to say before he speaks. They have worked together for only two and a half months, but it feels much longer.

In Mattmar they end up behind a truck with foreign plates. The driver is in no hurry; he is traveling at least ten miles below the speed limit.

"The limit is fifty here, for fuck's sake," Hanna mutters. "How hard can it be to read the signs?"

"We're not that short of time," Daniel says.

"Some people shouldn't have a license."

"Take the opportunity to enjoy nature." He can't help teasing her. "It's one of our few fringe benefits up here."

It works—Hanna smiles, and a little dimple that Daniel has never noticed before appears in her right cheek.

The road is lined with tall birch trees shrouded in rime frost. Suddenly the cloud cover opens up and the sun breaks through, making the white landscape sparkle. The sunbeams create a halo around the top of each tree, and the snow crystals shimmer like hovering fairies.

Daniel relaxes. The bad mood that has plagued him all morning fades away.

It is so beautiful here.

25

The sun is shining by the time Hanna and Daniel arrive at Torsten and Tarja Andersson's apartment, after just over an hour's driving.

Hanna parks on the street. It is a glorious winter's day, perfect for the beginning of the sports break. No doubt Lydia and her family are already out on the slopes.

They take the stairs up to the third floor. The Anderssons moved here fifteen years ago, after their children left home. Before that they lived outside Duved, not far from Linus's house.

Tarja opens the door when they ring the bell. According to their records she has just turned sixty-six and retired, but she looks at least ten years older. Her eyes are dull, her cheeks sunken.

She shows them in to the neat, spotlessly clean living room, where her husband, Torsten, is sitting in an armchair. He too looks somehow stunned. His face is gray.

"We're so sorry for your loss," Hanna begins. "We'd like to ask a few questions about Johan, if that's okay?"

Tarja's eyes immediately fill with tears.

"We can't understand any of this," she whispers. "Who would want to kill Johan? He was the nicest man in the world."

"That's exactly what we're trying to find out," Daniel assures her. "I realize things are very difficult right now."

They sit down opposite Johan's parents on a gray sofa with blue throw pillows.

"Tell us about your son," Hanna says warmly.

Tarja turns to her husband, but he doesn't speak; he simply stares blankly into space.

It isn't the first time Hanna has seen that kind of lost expression in someone who has been given the news of a death. It's as if grief fills the soul; there is no room for anything else because pain is occupying every corner.

The television is on, but the Anderssons don't seem to notice. Maybe the background noise helps when the silence becomes unbearable?

Tarja takes a deep breath. "Johan was our youngest boy. His brother, Pär, lives in Strömsund with his family. There are seven years between them."

Her eyes stray toward a desk on the other side of the room, where a number of family photos in black wooden frames are displayed. On the far right is Johan, standing on a sun-drenched Alpine peak in full ski gear. He has a number on his chest and is smiling broadly into the camera. He looks as if he's about twenty; he was already competing by then. Presumably he's just had a successful run.

He is beaming.

Hanna is beginning to understand why everyone talks about his joy of life and his warm personality.

"He was a much-longed-for child," Tarja goes on, pausing to draw a ragged breath. "He was the sweetest baby you could imagine."

"When did you last speak to him?" Daniel asks.

Hanna notices that his voice is much softer than usual. He can come across as very direct, almost boorish in certain contexts, but in difficult situations he shows a great deal of empathy. She has seen him patiently working with those who are deeply shocked in a way that few people can manage. At the same time, he is demanding and often uncompromising at work. Or downright argumentative, as he was with Grip this morning.

He is impressively skilled at adapting. She has never worked with a colleague who makes her feel so secure.

"I think it was last weekend."

"And how did he seem then?"

Tarja plucks at the sleeve of her cardigan. It is a little worn at the elbows; her pale blouse shows through the stitches.

"He was just the same as always. Just as cheerful and pleasant."

"He didn't say anything that struck you as odd? He didn't sound troubled or anxious?"

"No, not at all." Tarja blinks. "Should he have? Why do you ask?"

"It's just routine," Hanna says quickly.

"Right."

Hanna's words don't seem to have reassured Tarja. Now her fingers are plucking nervously at her skirt, as if her sorrow is so great that she can't keep still.

Hanna wonders how her own mother would react under the same circumstances. Would she grieve as deeply if it were Hanna who had died?

If it were Lydia, her mother would be devastated.

"How much contact did you have?" Daniel wants to know.

"Johan was very good at keeping in touch. We spoke once or twice a week."

"And how often did you see each other?"

Tarja bites her lip. "Once a month, maybe. Not as often as we would have liked. Johan always had a lot to do; it was hard for him to get away. We didn't want to be a nuisance . . ."

Her voice dies away. She takes a white handkerchief out of her pocket and gently wipes her eyes.

"What about Johan's business?" Hanna says. "Were things going well?"

"I think so. He was always out on some new job, everyone liked him."

The sound of the doorbell interrupts their conversation. Torsten barely reacts, but Tarja excuses herself and goes to answer.

She starts to sob as soon as the front door opens. Hanna hears the sound of low voices, and after a couple of minutes, Tarja returns with a tall man in his early forties. The resemblance between mother and son is striking—this must be Pär, Johan's brother.

It was a bonus that he was on his way to Östersund anyway, Hanna thinks; it has saved them a trip to Strömsund.

Pär holds out his hand and introduces himself. He too looks pale and strained, but he is calm. He is wearing a dark-green sweater and chinos. He is the principal at a high school and seems to have the calm authority necessary for such a role.

"We were just talking about Johan," Daniel says. "It's good that you're here—we have a few questions we'd like to ask you."

Pär nods. He fetches a chair and places it next to Tarja's armchair.

"When was the last time you spoke to your brother?"

"Friday. Actually, I was going to contact you to tell you about our final conversation, but I've been in shock since I heard the news. I couldn't think, it was as if I was enclosed in darkness. I just couldn't do it."

REBECKA

2019

OCTOBER

They have agreed to meet on the edge of the little forest a few hundred yards from the preschool.

Johan is already waiting when Rebecka, with her heart in her mouth, arrives during her lunch break. She doesn't dare go for coffee with him; she can't risk Ole finding out, even if that's all it is.

They have decided on a forest walk instead.

Anxiety is pulsating through her body, but it fades away as soon as she sees Johan's big smile. He looks so happy—Rebecka can't help being captivated. It is wonderful to be young and carefree, if only for a little while.

No stubble today. She wonders how those soft cheeks would feel beneath her fingertips.

"You came!" he says. She can hear the excitement in his voice.

"I said I would, didn't I?"

"I was worried you'd change your mind. I arrived way too early— I've been here for almost half an hour." He gives an embarrassed laugh. "To be on the safe side, so that we wouldn't miss each other."

He sounds so honest and straightforward, and so delighted that Rebecka can hardly breathe. She can't remember the last time someone spoke to her like that.

"You're lovely," he says.

"Thank you."

Rebecka couldn't put on anything special this morning in case Ole started asking questions, but she did apply a little mascara and lip gloss in the restroom at work. She will wipe her face clean before Ole comes to collect her this afternoon.

She is pleased that Johan has noticed.

They set off along the path, which quickly takes them out of sight of curious eyes. The temperature is just below freezing, and the first frost is shimmering on the trees. There is a thin layer of ice on the grass, and the leaves crunch beneath their feet.

Johan makes Rebecka relax.

She is often shy; she has never been the type of person who can easily chat to strangers. However, Johan asks questions about her job at the school and seems genuinely engaged in what she has to say. She describes the children, tells him how happy it makes her when they crawl onto her lap after their nap. Ole has never been interested, even when she still mistook his need to control her for love.

"Have you always wanted to work with children?"

"Ever since I was a little girl. Maybe because I don't have any brothers or sisters."

There is a pause in the conversation, but it doesn't matter. In Johan's company, the silence isn't uncomfortable.

"Do you have children?" Rebecka asks after a moment.

"No, unfortunately. But I've always wanted to be a dad." A shadow passes over Johan's face, a seriousness that she hasn't seen before. He gives himself a little shake, his expression melancholy. "Life doesn't always turn out the way you expect, does it?"

Rebecka knows something about that.

They carry on chatting. Johan listens without interrupting, as if everything Rebecka has to say is fascinating and important. Suddenly half an hour has passed—it feels like five minutes.

"I need to go back," she says, wishing she could stay.

"Already? Can't you stay a bit longer?"

Rebecka shakes her head. They are standing close together, their eyes locked. When Johan exhales, his breath forms a white cloud.

Rebecka stares at his lips as if she were in a trance. They are pale pink, soft and inviting.

She would like to kiss them.

Johan touches her elbow. Then he takes off his gloves and clasps her hand between his.

His skin is warm.

Her entire body is throbbing.

"I have to see you again," he says, his voice hoarse. "Please tell me we can meet very soon?"

26

How long has she been staring at the computer?

Marion glances at the clock; it is eleven o'clock in the morning, which means she has been sitting here for several hours. And yet she can't work, can't concentrate.

Her thoughts are tangled, fear is crawling all over her skin like ants.

She gets up from the desk in the small guest room that serves as an office. Dizziness makes her sway; she has to grab hold of the door frame to prevent herself from falling.

She should eat something, but she isn't hungry. She hasn't managed to force anything down over the last couple of days. The smell of food turns her stomach.

She hasn't spoken to her brother, Florian; she can't bring herself to call him after everything that's happened.

Her cell phone rings. She answers automatically, even though the last three calls were from the tabloid press.

"Good morning," says an unknown voice. "My name is Rafael Herrera, and I'm calling from the Åre police."

Marion's stomach contracts. *No more bad news, I can't cope with anything else.*

"Yes?"

"Do you have time to talk?"

She knows he can't see her, but she nods anyway. "Yes."

"I have a few questions about the business your husband co-owned with Linus Sundin."

Marion goes back and sits down at the computer. The cold blue light illuminates the screen; she can see her gaunt reflection.

"The thing is, we need a list of the company's clients. Sundin promised to send it over, but nothing has appeared. Would you be able to help?"

"Of course. Absolutely." Marion makes a note.

"We've also gone through Sundin's tax returns for the last few years. He seems to have opted to pay too little preliminary tax. As you're responsible for the finances, I'm wondering if you could explain how that happened?"

Marion slumps on her chair. This is exactly what she had been worried about.

For several years Linus has asked her to take too little preliminary tax when the salaries are paid. If she protested and insisted that this wasn't the right thing to do, he became aggressive, told her that he and Johan owned the business and she should do as she was told.

When she tried to discuss the matter with Johan, he said he didn't want another fight with Linus, not when everything was already so toxic. It wasn't the end of the world; only Linus would ultimately be liable for the residual tax. Once again, Marion told him it was wrong. They could end up with the tax authority on their case. What was she supposed to say to the auditors?

Johan refused to listen, and now she's sitting here with the police on the other end of the phone, wanting to know what was going on.

Will they hold her responsible? She is in charge of the books, after all.

Her heart is pounding. Johan is gone; he can't confirm that she tried to object to Linus's tax ruse. And Linus will never admit that he was the one who insisted on the low payment—instead he will blame Marion.

Linus can't stand her. He would be delighted if she went down for this. Stress races around her bloodstream as she tries to come up with an answer. The detective is still waiting on the line.

"I'm sorry, I'm not feeling very well," she says. "Can I call you back?"

There is a brief pause. "No problem—but as soon as possible, please."

Marion puts down the phone and rests her forehead on her hands.

As soon as she closes her eyes, she pictures Johan's bloodied body in the snow. She remembers every word the two police officers said on Saturday, when they told her how he had been found. She has barely slept since then.

The terrible images haunt her when she is awake and in nightmares when she is half dozing in bed. Johan, whom she loved so much. The man she thought she would be with for the rest of her life. They were supposed to grow old together, never part.

He was her other half, her soulmate. For his sake she left her homeland, her family and friends, and moved halfway across Europe.

Now she is all alone in ice-cold Sweden, with no one to turn to.

How did things end up like this?

Her gaze falls on the black cell phone next to the computer mouse. Sweat breaks out on her upper lip. She promised to call the detective back, but she has no convincing answers to his questions.

Why can't they leave her in peace?

27

The information that Pär Andersson had spoken to his brother as recently as Friday takes Hanna by surprise. This could be a key piece of the puzzle.

She doesn't take her eyes off him, sitting next to his broken mother. The father, Torsten, still looks as if he were in a world of his own. He has barely opened his mouth since she and Daniel arrived.

"You spoke to Johan on Friday? When?"

"At about five thirty—I was in my car, on my way home from work."

"How did he sound?"

Pär smiles sadly. "Happy and excited. As if he had too much energy."

Hanna recognizes the description from their conversation with Carl Willner. Something had made Johan so exhilarated that he could barely sit still.

But what?

"Did he sound scared?"

As soon as she has said it, she wishes she hadn't. Rule number one: Don't ask leading questions.

"No, not at all."

"What did you talk about?"

Pär looks away. The brothers must have been very alike; they both have an athletic build and regular features, but grief has taken its toll on Pär. He looks pale and haggard.

"He asked if he could come and stay with us."

"When?" Daniel says.

"More or less right away."

"Right away?"

"Yes. He wanted to come over on Saturday evening."

So the mysterious trip was to his brother's place in Strömsund. Hanna is relieved to have established where Johan was going.

"I was kind of taken aback. We've always been close, but Johan has never suggested a spontaneous visit like that. I explained that it wasn't very convenient, because we'd been invited out for the evening—the whole family."

"What did he say to that?"

"He asked me to leave a key so that he could let himself in."

"So he was pretty insistent?"

"Oh yes. And he asked if he could stay for at least a week."

That fits in with what they've already been told—Linus said Johan was intending to be away over sports break, if Hanna remembers correctly.

But why?

"Did he say anything about the reason for his visit?" she wonders. She is quietly hoping that he will have the answer, the reason why Johan was forced to leave Duved at such short notice.

Everything hangs on that question.

"The thing is . . ." Pär glances at his mother, as if he is worried about her reaction. "Johan told me he wouldn't be alone; he was bringing someone with him. I should have called you earlier, but as I said the news of his death came as such a shock. I haven't been thinking clearly."

"Who was he bringing with him?"

"He didn't want to tell me over the phone; he just said he would explain the situation when we saw each other." Pär takes a deep breath. "Then your colleagues contacted me the day before yesterday and said that Johan was . . . dead."

His face crumples, and he covers his mouth with his hand. Tarja pats his arm as her eyes fill with tears.

Hanna tries to process this new information. Johan was intending to head up to Strömsund to stay with his brother. Together with an unknown person.

Daniel asks the obvious follow-up question.

"Was Johan bringing a man or a woman with him?"

"I don't know."

"It wasn't Marion?" Hanna says, just to be on the safe side—although Marion has already stated that she didn't know anything about Johan's travel plans.

"It didn't sound like it."

"Can you remember exactly how he expressed himself? If you think back?"

Pär closes his eyes, concentrates.

"He said . . . I was going to meet someone who was important to him, but I mustn't tell anyone they were coming to visit. He made me promise before we ended the call."

REBECKA

2019

OCTOBER

It is four fifteen in the morning when Rebecka opens her eyes. The room is in darkness. Ole is lying on his back beside her, fast asleep.

Her ribs are aching; he'd pushed her against a chest of drawers the day before yesterday.

Ole's breathing is a reminder of the sacred marital vows she made before God. She must love and obey him for the rest of her life. He is a respected pastor who has now officially been chosen as Jonsäter's successor.

And yet she is lying here thinking of someone else.

Tears spring to her eyes. She buries her face in the pillow so that her sobs won't be heard. She can't risk waking Ole, can't risk arousing the least suspicion that everything is not as it should be.

How can a person be so happy and so unhappy at the same time?

When she thinks about Johan, it is as if a warm wave washes through her body. His gaze makes her forget everything. She just wants to sink into his arms and stay there. The fear she carries with her, the fear that has become a part of her like a second skin, melts away in his presence. He exudes a happiness and sense of security that are like nothing she has ever experienced before.

He brings back the joy of life, the joy that Ole has gradually taken away from her with his controlling behavior and violent mood swings.

She knows with absolute certainty that Johan would never hurt her.

In spite of all this, they have hardly kissed. He has mostly held her hand, and they have hugged, on the few occasions when they have stolen away for a secret forest walk.

She is too afraid to go any further. If Ole finds out what she is up to . . . Every time, she swears that she will never see Johan again, but it is impossible to resist. He keeps coming up with excuses to see her at work. First it was the toilet that needed fixing; then he tackled the pipes in the kitchen.

She has given him her phone number but told him to be careful. He is only allowed to text her when she is in school, and she quickly deletes every single message as soon as she has read it.

Ole knows her code—he chose it when she started her job and needed a phone of her own.

She doesn't dare think about the consequences if he discovers a message from Johan.

She peers out through the gap between the roller blind and the window frame. The first snow is on the way. The black October night lurks outside. The temperature is already below freezing, and the ice will soon settle. The long Norrland winter is coming, as heavy and dark as the confused thoughts that torment her every night.

There is no solution, no bright future to hope for as far as she is concerned.

She must forget Johan, even though he says they belong together, that he has never felt like this before.

Rebecka tries to suppress her tears, squeezes her eyes tight shut.

She mustn't see him again.

It will only lead to unhappiness for both of them.

28

They have stopped at a street kiosk to buy burgers, fries, and Coke after the visit to Johan's parents. As they walk back to the unmarked police car laden with fast food, Daniel offers to drive. It's only fair—Hanna drove all the way to Östersund.

He pulls out of the parking lot and heads for the E14. They are planning to go and see Linus again. Daniel puts his foot down as soon as they hit the highway. It is already quarter to one, and it has started snowing. The windshield wipers are operating at full speed. He overtakes an Audi before the road changes to a single lane.

Hanna seems lost in thought.

"We need to find out who Johan was planning to take to Strömsund," she says after a while.

"Stating the obvious . . ."

Daniel gives her a smile to lighten the atmosphere. The grief of Johan's parents and brother has crept beneath their skin; it was a relief to get out into the fresh air.

"Who would you take to your brother's if you were doing it in secret?"

"I'm an only child—I don't have a brother," Daniel replies.

Technically that's not entirely true. His father built a new family in Umeå after he had abandoned Francesca, Daniel's mother. She had left her extended family in Italy for his sake, but that didn't stop his father from calling her from work one day to tell her he had met another woman.

The following morning he was gone.

Daniel should have been too little to remember what happened, but certain snapshots remain in his memory.

His mother standing in the hallway, weeping, with the receiver in her hand. The only phone in the apartment was on the wall by the front door, and he can still see her leaning against the frame, her face crumpled in despair. He has a vague recollection of running over to console her, but his little arms reached only up to her waist.

She didn't even notice; she was too preoccupied with the conversation with his father.

Then it's a blank. He has a half sister, eight years younger, and a half brother, five years younger, whom he hasn't seen since he was ten. That was when the sporadic visits to his father stopped.

A quarter of a century has passed, and he hasn't spoken to his father once during that time, not even when his mother died in a hit-and-run accident in Sundsvall ten years ago.

Is he still alive? Daniel isn't sure. He pushes away thoughts of his father, as he has learned to do when his emotions get the better of him.

"Okay, let's think," Hanna continues. "Who did Johan want to take to Strömsund? It's hardly likely to be one of his normal friends. What do you think?"

Daniel shakes his head. "No idea."

"How about a lover?"

"Would he risk introducing a lover to his brother? A woman Marion knew nothing about?" Daniel overtakes another car, a Volvo this time. "To be honest, I don't see the point of going up to his brother's place if that were the case. If Johan was intending to leave his wife, then surely he could have done it without going away from Åre for a week? And why the secrecy?"

"Maybe he didn't want to risk Pär saying something to Marion by mistake, before he'd had the chance to tell her?"

"Why couldn't he have explained that to his brother?"

144

"Pär said that Johan didn't want to reveal the other person's identity over the phone. Which means it was too sensitive. And he made Pär promise not to tell anyone about the visit."

Daniel rests his left arm on the windowsill, silently going over the information in his head.

And suddenly he understands.

"I don't think this was about Johan."

Hanna looks up, reaches the same conclusion.

"He wasn't the one who needed to hide!" she exclaims. "It was the other person."

29

Hanna and Daniel reach Duved just before three. Hanna is still thinking about Johan's mysterious companion; maybe Linus knows something?

They find him in the kitchen of the white-painted house. No one answered when they knocked, but the door wasn't locked. Linus is wearing his blue overalls, sitting at the table with a glass of clear liquid when they walk in.

He quickly stands up and pours the contents down the sink, then offers them a seat. Hanna can smell the vodka on his breath. He looks worn out, his eyes are tired and bloodshot.

Raffe had called just before they arrived and informed them that Linus had taken out a number of payday loans totaling several hundred thousand kronor. He has also maxed out the credit on his bank card.

Linus is on the verge of bankruptcy—something he failed to mention on their previous visit.

"We have a few more questions, and we want honest answers this time," Daniel begins. The implied meaning hangs in the air: *Unlike last time, when you withheld important information.* "When did you last speak to Johan?"

"On Friday, when he stopped by."

"Are you absolutely certain?"

"Yes!"

"Perhaps you'd like to reconsider your answer," Hanna says. "We are now aware of your financial difficulties. You have enormous debts, and your house is mortgaged to the hilt. Plus, you have been paying too little tax on your income for a long time. You've been liable for residual tax for years."

"Who told you that?"

"We received information from the tax office," Hanna replies.

"Has someone been telling tales?"

She gives him an icy glare. "It would be better if you answered the question instead of worrying about that."

Her tone infuriates Linus Sundin. "Are you accusing me of something?" He leans across the table, clenches his fist in front of her face.

"Sit down!" Daniel roars, putting himself between the two of them.

Linus doesn't move.

"Sit down!" Daniel points to the chair, still acting as a human shield between Hanna and Linus, who eventually decides to cooperate. His expression is grim.

Hanna does her best to appear unmoved, but his outburst took her by surprise. Daniel's speedy reaction was very welcome, even though she is used to taking care of herself. She gives her colleague a grateful look. For a moment she thought Linus was going to punch her.

"We know you had a serious disagreement with Johan about the company finances," she says in a neutral tone. "You wanted to take out a far bigger salary, much more than the business could afford. According to a witness, you almost came to blows in the office."

She remembers Marion's assertion that she had never seen Linus behave so aggressively.

"So how do you explain that?" Daniel adds.

"It's crap." Linus folds his arms. "I presume it comes from Marion? She's never liked me." He sniffs loudly.

"Leave Marion out of this," Daniel says firmly.

Hanna has no intention of letting Linus off the hook.

"Are you denying that you have financial difficulties?"

"What's that got to do with anything? It's none of your business. It's private."

He slurs the last few words, and the smell of vodka is stronger now. The last time they met, he was more amenable, even though he seemed hungover. With a significant amount of alcohol in his system, he is a different person. If it's the booze that makes him belligerent, then they have every reason to believe what Marion told them.

"Johan Andersson's death means that you inherit half of his share in the company," Daniel points out. "That makes you the majority shareholder, with seventy-five percent. And it gives you the right to decide what happens to the firm's resources."

"Do you understand the implications?" Hanna asks.

Linus looks mutinous.

"It means you have a strong financial motive for the murder of Johan Andersson," Daniel clarifies.

"Are you accusing me of murder?" Linus doesn't sound quite so hostile now.

"Where were you between seven thirty on Friday evening and seven thirty on Saturday morning?" Hanna hardens her voice. After Linus's little performance, she is not inclined to proceed with caution. Maybe he'll fold if they go in hard?

"I was here."

"Is there anyone who can confirm that?"

"My wife was home—and my son."

"Were you sober when Johan showed up on Friday?"

Linus doesn't answer.

"The thing is, I'm wondering whether you were drunk, and so angry that you made your mind up to have it out with Johan, once and for all." Hanna pauses to let her words sink in. "Then one thing led to another. You started arguing with each other, and it all got out of hand. Maybe his death was an accident. Maybe you pushed him and he fell awkwardly, smashed the back of his head. But then you had to deal with the situation. You used his van and hid the body by Tångbölevägen so that nobody would suspect you."

The color has drained from Linus's face. He looks at Hanna with pure loathing; then he clamps his lips tight shut. He doesn't speak for quite some time.

"I'm not saying another word without my lawyer."

REBECKA

2019

NOVEMBER

The snow is sparkling in the golden afternoon sunlight as Rebecka drives to the little cabin in the forest. It belongs to a friend of Johan's and sits in an isolated spot just outside Kall.

In spite of her determination not to see Johan anymore, she couldn't resist. Not when the chance to spend the night together came up. She has prayed to God for help so many times, and at last it was as if he heard her. Completely unexpectedly, Ole informed her that he would be going away with Pastor Jonsäter.

Two days when she can breathe freely, without being afraid that he is going to hurt her.

He recently kicked her so hard in the back that there was blood in her urine the following day.

The situation is getting worse and worse, as if Ole intuitively realizes that she is longing for another man, even though he can't possibly know what is going on.

Rebecka tightens her grip on the wheel and tries to push away her dark thoughts. She wants to enjoy the beautiful winter landscape instead of worrying.

The red-painted wooden cabin is surrounded by shimmering, white, fresh snow. The sky is a perfect shade of blue. The sun's reflection bounces off the side mirror, making her smile.

Everything is like a dream. The prospect of a night with Johan is dizzying. She can hardly believe that it's really going to happen.

No one will find them here.

Rebecka is both terrified and blissfully happy as she parks the car and steps out into the dazzling whiteness. She hears the sound of an engine, and Johan's car appears around the bend. She starts laughing out loud; she can't help it, she is so excited. Eagerly she plows through the snow toward him, and as soon as he gets out of the car, she hurls herself into his arms. He loses his balance, and they fall over, still hugging each other.

They lie there like two snow angels, and he showers her with kisses.

Rebecka wonders if God can see her now.

If he is happy to allow her this moment?

Later in the evening they are lying in the narrow double bed in the cabin's only room.

Johan has lit a fire, and the orange-red glow of the flames lights up the walls. His temples are slightly sweaty, and his dark hair curls at the nape of his neck.

They have already made love several times. Made love in a way that Rebecka didn't know was possible, slowly and gently. Johan did his utmost to ensure that she too would experience pleasure.

For the first time in her life, she has had an orgasm.

Johan traces the line of her cheek with his index finger, then continues along her shoulder and down her collarbone. It is a simple gesture, but the tenderness almost moves her to tears. He is so gentle with her, so caring with every touch.

"I love you," he whispers. "I've never been as happy as this, not even when I won the Swedish junior slalom championship."

He gives an embarrassed laugh at the comparison. Rebecka smiles; he has told her about his skiing career. Maybe that was why she thought he seemed familiar the first time they met.

"I know this has happened really fast, but I love you," he repeats in a voice thick with emotion.

She looks into his blue eyes and knows that every word is true.

She swallows hard. She wants to say, *I love you too*, but fear stops her from speaking.

What will happen if she admits it? Will God punish her?

She caresses his cheek so that she won't have to say anything. The fire crackles, sparks fly into the air.

"You could leave him," Johan says slowly.

It's the first time he has mentioned the idea. Rebecka has tried to avoid talking about Ole, but Johan has managed to draw some information out of her. The rest he has put together for himself.

It is no secret that the church follows the teachings of the Bible, and that a woman must obey her husband. It has always been obvious to Rebecka that there are differences between men and women. Only recently she has begun to wonder why men make decisions and women conform to them.

Why she has so little control over her own life.

Johan's gaze travels down her body and stops at the fresh bruises on her back. She had hoped he wouldn't notice them, but the evidence of Ole's vicious kicks is clear to see.

"You can't allow him to treat you like this. Let me help you."

"Sh."

Rebecka doesn't want to waste the precious time they have together talking about Ole. Everything she has already belongs to him, but these twenty-four hours are hers and hers alone. She will not permit his dark shadow to take over.

"He doesn't own you," Johan continues. "We could be together, build a future." He places a soft kiss on her forehead. "I'm going to divorce Marion. We've grown apart; these days we're more like friends, or brother and sister."

In spite of the words, she can hear the guilt in his voice, and the fact that he is so troubled about his wife makes her love him even more. Johan is kind and considerate. A good man.

"I was very young when we met," he explains. "Only twenty-two. I didn't understand what real love was." He looks sad. "If we'd had children, maybe things would have been different, but it never happened."

Rebecka recognizes that longing, the dream of having a child. "Why not?" she asks.

"It just didn't work out. I guess we weren't meant to be parents. It's too late now—Marion is forty-four." Another sad smile. "I would have loved a houseful of kids, little rascals to take out sledding or on the slalom slopes. I've always dreamed of a big family."

His voice is quiet and loving; she could lie here listening to it for hours. She remembers how he consoled Frasse that day in school, how gently he picked up the little boy.

Johan would have been a wonderful father.

Then she sees Ole in her mind's eye. For the first time she is relieved that she has never gotten pregnant with him.

"I'm still very fond of Marion, but it's not enough to stay married. It wouldn't be fair—on either of us. Plus, she's never been happy in Sweden; she often says she'd love to go back home to Germany."

Rebecka curls up beside him, her head resting on his shoulder.

"I want to be with you," Johan says softly. "I can't think about anything else. You're in my mind all the time, the second I wake up and just before I fall asleep. I want us to be together forever."

He lifts her chin with two fingers, brushes her lips with his.

"Darling Rebecka, I want to have children with you. If that's what you want, of course."

Rebecka is incapable of answering. It is her greatest wish to be a mother, but it is impossible. She is barren.

Johan misinterprets her silence.

"We could adopt, given my . . . problem," he adds, suddenly tense. "Marion and I discussed the idea, but she didn't want to. You and I could try . . ."

Rebecka is fighting back tears. There is no one she would rather see as the father of her child. They belong together. It's as if she knew that when she first set eyes on him, as if fate had decided to pair them together against all the odds.

She buries her face in his chest, her throat constricted with tears. She would love to picture a life with him, but this can't go on. They must stop seeing each other. There can be no shared future for them, no rosy dreams of a happy ending.

She might be able to fool him, but not herself or Jesus. Her future is already set. She is Ole's wife. The wife of the pastor.

This night is all she can allow herself.

Tomorrow she will return home, continue to help out within the church and spread God's word on Earth, along with her friends and relatives.

She cannot break free, not even for Johan's sake.

This day and night together are a precious gift, nothing else.

It will sustain her for the rest of her life.

30

The sun has set by the time Hanna and Daniel return to the station for a quick briefing.

Daniel heads for the conference room. It has been a long day, with a lot of driving. He rubs his eyes. After the meeting with Linus Sundin, he ran out of energy. He had hoped that the guy would break down, but instead he'd demanded a lawyer.

As far as Daniel is concerned, that's the behavior of a guilty person.

Linus was clearly less than sober and became noticeably aggressive. This was a side of him they hadn't seen before. They have discussed the chances that Linus could be the perpetrator, given the brutality of the way Johan was murdered, and right now Daniel has no difficulty imagining that possibility.

A drunken Linus could easily be the killer.

The door opens, and Anton and Raffe come in, followed by Hanna with two mugs of steaming tea. She gives one to Daniel and sits down beside him.

"I've added milk, just the way you like it."

He gives her a grateful smile.

Anton takes out his notepad. "We have a reliable witness who's been in touch concerning Johan Andersson's van," he begins.

"Great," Daniel says. They really need some good news.

"The father of a teenager saw it parked on Klubbvägen, to the south of the recycling center in Staa, at about nine o'clock on Friday evening.

He was driving his daughter and a friend to a party nearby. When he went back at midnight to pick them up, it was gone."

"Perfect," Hanna says. "That confirms our time frame."

"He said he'd noticed the van because he'd contacted the company to fix a toilet back in November. He recognized the name," Anton adds.

"Carina said she thought the body had been moved to Tångbölevägen around midnight," Hanna reminds everyone, "given the amount of snow that was covering it. That fits perfectly. So, after Johan's visit to Linus, the van was driven back to Staa, but not to Johan's home on Dalövägen. Instead, it was parked on Klubbvägen for a while."

"I wonder why?" Raffe says, digging a tin of snuff out of his pocket.

"If there's an electronic logbook in the vehicle, we might find out," Daniel says. Carina had promised to check, but they've heard nothing yet.

"Maybe the perp panicked and needed time to think?" Hanna suggests. "If Linus killed Johan in a fit of rage, he wouldn't have had a plan in place."

"Maybe," Daniel concedes. The afternoon encounter with Linus had been revealing in many ways. He seems to have poor impulse control, especially when he's been drinking.

Anton strokes his chin. "I wonder if Johan was already dead by that stage. Or if he was lying on the floor of the van, beaten and bloody, and died later?" His eyes are drawn to the photographs of Johan's battered face on the wall. "I hope the poor bastard was unconscious at least. So he didn't suffer."

A painful silence fills the room.

"After stopping off at Tångbölevägen, the killer presumably drove to Lake Gev," Hanna says after a minute or so. "Since it was hidden by the old barn where it was found yesterday."

Daniel can see the entire chain of events now. They are beginning to get a clear picture of the situation and how it developed. With one important exception.

Who was driving the van?

31

A wonderful aroma of game stew fills the house when Hanna gets back to Sadeln. It's an unusual feeling, to be greeted with a hot meal.

Lydia is in the kitchen, wearing a brown leather apron. As usual she looks both chic and efficient, in a gray knitted polo-neck sweater and dark-blue designer jeans. Even her hair looks perfect, in spite of the fact that it has probably been stuffed inside a ski helmet all day.

Hanna becomes acutely conscious of her own lack of makeup. She didn't bother with mascara this morning; she simply pulled on her clothes and ran.

"There you are," Lydia says with a big smile. "Wonderful—dinner is almost ready."

"Thank you so much—I'm starving!" Hanna sniffs the air appreciatively. "You know, you don't have to wait for me in the evenings. I'll be working odd hours all week—this new case is taking up a lot of time."

Lydia is a lawyer and knows better than to ask her sister about an ongoing homicide investigation. Instead, she tastes the stew and smacks her lips.

"Where are the kids?" Hanna asks.

"Richard took them to Copperhill for a swim. They'll be back any minute."

It sounds perfect. The Copperhill hotel, which is only five minutes away by car, has a fantastic pool complex.

"Shall I set the table?"

Hanna opens the drawer containing the heavy stoneware dinner plates and takes out five, along with glasses and cutlery.

"By the way, Mom called," Lydia says over her shoulder.

"Right."

Hanna's heart sinks. What has her mother told Lydia this time?

"She said you were annoyed with her the other day."

"I wonder why," Hanna mutters.

She knows she sounds childish, but she is still hurt that her mother has chosen to keep in touch with Christian. To take his side instead of her daughter's. Hanna has no children, but if she had, she would never do that to them.

"What does it matter?" she goes on. "She prefers talking to you anyway."

The last comment is unnecessary; it isn't Lydia's fault that she has always been the favorite. Ulla had never intended to have more than one child; the family was a perfect little trio until Hanna came along, totally unplanned.

On top of that, she and her mother are like yin and yang. It isn't only their personalities that differ; they also have completely opposing values. Her mother's world is all about the superficial, how others see her. Therefore, life must be perfect, and that includes all members of the family.

Lydia, with her law degree, is a shining example of the success that can be achieved. While Hanna, with her career in the police department and her determination to stand up for abused and vulnerable women, is something of an embarrassment.

Her mother has even taken the assault in Barcelona, which Hanna still finds traumatic, as an affront. Not because Hanna was physically attacked and injured, but because deep down Ulla is ashamed of having a daughter who was raped. It is an attitude toward women that is a million miles from Hanna's. Sometimes she thinks it might be better to cut all contact with her mother—would that be easier for all concerned?

Lydia sighs and opens the oven door to check on a tray of potato wedges.

"Sorry, but you know what she's like," Hanna adds. "If I call her, there's always something that's not good enough. If I don't call, she complains to you."

She doesn't mention the dinner with Christian; she hasn't got the energy to bring that up right now. She slams the last of the knives and forks down so hard that everything on the table rattles. "Whatever I do, it's not good enough."

"That's not true."

"It is." Hanna can't help the sharpness in her tone. "Mom doesn't like the fact that I'm single, it doesn't fit her image of a happy, successful family. She's also upset that Christian and I broke up, because he was the perfect son-in-law—at least according to her. It wasn't my fault, but she still took it personally."

The very thought of Saturday's conversation makes her angry and disappointed. She goes back to the table and sets out the paper napkins. Irritatingly, tears spring to her eyes. Mom has hurt her far too often. It has taken Hanna years to build up a hard shell as self-defense; she feels better when she avoids close contact.

Thank God her parents now live in Spain, so that strategy works pretty well.

"She's getting old, you know," Lydia says.

"She's only seventy-five."

"Couldn't the two of you try and make peace?"

Lydia comes over, squeezes her shoulder.

"Can we drop the subject?" Hanna grunts. Her vision has become cloudy; she has to blink several times to see clearly again. "I need to go to the bathroom," she says, and walks away.

32

There is a long line at the checkout in the ICA store in Duved.

Anton has tossed a few random items into his basket, including spaghetti and a pack of meatballs that he can fry. For once he can't be bothered to work out the carbs or think about training, he just wants to go home, eat, and go to bed as soon as possible.

His ears are humming with exhaustion. No more nights with four or five hours of sleep; tonight he has to turn in early.

With the bag of groceries in one hand, he cuts across Karolinervägen. He can't help glancing over at Carl's apartment block a few hundred yards to the east. Duved is a small place—he doesn't understand why they haven't met before. Then again, Anton is a few years younger, and Carl has been living in Gävle for a while.

It is cold and dark as he walks through the whirling snow toward his own apartment. He is shivering, but the urge to take a detour past Carl's place is powerful.

It would only be a few more minutes.

He hesitates, then changes direction.

He stops in the parking lot opposite the main door and puts down his bag. Rubs his hands together for warmth. The temperature has dropped even further; it is now minus fifteen Celsius. Rows of icicles like sharp fangs hang from the roof above Carl's window on the second floor. The transparent ice shines in the glow of the streetlamps. The apartment is in darkness; it doesn't look like anyone is home.

Anton realizes it doesn't matter. He shouldn't be here; he can't have any contact with Carl as long as the investigation is ongoing.

What the hell is he doing here?

With a sigh he bends down to pick up the bag—then someone calls out his name.

"Anton?"

Carl is coming toward him from the church across the way. He is wearing a dark-blue woolen hat; snowflakes have settled to form an extra layer over the knitted pattern, giving the hat a fluffy, almost cute appearance.

Carl looks every bit as good as yesterday.

"I thought it was you." He sounds pleased.

Anton actually blushes. He can't remember the last time that happened. "I just wanted to . . ." He is lost for words. What did he want to do? He doesn't have a satisfactory answer; he just knows he ought to walk away before he makes even more of a fool of himself. "It was all a bit of a mess yesterday," he says, his cheeks burning.

Carl's serious expression doesn't help. "Why didn't you tell me you were a cop?"

Anton doesn't have a satisfactory answer to that either.

He usually tries to avoid mentioning his profession when he meets someone for the first time. He has learned that people either distance themselves or ask dozens of questions. Or he is subjected to a lecture about everything the police ought to be doing better.

"I hadn't expected to meet you within the framework of a homicide investigation," he says. It doesn't sound particularly friendly or apologetic. It's also pretty clumsy, given that Carl has just lost his best friend. Anton immediately regrets his words.

Carl looks both taken aback and hurt.

"I just mean that I was as surprised as you," Anton adds hastily, with the feeling that he has made things worse. "I'm sorry; I didn't intend to be so tactless."

He turns away. The wind picks up a torn plastic bag from the ground and whirls it into the air. It is carried along the street before being swallowed up by the darkness.

Anton would also like to be swallowed up by the darkness right now.

"I'm sorry," he says again. "I wouldn't hurt you for the world."

Carl shivers, stamps his feet up and down a few times.

"It's okay." He hesitates, then goes on. "Would you . . . like to come up for a chat?"

That's the last thing they should do.

But Anton nods and follows Carl toward the main door.

REBECKA

2020

JANUARY

At long last the Christmas break is over. It is dark when Rebecka unlocks the front door of Little Snowdrops. The January morning is bitterly cold, and frost frames the windowpanes. Yet relief floods her body as she steps inside.

It is time to get back to work, and she has longed for this day. Even though she has had her hands full with all the church events to celebrate the birth of Jesus, she has hardly been able to stand it. The eyes of the faithful fixed on Ole as he preached or explained the meaning behind a passage from the Bible have felt like a mockery, just like the hymns and carols she had to join in with.

The air in the Light of Life has become too thick to breathe.

She longs for Johan in every waking moment. The fact that she has refused to see him since that day and night at the cabin in November has made no difference. It has taken an enormous effort of will to resist. He is the love of her life, but there is no other way.

They have no future together.

Ole is her husband.

But she misses Johan desperately. It is like a physical pain, an open wound that will not heal unless he's close to her. She has prayed to

God every night, pleaded with him to help her, to free her from this forbidden love.

She cannot do it alone.

Every aspect of her life makes her think about Johan—the way he looked at her, the way he touched her. The hours they spent lying side by side on that wonderful night.

When Ole reaches for her body in the darkness of the bedroom, she has to bite her lip in order to hide her disgust.

She tries to think of this as her penance. Her cross to bear. She *must* banish all thoughts of Johan. Every day is a struggle, and at the same time the situation with Ole is getting worse and worse. She has done her best to please him, but there were several incidents over Christmas. Ole seized on the smallest excuse to punish her.

If he found out about her relationship with Johan . . .

The hairs on her arms stand on end.

She has no idea what he might be capable of. She has given up hoping that he will change. The violence is steadily increasing, as if he has crossed a line that used to hold him back.

She hangs her coat on its usual hook and lets out a groan. Her upper arm is sore after the latest quarrel. The marks of Ole's iron grip are clearly visible on her skin, and her neck and shoulders ache. She is so tense these days; she can't relax. As soon as Ole is anywhere near her, the muscle memory reacts. Her body stiffens, everything contracts.

Rebecka takes off her hat, shakes out her hair.

She is grateful to have a whole day at Little Snowdrops to look forward to. The preschool is her haven, the only thing that keeps her going. Sometimes she dreams of a different life—a life like the one Maria has, making her own decisions. Presumably Maria also has control over her own money. Rebecka's salary is paid directly into Ole's bank account.

Johan's words have stayed with her.

You can't allow him to treat you like this.

Easy to say, but what can she do? Her fate is already determined. She belongs to the Light of Life. She will walk through the valley of the Lord for the rest of her life.

God is testing her.

Besides, who would believe her if she took courage and told the truth about Ole, why she wants to leave him?

Everyone else thinks he's wonderful.

The rooms are silent and deserted. Rebecka relaxes for the first time in weeks. Advent stars still hang in the windows, their warm glow preserving the Christmas atmosphere. Maria won't be here for half an hour, so she has a little while to herself.

She goes into the staff room and makes a cup of coffee. It smells funny. She wrinkles her nose, puts down the cup, and checks the jar. Is it out of date? No, it's fine, nowhere near the expiration date.

A wave of nausea rises up from her stomach. She just makes it to the toilet before she throws up. It is a few minutes before she feels able to stand up; even then she has to hold on to the basin with one hand while she rinses her face with the other.

She looks in the mirror; she is pale and hollow eyed, in spite of the Christmas fare that made her put on weight. Ole has commented more than once on how fat she is getting. Her pants strain over her belly, most of her clothes don't fit properly. She has promised herself that she will stay away from cakes and cookies from now on.

The very thought of food almost makes her vomit again.

Her eyes are drawn to the area around her navel. It is protruding slightly. Over the past few days, her bra has felt uncomfortable too, as if it is too small. Surely, she can't have eaten that much?

A thought comes creeping into her mind, so unimaginable that she can hardly put it into words. She covers her mouth with her hand, stares at the reflection of her ashen face.

Could she be . . . pregnant?

Her legs won't hold her up. She sinks to the floor, rests her head on her knees. Takes several deep breaths.

Her pulse is racing.

It's impossible, it can't be true. She has been married to Ole for seven years without getting pregnant. She has never even had a miscarriage with him. How could it have happened now?

Unless . . .

There can be only one explanation.

Feverishly she counts on her fingers. Six or seven weeks have passed since she spent the night with Johan. It didn't occur to her to use any kind of protection; she knew that she was infertile. Besides, Johan had told her that he couldn't have children either.

And yet all the signs are there.

She hasn't had her period for a while. She is sometimes irregular, so she hasn't given it any thought. Plus, the situation with Johan has filled her mind.

She runs her fingertips over her belly. Could there be a little life in there?

She gets to her feet again, looks in the mirror. Pulls up her sweater so that she can see better.

From the side there is no doubt that her stomach is sticking out in a way that it never normally does.

Her breasts are bigger too.

It is a disaster, and yet she is overwhelmed by joy, smiling and laughing. She has wanted to be a mother for so long, she has dreamed of a baby of her own for many years. Sometimes she has crept away and cried when she has seen others with their little ones or pregnant bellies.

To think that she is going to be a mother too! To think that God has granted her such a gift!

The fear catches up with her.

She might not have counted exactly, but she knows roughly when she had her last period. And in the weeks following the night in the cabin, she managed to avoid Ole's advances, because she couldn't stand the idea of him inside her.

This has to be Johan's child.

Nothing else makes sense.

She and Ole have been trying for years. The likelihood that the two of them would get pregnant right now is vanishingly small. She has actually read about the phenomenon: a couple who can't have a child together can surprisingly become pregnant when they meet someone else.

Astonishingly, this must be what has happened to her and Johan.

Rebecka's entire body begins to shake. She is pregnant by Johan. Panic stricken, she covers her face with her hands and begins to whimper as tears fill her eyes.

Ole must never find out that she is carrying another man's baby.

She knows him so well by now; he has become more and more controlling and violent. If her secret were revealed, his rage would know no bounds.

If Ole finds out the truth about the child, there is no knowing what he might do.

To her and to Johan.

33

Daniel has barely finished eating when Ida gets up from the table and places her plate in the dishwasher. She had to prepare dinner because Daniel got home so late; he usually takes care of the evening meal. He must try to leave work earlier tomorrow—maybe he could cook pasta pomodoro with fresh basil, which is a family favorite.

He realizes that Ida is still standing by the sink, with her back toward him. She has said very little all evening, come to think of it.

"Are you okay?"

Ida turns around; he doesn't like the expression on her face.

"It's not going to be like December, is it?" The tension in her voice is unmistakable. "When you were never here?"

He gives her a reassuring smile. "Don't worry. I promise I'll do my best."

There is no guarantee that he will be able to keep that promise, but he can't tell her that—not when she seems so upset.

"Everyone is talking about Johan's murder," she says. "The head of tourism was interviewed on TV today. He said it's important for the whole area that the crime is cleared up as quickly as possible. Doesn't that mean you'll be working all hours?"

Ida is right. Daniel is well aware from his time in Gothenburg that homicide investigations have a tendency to swallow up every waking moment.

"What if you put yourself in danger?" she goes on, her voice trembling. "They said the murder was unusually brutal. It sounds like chasing the killer could be risky."

"I've got everything under control. And we have more resources this time—Hanna is on board right from the start. That will make a huge difference; she has a lot of experience from working with the City Police in Stockholm."

"I don't care about Hanna!" Ida is practically yelling now. "It's you I'm worried about—don't you understand?"

"Sweetheart . . ." He stands up, goes over to give her a hug, but she knocks his arms aside. The angry tears spill over.

"You're gone for hours and hours, and I get stressed and scared. I tried to call you twice today, and you didn't answer."

He was interviewing both times, first with Johan's parents, then at Linus's house. He couldn't speak to her then, not in the middle of a sensitive conversation. Of course, he should have returned her calls, but he and Hanna had spent the drive back to the station analyzing what they had learned; then he had gone straight into a meeting.

"I'm sorry. I didn't mean to upset you. Hanna and I were interviewing and   "

Ida interrupts him. "So, she was there too? It's nice that she gets to see you at least!"

In an instant she has switched to anger and sarcasm.

Daniel has probably mentioned Hanna a few times over the last couple of months, maybe even praised her now and again—but that's all there is to it. She played a key role in the Amanda Halvorssen case, for which she paid a high personal price.

He feels a surge of irritation, although he really doesn't want to quarrel tonight. Why is Ida picking on Hanna? She has nothing to do with this. On the contrary—without her input he would have to work even longer hours. However, he knows this isn't the right moment to point that out.

"Don't you understand how difficult this is?" Ida's voice is thick with tears. "When you don't pick up and I'm sitting here wondering if that means you've been hurt? Wondering if someone is going to show up at the door and tell me that something terrible has happened . . ."

"Oh, Ida . . ."

Daniel makes another attempt to embrace her, and this time she doesn't resist. She rests her head on his shoulder and lets out a muffled sob.

"You don't need to be scared," he whispers in her ear. "I promise to be careful. Nothing is going to happen to me."

Ida nods as a scream comes from the crib.

"I'll see to her," he says quickly. "You have a rest—maybe take a bath?"

"It's fine."

She gives him a shaky smile and heads for Alice's room. Daniel sits down at the table with the strong feeling that the conversation nearly spiraled out of control. However, at least he didn't lose his temper. It seems as if Ida is becoming very agitated. It's not a good sign when she drags Hanna into their discussions.

With a sigh he picks up his plate.

He really does try, all the time. And yet it is never enough.

34

Marion is dozing on the sofa when she is woken by a strange noise.

It sounded like a thud outside the front door.

She looks around, confused. She must have nodded off in the living room. What time is it? The house is in darkness, but the sky has cleared, and a pale half-moon is shining in through the window, casting a ghostly light over the furniture.

Could it be midnight already?

Before she can check, she hears something else from the hallway— the door handle is rattling.

Someone is trying to get into the house.

The hairs on her arms stand up. She curls into a ball, closes her eyes, tells herself it's fine; if she just lies here and pretends she isn't home, maybe whoever it is will go away.

The sound of the doorbell slices through the silence. Marion dares not move.

The bell rings again, for a long time.

Her heart is pounding. She can't remember where she put her phone, and she is too scared to get up and look for it.

It seems as if the stubborn ringing is making the entire house vibrate. She can't bear it. She gets up and creeps toward the hallway. Through the frosted glass in the front door, she sees a tall shadow on the steps.

A bolt of shock shoots through her body. It looks like Johan. *Oh my God—has he risen from the dead?*

Then she hears a voice bellowing outside.

"Open the fucking door!"

Marion inhales sharply.

"I know you're there!"

Linus. He sounds just as angry as that time in the office, when she thought he was going to punch Johan. He hammers on the door, then rings the bell again.

Marion looks around. She has nothing to defend herself with. She glances over at the wide window in the living room, the glass doors that open onto the terrace. If he smashes them, he will be inside in seconds.

The constant ringing reverberates off the walls.

"Open this fucking door!"

Linus's powerful figure looms up outside; the front door shudders as he bangs on it with his fist. In the glow of the outside light, Marion can see his shadow moving back and forth, like a deranged ghost searching for a way in.

She presses herself against the kitchen wall; she is so frightened that her whole body is shaking. Her gaze travels over the kitchen counter, and there, to the right of the stove, is the knife block Johan received on his thirtieth birthday. He did most of the cooking; she has never been particularly interested.

Her throat constricts at the thought that they will never eat dinner together again.

"Open the door or I'll kick it in!"

Instinctively she reaches for Johan's favorite knife from the middle of the block. The broad blade shines in the moonlight. Johan was meticulous when it came to keeping his knives sharpened.

She clutches the knife in her right hand.

"Open the door, you stupid bitch—I'm going to get in one way or another!"

Marion hesitates, then goes into the hallway. She quickly turns the latch and steps away in a single movement, keeping the knife behind her back. She isn't sure if it will provide security or simply make things worse.

Her fingers are slippery with sweat.

Linus flings the door wide open, and an ice-cold wind sweeps in. He staggers toward Marion, his face bright red, his eyes burning with rage.

"You bitch—how the fuck could you set the cops on me? Do you realize what you've done? They showed up at my place today!"

Spittle flies through the air, and a few drops land on Marion's cheek. She doesn't dare wipe them away; she simply holds on to the knife.

It is hurting her palm.

"The cops are going to frame me, and it's your fucking fault!"

"I haven't said a word," Marion stammers.

Linus moves nearer until there are only inches between them. His breath stinks of booze. At close quarters she can see how bloodshot his eyes are. Not only is he beside himself with fury, he is very drunk.

Marion has never seen him so mad, but she remembers how frightening the incident in the office was—when she thought he was going to lose control and attack her.

She is sobbing now, with her mouth open.

If only Johan was here.

35

Anton cannot sleep—what the hell has he done?

He is lying on his back in the double bed, with Carl beside him. Carl must have been asleep for at least an hour, but Anton can't switch off his mind.

Everything he had promised himself disappeared as soon as he walked into the apartment and was alone with Carl. The attraction was too strong; he couldn't resist. He wanted him.

Now he really is in trouble.

If his colleagues find out about this . . . He might have jeopardized the entire investigation.

He has to leave. Get out of bed, gather up his clothes, and go home. He should have left a long time ago, but his body is resisting. It doesn't want to go out in the cold. It wants to stay the night, wake up in the same bed as Carl. Have breakfast together.

Anton has yearned for a man like this for such a long time. He clutches one corner of the sheet. This is insanity. He can't embark on a relationship right now. He can't even risk being seen with Carl. They have already crossed the line. He is a police officer and is expected to show good judgment, in both his professional and personal life.

Now here he is, having gone against all his principles.

He gazes at Carl's sleeping body. He is lying on his stomach, with his leg drawn up to the side. One arm is tucked under the pillow, the other outstretched.

Anton could look at him for hours. Carl is beautiful in the pale moonlight. His back is well shaped and muscular, his skin invitingly soft and warm. He has a black scorpion tattooed on his left shoulder.

Anton leans over and brushes the back of Carl's neck with his lips. Carl takes a deep breath but doesn't stir.

This wasn't supposed to happen. He only meant to stay for a little while, explain why things were so awkward during yesterday's interview. Let Carl see him the way he'd been on Saturday, the real Anton rather than the formal police officer.

But they'd started kissing almost as soon as they got through the door.

Like two horny teenagers.

Anton sighs. Afterward they sat in bathrobes and ate the meatballs and spaghetti he'd bought earlier. It wasn't exactly a gourmet feast, but they were both hungry, and cooking together felt natural. They divided up the tasks, didn't get in each other's way.

Everything is easy with Carl—it's as if they've known each other for years. Anton's emotions have already begun to develop; he wants to protect him and support him, not least because Carl has just lost his best friend. Anton can't imagine how that feels.

No doubt that was why he asked so many questions about the case. Did they have a suspect, how had the murder been committed, what had actually happened to Johan?

Anton did his best to avoid concrete answers. It's bad enough that he's spent the night with an important witness; he definitely can't share confidential information. At the same time, he wanted to reassure Carl, console him in this terrible situation.

Eventually Carl seemed to realize what he was trying to do.

Anton shuffles, gets more comfortable. He's sure that Carl didn't mean any harm. He is still deeply shocked and upset. Besides, he was one of the last people to see Johan alive; it's only natural that he feels involved, wants to know how the investigation is going.

His phone is on the nightstand on top of a book. When Anton reaches out to check the time, he notices that it is a hymn book. Is Carl religious? He hasn't mentioned it.

Almost midnight. He really must leave. He can't stay here until morning. Duved is a small place. It would be impossible to explain away if anyone saw him.

He has to keep his distance from Carl.

At least until Johan's murderer is caught.

REBECKA

2020

FRIDAY, FEBRUARY 21

"Are you okay?" Maria asks.

She and Rebecka are in the staff room, grabbing a quick coffee. It's afternoon, and most of the children have already been picked up ahead of the weekend.

"You've been so down lately," she goes on. "Ever since Christmas, to be honest."

Rebecka shakes her head dismissively. "I guess I'm just tired." Maria is kind, but she can't do anything to help. No one can. Her belly is growing by the day, and soon she won't be able to hide it any longer. Her blood pressure is also too high. She has secretly visited the health center a few times to have some tests. On the last occasion the doctor sounded worried but said he would get back to her as soon as the results came through.

She doesn't know what to do. She can't contact Johan, that would just make things worse. For three long months she has ignored him completely. She hasn't replied to a single text message; she has simply deleted them immediately.

It is no good turning to her parents. They will never take her side, and her father's reaction is all too easy to predict. Rebecka can almost hear his angry voice if he finds out. A wife must obey her husband and remain faithful to him.

How can she reveal to her father that she is nothing more than an adulteress?

She doesn't dare even contemplate Ole's rage if the truth comes out. Not when he already abuses her for minor matters such as socks going missing in the wash or too much salt in his food. She is also increasingly worried that he will harm the baby. What if his kicks damage the fetus?

Every night she lies in bed wondering whether to tell him she is pregnant. Behave as if it's his child. Pretend to be delighted.

But every morning her courage fails her.

Maria glances out the window. "Our handsome plumber is back again—I wonder what he wants today?"

Rebecka gives a start when she sees Johan's white van in the parking lot. Her heart stops beating—then she sees his face through the windshield, and it feels as if it will burst with happiness.

She has missed him so much. They haven't spoken since that night in the cabin. She chose not to tell him about the baby, because she is so afraid of the consequences—but oh, how she has longed for him!

Johan is striding toward the door.

"Can you let him in?" Maria says. "I need to go to the bathroom."

Rebecka tries to pull herself together. "No problem."

The cold sweeps in as Johan steps inside. His thick jacket is unbuttoned. His usually cheerful expression is gone; he is clearly under strain, and there are dark circles beneath his eyes.

"I have to talk to you," he says quietly.

"No." Rebecka can't look at him. If she meets his gaze, it will be too difficult. It is already so painful. "Leave me alone. Forget about me."

He takes a step closer and grabs her wrist, his fingertips burning her bare skin and reawakening all the memories she has tried to bury.

"Please, Rebecka. Don't do this to me."

She is so close to tears that she can't make a sound.

"I've been trying to get a hold of you for months. Why are you avoiding me? What have I done?"

Rebecka swallows hard. "You . . . you haven't done anything. This isn't about you."

"So what is it about?"

Out of the corner of her eye, Rebecka sees that Maria has reappeared and is watching them thoughtfully. Two five-year-olds are chasing each other around the hallway, yelling at the top of their voices.

This is no good.

Johan is still holding her arm. She moves back, shakes off his hand. "Go away. We can't meet again."

"Why not?"

Rebecka is breathing heavily.

"We love each other," Johan says, a little louder now.

She can't bear it. The despair in his eyes is like a knife twisting inside her. She knows she shouldn't spend a single minute more in his company, but she can't control her feelings. Her voice betrays her.

"I'll meet you on the edge of the forest in fifteen minutes."

Johan looks searchingly at her, with a mixture of relief and anxiety. "Promise?"

Stress is pulsating through Rebecka's body. She must get him out of here before they attract even more attention. A parent could show up at any moment, someone who might tell Ole what they've seen.

She isn't safe anywhere.

"Yes. I promise. As long as you leave right now."

36

Daniel feels as if he has slept for no more than fifteen minutes when Alice wakes up, even though the alarm clock tells him that two hours have passed. He groans quietly to himself but manages to slide out of bed and scoop her up before she disturbs Ida.

With his daughter in his arms, he heads for the kitchen and warms up a bottle in record time. Soon Alice is eagerly sucking away at her formula. When he sees her contented expression, he knows that it was worth getting up, even though his entire body aches. He loves it when it's just the two of them; he has been longing for this all day.

She smells of freshly bathed baby.

He inhales the sweet scent and settles down in the armchair in the living room. It's nice to sit here in the dark, with only a table lamp glowing in the corner.

His thoughts drift away as they often do. He wants to be present in this moment with his child, and yet he can't quite turn off the day's events; they are playing in his mind like a movie. His brain continues to process the information, and there is nothing he can do about it.

He is relieved that it didn't erupt into a new quarrel with Ida and he was able to control his temper. At the same time he is torn; he would have liked to stay much later at the station this evening. There is still a lot to discuss with the team, he needs to find new angles, study every piece of the puzzle.

He would like to sit quietly with Hanna, go over everything one more time. He can't stop wondering about Johan's hastily planned trip to

Strömsund. There must have been a good reason, probably connected to the person he was intending to take with him. The mysterious stranger.

The more he thinks about it, the more convinced he becomes that he or she knows something of vital importance. Why else would his or her identity be so sensitive that Johan wouldn't even tell his brother over the phone?

He remembers another point that Raffe mentioned just before Daniel came home.

At lunchtime Marion had sent over a list of the firm's latest jobs. Johan had spent most of the previous week at a construction site in Sadeln. Raffe had contacted the foreman, and according to him, Johan had left early on Friday afternoon, even though they were behind schedule. Apparently, he had been going to a preschool called Little Snowdrops in Ånn; the name of the school was also included in Marion's list.

Ånn. It's hardly even a village, just a collection of buildings and an old train station. If Daniel remembers correctly, there are no more than seventy residents—just enough for a preschool, but too few for a grocery store or a restaurant. A short distance away is Camp Ånn, a center that is used to train volunteer military reserves and members of the home guard.

The hamlet lies in the opposite direction from Sadeln, approximately twenty-five miles from the site where Johan was working and twelve miles from Staa, where he lived.

That's quite some distance. If he went over there late in the day, on a Friday afternoon, it must have been important.

Alice's head has slipped down into the crook of his arm. He adjusts her position so that she can finish off her formula.

There must be a contact person at the preschool that they can speak to. Maybe Johan mentioned something while he was there, a clue that might throw light on the sudden trip to Strömsund?

Daniel puts down the empty bottle and carries Alice into the bedroom. He places her in the crib below the window. Her eyelids are already drooping, her body is relaxed. She almost fell asleep in his arms.

Ida hasn't moved. She is lying on her side with her eyes closed. Her long hair is spread across the pillow, and one shoulder of her T-shirt has slipped down.

She is so beautiful.

A sudden tenderness comes over him. He gently caresses her cheek, and she lets out a little whimper before turning over. He gets back into bed and nestles close to her so that he can feel the warmth of her body.

Everything is going to be all right between them, he tells himself. They're going through a phase; it happens to all new parents from time to time. It's hard work with a baby, especially when it's the first. They are still learning how to be a family.

And yet there is something that gnaws at him.

It takes a long time before he falls asleep.

37

A thousand thoughts whirl around inside Marion's head as she cowers before Linus's powerful figure. He is so tall. And well built. She is no match for him, even with a knife in her hand.

He can do whatever he wants.

Her eyes dart from side to side, searching for an escape route. It's too late to hide, but the bathroom door is ajar. Maybe she can slip under his arm and seek sanctuary in there?

But there's no lock, just a simple hasp. He could easily push the door open with his shoulder.

The stress is making her field of vision shrink.

If Johan were home, Linus would never dare to treat her like this. *But Johan is dead.*

"Get out," she says hoarsely. She is doing her best to keep her voice steady, to hold the hysteria at bay so that Linus won't realize how frightened she is. When he's this drunk he is totally unpredictable, he has no boundaries.

She has seen him change in an instant before.

He is capable of anything.

An icy wind is blowing in through the open front door, but she is too scared to ask him to close it.

"You're wasting your time here," she continues. "I haven't said a word to the police. Go home to your family."

Linus isn't listening to her. He is in a world of his own, and the only thing buzzing around in his brain is the list of imagined injustices.

He wants one thing, and one thing only.

To take out his anger on her.

"Do you really think you can get away with this?" he hisses.

"I'll call the police if you don't leave right now."

"I thought you'd already done that."

There is so much venom in the comment that Marion gasps.

Linus gives her a hard shove. She almost falls over but manages to grab hold of a door frame and keep her balance, still with the knife behind her back.

You mustn't end up on the floor, an inner voice tells her. *If you're lying down, you'll be even more vulnerable.*

When Linus reaches for her again, Marion brandishes the knife, points it straight at his chest. Virtually every muscle is trembling, but miraculously she manages to keep her hand steady.

They are only twelve inches apart. One sudden movement and the blade will penetrate his heart.

She can smell the sweat from his armpits.

"Get out," she says again.

He is staring at the knife as if he were hypnotized.

"I'm warning you, Linus."

Still, he doesn't move. Only when she pretends to lunge at him does he take a step back, then another. Rage gives Marion fresh strength.

"Get the fuck out of my house!" she yells.

Linus's face contorts. "You'll regret this! You don't get rid of me that easily!"

Marion raises her hand. "You've done enough damage to me and Johan!"

"I'll be back!" he shouts, and suddenly he's left the house. A car door slams, followed by the roar of an engine. Snow spurts up around his spinning tires as he drives away.

Through the open front door, Marion watches his red rear lights disappear down the road.

She takes a ragged breath. Her legs give way; the knife falls to the floor with a clatter. She drops to her knees and buries her face in her hands.

For several minutes she rocks back and forth, incapable of getting up. Eventually the icy blast from the door brings her to her senses. She drags herself to her feet, staggers over, and manages to close it by leaning on the frame for support. With one last huge effort, she turns the key and weaves her way to the sofa, where she collapses.

The blackness of the window overlooking the terrace gapes at her. Marion sobs into the darkness. She has never felt so alone in her entire life.

One single thought echoes through her mind.

He said he'd be back.

REBECKA

2020

FRIDAY, FEBRUARY 21

Rebecka is hurrying toward the edge of the forest where she has arranged to meet Johan. *This is insane.* She is doing exactly what she shouldn't be doing, what she promised herself she wouldn't do: she is going to be alone with him again.

And yet her heart rejoiced as soon as she saw him. She has longed for him so much.

She gabbled an excuse to Maria, said she had an errand to do, then practically ran out of the door.

She can see Johan's tall figure in the distance. He is waiting for her in their usual place, by the path where low-growing fir trees hide them from view. The sight of his unhappy face breaks her heart. How can she make him understand that he must leave her alone when the only thing she wants to do is throw herself into his arms and tell him about the baby?

His devastated expression didn't make things any easier. Johan, who is always on the brink of laughter.

The winter sun is hiding behind thick clouds. Icy flakes fill the air and cover the trees in a melancholy mist.

Or maybe it's her tears that are making it hard to see properly.

"At last!" he exclaims, reaching for her.

Rebecka backs away; she can't afford to feel his arms around her, or she will never be able to go through with this. She has to make him realize that it's over between them.

"We can't see each other anymore," she says firmly, doing her best to sound unmoved.

He looks like an upset child. His face is naked and defenseless, his pain raw and tangible. It is her fault. She is the one who has caused him such suffering. She prays for the strength to do what she has to do. She reminds herself that God is testing her, as he has done so many times in the past. She must remain strong in her faith.

"I love you," he says. "I want to live with you."

"That's not possible."

"Why not?"

Rebecka's desperation is intensifying. Why is he making this so difficult? She swallows hard.

"I will never be able to leave Ole. Or the church. I have promised before God that I will be faithful to my husband for the rest of my life."

Johan doesn't seem to be listening—or he doesn't want to listen.

"Why?"

"I've told you—it's impossible."

Johan gazes at her for a long time, as if he is trying to read her innermost thoughts. For a second Rebecka thinks that he is doing exactly that, and he knows she is lying.

He isn't wearing a hat; his brown hair is covered with snowflakes. They melt slowly and are replaced by fresh, perfect ice crystals that land and settle.

She wants to brush them away with her fingertips, but she dare not get so close to him. The risk of losing control is too great. Instead, she pushes her hands deep in her pockets and digs her nails into her palms.

Something flickers in Johan's eyes, as if he has made a decision.

"Okay then—I'll leave you in peace."

The words cut her like a knife, even though she is the one who has driven him to this.

"On one condition."

She nods.

"Look me in the eyes and tell me you don't love me."

Rebecka takes a deep breath. She has made such an effort to push him away; she has made her voice cold and dismissive. She can't break down now.

But he is asking for the one thing she cannot give him.

She opens her mouth to answer. Nothing comes out. She can't do it.

"Just say it." Johan's voice is rough. "Then I'm gone—I promise I'll never bother you again."

Rebecka falls apart. Her face crumples, and the tears she has tried so hard to hold back spill over.

"I love you, Johan. I love you so much. I would give my life to be with you, but it's out of the question. It's too dangerous."

In one stride he is with her, wrapping her in his arms. He presses her so tightly to his chest that she can hardly breathe. It doesn't matter. She wants time to stand still; she doesn't want to be parted from him now that they are finally together again.

After a while he loosens his grip and looks at her searchingly.

"What are you afraid of? Is it Ole?"

Rebecka turns her face away, overwhelmed by shame. It is her husband they are talking about.

"He could do . . . anything," she admits. "If he finds out what we've done."

Johan shakes his head. "Darling Rebecka, he can't do us any harm."

He has no idea how bad things are. Johan has never seen Ole when the rage takes over, when he transforms from the charismatic pastor into a violent bully as soon as the front door closes.

Johan is a good person—how could he understand the psychology of a man who deliberately assaults his wife?

And now she has the child to think of.

"You can't stay with him because you're scared of him," Johan goes on, tightening his embrace once more. "He can't be allowed to get away with hurting you."

"You don't know what he's like . . ."

"We live in Sweden, Rebecka—you are not his property. It's only in the Bible that women are stoned for leaving their husbands. Everyone has the right to divorce."

Johan is wrong. She didn't want to tell him about the pregnancy; it won't make the situation any easier if he knows. However, it seems to be the only way to make him understand how desperate she is, and why their relationship must end at all costs.

"For God's sake Rebecka—we can fix this. I promise."

He takes hold of her shoulders, and she looks into his eyes.

"Stop, Johan! I'm pregnant."

He is lost for words. His eyes travel to her belly and rest there for a few seconds; then he hugs her again and kisses her forehead.

"It doesn't matter. I love you so much, I can take care of you and the baby. There's no need to worry."

He doesn't realize that he is the father. Before Rebecka can speak, he takes a step back, frowning.

"Are you sure it's Ole's?"

She can't lie about this. "It's yours. I'm in the fourth month."

Time stops. In the far distance she hears a train braking, then sounding its whistle in the twilight.

Johan opens his mouth, closes it again.

"Are you sure?" he says eventually.

She nods helplessly. "It must be. There's no other explanation. It can't be Ole's."

Johan blinks several times, as if he can't let himself believe what she has just said. Then his expression changes, his eyes are shining, his smile is broader than ever before.

"That's fantastic!" He kisses her cheek. "You're fantastic!"

His reaction makes her laugh with relief. She remembers their night in the cabin, how wonderful it was. The best day and night of her life.

Their child was conceived in a rush of happiness.

He takes her hands in his.

"You *have to* leave him." There is a new gravity in his tone. "I don't want you to go back home. You need to get away from him today."

The afternoon sun is disappearing behind the treetops, and the temperature is dropping fast. Johan's face is in shadow, but Rebecka can see the concern in his eyes.

"I mean it—you have to leave Ole immediately. I'll help you."

"Today? That's not possible."

She can't do it—God is watching her.

"Rebecka. Think about our child."

She tries to think, but there is only chaos in her mind. Everything is happening too fast; her head is spinning. She has no idea what to do. Besides, this isn't only about her and Ole—Johan is married too.

"What are you going to say to Marion?"

"I'll take care of Marion; don't you worry about that. She's a sensible woman with a warm heart. She'll understand, I'm sure of it. It's a long time since we were a couple."

Rebecka sees the love in his eyes. For her sake, he is prepared to walk away from everything.

A strand of hair has escaped from her hat; tenderly he tucks it behind her ear.

"Listen to me. It's essential that you don't stay under the same roof as that man."

He is right. There is bound to be more violence. She is already afraid that Ole will kick her so hard in the belly that the baby will be hurt.

An ice-cold gust of wind whirls by as she tries to reach a decision. Suddenly she is acutely aware that she is freezing cold. The wind is hard and sharp against her cheeks; her fingers are growing numb. She stamps her feet up and down to get the circulation going, hears the snow crunch beneath her boots.

She ought to get back to the preschool; she has already been gone for way too long. It's Friday, and it's almost four fifteen.

"I don't want you to sleep there for one more night," Johan says firmly. "You mustn't stay over the weekend if you're so frightened of him."

Rebecka knows that she can trust Johan; he only wants what is best for her. It's such a relief to let him take over. She is exhausted by all the emotions racing around her body; she can't think clearly anymore.

"I have to gather up my things," she says. "I can't just disappear."

"I'll pick you up this evening. Could you get to the parking lot on Björkvägen? It's pretty close to your place."

Rebecka nods, dizzy with excitement, trying to get her brain to work.

"Tomorrow would be better," she says.

Johan frowns. "Why?"

"Ole won't be at home. He's leading a Bible evening at the church." Johan clearly isn't keen.

"It will be much easier for me to get away then," Rebecka goes on. "Otherwise, he's bound to see me packing."

Eventually Johan gives in. "Okay. In that case I'll pick you up at the parking lot at seven o'clock tomorrow evening. We can go to my brother's place in Strömsund. It might be sensible to stay away for the next week or so, give everything the chance to calm down."

Rebecka looks at her watch. "I have to go."

Johan pulls her close and kisses her for a long time; then he gently caresses her stomach. There is something reverential about the movement, and he has tears in his eyes.

"We're having a baby." His voice is thick with emotion. "You and me. We're going to be a little family."

Rebecka pats his cheeks. She can hardly believe that she has just promised to leave Ole. Her parents will probably never speak to her again—nor will her relatives, or Lisen.

God is bound to punish her, but for Johan's sake she is prepared to pay the price.

For the sake of their unborn child.

"See you tomorrow," he calls after her with so much love that she too begins to cry.

TUESDAY, FEBRUARY 25

38

A pale winter sun is spreading its light over the Åre valley as Hanna and Daniel head toward the preschool in Ånn. It is twenty past eight, and they have just finished the morning briefing with Östersund.

Hanna curls up in the passenger seat. Dinner yesterday evening was very pleasant, once Richard and the children got back from Copperhill, but she slept badly; the night was filled with uneasy dreams about her mother and Christian. When she woke at five thirty, she gave up and came in to work early.

Daniel backs out of the parking lot. The road is covered in thick snow; the plow hasn't made it this far yet. A pedestrian has plodded along by the sidewalk, the deep footprints clearly visible.

There is hardly anyone around, and it's nice to be free of the sports break tourists. Yesterday the large parking lot outside the liquor store was full, and for once the vehicles crawling around searching for a space weren't Teslas with Norwegian plates.

"I can't stop thinking about Johan's van up by the lake," Hanna says to break the silence. "How the driver got back."

Daniel gives a start, as if he were somewhere else entirely. He does that sometimes, disappears into his own thoughts. As they often travel together between Åre and Östersund, Hanna has gotten used to it.

"Sorry, what did you say?" He pushes back a lock of dark-brown hair from his forehead. It is slightly too long; he could do with a haircut. At the same time, it gives him a softness, taking some of the sting out of the sternness that can dominate his character.

Viveca Sten

"If we assume that it was Linus Sundin who drove the van up there, then someone must have picked him up. How else would he have gotten home?"

"Sounds reasonable."

"How about his wife?"

"Sandra?"

"Yes."

"Why would she have done that?"

"To protect the family, of course." As far as Hanna is concerned, it's a simple calculation. "They have a little boy together. If Linus goes to jail for Johan's murder, then Sandra will be left alone with the child. It's enough of a motive for me."

The wife is the simplest option—who else would Linus have turned to?

"This is my thinking," she goes on. "Linus and Johan started to argue when Johan arrived, the argument spiraled out of control, and Johan could have been dead as early as eight o'clock. He might even have died in the Sundins' kitchen." She pauses to gather the threads of her reasoning.

"Linus throws him in the back of the van, but he's left with a major problem: What is he going to do with the body and the van? If he dumps the body, then hides the vehicle, he has no transportation—so he persuades his wife to help."

Daniel's attention is firmly fixed on the road ahead. They have just passed Tångböle, where Johan was found on Saturday.

"So why was the van parked on Klubbvägen?"

"To gain time." Hanna has spent the early morning going over a possible scenario. There was no opportunity for discussion yesterday before the team went their separate ways. "I don't think it was any more complicated than that. He needed to work out what to do, and there are still plenty of people out and about at eight o'clock in the evening. It was easier to get rid of Johan's dead body later on, without anyone seeing him."

They pass the sign for Ånn, and a collection of red wooden houses appears. Daniel takes a right and follows a narrow track up a steep hill.

"I believe Sandra picked Linus up from Klubbvägen in the family car; then they went home and waited for a few hours before dumping the body."

They have reached a red single-story building—Little Snowdrops.

"We should go and speak to Sandra when we're done here," Hanna concluded.

Daniel parks a few yards from the entrance.

"Fine by me, but what if Linus isn't the guilty party? How about Johan's mysterious companion?"

"You mean the person he was planning to take to Strömsund?"

"Exactly. Maybe Johan left Linus's house just after eight and headed to Klubbvägen to meet this person. Something went wrong, leading to Johan's death. His companion waited for a few hours, then drove to Tångbölevägen and dumped the body." Daniel switches off the engine. "It's very similar to the situation you described, except that we're talking about a completely different perpetrator."

Hanna gives him a look.

"Weren't you the one who was pretty convinced Linus was our man?"

"I'm not saying he isn't, just that we shouldn't jump to conclusions too soon. It's only a few days since Johan was found. We don't even have the autopsy results yet."

Hanna knows he's right. This is one of the things she likes about Daniel, the fact that he is always ready to consider new angles. For him it's never about prestige; there is no point in clinging to one hypothesis if another possibility presents itself.

"In that case," she says as she unfastens her seatbelt, "the question is how do we get a hold of this mysterious stranger?"

Daniel grins for the first time today.

"It's called police work, my dear colleague."

39

They are met with the sight of children's snowsuits hanging neatly on hooks and boots lined up on the floor as they step across the threshold of Little Snowdrops preschool. Daniel notices all the colorful drawings displayed on the walls, and the aroma of freshly baked buns filling the air.

"I guess you'd better get used to this kind of environment," Hanna says with a smile. "It won't be long until Alice is in school."

"We're not quite there yet."

Alice is only five months old. The plan is for Ida to stay home with her until she reaches eight months; then Daniel will take over. He is due to go on paternity leave in May. It's something of a cliché for the man to take his parental leave over the summer, but it just worked out that way. Also, work is significantly quieter during the low season.

He looks around for someone to speak to. When he double-checked the list of the plumbing firm's clients and jobs, it showed that Johan had been here many times during the fall. Then there was a break in December and January until last week's visit. It may not be important, but Daniel wants to find out what was going on. Something must have made Johan Andersson drive all the way from Sadeln to Ånn on Friday.

As if summoned by his thoughts, a fair-haired young woman in a moss-green sweater appears. Daniel shows his ID and explains that they have a couple of questions. Is there a room where they can talk in private?

She seems taken aback but shows them into the staff room. On the counter along one wall, there is a microwave and a coffee machine, the pot half-full. In the middle of the room, there is a round table with a beautiful blue hydrangea in a pot.

"Help yourselves to coffee—I just have to tell my colleague I'll be away for a little while."

Daniel pours himself a cup, but Hanna doesn't want one. They sit down at the table, and the teacher returns in no time.

"Sorry—we're short staffed this week, so it's all a bit hectic." She holds out her hand. "Maria Törnlund—how can I help?"

"We'd like to ask about a workman who seems to have been here quite a bit during the fall. His name is Johan Andersson, and he's from a firm called Andersson and Sundin Plumbing."

"I know who he is. As you say, he's been here several times. He's the one who was such a fantastic downhill skier back in the day. Is something wrong?"

"He's dead," Hanna informs her. "Murdered."

Maria's hand flies to her mouth. "What? What are you saying?"

"You might have read about it in the paper," Daniel says. "A man was found by the roadside in Tångböle on Saturday."

"Oh my God . . ."

Maria inhales sharply, her eyes fill with tears. It's not the first time Daniel has seen this kind of reaction. For most people news like this is impossible to process. The fact that a person they've seen alive has been found murdered just doesn't make sense.

"I can't believe it's true—he was here on Friday! I didn't link the murder to him. I've been away for the weekend, I haven't really caught up with the news."

"No problem," Daniel reassures her. "But we do have a couple of questions about Johan's last visit."

Maria looks guilty, although it's hard to imagine why.

"I'm not really the right person to speak to," she says. "He had a lot more to do with my colleague, Rebecka Nordhammar."

40

Heavy gray-blue clouds are lurking behind the peaks of the mountain known as Snasahögarna, but the morning sun is shining brightly over Åreskutan, where Marion has made her way by using climbing skins attached to her broad cross-country skis. She left the house early this morning and hasn't stopped, following the route from the VM8 lift in the valley all the way up to Åreskutan.

She has never attempted such a long ascent before. She is dripping in sweat beneath her clothes, and her thigh muscles are aching. It has taken every ounce of energy to reach the peak—but at least her brain has been able to rest for a few hours.

That was what she longed for when she set off. She had to fill her head with something other than the images of Johan's badly beaten body and Linus's furious face. The only thing she could come up with was to wear herself out completely, and it is a relief to feel her heart pounding from physical effort.

Rather than fear.

She is safe up here. No one can get to her.

Marion leans heavily on her poles and allows her gaze to sweep across the mountains to the southwest. It is a magnificent sight, and it gives her fresh strength, almost makes her forget the horrific reality.

Way down below, at the bottom of the valley, she can see the oval expanse of Lake Åre, with a covering of snow that looks like white icing. Its outlet meanders slowly out of sight, past Berge, Ängena, and Duved. By the time it reaches Staa, where she lives, it is no more than a brook.

Even farther away in the distance, she glimpses Norway.

Last year she and Johan visited Norwegian friends in Trondheim. The drive took only a few hours. If she closes her eyes, she can picture Johan's face, glowing with anticipation; the laughter over dinner as they joked about Norway's unofficial national dish, lamb-and-cabbage stew.

Marion pushes away the memory and turns her face up to the sun.

For once the air is still. The only evidence of the strong winds that normally blow up here is the remarkable snow formations everywhere. The wind has compressed the snow into weird shapes, building on top of the drifts. Some hang over the edge of the precipice at such impossible angles that it seems they might collapse at any moment.

She inhales deeply, fills her lungs. She has always adored the mountains, always felt more at home outdoors than indoors. This has been her safe place.

Åre isn't like the Alps, where she grew up. There are no ten-thousand-foot slopes here, no endless downhill runs, but she has come to love the Swedish mountains. It is a different kind of love, more about being at one with nature than crazy off-piste adventures in dangerous ravines. Instead of the hunt for the perfect powder snow, she has become captivated by cross-country skiing, the feeling of silently gliding along through the fir trees as the sun filters down through the branches.

She and Johan often went out together, and she learned to cover the twenty-mile circuit in more or less the same time as him. Sometimes they would head off to Ul:ådalen when the winter cold gave way to the milder temperatures of the early spring.

She has come to love Sweden as she loved Johan.

The pain claws at her breast.

Marion bends down and removes the climbing skins so she can ski down. The hairy surface is a mixture of nylon and mohair, which provides the best grip and lasts the longest.

A great weariness comes over her. She didn't get much sleep after Linus's intrusion, just a few restless hours on the sofa. Terrifying thoughts whirled around her mind as soon as she closed her eyes.

Maybe she should contact the police, tell them what happened, but who knows what that might lead to? The consequences could be serious. She is not prepared to take the blame for Linus's financial mistakes, or to be the scapegoat for his poor judgment.

Then again, he is dangerous and unpredictable. Last night she almost believed he was going to kill her. What will she do if he comes back, if he tries to get into the house again? Can she even face staying there tonight?

If not, where will she go?

Marion is overcome by a sudden impulse to simply lie down in the snow. Never go back. Then she takes a deep breath and pushes the straps into her rucksack. When she gets home, she will call her brother, talk through the whole thing.

Florian is wise—he will help her.

41

Hanna can hear the children playing on the other side of the staff-room wall. There is something so innocent about the sound, the voices and the laughter.

"You said we ought to speak to your colleague Rebecka Nordhammar," Daniel says to Maria. "Could you go and get her, please?"

Maria shakes her head. "I'm afraid not. She called in sick—that's why there are only two of us here."

"Do you know how long she's going to be off work?"

"I'm not sure. The rest of the week, maybe?" Maria plucks at the table mat under the plant pot. "Actually, it was her husband who phoned, not her. Yesterday morning."

Hanna frowns. It's probably nothing to worry about, but the information triggers something within her.

"Rebecka's husband?"

"Yes, Ole."

"Did he say what was wrong with her?"

Hanna can't help asking the question. Why would a grown woman let her husband call on her behalf to say she's sick? That's the kind of thing parents do for their children in school.

"Just that she had a temperature and wouldn't be in. Why?"

"She must have had an incredibly high temperature if she couldn't make the call herself."

Maria looks as if she has been thinking along the same lines. She lowers her voice.

"I probably shouldn't say this, but I get the impression that Rebecka's husband is quite . . . controlling." She looks embarrassed, tucks a strand of hair behind her ear. "I mean, Ole's really nice, but he always drives her to work and picks her up at the end of the day. He's done that more or less every single day since she started here two and a half years ago. It's pretty odd, because he never comes in to say hello; he just sits out there waiting."

Maria looks at Hanna as if she really wants to say, *It's kind of creepy.*

Hanna feels the old rage spark inside her. During her years with the City Police in Stockholm, she met plenty of men who wanted to control their women. However, the Nordhammars' marital situation has nothing to do with her. They have come here to find out about Johan Andersson, not to dig into a marriage with a skewed balance of power.

"They're religious," Maria continues. "Rebecka and her husband belong to the church known as the Light of Life—have you heard of it? I think Ole is a pastor, actually."

The name is not familiar to Hanna, but Daniel nods. "I believe it's a pretty conservative movement?"

"Yes," Maria says. "I've read up about it since Rebecka came to work here. The church has been in this area for a long time and has a sister organization in Norway. It's very . . . traditional."

"What does that mean?" Hanna asks.

"They use the Bible as their most important guide. It's the central authority. Members have to follow its rules as far as possible. More or less to the letter, if you understand what I mean."

Maria's disapproval is clear.

"So, it's the man who holds the power?" Hanna can't disguise her contempt. There always seems to be an excuse for men to rule over women. Daniel gives her a warning look, but Maria agrees.

"Something like that. When Rebecka started with us, I asked her several times if she'd like to meet up for a glass of wine after work. At first, I thought she didn't want to, but as time went by, I realized that her husband wouldn't allow it. That she'd have to ask him for permission." Maria rubs her wrist. "I don't think she even dared ask. To be honest, I've been worried about her, but whenever I try to broach the subject, she says I'm being silly."

Hanna feels the familiar frustration. She has seen this kind of behavior before, men who rule their wives with an iron hand. Men who demand precedence on every occasion. Sometimes it remains as an exaggerated need for control with constant monitoring; sometimes it spirals into serious violence.

Home is the most dangerous place for women, according to all the statistics.

Daniel clears his throat, gestures discreetly toward the clock on the wall. They have already been here for over fifteen minutes. Hanna would like to ask Maria a few more questions about her colleague, but that's not why they're here. Time to move on. However, she does make a mental note to speak to Rebecka when she gets the chance. There is help available for vulnerable women.

"Back to Johan Andersson's visits," Daniel says. "Was it only Rebecka who dealt with him?"

Maria nods.

"Any idea what kind of mood he was in on Friday?"

"I'm afraid not. I didn't speak to him at all."

"Why was he here?" Hanna asks.

"I don't know. We had quite a few problems with the plumbing back in the fall, so he came over quite often. I thought everything was fine now, so I was surprised to see him on Friday. I didn't even know anyone had asked him to swing by."

"How long did he stay?"

"Ten minutes maybe. Not long, anyway."

"And he only spoke to Rebecka?"

"Yes. In the hallway."

Hanna glances at Daniel, but he is scribbling on his pad. This doesn't make sense. Why would Johan drive all the way from Sadeln to speak to Rebecka for such a short time?

"Could we have Rebecka's phone number?"

"No problem."

Maria takes out her phone and finds the relevant contact details. Hanna jots down the number and gives Maria her card.

"I have actually tried calling her," Maria says. "But there's no answer—it just goes straight to voicemail."

Daniel gets to his feet. "Thank you for your help. If you hear from Rebecka, could you ask her to get in touch with us?"

"Of course."

Maria accompanies them to the door. Just as they are about to leave, Hanna notices that she pauses, as if she has something more to add—but then she simply raises her hand and waves.

As soon as they reach the E14, Hanna tries Rebecka Nordhammar.

"Hi, you've reached Rebecka," says a slightly subdued voice. "Please leave a message after the tone."

Hanna explains who she is and asks Rebecka to call her back as soon as possible. Then she turns to Daniel, who is screwing up his eyes even though the sun visor is down. The gray-blue clouds that had threatened to roll in from Norway earlier on have been replaced by brilliant sunshine.

"No reply. I'll have to try again later."

"Okay."

"I have a feeling that Rebecka could be important—especially after what Maria said."

Daniel nods in agreement. They are on their way to the beauty salon where Linus Sundin's wife, Sandra, works. They plan to question her about where her husband was on Friday evening. Whether she will be prepared to talk to them is anyone's guess, given Linus's attitude the last time they saw him.

However, Hanna has no intention of forgetting about Rebecka Nordhammar's home circumstances. When she manages to speak to her, she will ask what Rebecka and Johan talked about on Friday afternoon—then she will raise the issue of what is going on with her husband.

REBECKA

2020

SATURDAY, FEBRUARY 22

The snowflakes are whirling through the air at the parking lot on Björkvägen, where Rebecka is waiting for Johan. She has hardly slept over the past twenty-four hours, her nerves are in shreds. She is about to take an irrevocable step that will change everything.

She is going to leave Ole and start a new life with Johan.

For the sake of their child, the little miracle that is growing inside her.

She places a protective hand on her belly. Her child will be raised in a secure home with its real father, not a violent man of God. She knows she is doing the right thing, however hard it might be to go against her upbringing.

She checks the time again. Seven thirty; Johan is very late. She has already been here for half an hour. She stamps her feet up and down, trying to generate some warmth. It is very cold; she can feel the icy air in her nostrils.

Where is he?

At last she hears the sound of an approaching vehicle. Rebecka sighs with relief. She wants to be far away before Ole arrives home and discovers that she has gone.

The car turns in and stops. The headlights blind her at first, but she can just make out a dark figure getting out of the driver's seat.

Something isn't right. The height is wrong, the posture is different. *That's not Johan.*

Rebecka is frozen to the spot. The man who has just climbed out of the car is Ole, and he is walking toward her.

It can't be. It's impossible.

Her heart is racing.

Johan is supposed to be picking her up. For his sake she has packed the essentials and sneaked away. Ole is supposed to be in Snasadalen, leading a Bible study session. That was why she postponed her escape from Friday to Saturday. So that he wouldn't catch her.

And yet here he is, standing in front of her in the snow, his eyes burning with such rage that she has to look away.

"What are you doing?" he hisses.

Rebecka is incapable of making a sound. A minute ago, her teeth were chattering because of the cold; now her body is shaking because of pure fear. She ought to run, flee into the forest, but she can't move.

She has had nightmares about a situation like this.

Ole's jawline is rigid. His eyes are burning, his face is so contorted that he is barely recognizable.

Every boundary seems to have disappeared.

Rebecka feels the panic rising. What is he going to do to her?

A bitterly cold gust of wind sends the snow whirling into her face. Ole's coattails fly out behind him like big, black bat wings.

The wind howls in Rebecka's ears.

He knows.

"You are a harlot," Ole says. "God has seen you."

Rebecka can barely remain upright, her legs are about to give way. The bag drops from her hand and lands on the snow.

How has this happened? How could Ole know that he would find her here on Björkvägen? At this particular time? She has been so careful; she hasn't told anyone about her plans, not even her mother or Lisen.

And she has brought only a few things with her, as much as she could fit into an ordinary bag.

Then she realizes. He has tracked her via her phone. Ole knows her code, he has known exactly where she was all along.

Has he also read Johan's text messages? She has deleted them all, but maybe she wasn't quick enough?

She looks around in desperation, willing Johan's white van to appear and rescue her.

The passenger door of Ole's car opens, and another man climbs out. Pastor Jonsäter. He watches them from a distance but shows no sign of intervening.

He has come to help Ole bring her home.

There is no escape.

When Ole grips her arm and pushes her toward the car, Rebecka does not resist. There is no point. All her efforts have been in vain. How could she have believed she would get away?

Ole pushes her into the back seat. They drive toward the E14. It isn't cold inside the car, but Rebecka is shivering violently. Her upper arm is hurting where Ole grabbed her.

Nothing makes sense.

Why didn't Johan come? They had arranged to meet at seven. She waited for half an hour. Where is he?

Rebecka doesn't want to believe that he has changed his mind, decided to stay with Marion, but of course that could be the case. Or has Ole made Johan abandon her?

Could Ole have done something to him?

She can't suppress a gasp. Ole has hurt her many times, but she has never seen him like this. What if he has done something terrible to Johan?

She places a hand on her belly, tries to find new strength.

Ole is talking quietly with Jan-Peter Jonsäter. She can't hear what they are saying because of the noise of the engine. She hardly dares look at Ole, and the pastor hasn't yet said a single word to her.

The car jolts as they turn onto a narrower road. After a few minutes they stop, and Rebecka realizes that they are in Handöl, outside the Jonsäter family's beautiful turn-of-the-century home.

The pastor unfastens his seatbelt, reaches for the door handle.

Rebecka sits up straight. He is going to leave her alone with Ole. He must have seen how angry Ole was, how roughly he treated her— and yet he did nothing.

She watches as he gets out of the car and disappears into the house. *Stop!* she wants to yell. *Don't leave me with him!*

The words die on her lips. Jonsäter will never take Rebecka's part. If he had any sympathy for her, he wouldn't have come along to stop her from leaving.

It is the men who rule the roost in the church, and in his eyes she has sinned against both God and Ole. How Ole chooses to deal with her is a matter between man and wife.

Ole floors the gas pedal and heads back toward the E14, where he takes a left instead of a right. Rebecka doesn't understand; they live in the opposite direction.

When she looks up, she meets Ole's black gaze in the rearview mirror, so full of hatred that she cowers in her seat.

Tears pour down her cheeks. She is in no doubt that Ole is going to punish her.

He will do it in God's name.

There is no forgiveness to be had.

42

The beauty salon where Sandra Sundin works is in the town square in Åre, right next to the black building housing the funicular railway's valley station, dating from 1910.

As they arrive Daniel sees the carriage setting off for Fjällgården, the hotel that lies approximately six hundred feet higher up the mountain. The railway is a reminder of days gone by. The inspiration came from Davos in Switzerland, and the plan was to create a Swedish ski resort that could compete with European winter destinations. A modern way of getting up the mountain was needed so that visitors didn't have to trudge up the slopes, carrying their heavy skis.

"I've traveled on that a few times," he says, pointing to the carriage, which is just disappearing from view.

Hanna laughs, a nostalgic look in her eyes. "Me too. It's fantastic that it's still running. We used it every winter when I came here as a child."

Daniel remembers Hanna telling him that she and her family always spent the February sports break in Åre.

They make their way toward Sandra's salon and meet three men coming from the opposite direction. They are carrying their skis over their shoulders and moving with the clumsy, uneven gait that goes with a slalom suit and flat, rigid-soled boots.

Daniel feels a stab of longing to be out there on the piste. The clouds have broken up, and the slopes are bathed in sunlight. The sky is clear blue behind the white mountaintops, where enthusiastic skiers are making the most of the perfect weather.

It's been quite a while since he tackled a slalom run. Life has been so busy since Alice's arrival. Occasionally he and Ida have set off on their cross-country skis with Alice in a sled, but that's all. They haven't had time for anything else, even though downhill skiing is their favorite sport. Ida worked as an instructor for several years, and to tell the truth her technique is much better than his.

No doubt she misses it even more than he does.

He glances up at Åreskutan. The air is so clear that he can see the top station; the red funicular carriage is just arriving, its passengers ready to disembark.

The mountain is calling to him.

He loves to stand up there, especially in the mornings when the slopes are deserted. He prefers to ski down the back route, escaping most of the tourists.

The feeling as his skis glide over fresh snow is unbeatable.

You can never relax because you can't predict what is hiding beneath the snow cover. Sometimes you see a rock at the last minute and have to veer to one side, sometimes a wind-flattened tree appears without warning. Choosing the best route between crevices demands total concentration.

In spite of the rules about not going off-piste alone, that is exactly what he loves to do. He can set his own pace without having to take anyone else's wishes into consideration. It is a special kind of freedom that he loves: total independence, being at one with nature.

Johan must have felt that way too. He was such a talented skier, and of course he grew up in Duved. But he will never stand at the top of Åreskutan again, gazing out over the valley . . .

"Are you coming?" Hanna shouts from several yards away. She is just opening the door of the salon.

With one final glance at the mighty mountain, Daniel hurries to catch up with her.

REBECKA

2020

Ole drives in acrimonious silence.

Time has no meaning.

Rebecka has no idea where they are, or what time it is. Ole took her phone off her before he pushed her into the back seat, and she can't see her watch in the darkness. All she knows is that they have left the E14 behind them.

She is alone with Ole, and everything is lost. The dream of a different life no longer exists.

The car speeds along narrow tracks, with tall fir trees looming up on both sides. Nothing changes, mile after mile. Rebecka tries to orient herself, but it is pitch black outside, and there is no street lighting. She hasn't seen any signs or buildings that might provide a clue.

Could they have crossed the border into Norway?

She is so confused; she doesn't remember if they went through Storlien. After they dropped off Pastor Jonsäter, she fell into a kind of trance. She curled up and closed her eyes, thought about Johan in order to shut out the world around her.

They are traveling much too fast. The car skids on every bend, and Rebecka is fighting nausea. She can't be sick in the car. Ole is so particular about the upholstery—that would make everything even worse.

"Where are we going?"

No response.

"Where are we going?" she repeats, louder this time.

"Shut your mouth, you filthy bitch!" The words are like the crack of a whip. "Otherwise, I'll stop right now and show you what God does to whores like you!"

After that Rebecka dare not open her mouth. She has never seen Ole so angry. His shoulders are hunched, he is gripping the wheel tightly. She mustn't annoy him even more.

She whimpers quietly and looks out the window. Could she open the door, throw herself out?

Another bend causes the car to judder so violently that she lets out a gasp. It's too risky at this speed; the baby could be hurt.

Plus, it is bitterly cold. The snow might cushion her fall, she might be able to flee into the forest and hide, but she would freeze to death within a few hours.

Despair fills her heart.

No one knows where she is. Johan didn't come to meet her.

She is totally at Ole's mercy.

43

As they leave the beauty salon, Hanna thinks that the conversation with Sandra Sundin was a real disappointment.

She and Daniel stand in the middle of the square, the snow sparkling in the bright sunlight. She has to shade her eyes with her right hand in order to see properly. The place is crowded with people enjoying the fine weather.

"Sandra didn't tell us anything we didn't know," she says with a sigh. "She admitted they're having financial problems, but that wasn't exactly news. I suppose we could say that her information strengthens Linus's motive."

Daniel shrugs. "What did you expect? Linus refuses to speak to us without legal representation, so obviously his wife is going to protect him as best she can."

Hanna had still hoped for a better outcome. "She must have known Johan for a long time. I thought she might step up and help us for his sake."

"And drop her own husband in the shit?" Daniel gives a wry smile. "Forget it. We're not going to get anywhere with Sandra right now." He looks around, points to Werséns diagonally opposite. "How about a pizza? We should eat before we go back to the station."

No one makes pizzas as delicious as Werséns, and Hanna is starving after a long morning.

"Sounds like a plan."

She leads the way and opens the door. The place is packed, and they have to virtually fight to get through to an empty corner table. Hanna can't wait for this week to end, even though she used to come to Åre with her parents for the sports break. Back then she didn't realize how much of an invasion it was for the local population. The busy restaurant is more reminiscent of a European city than a small town in Norrland.

When the food arrives, Hanna practically falls on her "hunter's" pizza, which is generously loaded with sautéed reindeer, chanterelles, and horseradish sauce. They are virtually the only diners who are not dressed in skiing gear or are on vacation. And it feels as if they're the only ones drinking alcohol-free beer with their meal.

"God, I was so hungry," she says apologetically.

Daniel smiles; he is enjoying his pizza too. He went for a more Italian option with truffle salami, arugula, and Parmesan.

"It's cool," he says. "This is delicious."

To be on the safe side, they avoid talking about the interview with Sandra, although Hanna is going over the conversation in her mind. The restaurant is too busy, the tables too close together. The last thing the investigation needs is gossip based on someone eavesdropping on a private discussion.

She notices that the woman at the next table, who is drinking rosé wine and wearing a chic gray fur poncho, has glanced at them curiously several times. Hanna nods in her direction and says to Daniel out of the corner of her mouth, "Do you think she knows we're cops?"

He looks discreetly at their neighbor, who now seems to be fully absorbed in her phone.

"Does it matter?"

Hanna shakes her head and shovels down the last piece of pizza. They don't wear uniforms, but people often suss out their profession. That's just the way it is—many of their colleagues say the same thing.

After they've eaten, they head back to the car. Every parking space around the square was occupied, so they'd had to leave it in the parking lot by the train station.

This afternoon there is a briefing via video link with Östersund. Hanna is hoping that the autopsy results will be in, so that they can find out what really happened when Johan was murdered.

44

Daniel pushes open the door of the conference room, a cup of coffee in his hand. The whole team is meeting up via video link, and as usual they start by going over the current situation. Jenny Ullenius is there too, as is common practice for the prosecutor in homicide investigations.

Just like yesterday, she is dressed entirely in black.

Birgitta Grip asks what steps have already been taken; then she hands over to Ylva Labba.

The forensic pathologist is at her desk in an unbuttoned white coat. Her dark hair is shorter than the last time Daniel saw her; it is beautifully cut in a bob that ends at her jawline. It brings out her high cheekbones, but at the same time it makes her look harder, colder, more remote.

Daniel values Ylva's competence, but he will never understand why a doctor is drawn to pathology. Why specialize in mutilated and dead bodies when you could work with the living? In some of the homicide cases he worked on in Gothenburg, the mere sight of the mistreated victims almost made him throw up. He felt the same on Saturday when he first saw Johan's body.

Ylva begins her report, and Daniel listens attentively.

"We have established that Johan Andersson died as a result of a serious head trauma to the left parietal bone, which protects the parietal lobe. The occipital lobe was also damaged to a certain extent."

She continues with a technical description of blood stasis, crush fractures, multiple bone fragments, and the effect on the vital functions of the brain. Daniel has heard this terminology in other contexts, but sometimes he finds it difficult to keep up. The conclusion is more or less the same as when they found the body: Johan's death was caused by several hard blows to the back of his head, crushing his skull and destroying key parts of the brain. He would have died almost instantly and had presumably been dead for between six and twelve hours when the body was discovered.

"What can you tell us about the murder weapon?" he asks when Ylva has finished.

"I believe it's some kind of flat tool, judging by the appearance of the injuries and the effect on the surrounding skin."

"Could you be more specific?" Raffe wonders.

"I'm leaning toward a small hammer."

A hammer? That's something you'd find in virtually every household in northern Jämtland, Daniel thinks. Talk about searching for a needle in a haystack . . .

"What about the other injuries?" he says. "How did they come about?"

"That's trickier to determine."

Ylva brings up an enlargement of Johan's battered face, which immediately fills Daniel with horror. Seen at close quarters it is clear how severely Johan was beaten before his death. Skin and blood vessels are torn, and his nose is at a very strange angle.

"Shit." Raffe can't help himself.

Ylva comments on the image in a matter-of-fact tone of voice.

"The victim had a fractured nose, injuries to the right cheekbone, and crush damage across his entire face."

Daniel allows this to sink in; then Hanna puts into words what they are all thinking: "You mean he was tortured?"

Raffe shuffles uncomfortably in his seat.

"I can't confirm that with any certainty." Ylva pauses. "It's not easy to establish an exact timeline, because the body was exposed to the cold for many hours." She flicks through a pile of papers in front of her. "However, I do believe that most of the facial injuries occurred in quick succession. The damage to the right cheekbone is consistent with a powerful blow from a clenched fist; this is indicated by the appearance of both the skin and the underlying tissue. However, the cause of the other injuries is less clear."

"Could you try?"

"One hypothesis is that after the first blow was delivered, he fell down face first, unable to save himself because his hands were already tied behind his back. The number of superficial grazes supports this theory; they are evenly distributed, as if they were all sustained at the same time. I can't say with any certainty whether he broke his nose before, after, or as a result of the fall."

"What about the timing of the facial injuries and those to the back of his head?" Anton asks. He is sitting with his arms folded and looks just as tired as he did yesterday, with dark circles beneath his eyes. Daniel has rarely seen him so apathetic. Something is wrong, but right now he doesn't have time to work out what it is.

"That's also a difficult question, but I am prepared to say that they happened quite close together."

Daniel is disappointed; he had hoped for more definite answers from the pathologist. He knows she is doing her best, though, and she did prioritize the case—otherwise they would have had to wait much longer for the autopsy.

Ylva looks at her watch.

"I think that's all the information I can give you. I really ought to . . ."

Hanna is frowning. "One last question. Was Johan under the influence?"

Ylva shakes her head. "There is no trace of alcohol or chemical substances in his blood."

That fits with Carl Willner's assertion that Johan drank only a low-alcohol beer at Pigo.

Ylva vanishes from the screen, and Grip taps her pen on the desk several times to attract everyone's attention.

"Where are we with the van?" she says to Carina. "Have you found the electronic logbook yet?"

Carina adjusts her earbuds. "Yes and no. There is a log, but we haven't managed to access the information yet. I'll have to get back to you on that."

"There were toolboxes in the van, weren't there?" Daniel tries to picture the interior. "Could you check if there's anything missing? It would be interesting to know whether the weapon came from Johan's own equipment." He looks around. "I'm thinking that might give us a sense of how spontaneous the murder was—whether the perpetrator grabbed the first thing that came to hand, or whether he brought the weapon with him."

Grip nods approvingly at the suggestion. "How about the phone calls? Any progress?"

Johan's cell is still missing. They've asked the phone company for a list of everyone he has been in contact with over the past six months.

"Still waiting," Raffe says.

Daniel silently summarizes the course of events:

They know that Johan arrived at Linus Sundin's house at twenty to eight on Friday evening. Sandra had tried to say as little as possible when they spoke to her earlier, but she had given away the fact that there had been considerable tension between the two men. She also confirmed that Johan stayed for twenty-five minutes at the most.

The question is whether things got out of hand there and then. Did they start brawling in the kitchen?

According to Sandra there was no physical violence during Johan's visit, but she could be lying. It wouldn't be the first time a woman has lied for the sake of her husband.

Daniel is finding Linus's insistence on the presence of his lawyer increasingly suspicious.

If they could go through his house, with everything Carina has at her disposal, it wouldn't be hard to find evidence of a fight. Blood that has been scrubbed away can be seen with infrared light. A good CSI can find traces of hair and bone.

"We ought to search Linus's house," he says. "Send in the CSIs, dogs, the whole lot."

Grip doesn't look particularly enthusiastic. Nor does the prosecutor.

"We're talking about a family with a child, where the suspect has no criminal record," Grip points out.

Daniel is well aware of that, but he's not giving up. "Linus had both motive and opportunity. He's refusing to cooperate without legal representation."

"It's too soon."

"It's not as if we have any other suspects lined up."

"We can afford to wait another day."

"What's the problem?" Daniel says, a fraction too loud.

Jenny Ullenius frowns.

"We don't have enough to go on," Grip says.

Daniel understands why she is so hesitant. It's called the proportionality test. A measure must not be seen to be disproportionate in relation to its effect, according to the rule of law.

"We have no forensic evidence whatsoever linking Linus Sundin to the murder," Ullenius says firmly. She's hardly said a word so far—why does she have to take Grip's side now?

"Surely that's the point of a house search? To find new evidence?"

Daniel can hear how aggressive he sounds. Grip stares at him from the screen with a look that could freeze the blood in his veins.

"Bring me something new and we'll talk about it again."

45

It has taken Ida forty-five minutes to get Alice dressed and settled in the stroller for a walk. By the time they finally get out onto the street, she is sweating beneath her down jacket.

She heads for the village, where she is meeting Tove, one of her best friends, for coffee.

The square is busy when Ida arrives. A pop-up bar has been set up in front of the Stadium Store, and a long line of people are waiting to buy beer and steaming-hot mulled wine. Ida negotiates her way past piles of snow to reach the café. Alice has fallen asleep, so Ida finds a spot for the stroller right by the window so that she can keep an eye on her.

She stands there for a moment contemplating her daughter. Alice is so beautiful, lying there with her eyes closed. Rosy cheeks, long eyelashes. Her mouth is like a tiny rosebud. An intense wave of love floods her body. It is incomprehensible that she was once unsure about becoming a mother; what was she thinking?

She goes inside, and Tove waves at her from a corner table—all the others are occupied.

"So many people!" Ida exclaims as she gives Tove a hug.

"Typical sports break," Tove replies with a smile.

As usual the café smells amazing. There is a tempting display of freshly baked cakes and cookies by the till. They each order a latte and a slice of chocolate cake.

"Have you heard that they're closing the ski resorts in Northern Italy?" Tove says when they've been served.

Ida shakes her head. She has hardly seen the news or read the papers online over the past few days, mainly because she doesn't want to hear any more about Johan's murder. Things are already bad enough, and she is worried about Daniel's safety. Who knows what can happen when he's hunting a killer? Daniel is so conscientious, even when he ought to put himself first. Especially now he has a baby daughter.

Tove continues along the same lines.

"It's that coronavirus from China—it's spreading. They're closing virtually everything to stop the infection—the entire lift system. And the schools."

"Surely they can't shut down an entire ski resort?" Ida protests, taking a sip of her coffee, which has a delicious, nutty aftertaste. "How does that work?"

"People are being told to stay home and keep their distance from anyone who isn't part of the family."

"That sounds crazy. Is it even legal?"

"Apparently. Unbelievable . . ."

Ida turns her head, looks out the window. She sees the square crowded with skiers, thinks about the après-ski, the long lines that form at the lifts, the cable cars where people are packed together like sardines. Åre relies on its tourism—a good ski season is vital for local businesses.

Her own job as an instructor depends on it.

"I hope it doesn't come here," she says with a shudder.

Tove stirs her latte. "So, what do you think about the murder of Johan Andersson? Isn't it awful? I presume Daniel isn't home much right now."

"No."

Ida takes a big bite of her cake. She has to have some consolation when Daniel is away so much. At the same time, she knows she should be proud of him. Johan's death is a terrible crime that needs to be solved.

She does her best not to complain.

"He's working all the time," she adds. "We've barely exchanged a word over the past few days."

Tove places her hand on Ida's. "It can't be easy." She glances around, as if she wants to be sure that no one is listening. "I don't know if I should tell you this, but I happened to see Daniel at Werséns today."

Ida looks up. How come Daniel has time to go to a restaurant when he's working nonstop?

"He was having lunch with a brown-haired woman about the same age as him," Tove informs her. "They seemed to be enjoying themselves." She hesitates, looks deep into Ida's eyes. "Don't take this the wrong way, but . . . is everything okay between the two of you?"

REBECKA

2020

The car stops abruptly, rousing Rebecka from her trance. She peers out the window, but all she can see is darkness. And snow. Gradually her eyes adjust, and she is able to make out the contours of a building, an empty field, and dense forest in the background.

She is desperate for a pee but tries to hold on.

Ole gets out, retrieves a snow shovel from the trunk. Rebecka hears a click as he locks her in. They have pulled up on the road; it is impossible to drive up to the house because of the snow.

She watches him go, wide eyed.

Furiously he clears a narrow pathway from the road to the door; then he goes inside and switches on the light, revealing a two-story wooden cottage. It is very shabby; the paint is flaking, and several roof tiles are missing.

Fear shoots through her body with renewed strength.

Why are they here? What is he planning to do?

She is shivering now, the engine is off, and the temperature inside the car is dropping fast. It must be at least minus twenty Celsius outside.

The door is yanked open, and Ole signals to her to get out.

Rebecka obeys; there is no alternative. Silently she picks up her bag and trudges after him. They enter a chilly hallway with cracked linoleum on the floor. The air smells musty, closed in. A kind of old man's smell, a mixture of ingrained dirt and stale urine, assails her nostrils.

On the wall there is a large crucifix with the figure of Jesus in faded colors. His empty eyes stare blankly at Rebecka. She would like to fall to her knees and beg him to save her, but she knows there is no point.

She has figured out where they are. Ole has driven to his maternal grandfather's home, north of Meråker. His grandfather passed away several years ago, and because his wife is dead, just like Ole's mother, he inherited the cottage. Ole has talked about it occasionally, but Rebecka has never been here before.

They are in Norway.

The realization makes her sway. This is a remote and isolated spot; any hope of someone coming to rescue her is gone. Ole has brought her to a place where he can do whatever he wants.

She remembers the worst incident, six months ago, when she believed he had lost control and was going to kill her.

His hard hands gripped her throat, she couldn't breathe. Everything went black.

He didn't let go until she fainted.

Might he do that again tonight? There is no one here to stop him, but this time there would be two lives at stake. If she dies, her child will not survive.

Ole doesn't take his eyes off her.

It seems absurd, but Rebecka has to ask for permission to pee. She can't hold on; any second now she will wet herself.

"Bathroom?" she whispers.

Ole points to one of the doors. Rebecka hurries inside, feeling as if her bladder is about to burst.

The tiny bathroom is as filthy as the rest of the house; it smells disgusting. There are dark cracks in the toilet bowl, and yellow stains disappearing into the U-bend.

When she has finished, she can barely drag herself to her feet. She reaches out, places a hand on the wall for support.

She is terrified of going back into the hallway, but she has no choice. There is no lock on the bathroom door. Ole could simply fling it open and drag her out.

With trembling fingers, she pulls up her pants and buttons the fly. In the cracked mirror she sees the fear on her face.

Then she pushes down the handle and leaves the bathroom.

46

It is almost six thirty. Hanna is still at the police station; she has just texted Lydia to say that she won't be home for dinner. She is about to leave yet another message for Rebecka Nordhammar when she sees that Daniel is packing up his things.

She gets up and goes along to his office.

"Rebecka Nordhammar's phone is still switched off," she says from the doorway. "I just tried again."

"Leave it until tomorrow," Daniel says tersely. He sounds as if he is still smarting from Grip's reprimand. Hanna has found herself in similar situations, but sometimes you have to roll with the punches when the boss doesn't agree.

"Shouldn't we go and see Rebecka?" she ventures. "To be on the safe side?"

Daniel isn't listening; he seems stressed.

He waves his phone. "I have to go—Ida just called."

Hanna returns to her desk, and a minute or two later, Anton passes her door. "I'm out of here," he says with a cheerful wave.

Hanna waves back, then focuses on her computer once more. It's strange that Rebecka isn't answering and hasn't called back, particularly in view of all the messages Hanna has left. She reaches for her notebook and finds Maria Törnlund's number, hoping against hope that Rebecka has been in touch with her instead. It's worth checking at least.

Maria answers right away, and Hanna explains why she's called.

"Sorry, no—Rebecka hasn't been in touch. I haven't spoken to her since Friday." Then she takes a deep breath, as if she is bracing herself. "There's something I maybe should have told you . . ." Maria hesitates. "But I didn't want to make the situation worse."

"I'm happy to listen," Hanna says to help her along.

After a brief silence, Maria continues, "I'm afraid that Rebecka isn't really sick, but that Ole has done something to her," she says, falling over her words. "Do you understand what I mean?"

"I do." Hanna picks up her pen.

She understands exactly what Maria means. After seven years with the Domestic Violence Unit in Stockholm, she has no problem getting her head around toxic relationships. She has seen way too many examples.

"I think it's been going on for a long time. I once happened to see Rebecka's forearms when she rolled up her sleeves to do some painting with the children. She had huge black-and-purple bruises—the sort of marks you get when someone grips you too tightly." Maria almost sounds as if she is speaking from experience. "And there were plenty of other occasions when I thought she'd been mistreated. I tried to talk to her about it, but she didn't want to. And she was very careful never to roll up her sleeves again."

She falls silent. Hanna makes detailed notes but doesn't attempt to prompt Maria.

"Maybe I should have come straight out and asked her what was going on, but I didn't dare." Hanna can hear the guilt in her voice. "It seemed too . . . intrusive. And her husband made such a good impression, at least in the beginning. It was hard to believe that he would . . ."

"What happened then?" Hanna asks.

"I think . . . I think the violence escalated. Rebecka became more and more downhearted. I did the best I could, talked about a friend in a similar situation who'd gotten help. Another time I left some leaflets about protection for abused women on the table in the staff room. I thought she might pick up one of them, see that there was help available."

"And did she?"

"No—they were all still there at the end of the day. But maybe she looked at them?"

Hanna knows what a difficult dilemma it is, fearing that a friend or relative is being subjected to violence in the home but having no concrete evidence. It's hard to know what to do. Many people choose to keep quiet, afraid to interfere or to make baseless accusations. Not appearing to be too nosy is part of the Swedish psyche. And sometimes people are worried about making things worse for the vulnerable person.

It is brave of Maria to share her suspicions with the police.

"There's something else," she says. "The reason why I'm so concerned about Rebecka."

"Go on."

"I think Johan and Rebecka were . . . fond of each other."

Hanna is taken aback. "You mean they were in love?" She wants to be sure that she hasn't misunderstood.

"There was something about the way they looked at each other when he was here on Friday. His hand was on her arm, and the expression on his face . . . Johan seemed devastated."

Hanna writes down every word.

"A little while after he'd gone, Rebecka disappeared. She was away for half an hour, even though we were closing up for the day. When she came back she was turned upside down, couldn't concentrate at all. I'm wondering if she sneaked away to meet him."

"Thank you so much for sharing this information, Maria. It's invaluable."

"Yesterday Rebecka's husband called and said she was sick. And she didn't answer her phone when I tried to contact her a few hours later.

My mind was spinning. I'm wondering if Rebecka and Johan were having a secret relationship."

Hanna can hear the fear seeping through Maria's words.

"What if Ole found out?" Maria is on the verge of tears. "What if he's done something terrible to Rebecka?"

REBECKA

2020

The stress fills Rebecka's ears with a buzzing noise when she emerges from the bathroom.

Ole is waiting for her in the run-down kitchen. On the table is an old Bible with a black cover and ornate lettering.

He is standing in the middle of the floor with his arms folded. There is no warmth, only disgust in his eyes. His apparent calmness terrifies her.

He gestures toward one of the chairs. Rebecka understands—he is going to conduct a trial. She is the accused, while he will act as both prosecutor and judge.

"You have *one* chance to tell the truth," he says in a monotone.

It's as if he is facing a complete stranger, not the wife he has lived with for seven years. Rebecka grips the edge of the chair, overwhelmed by blind panic. She can't tell him about Johan, about their relationship— but if she lies and it turns out that Ole already knows she was having an affair, then she is lost.

She stares at Ole's face, searching for a clue, anything that will help her to reach a decision. Is this simply a cruel game of cat and mouse? Everything depends on her giving the right answer.

The life of her unborn child.

"Ole. Don't do this—please."

"One chance." His jaw is clamped together.

"What do you want to know?" she whispers. It is hard to speak properly. Her throat is thick with tears, her nose is running. She is struggling to hold back her sobs. Ole has always hated it when she cries.

"You lied to me." The look on his face is ice cold. "You said you weren't feeling well. You said you were going to go to bed early—to get out of coming to church with me. Instead, you packed a bag and left the house." He gives her a sarcastic smile. "What were you doing in the parking lot?"

Rebecka tries to work out what he wants. Is she supposed to admit her infidelity?

Probably—he wants her to confess her sins out loud, like they do in church. She glances at the heavy Bible. She has sinned, she already knows that.

She coughs to give herself a little more time.

"I . . . ," she begins, but the words won't come. Fear of saying the wrong thing makes her incapable of going on.

"Yes?"

Ole moves toward her. He grips her chin and twists, so hard that she can hear the bones crunch.

"The truth—out with it."

It feels as though her chin is being dislocated. She can't suppress a cry of pain.

"Shut the fuck up."

"Wait! I'll tell you!"

Tears pour down her cheeks as Ole lets go. He steps back, gives her a challenging look.

"I was going away," she gasps, determined not to mention Johan's name.

"You were leaving me?" He practically spits out the question.

There is no point in denying it.

"Yes," Rebecka whispers, lowering her head.

"I am your husband. You promised before God that you would love and obey me. Your body belongs to me!"

"I know."

The air is thick and heavy with rage.

Something wet seeps into Rebecka's panties, even though she has just been to the toilet. Fear makes it impossible to control her bladder.

She lets out a sob.

Ole clenches and unclenches his fists. Rebecka can already feel his grasp around her throat, the lack of oxygen as he squeezes harder and harder.

She can already hear the ringing in her ears, just like last time.

He is going to kill me.

47

Hanna rests her chin on her hands as she thinks about the conversation with Maria Törnlund.

The station is quiet; Hanna's office is the only one with the lamp still on.

Maria's revelation about a possible love affair between Johan and Rebecka could influence the entire course of the investigation. In fact, Rebecka could be the key to the attack on Johan—and she might also be a victim in this story.

The description of her controlling husband triggers all of Hanna's red flags. It's like a checklist of signs of a destructive relationship.

She types "Light of Life" into the search box. The screen immediately fills with hits.

According to Wikipedia, the church has existed in Jämtland since it was founded in the fifties in Snasadalen, an area close to the Norwegian border. The religious body consists of around a hundred members and belongs to the Evangelical Free Church. Most of the members live between Storlien and Järpen, while the parish hall is still in Snasadalen.

When Hanna searches with the help of Google Maps, she discovers that it lies at the foot of the mountain known as Snasahögarna, a short distance beyond Handöl.

The Nordhammars live in Enafors, no more than ten minutes away.

She keeps going and finds a home page. They're clearly not so old fashioned if they have an online presence. A pale-green banner appears, adorned with a white cross. The text beneath outlines the church's sacred mission: to make Jesus known and loved among all the people on Earth. The church is a loving community, blessed by God. When we choose Christ, we choose one another in faith, hope, and love. By following the Lord and carrying out his work together, the aim is to encourage more people to take him into their hearts.

It sounds like a biblical idyll, but Hanna notices that all the pastors are men, and that the woman's role is described only in terms of nurturing and supporting. She is praised as a wife and mother.

It is obvious that women are seen as vessels to produce children rather than individuals with the right to make their own decisions.

The more Hanna reads, the more unpleasant she finds the whole thing—and the more her concern for Rebecka's safety grows.

Every tab on the home page reveals new paeans to God's love, and how the spirit of Jesus permeates the church. The members must not put themselves first, but serve others, take heed of one another's needs, gain strength through prayer and worship.

It's like a never-ending religious cycle.

She finds a section outlining the structure of the church. Members belong to different family groups that meet in their homes. They are also required to help with a range of tasks, such as looking after various locations, running Bible study groups, and providing coffee after services.

Hanna is prepared to bet that women are expected to carry out most of these activities.

In her world this is called the unpaid workforce.

One particular highlight is the "housewives' breakfasts," shared meals with the emphasis on beautifully laid tables, a Christian atmosphere, and the promotion of mutual trust. Hanna shakes her head. Do they realize they're living in the twenty-first century?

She leans back in her chair. The lyrical descriptions of a blissful existence under God's protection don't exactly match what Maria Törnlund told her about Rebecka's life. Her husband driving her to and from work every day. The fact that she had to ask for permission to go out for a glass of wine. The bruises she tried to hide.

That kind of control does not bear witness to love or to the safety of women.

The more Hanna reads about the Light of Life, the more cultlike and oppressive their message seems to be. She thinks back to the Pentecostal sect in Knutby some years ago, where blind obedience to the pastors and the woman known as the Bride of Christ led to murder, abuse, and sexual exploitation.

She googles "Ole Nordhammar" and sees a picture of an attractive man with a firm jawline. He looks as if he's about forty, with regular features and thick dark hair. There is something about his eyes . . . They capture her attention in an almost hypnotic way.

Is this the image of a wife beater?

Hanna studies the photograph, even though she knows there is no such thing as a "typical" appearance. The truth is that most abusers look perfectly normal; they are neither especially handsome nor ugly. Their common denominator is the psychological profile, the need to exercise power and control, often compensating for injustices they have experienced earlier in life.

She searches for a picture of Rebecka Nordhammar but finds nothing. She doesn't seem to be on any social media platforms, but maybe that's not so strange? If the church is as conservative as it appears to be, then that kind of self-glorification is probably not allowed.

She sends a quick text to Maria, asking if she has a photo of Rebecka.

It really would be good to speak to her face-to-face. All of Hanna's instincts are telling her that this is important, given how worried Maria was about Rebecka's safety.

And her suspicions about a relationship with Johan.

A tiny idea takes root. Hanna glances at the clock on the wall. It's only six forty-five.

Not too late to drive over to Rebecka's home in Enafors right now.

48

Anton hurries toward the parking lot. He has spent most of the afternoon contacting Johan's friends and acquaintances, and now he is late for the jazz band rehearsal that takes place on Tuesdays.

He is about to unlock the car when he hears his name. When he looks up, he sees Carl standing outside the health center, which is housed in the same building as the police station.

"Hi," Anton calls out, then goes over to the wide steps where Carl is waiting. To be on the safe side, he looks around but can't see any of his colleagues. "What are you doing here?"

"I'm just taking a few tests before they close." Carl nods toward the health center, where a nurse dressed in white is just passing the glass doors. He steps closer to Anton. "Where did you go last night?" he says, lowering his voice. "You were gone when I woke up this morning."

Anton shifts uncomfortably from one foot to the other. He had intended to write a note but couldn't work out what to say. Also, he didn't want to leave anything that could betray the fact that he'd been there for personal reasons.

The look in Carl's eyes makes Anton think about anything but ethics and cautionary measures. A pang of longing shoots through his body as he remembers Carl's naked back in the soft moonlight. The warm skin he brushed with his lips.

Carl reaches out and gently touches Anton's shoulder.

"I enjoyed yesterday," he murmurs. "I was wondering if you'd like to have dinner later in the week?"

Anton swallows. He would love to do that. More than anything he wants to throw his arms around Carl and go home with him right now—but he knows how that would look.

Hanna hasn't left yet. She has met Carl and would definitely recognize him if she saw him standing here with Anton. He thought she'd already had her suspicions about their relationship on Sunday, and earlier today Daniel had asked if Anton was okay. He'd brushed the question aside, but there is a limit to how many excuses he can get away with.

He would like to talk to Carl about all this, but he is short of time. He can't get tangled up in a long explanation about the case right now or how he ought to behave as a police officer. Hanna or some other colleague could show up at any moment and see them talking to each other.

"Can I get back to you on that?" he says in an indifferent tone.

Carl stiffens, withdraws his arm. The warmth in his eyes disappears, and he looks both hurt and disappointed.

Anton can't really blame him. He is acting like a complete ass, toward a man who is grieving for a close friend. Anton isn't exactly helping.

"Okay," Carl says, his voice flat. "I understand." He zips his down jacket up to the top. "I've actually got a lot to think about at the moment. This business with Johan . . . I was just on my way to church to plan a memorial service for him. There are a lot of people who miss him."

Anton hates how he must give Carl the cold shoulder, but he needs to get away from here before anyone sees them. He looks demonstratively at his watch, making it clear that he is in a hurry.

There is a painful silence.

"By the way, how's the investigation going?" Carl asks. "I heard someone questioned Sandra at work."

Anton frowns. "How do you know that?"

"Do you seriously suspect Linus?" Carl goes on.

Anton does his best to keep the mask in place, not to reveal how close to the truth Carl is. But Carl moves closer, grabs Anton's arm.

"Do you think Linus is behind this? Seriously?"

"I'm sorry," Anton says, blocking out all his emotions. "I'm not allowed to discuss the case."

He hurries away before Carl can ask any more questions.

He couldn't hate himself more.

49

The drive to Enafors takes longer than expected.

The place is even smaller than Ånn, but there is a train station, and the line from Sundsvall to Storlien cuts through the village. And it's not far from Snasadalen, where the Light of Life is based.

According to the map it is just over twenty-five miles, and the trip should take about forty minutes. However, the road is dark and winding, even though it is the same E-route that continues to Norway. Plus, Hanna goes the wrong way. She has to turn around and go back to find the right exit.

The one that leads to the Nordhammars' house.

On the way she has time to think. Could her unannounced visit put Rebecka in more danger? If she is living in a sect that exercises strict control, her safety could be adversely affected by Hanna showing up, especially if Ole finds out that she is asking questions about Rebecka's relationship with Johan. But given what Maria told her, she dares not wait. Not doing anything could be equally risky.

A murderer is hiding in the shadows. Rebecka could be in possession of vital information.

Hanna will just have to be careful.

The house in Enafors is in darkness when she arrives. It isn't even eight o'clock yet; surely they can't have gone to bed? According to the public records, there are only two people living at this address, as Ole and Rebecka don't have any children.

Hanna switches off the engine and gets out of the car. She pauses for a moment, gazes at the red two-story wooden building with white window frames. A narrow path leads to the black front door, where a solitary lamp spreads a cold light.

The road ends here. The house is by itself next to a small turning area, which is mostly covered by a large heap of snow. Beyond the garden there is nothing but forest and a common. On the way, Hanna drove past a few houses and a rusty trailer, but there are no neighbors within sight.

She examines the immediate area closely. Judging by the tracks in the snow, a car ought to have parked here recently. She can see the broad marks where it backed out of the drive and swung around.

Does this mean that the husband has gone off somewhere?

Is Rebecka home alone?

She cranes her neck to look at the upper floor. It is reasonable to assume that Rebecka is resting in bed, if she is too sick to call work or even answer her phone.

Are the blinds pulled down? She can't be sure.

She goes up to the front door and rings the bell. The sound echoes through the house, but no one comes. She tries again, with the same result.

The silence is oppressive. Hanna is breathing more heavily now. Did she do the right thing, coming here by herself?

Her gut instinct says yes. Rebecka could be a key figure in the case, and she might not be sick at all, but in danger.

Hanna takes out her phone and calls Rebecka's number while pressing her ear to the door.

Not a sound.

Her mind is whirling. If Rebecka really is unwell, she might have switched her phone to silent and doesn't realize that Hanna is trying to reach her. That seems unlikely, though; these days most people keep their phone close at hand. At some point Rebecka ought to notice how many missed calls she has. Hanna must have left seven or eight messages by now. She presses redial, but once again the call goes straight to voicemail.

Hanna puts her phone away. After a brief hesitation she reaches out and tries the door handle.

Locked.

What is going on with the Nordhammar family?

Where is Rebecka?

Far away a lone dog howls. It sounds ominous and strengthens Hanna's feeling that something is wrong. She decides to go around to the back of the house.

As soon as she leaves the pathway that has been cleared, progress becomes difficult. The snow is deep, the icy crust breaks with every step. In no time her calves are freezing.

Finally, she reaches a wide veranda overlooking the common. She places one hand on the wooden railing and looks up at the veranda door. It is made of glass; she should be able to see inside if she presses her face close.

An inner voice tells her that she ought to leave it, go home and come back in daylight with Daniel. That would be the safest course of action, possibly for Rebecka too.

But she could be lying injured in there, alone and abused, in desperate need of help.

Hanna is breathing faster. She can see the white mist in front of her mouth with every exhalation. She can't stand here like this, she has to make up her mind.

Go home or try to get into the house.

The darkness throbs around her. She can almost hear her conflicting thoughts in the silence.

She feels as if icy fingers are touching her forehead.

With one last look around, she sets off up the steps.

50

The icy cold nips at Hanna's cheeks as she peers into the dark house. She presses her face against the veranda door and screws up her eyes to see better. She is looking into a living room; she can just make out a sofa, two armchairs, a coffee table, a floor lamp, and a bookcase.

There are no lights on anywhere. The house seems empty, lifeless.

She takes out her phone and switches on the flashlight. She shines it into the room but discovers nothing new apart from a Bible in the middle of the coffee table. It is demonstratively visible, as if to remind everyone of God's canon.

The feeling that no one is home is growing stronger.

Hanna takes a deep breath, inhales the smell of snow. There are many smells in Stockholm, and everything gets lost in a thick porridge. Up here where the air is cold and clear, it is quite different. Icy and crispy, with hints of salt.

She sniffs again and becomes aware of something more unpleasant, rotten planks in the wooden walls. As rotten as the old-fashioned values that permeate the Light of Life.

Hanna glances around. The shadows are lurking beyond the garden, the dense trees become one with the background. The silence is both inhospitable and intrusive. Rebecka has lived in this desolate place since the age of nineteen, when she married Ole.

Should Hanna try to get inside, or leave? She shivers and stamps her feet up and down. Her earlobes are aching with the cold. Entering the property without permission is a bad idea. It's against all the rules;

she does not have the authority to do it. If she is caught, it would be regarded as professional misconduct.

And yet she is convinced that it's the right thing to do. To be honest, it wouldn't be the first time she's pushed the boundaries. All police officers do the same thing sometimes—at least that's what she tells herself. You can't always follow the regulations to the letter—you'd never make any progress in an investigation.

If Rebecka is lying in there badly hurt, then Hanna would never forgive herself for not taking action.

Decision made. She's here now; she can't, won't back off.

She reaches out, tries the door handle. Locked. The window is also closed and impossible to open.

Has she got the nerve to smash a pane of glass?

Before she can make up her mind, the silence is shattered by loud, aggressive barking echoing among the trees. The howling came from a long way off before, but now the dog is much closer.

Hanna turns, tries to determine where the sound is coming from. The dog barks again, louder this time. It's definitely heading in her direction. It's too risky to stay; she doesn't have her service weapon with her.

As a fresh burst of barking fills the air, Hanna runs down the steps. It is equally difficult to make her way through the deep snow as she heads back to the car. She is moving as quickly as she can, but it's still much too slow.

She rounds the corner of the house and sees a huge dog racing along the road. It looks like a Doberman, and it must weigh around seventy or eighty pounds. It is barking nonstop and increases its speed when it sees her.

Her heart is pounding.

The dog is only a few yards away as Hanna hurls herself at the car. She yanks open the passenger door and just manages to get in and slam it shut before the beast attacks. She curls up in the seat, staring at the threatening jaws outside the window. Saliva trails from the sharp teeth; the hard claws scratch furiously at the paintwork, making a loud scraping sound.

In the distance she sees a man running toward them, which rouses her from her paralysis.

She can't be caught.

At lightning speed she wriggles across to the driver's seat and starts the engine. She performs a desperate, uncontrolled U-turn, floors the gas pedal, and drives away.

When she passes the dog's owner, she lowers her head so that the man won't be able to recognize her. He is wearing a thick hat and has a scarf pulled up over his chin; it is impossible to see his face.

She glances in the rearview mirror; the dog is still standing there, frozen to the spot and barking hysterically.

51

The rehearsal room is in the cellar of a terraced house on Lienvägen. Bobo, the band's informal leader, lives here; he has installed soundproofing so that they can practice without driving his family insane.

Anton has played with the same group of guys for almost five years, and they usually meet once a week. They are happy amateurs, but from time to time they get a paid gig at various venues in the area. There are still those who appreciate an evening of fine jazz rather than chart-topping house and dance music.

He is the last to arrive, carrying his saxophone case. Bobo welcomes him.

"I didn't think you'd make it, what with the murder of Johan Andersson. What a terrible thing." He shakes his head. "How's it going? Do you have a suspect?"

Anton gives him a weary smile, trying to convey a simple message: *Can we talk about something else?*

He understands that people are both worried and upset. His own mother called earlier; the family knows Johan's parents. But it's been a tough few days, on both a personal and a professional level. All Anton wants to do right now is sit down, play for a few hours, and avoid thinking about anything but the music.

Especially after the unexpected encounter with Carl. Anton is still ashamed of his behavior, the distance he felt compelled to enforce. He sighs. What's done is done. He says hi to the other guys—Nisse on drums, Charlie on double bass—and sits down. He's brought the big tenor sax today; pitched in Bb, it gives a deep, rounded tone, perfect for the melancholy sound of jazz. Its warmth evokes images of smoky nightclubs and trendy cocktails, gentlemen in smoking jackets and elegant ladies with a cigarette holder at the corner of their mouth.

Tonight, he simply wants to sink into that atmosphere, forget about Carl.

He runs his hand over the instrument. He has played ever since he was in grade school, learned to switch between the tenor sax and the smaller alto sax, pitched in Eb.

The ceiling light is reflected in the rose-colored brass as he slips on the strap and places the saxophone in front of his chest. He tries a few notes, allows the heartrending sound to express everything he couldn't say to Carl an hour ago.

Bobo, who is on keyboard, raises his hand to indicate that it's time to begin.

"We'll start with 'Take Five,'" he says.

It's a classic in D minor from the fifties, recorded by Dave Brubeck with the saxophonist and composer Paul Desmond. It is played in four-five time and has one of the most beautiful sax melodies in the jazz canon. It was written for the alto sax, but tonight the tenor will have to do.

Charlie plays the soft introductory drumbeats; then Bobo joins in with the familiar piano chords.

Anton places his lips to the mouthpiece and fills his lungs with air. He is usually able to lose himself in the music; it has often been his sanctuary, particularly when he has been plagued by doubt or has brooded for too long over his sexual identity.

But this time he sees only Carl's face before him as his fingers touch the keys.

52

It is almost ten o'clock by the time Hanna gets back to the house in Sadeln.

On the way home from Enafors, she stopped in Duved to have something to eat and compose herself. That crazy dog had frightened her; she doesn't want to go home and let Lydia and Richard see her with nerves so obviously shattered.

Hanna knows her sister; it would inevitably lead to a whole raft of questions. Instead, she sent a brief text saying she'd be back late from work.

She creeps into the lower ground floor via the skiing entrance and goes straight to her room to avoid anyone seeing her. She has just started to get undressed when there is a gentle tap on her door: Lydia. She is barefoot, and for once she is wearing a faded-blue college sweatshirt, the kind Hanna might pull on.

"Are you okay?"

"Fine," Hanna replies.

Her sister looks at her with a certain amount of skepticism. "Sure?"

Hanna takes off a sock. "It's been a long day, that's all. I left at six this morning."

Lydia leans against the door frame. "Do you have to work so hard?" She sounds worried.

"Sometimes it's necessary." Hanna tries to smile, but it ends up as more of a grimace. She is bone weary, and she can't stop thinking about

Rebecka. Her concerns have only grown since the visit to Enafors; that dark, deserted house fills her with foreboding.

"I wondered if you'd like a glass of wine or a cup of tea? I assume you've eaten? Richard made a big lasagna, and there's plenty left if you're hungry."

Lydia's kindness makes Hanna smile. It's an unfamiliar but very nice feeling to be taken care of. She hasn't experienced that for a very long time.

Her big sister has always been like a mother to her.

"That would be great—just give me a few minutes. Tea rather than wine, please—I have to get up early tomorrow too."

Since that time in December when life was such a mess, Hanna has cut down on her drinking. She thought it would be difficult, but in fact it was easy. With the chance of a new life and a new job in Åre, the compulsion to drink simply faded away.

Over the past couple of months, she has barely touched a wine bottle.

Hanna goes upstairs to find a fire crackling in the generous hearth. Lydia has set out teacups and saucers with a floral pattern on the table and lit candles in various lanterns. There is also a jar of honey and a plate of freshly baked cinnamon buns.

It smells wonderful.

"Have you baked?" Hanna wonders.

"Hardly. Credit where credit is due—these are from the local bakery. They're delicious."

Hanna sinks her teeth into one of the warm buns. Lydia is absolutely right—it tastes divine. As Hanna chews, she feels her shoulders drop. Before she goes to sleep, she needs to review the events of the day, but right now that can wait. It's nice just to sit here with Lydia and switch off from work for a while.

"Where's everyone else?"

Lydia nods in the direction of the main bedroom.

"Richard's already gone to bed. He was tired; he's been skiing on the back slopes of Skutan all day with some friends and a guide. I'm assuming the kids are in their rooms with their iPads." She gives a resigned laugh. "There's no point in even trying to limit that kind of thing anymore. They do what they want, regardless of what I say."

It's not like Lydia to admit she's beaten. Hanna is reluctantly impressed by her niece and nephew. Come to think of it, they do take after their mother.

She sips the pale-yellow tea that Lydia has poured. It is made from turmeric, which apparently is the latest trend within the practice of yoga and well-being.

Lydia does a lot of yoga.

"How are you really?" Lydia asks, tilting her head to one side. "After everything that's happened since you left Stockholm?"

Hanna hasn't really thought about it. The last two months have gone surprisingly quickly. She is happy in Åre and enjoys working with the team up here. At the beginning she was worried that Anton might feel as if she was treading on his toes, but he doesn't seem to mind.

She has clicked with Daniel in a way that she never dared hope was possible. He often asks for her opinion and is happy to take her along on cases. Sometimes the best part of the day is when they're sitting in the car, chatting.

She likes his slightly terse style, which hides a deep empathy. He is also very interested in cooking, thanks to his Italian heritage. He has told her that his mother, Francesca, was a fantastic cook, and he can spend an entire journey from Åre to Östersund discussing different kinds of olive oil or the best way to keep Parmesan cheese.

"I'm . . . great," she replies. "Much better than I thought I'd be."

"That's excellent, because I have some good news." Lydia smiles mysteriously. "Christian has agreed to give you forty percent of the increased value of the apartment in Solna."

Hanna does a quick mental calculation. It's a lot of money; it should be something in the region of . . . half a million kronor, if not more.

"Wow! You're amazing!"

Lydia grins. "It's the least he can do. He behaved like a complete shit toward you."

She sounds like a judge delivering her verdict. Hanna can't help smiling too. The next time she meets a guy—if she does—she is determined to sort out a legally binding contract before they move in together.

"He did," she says, adding a spoonful of honey to her tea. "But it wasn't only his fault that we broke up. We just weren't very well suited."

She gazes at the candle in the closest glass lantern. The flame is moving hypnotically back and forth, its slender blue heart surrounded by an orange-and-yellow aura. Christian's betrayal still hurts, but she realizes that she is over him. Her time in Åre has helped her to heal.

"I should never have gotten together with him," she confesses, talking to herself as much as to Lydia. "We have completely different goals and values. His new girlfriend suits him much better."

"So why did you stay? You stuck it out for five years," Lydia says.

Hanna chews her lower lip. She's wondered the same thing herself over the past few weeks.

Christian pursued her relentlessly at the start. He was something of a Prince Charming, and she was probably more flattered than was healthy. Plus, her mom and dad adored him from day one; it was the first time they'd liked any of her boyfriends, and it made her feel accepted by them.

"He was a big hit with our darling mother," she says in a failed attempt to brush aside the question with a joke. "I think she's more upset than I am that we broke up."

"Fuck her," Lydia snaps with unexpected venom.

Hanna laughs but can't hide her bitterness. "Easy for you to say."

Lydia has always been the apple of her mother's eye, and they both know it. Hanna has no intention of complaining; it's not Lydia's fault that their parents have always favored her.

"You know what she's like." Lydia reaches across the table and squeezes Hanna's hand. "I'm so sorry about the way she's treated you. The way she behaved when you were growing up. You do know how I feel?"

The pleading tone in Lydia's voice comes as a surprise. In the glow of the candles, the pain of a guilty conscience is written all over her face and in her blue eyes.

A lump forms in Hanna's throat. Her sister has always been the anchor in her life, even when she was at her most difficult and traveled around Europe, to her parents' horror. Or when she applied to the police academy, against their express wishes.

It was only Lydia who encouraged her back then.

After the attack in Barcelona, when her much older, revolting boss forced her into a cramped cellar with an earth floor and raped her, it was Lydia she turned to.

Hanna has never blamed her sister for the situation when they were growing up—the fact that their mother didn't seem to care about her younger daughter or that their father was so conflict averse that he never stepped in.

Now she understands with a sudden flash of insight that Lydia blames herself.

"It's not your fault." She squeezes her sister's hand in return and gives her a sad smile. "It's never been your fault."

Lydia's eyes fill with tears.

"The thing is . . . it doesn't feel that way."

She blinks several times and pushes back a strand of hair from her forehead. With her ponytail and her faded sweatshirt, she is far from the image of the successful lawyer, talking about women's empowerment and being interviewed on the news about landmark legal cases.

Her expression changes, as if too many unhappy memories are filling her mind.

"I've always had a guilty conscience about you. There was so much unfairness. I wanted to put it right, but I didn't know how—apart from stepping in as a kind of buffer and trying to give you what Mom couldn't."

"It wasn't your responsibility."

Lydia clutches her cup between the palms of her hands.

"It was as if . . . I got everything and you got nothing. I was the eldest, so all the attention was focused on me. By the time you came along, Mom and Dad were both older and more tired. I had an easy time in school, because I was a good student; I didn't have to try particularly hard. When I was twenty-three I was lucky enough to meet Richard, and since then both our careers have gone very smoothly. While you met Christian, who behaved like a total jerk. We're also very comfortable financially, while you're working twenty-four seven for a ridiculously low police salary."

Lydia's comments are a surprise. Hanna never imagined that her sister thought that way. Why should she blame herself for the way their mother behaved? How can she think that Hanna would feel any resentment toward her, after all that Lydia has done for her?

"You don't need to apologize," she says. "This is between me and Mom, not the two of us. You and Richard have worked incredibly hard to get where you are." She waves a hand, encompassing the impressive decor. "And you're also very generous. I've lived here for weeks without paying any rent."

Lydia lets out a snort. "It would never occur to me to ask you for money."

"Well, I'm very grateful." Hanna raises her cup, toasting her sister.

Lydia's voice is steadier now. "Anyway, I don't understand Mom and Dad's attitude toward you and me. Or rather Mom's. She's the one who rules the roost in our family."

Hanna isn't going to argue with that.

"I've thought about it a lot since I had children of my own." Lydia's voice is trembling with indignation. "I don't understand how you can treat siblings differently. I look at Linnéa and Fabian and I love them to death, both of them. How can you love one child more than the other? How can you let yourself do that?"

Obviously, some people can, Hanna thinks. Their parents are a shining example.

"Above all, I don't understand how you can show it as openly as Mom does," Lydia continues.

It hurts, even though it's true. Lydia is putting into words what Hanna has known for a long time, and yet it is astonishingly painful to hear what has lain hidden deep down inside her. It is so shameful that she has barely been able to face up to it herself.

Her mother loves Lydia more. It is a wound that might never heal.

But it's not Lydia's fault that Hanna's relationship with her mother is so toxic, and above all, it is not her sister's job to compensate for it.

Lydia has always been there for her. Hanna quickly gets to her feet, goes around the table, and gives Lydia a big hug. "Thank you," she says, and means it with all her heart. "You're the best big sister anyone could ever have."

REBECKA

2020

SATURDAY, FEBRUARY 22

When Rebecka looks up, Ole is standing there with a clenched fist raised.

She closes her eyes, tenses her body as she always does when he turns to violence. She keeps both arms in front of her belly. She has to protect her child; it's the only thing that matters.

The hard blow to the middle of her chest knocks her off her feet. The chair falls over with a crash, and Rebecka lands on her hip on the wooden floor.

She can't breathe, and her side is burning. It is incredibly painful, and she can't suppress a loud groan. Instinctively she curls up to save her baby.

"Please," she hears her own voice shouting. "Please stop."

"You are a harlot," Ole roars. "A damned harlot who must be punished!"

A vicious kick in the back makes Rebecka cry out. She is lying on the kitchen floor and tries to pull herself up with the help of the chair leg, but another kick knocks her off balance again.

Something wet is running from her nose. The taste of blood fills her mouth.

Ole is going to kill her.

She calls out his name, hoping to appeal to his sense of reason, but he doesn't seem to hear her.

With the last of her strength, she yells, "Think about the baby!"

Somehow the words penetrate his brain, because suddenly the blows stop.

Rebecka can't move. She stays where she is, whimpering in pain. When she opens her eyes, Ole has stepped back. He is breathing hard, his knuckles are red with blood.

Her blood.

"The baby?" he gasps, edging away until he reaches the counter.

"I'm pregnant," Rebecka whispers.

Ole stares at her, disbelief written all over his face.

"Is that true?"

"I swear."

She looks around desperately, catches sight of the Bible on the table. Pulls herself up into a half-sitting position and reaches for it.

"I swear on the Holy Scripture," she says, holding it up in the air. "As God is my witness." Blood is still pouring from her nose, and she wipes it away with the other hand. "You have to believe me. I'm three months pregnant."

Despite the situation she has the presence of mind to subtract a few weeks. If she tells the truth, Ole will be able to work out that he is not the father.

"Is it mine?"

"Of course it's yours!"

Her life hangs on her ability to convince Ole that he is the father; otherwise she will never get out of here alive.

He is still breathing hard. "Why didn't you tell me?"

"I didn't dare . . ." Fear makes her voice hoarse and rasping. "I was afraid of having a miscarriage. I didn't want to say anything until I'd made it past twelve weeks."

She doesn't know if he believes her, but she can see in his eyes that he's wavering. At least he's not certain that she's lying. If she can just sow a seed of doubt in his mind . . . If he thinks it's his child, after all these years together, then he won't kill her tonight.

She has to win time. Win his trust.

"I was so happy," she lies, amazed that she can do this under the circumstances. "But I didn't want to risk disappointing you if things went wrong."

Has she succeeded? His face softens a fraction; there is less aggression in his stance.

Then that look of utter contempt is back.

"Is it *his*?"

Ole doesn't mention Johan's name, but Rebecka feels as if the floor is giving way beneath her.

"What do you mean? There's no one else."

He takes a step toward her, and she recoils, but just as she thinks he is about to attack her again, he stops himself. His jaw is working, as if he is about to say something but can't make up his mind.

He grabs her wrist, pulls her to her feet, drags her out of the kitchen and up the stairs to a small bedroom, where he pushes her down onto the bed.

"I need to think," he mutters. "I have to pray to God for guidance."

He is gone before Rebecka has time to react. The sound of a key turning in the door makes her shudder.

A few minutes pass; then she hears a bang as the front door slams shut. She drags herself over to the window and sees how the car drives off along the road. The beam of the headlights quickly disappears in the dense darkness.

Rebecka can't suppress a sob. Ole has left her alone in this cold, damp cottage. It can't be more than twelve degrees Celsius indoors, and she has nothing to eat or drink.

On the wall opposite there is a framed piece of embroidery. Two lines in Norwegian, surrounded by faded cross-stitch flowers.

Herren er min hyrde, jeg mangler ikke noe.

"The Lord is my shepherd, I shall not want." Psalm 23. David's psalm.

The words are another slap in the face.

What would the Lord say about her situation now when everything has been taken from her?

She sinks down onto the bed and wraps a blanket around her, even though it smells moldy. She is aching all over. Cautiously she lets her fingers feel their way over her body; nothing seems to be broken, she is just in terrible pain, especially from her hip. She thinks she managed to shield her belly from Ole's kicks. Whatever has happened to Johan, she must protect their child. Nothing else matters.

Rebecka falls to her knees and clasps her hands in prayer, although deep down she has started to wonder whether there is any point.

"Jesus, help me," she whispers into the darkness. "Save us."

WEDNESDAY, FEBRUARY 26

53

It is almost dawn when Hanna parks on Kurortsvägen by the police station. She has slept for seven hours and feels both rested and focused. It was good to have a one-on-one conversation with Lydia last night; the dark thoughts surrounding her childhood are beginning to dissipate.

She has made a decision on the way to work. They have to go to the Nordhammars' house straight after the morning briefing. Her gut instinct is telling her that Rebecka is central to the investigation.

She swipes her pass card and walks through the door. She is the last to arrive today; everyone else is already in the conference room. There is barely time to pour herself a coffee before the meeting begins.

Daniel summarizes the current situation; then they go around the table.

Raffe has continued to dig into Linus Sundin's finances, along with one of the investigators in Östersund. He reports on frequent contacts with the bank and companies that offer payday loans.

"Sundin has just defaulted on one of those loans, and the lender is threatening him with the Enforcement Authority. It doesn't look good."

When he has finished speaking, he discreetly removes the plug of snuff from beneath his upper lip and wraps it up in a paper napkin.

Daniel hands over to Anton, who has followed up on the interviews with Johan Andersson's circle of acquaintances.

"I've spoken to several of Johan's friends in addition to Carl Willner, including those Johan was due to meet at Pigo on Friday evening. Unfortunately, he hadn't mentioned his plans to go away."

Anton goes on to share the information he has acquired. Two of the men confirmed that Johan was frustrated about the situation with Linus; clearly Carl Willner wasn't the only one who had heard about the difficulties between the joint owners of the company.

The sun breaks through the clouds and shines in through the window. The sudden burst of light divides Anton's face: one half is illuminated, the other half in shadow. Hanna thinks back to the interview with Carl Willner the other day and how uncomfortable Anton seemed.

Daniel nods to Hanna. Should she mention her visit to Enafors? She isn't sure how her colleagues will react if she reveals that she went there on her own initiative late at night.

She chooses a middle way, reporting back on the meeting with Maria Törnlund at the preschool and their telephone conversation yesterday evening, Maria's suspicions about a relationship between Johan and Rebecka. Then she talks about her research into the Light of Life. She also gives some statistics about coercive control and highlights the fact that Ole Nordhammar insisted on driving his wife to and from work every single day. Finally, she points out that Johan didn't actually have a work-related reason for being at Little Snowdrops on Friday and that—according to Maria—he seemed devastated.

Suddenly Raffe reacts, interrupting Hanna in midsentence.

"This Rebecka Nordhammar—do you happen to have her cell phone number?"

"I do."

Hanna takes out her phone, brings up the number on the display.

Raffe taps away on his laptop. "Hang on . . . This might be a long shot, but just let me check something."

His fingers fly across the keyboard; then he turns the computer so that everyone can see. An enlarged document fills the screen—row after row of numbers. After a moment Hanna realizes that they are looking at a list of phone calls—columns of numbers and the time and length of each call.

"This is from the telecom company and relates to Johan's cell phone," Raffe explains. "It came through late yesterday." He turns the laptop around again and finds another document showing more numbers and times.

"These are the subscribers with whom Johan had contact by text message over the past six months. I haven't had the chance to go through them yet, but it's obvious which numbers occur most often."

Hanna stares at the list.

"Three appear frequently during the fall," Raffe continues. "Both when it comes to calls and text messages. One is Marion's, the second is Linus's."

"And the third?" Hanna says, although the answer is right there in front of her.

"It seems to be Rebecka Nordhammar's, if the number you have is correct."

It is. Hanna has called it so many times that she knows it by heart.

"Interesting," Daniel says. "That gives us a concrete link between Johan and Rebecka."

"Can I take a closer look?" Hanna leans forward. Now that she knows what she's looking for, the pattern is clear. Rebecka and Johan exchanged texts on a regular basis. It began in September, continued in October, and escalated in November. Then it stopped.

"Is there a period missing?"

Raffe frowns, his dark-brown eyes peer at the screen. "What do you mean?"

"Here," Hanna says, pointing to the left-hand column. "From this date in November, it's only Johan sending texts to Rebecka." She scrolls down. "He didn't receive a single message from her after that."

Raffe leans closer. "You're right," he says, sticking his pen behind his ear.

"Can you bring up the list of phone calls again?"

Raffe obliges, and Hanna quickly scans the columns.

"Look—from that date in November, it's the same story. Johan calls Rebecka, but she doesn't pick up or call him back."

Raffe gives her an appreciative glance. "Well spotted."

"So," Hanna says. "Johan and Rebecka had a period of frequent contact over the phone for just under three months, from September to the middle of November. Then it stopped abruptly. Johan continued to call and text Rebecka for several weeks until Lucia in mid-December, but she didn't respond. Then silence."

"She ghosted him," Anton says. "If we assume they were having an affair—she finished it."

"Exactly." Hanna links her hands behind her head and thinks out loud. "And then, last Friday afternoon, Johan shows up at the preschool to talk to Rebecka. Maria Törnlund sees them from a distance; they seem to be having an intense and emotional discussion, and he appears to be very upset."

"The following day, Johan is dead," Raffe adds. "And two days later, Rebecka's husband calls to say she's too sick to come to work."

"And now no one can get a hold of her," Hanna says.

"Could we assume that Rebecka is the person Johan was planning to take to Strömsund?" Daniel wonders.

"I think so." Hanna allows herself a little smile; they are on the same page. "It definitely looks as if Johan and Rebecka were having a secret relationship during the fall. What if his visit to the school on Friday was one last desperate attempt to persuade her to leave her husband?"

"You mean they were about to run away together to his brother's house?" Anton sounds skeptical. "Isn't that a bit too much like the plot of a romance novel?"

Raffe grins.

"That doesn't necessarily mean it's not true," Hanna points out.

Daniel gets to his feet, goes over to the whiteboard, and picks up a dark-blue felt-tip pen. He writes down Rebecka's and Johan's names, with a double-pointed arrow between them. Then he adds Linus's name and another arrow connecting Johan to Linus.

"Where does Marion fit into all this?" he says, adding her name in capitals.

Hanna lets down her hair and puts it up again while she considers the question. Marion didn't give any indication that Johan was planning on leaving her. According to her, she and Johan had a happy marriage. She had nothing but positive things to say about her husband, even though she was shocked and upset.

"Maybe Johan hadn't had time to tell her he was leaving. Maybe he was killed before he had the chance?"

"Could be," Daniel concedes. "It's possible that he was intending to speak to her on Saturday, just before he left." He studies the board. "What else do we know?"

Anton frowns, presses his fingertips together.

"We know that Johan meets Rebecka between three and four o'clock on Friday afternoon. Then he calls his brother at five thirty and says he's coming over late on Saturday evening, accompanied by an unknown person. After that he has a beer with Carl Willner at Pigo. According to Carl he isn't his usual calm self; he is described as restless, wired. He also leaves earlier than they'd arranged. The last time he is seen is at Linus Sundin's house, shortly after eight. Just under twelve hours later, he is found dead in Tångböle."

"Excellent summary," Daniel says.

Hanna takes over. "It seems to me that Johan's restlessness stems from the fact that he had finally talked Rebecka into leaving her husband. Johan was the persistent one, we can see that from the list of phone calls and text messages. If she unexpectedly agreed, then that would explain the sudden trip. Johan made one last attempt to win her over, and she said yes."

"Unless the polar opposite is true," Anton says.

"What do you mean?"

"What if Johan was stalking Rebecka, and the silence between them was because she'd finally managed to get him to leave her alone?"

Hanna doesn't answer. Of course, there is a different way of looking at the situation. That's always the case; it's important not to lock in to one particular theory too early on. But everything she has heard about Johan contradicts that interpretation. Every single witness has talked about his warmth, his positivity. He was a kind, considerate, and empathetic friend who didn't become bitter in spite of his skiing career being brought to an end so abruptly and unfairly.

Could Johan be a crazed stalker? She doesn't think so.

Raffe seems to agree. "To be honest, I find that hard to believe. There's nothing in Johan's background to suggest such behavior."

"Okay," Daniel says. "Let's assume we're looking at a love story, and Rebecka was the person Johan was intending to take to Strömsund . . . Why did it have to be kept secret?"

That seems crystal clear to Hanna.

"Because she was terrified of her husband, of course. Everything we've heard about Ole Nordhammar suggests a man with a powerful need to exercise control and a marked tendency toward violence."

She pauses, thinks back to what Maria Törnlund told her.

"Her colleague said she'd seen bruises on Rebecka's forearms. Her behavior when Maria tried to raise the issue is also typical of women who have suffered domestic violence. They are ashamed and embarrassed and try to hide what's going on instead of accepting help. If Ole is a man who beats his wife, then he's hardly likely to have become less dangerous if Rebecka told him she was planning to end the marriage." She finishes off her coffee, which doesn't taste too good. She usually takes milk, but they'd run out.

"In my opinion, Rebecka wouldn't dare let her husband know that she was intending to leave. Johan was careful not to take any risks either—that's why he didn't tell his brother who he was bringing with him."

"Sounds reasonable," Daniel agrees. He turns back to the board and adds Ole Nordhammar's name, with an arrow connecting him and Rebecka. "So, what do we know about the Nordhammars?"

Hanna had gathered quite a lot of information before setting off for Enafors the previous evening.

"Ole Nordhammar is one of the pastors in the church known as the Light of Life. He's fourteen years older than his wife and grew up within the church. They married in 2012, when Rebecka had just turned nineteen and he was thirty-three. Ole was employed as a trainee accountant with a small company in Järpen until 2017, but over the past few years, he has mainly devoted himself to the work of the church. The couple have no children, and they live in Enafors."

She pauses for breath. Maybe she should tell Daniel about her visit after the meeting?

"Rebecka is twenty-six now. Her parents are also active within the church and live in Storvallen, near Storlien. She followed the childcare and leisure program at the high school in Järpen and started work at the Little Snowdrops preschool three years ago. Before that she appears to have been a stay-at-home housewife, even though the couple don't have any children of their own, as I said."

The final comment is her own observation, but she feels it contributes to the overall picture of Ole Nordhammar. She finds it hard to believe that Rebecka would have chosen to stay home full time at such a young age, even if her faith is important to her. It must have been lonely, rattling around in that isolated house in Enafors while her husband went off to work.

Once again, this behavior fits the typical profile of a controlling partner. It rarely begins with violence; instead, it is a matter of socially isolating the woman until she has nowhere to go. Only then, when her self-confidence has been destroyed and she is totally dependent on her husband, does the mental abuse mutate into physical violence.

"That's what I know so far," she concludes.

Picking up a red pen, Daniel draws a dotted line between Johan and Ole, then circles Ole's name.

"If this theory is true, then there is another person with a strong motive for attacking Johan Andersson," he says before sitting down. No one in the room seems inclined to disagree. "We need to track down Ole and Rebecka Nordhammar right away."

The image of the dark and deserted house in Enafors comes into Hanna's mind.

The feeling that Rebecka was no longer there.

"That might be trickier than you think," she says.

REBECKA

2020

SUNDAY, FEBRUARY 23

Johan is sitting on the edge of the bed. He takes Rebecka in his arms. She is still half-asleep, but it is enough to smell his familiar scent to know that she is safe again.

Darling Johan.

He caresses her gently, rocks her to and fro as if she were a little girl.

"I'm here now," he whispers tenderly. "I love you. There's nothing to be afraid of anymore. I'm going to take care of you and our baby."

The tears begin to flow beneath her closed eyelids. Johan came in the end; he didn't let her down.

He will help her escape from this place.

Rebecka leans forward to get closer and bumps the wall with her shoulder. She opens her eyes and realizes that she is still locked in the horrible bedroom.

The nightmare is not over. Johan existed only in her imagination. She is aching from Ole's kicks and blows.

The happiness of a few seconds ago gives way to darkness. It is pointless to fight. She ought to get up, try to find a way out, but her body refuses to cooperate. Everything hurts; she has no strength left.

The daylight seeps in through the dirty window; it must be Sunday. She closes her eyes, sinks back into an uneasy sleep.

The next time Rebecka wakes up, it is still light.

She is desperate for a pee and sits up. When she looks around, she sees an old metal bucket just inside the door and a plastic bag tossed on the floor beside it.

She grabs the bucket and does what she needs to. At first, she is too scared to check if there is blood in her urine; then she decides to take a look. The color is normal, and she feels an overwhelming sense of relief. There is no sign that her pregnancy has been adversely affected by the assault.

Her child is still alive.

Nothing else matters. She has to get through this for the sake of her unborn baby.

She reaches for the plastic bag and finds two bottles of water, a loaf of sliced bread, and a smoked sausage. Ole must have come back and left it while she was asleep. She doesn't care why; right now, she is too hungry and thirsty to speculate.

She uncorks one of the bottles and drinks so greedily that the water runs down her chin. Her lips are cracked, her throat as dry as dust. When she has had enough, she sinks back down onto the bed. She catches sight of the embroidery again; she tries to say a prayer, but the words refuse to come out. There are too many questions swirling around in her mind. How long is she going to be imprisoned here? Surely Ole can't keep her locked up forever?

Or can he? Maybe she will never be let out.

She tries to think about Johan. About how her parents or Maria ought to be wondering where she has gone, but it doesn't help. She is overcome by a wave of fear so strong that it takes her breath away; she is gasping for air.

The room shrinks, the walls lean inward. The ceiling is about to crush her, and little black dots appear in her field of vision.

Rebecka closes her eyes and lets out a loud groan. She clenches her fists and digs her fingernails into her palms with such force that the skin almost breaks.

The pain helps, strangely enough. Somehow it is possible to breathe again. She draws air into her lungs with long, shuddering breaths. After a while she dares to open her eyes.

The room looks like it did a moment ago.

She wraps her arms around herself, hugs her upper body. She tries to recall the sensations from the dream about Johan, to pretend that he is holding her, stroking her hair.

She cannot give in and become hysterical, she must keep a clear head.

For the sake of their child. She repeats it like a mantra.

For the sake of their unborn child.

54

They have passed Ånn and should soon reach Enafors. The clock on the dashboard shows five to nine; the morning briefing was longer than usual. Daniel feels well rested; Alice had a good night.

Hanna clears her throat. "There's something I need to tell you."

Daniel gives her an inquiring glance.

"Don't get mad, but I did something on my own initiative last night. I went to Rebecka Nordhammar's house. Just to check it out."

Daniel feels a familiar stab of irritation. "On your own? With no backup?"

"Er, yes." Hanna sounds guilty. Before Daniel can say anything else, she adds, "There was no one home, nothing happened."

It doesn't take a genius to work out the possible consequences. If their suspicions about Ole Nordhammar are justified, things could have gone very badly. What if he'd been home when Hanna showed up?

"Did you know that before you set off? That the house was empty and Ole wasn't there?"

"Not exactly."

Daniel sighs. "You do realize you should have cleared it with me first?"

"I do." Hanna hangs her head. "But I was so worried about Rebecka after the conversation with her colleague. I didn't think it was safe to wait until today."

A sharp bend a hundred yards up ahead forces Daniel to slow down. The sun is shining, but there has been a heavy fall of snow overnight, and the asphalt is covered in a thick layer of white. The traffic report on the radio has just informed listeners that a truck has skidded off the road up by Krokom.

His irritation fades. Hanna's intuition and her ability to act quickly have often moved them forward, as in the Amanda Halvorssen case, even though her actions almost led to a catastrophe on that occasion. He isn't pleased about her little trip, but at least she has been honest and told him about it.

"Can we agree that this is the last time you take off like that without talking to me first?"

"Absolutely. I promise."

The answer comes instantly, almost before he has finished speaking. At the same time Hanna's phone buzzes. She holds it up so that he can see the display. "Look—a photo of Rebecka."

Daniel sees a young blond woman surrounded by children, then immediately turns his attention back to his driving.

"I asked Maria Törnlund to send over a recent picture," Hanna explains as she stares at Rebecka's face. "I wonder what it's like, growing up with such strong Christian ideals. Does it make you more vulnerable, more easily influenced? You can almost see that she's a believer."

In spite of his frustration at Hanna's actions last night, Daniel has to smile at the sweeping generalization. "Are you basing your analysis on the photo, or on what you already know?"

She laughs, and the atmosphere between them is back to normal.

"Isn't everyone who lives within some kind of sect being manipulated in a way?" Hanna says. "Although there is a difference between joining a sect and being born into it."

Daniel isn't sure that it's entirely fair to describe the Light of Life as "some kind of sect." A quick check in the police database hasn't highlighted anything noteworthy. There is nothing suspicious about its leaders. There are plenty of free religious churches that operate without unhealthy elements.

The Light of Life isn't necessarily to blame for the fact that Ole Nordhammar might be a man who abuses his wife.

"What do you mean?" he asks.

"People who join a sect are hardly expecting to be manipulated, but it seems to me that they must have a hollowness within them. They lack a higher purpose, maybe a sense of connection. A feeling that they have been put on this earth to achieve something."

Daniel remembers that Hanna took several courses in psychology in college, which gives her real insight into the issue—much better than anything he can offer.

"And that's exactly what religious organizations like the Light of Life provide," she goes on. "They make people feel important and needed—that's part of the attraction. Combined with a burning faith, of course. It gives you a chance to make a difference."

As a police officer, Daniel recognizes something of himself in what she is saying. That's why people join the service—to make a contribution, to feel needed, to be able to help others.

That's the way it is at the start, anyway.

"If you were told that you could be free of all your problems and your pain, and save the souls of others at the same time . . . Who could resist?"

Daniel isn't sure if Hanna is asking him the question or if it's rhetorical.

Presumably anyone can become ensnared in a sect if the right psychological tools are used. Perhaps it's the same mechanism that is increasingly being used to recruit young teenagers into serious gang crime. Once again, the temptation is to find a sense of belonging, a connection, the opportunity to feel special, chosen.

"Turn right," Hanna interrupts his train of thought.

They have arrived in Enafors. Daniel signals, leaves the E14, and takes a narrow track. He isn't quite done with their discussion.

"You said there's a difference between those who join an organization and those who are born into it, like Rebecka."

"Yes. I see that as something else entirely." Hanna's voice is firm and clear. "If we take Rebecka as an example, she has been brought up within the church ever since she was a child. It's the only life she knows. If she were to break away from the Light of Life, then presumably she would also lose contact with her family and friends. That's how this kind of organization works—that's why it's so hard to leave."

"And yet it seems as if she was about to do just that."

Daniel stops the car as they reach the end of the road. They've arrived at Rebecka's house.

"Which says a lot about the powerful emotions that must have been involved," Hanna replies.

55

By daylight the house seems smaller. It is also in a worse state than Hanna realized last night; the overall impression is one of desolation and abandonment.

"It would be a good sign if there were a car on the drive," she says to Daniel. "The place looks deserted."

She hopes the aggressive dog isn't around. She has decided not to say anything about it to Daniel; it seems unnecessary to explain how close she came to being attacked or why she drew the attention of the dog in the first place.

They ring the doorbell, but Hanna isn't expecting anyone to answer. After a minute or so, Daniel tries again; then he knocks on the small glass panel in the upper part of the door. He steps back and looks at the upper floor.

"Hello?" he shouts, hands cupped around his mouth. "Anyone home?"

Hanna takes out her phone and calls Rebecka's number, but once again it goes straight to voicemail. She must have left a dozen messages by now, asking Rebecka to contact her. She is becoming increasingly convinced that Rebecka is in danger.

"I don't think they're in," she says. "The place feels deserted."

"You're probably right."

"Let's go round the back," she suggests, following the tracks she'd left the previous evening. When they reach the veranda, she goes up the steps to the glass door. It's easy to see into the living room now. There is a navy-blue sofa suite and a large rag rug beneath a square wooden coffee table. A dark oak dining table with ornately carved chairs stands at the other end of the room.

Hanna notes the details, from the hand-crocheted cushion covers to the pale-blue curtains. The walls are adorned with paintings in gilded frames; it's all very old fashioned.

It's hard to believe that a young woman like Rebecka, who is only twenty-seven, would decorate her home like this.

Hanna suspects that she knows how things stand. She's gathered from public records that Ole Nordhammar's mother died of cancer several years ago, and his eighty-four-year-old father moved into assisted living in Duved. Ole has no siblings. This must be his parents' house, which is why it looks so drab and dated. Rebecka is living among her in-laws' old furniture.

Given the picture Hanna has formed of Ole's personality, it seems perfectly logical in a depressing way. Rebecka has had very little say in what her own home looks like.

Hanna has met his sort before.

Something is niggling at the back of her mind, a memory from yesterday that she can't quite get a hold of. She stares into the living room one more time.

"Seems empty to me," Daniel says. "Shall we go?"

Then she realizes.

Yesterday evening there was a heavy Bible on the coffee table. This morning it has disappeared.

Someone must have been here overnight.

56

After the visit to the empty house, Daniel suggested going to see Rebecka's parents, so now they are on their way to see Stefan and Ann-Sofie Ekvall in Storvallen. Their farm is close to the Norwegian border, about fifteen minutes from Enafors.

While Daniel is driving, Hanna looks up Ole Nordhammar's phone number. He doesn't answer, which serves only to increase her sense of foreboding.

They pass the bus station and reach a collection of red-painted buildings. Daniel parks in front of the farmhouse, next to a barn.

A woman in her early fifties, her hair peppered with gray, opens the front door. She looks alarmed when she hears that they are from the police, but before she has time to say anything, she is joined by a weather-beaten man of about the same age.

This must be Rebecka's father. Hanna can see the resemblance from the photo Maria sent her.

"May we come in? We have one or two questions about your daughter, Rebecka."

Ann-Sofie's hand flies up to her throat, where a tiny silver cross hangs from a fine chain.

"Has something happened?"

"We'd just like to ask you a couple of questions," Hanna repeats in a reassuring tone of voice. "But it might be better if we could come in and sit down."

Ann-Sofie leads them into the kitchen. Hanna wonders how many kitchens and living rooms she has seen during her career, usually clutching a cup of coffee made hastily and anxiously by the homeowner.

Rebecka's mother busies herself with the coffee machine; Stefan Ekvall sits there with his arms folded. Hanna notes that he is a big man with an air of authority. She has only been here for a few minutes, but she has no doubt who is in charge in this house.

From time to time Ann-Sofie glances anxiously at him, as if to check that she is behaving properly and isn't going to be chastised by her husband.

Hanna wonders about their involvement in their daughter's decision to get married at such a young age, to a man fourteen years her senior.

"Shall we begin?" Stefan says as his wife continues her preparations in the background. "What's this about?"

57

Anton is busy checking the information that has come in via the special telephone hotline. Nothing useful so far, but the next note on his desk is about a witness who heard Linus making aggressive comments about Johan.

He contacts the caller, a woman called Elin Algren who works as a dental nurse in Järpen. It transpires that she was at the same outdoor bar as Linus only a week before Johan's death.

"What made you react when you saw Linus?" Anton asks.

"I wasn't eavesdropping—he was talking so loudly that he was practically yelling. It was impossible not to overhear."

"Do you remember how he expressed himself? The more specific you can be, the better."

"He was swearing, going on and on. That's what first caught my attention—he sounded so angry. He kept repeating 'fucking Johan' and 'fucking Marion,' something along those lines."

Anton notes down that Linus has displayed open hostility toward the Anderssons, which backs up Marion's assertion that he became aggressive during the quarrel at the office.

"Okay—what else did he say?"

There is a brief silence, as if Elin is trying hard to remember.

"I'm not sure. I'd gone to the bar to order a glass of wine, and when I got it I went and sat somewhere else. But I think Linus said that Johan and his wife were on his back all the time, that he never had any peace."

Anton continues typing up his notes while Elin is speaking. Her information says a lot about Linus's character.

"Roughly how long were you standing near Linus?"

"Maybe ten minutes—no more than that."

"And what state was he in?"

Elin gives a nervous laugh. "He was very drunk, red-faced, couldn't focus his eyes. He was almost slurring his words. Linus certainly wasn't sober."

"Was he aggressive?"

It's a leading question, but Anton chooses to ask it, given what Marion told them earlier.

"He seemed very . . . belligerent."

Anton asks a few more questions, but Elin has told him everything she knows.

"One more thing—what made you contact us?"

"Well . . . I know who both Linus and Johan are. Åre is a small place. I also know Linus's wife, Sandra. When I saw that Johan had been murdered, I went onto the police Facebook page, and it said that if anyone knew anything, they should get in touch." She takes a deep breath. "I kept wondering whether to call you . . ."

"I'm very pleased that you did," Anton says to reassure her.

"Can I ask you something?"

"Of course."

"You won't tell Linus that I've spoken to you, will you?" There is no mistaking the anxiety in her voice. "I can remain anonymous, can't I?"

"There's no need to worry about that. Not at this stage."

Anton checks Elin's contact details and thanks her for her help before ending the call; then he sits there holding the phone and staring into space. Outside the window the sun is shining, but there has been a severe weather warning on the radio. Storm-force winds from Northern Norway are moving in over Jämtland.

Anton doesn't know what to believe.

Hanna seems convinced that Ole and Rebecka Nordhammar are the hottest lead right now. She has come up with a detailed theory about a love affair between Rebecka and Johan, combined with a jealous husband who has lost his mind.

But is that reasonable? Sometimes Hanna tends to get carried away, particularly when domestic violence is involved, due to her experience in that field with the Stockholm City Police.

He is by no means certain that Ole Nordhammar is the man they're looking for. There is still a great deal pointing to Linus Sundin. He had a strong financial motive, and he definitely has the physical strength that was needed to take Johan's life. More than one person has spoken about his temper, and he has a well-documented habit of drinking too much alcohol.

Who knows what might have happened in the heat of the moment if he lost control?

REBECKA

2020

MONDAY, FEBRUARY 24

Rebecka is lying on her side on the bed. It is light outside, which means that another night has passed since she was brought to the cottage in Norway. Her sleep has been intermittent and uneasy, filled with nightmares about Ole and what he might do to her when he comes back.

She isn't hungry but knows that she ought to eat. She needs nutrition; otherwise the child will not survive.

Johan's child, the child they will raise together, if she can just get out of here.

She can't suppress a sob, but then she sits up and rummages in the bag. She forces down some bread and a slice of sausage, even though it makes her retch. Then she drinks some water and feels a little bit more energetic.

She is thinking more clearly now.

On Saturday she really believed that Ole was intending to kill her. He seems to have changed his mind, at least temporarily, since he has brought food and water. It must be because of the pregnancy. He stopped hitting her when she told him about the baby. That was when he dragged her upstairs and locked her in the bedroom.

She has been granted a period of respite, but who knows how long it will last?

Somehow, she must escape before he returns.

Think. Maria will have missed her when she didn't show up for work this morning. She is rarely sick; her colleague should react, try to get a hold of her.

But Ole could come back at any moment.

She goes over to the filthy window. It isn't very big because of the sloping roof and is divided into four leaded panes. Maybe she can crawl out that way?

Her body is stiff, but she leans forward to see how far it is to the ground. The sight makes her feel dizzy—it must be ten or twelve feet, if not more.

It's too high. She risks breaking her legs, or worse—harming the child. It's not worth the risk of ending up lying on the ground in the cold, maybe in a poorer state than she is in now.

She would freeze to death within hours.

And it has started to snow. Visibility will drop to almost nothing when it gets dark. The dense forest of fir trees surrounding the cottage frightens her, and she has no idea how to find her way to civilization. Ole told her in the past that the place was isolated, but she hadn't appreciated how remote it is. She has no idea how Ole's grandfather coped, living all alone in this ramshackle dump.

Her eyes are drawn to the locked door. She has to get it open, that's the only way.

She examines every inch of the room. Apart from the bed, with its smelly blanket and stained pillow, there is a chest of drawers against the wall.

Rebecka opens each drawer in turn. The top one sticks, but eventually gives in with a loud scraping sound. She finds piles of motheaten clothes and puts on two substantial sweaters, even though the smell practically suffocates her.

The lower drawers contain only rubbish and old newspapers, nothing that can help her.

She kneels down and peers under the bed; the floor is thick with dust bunnies.

There is also a pine nightstand with a hymn book on the shelf, but when she opens the small drawer, she sees it.

A sewing kit . . . with a slender crochet hook. Maybe she can use it to pick the lock? Get out of the house before Ole comes back. She has no idea where she will go after that, but surely there must be people somewhere who will help her?

She rubs her belly to gain fresh strength.

Then she crouches down by the door and pokes the crochet hook into the keyhole.

58

Ann-Sofie Ekvall can't settle. She has only just sat down at the kitchen table when she leaps to her feet again, pouring everyone coffee, then fetching a plate of homemade cookies and asking if anyone takes milk.

She puts the milk on the table, sits down, and immediately gets up again to fetch sugar, even though no one has asked for it. On the way back she wipes the draining board, which is already spotless and shining.

Her restlessness is making Hanna nervous. She would like to tell Rebecka's mother to sit down so they can start talking.

At last she sinks down on her chair and stays put.

Stefan Ekvall's eyes are fixed on Daniel. He barely seems to register Hanna's presence.

"You have questions about our daughter?" he says.

Hanna wonders if he deliberately used *du*, the singular form of *you* in Swedish, in order to diminish her presence. She doesn't like the way he is directing all his attention to Daniel, even if she suspects that female police officers aren't met with approval in the conservative congregation.

Stefan is confirming all her preconceived opinions about the view of women within the Light of Life. It is painfully clear that he is the head of this household.

His wife hardly dares to speak.

However, it is important to keep an open mind. She mustn't allow her own prejudices to get in the way of the investigation. What she has learned so far about the Light of Life indicates a strongly patriarchal organization, but that doesn't necessarily mean that any crimes have been committed.

Daniel opens his notebook to a clean page.

"My colleague and I are here because we have been trying to get in touch with Rebecka for several days."

He emphasizes the word *colleague*, for which Hanna is grateful.

"She hasn't been at work since Friday. We've just been to her house in Enafors, but it's empty."

Daniel explains that although Rebecka called in sick, she doesn't appear to be at home. They have called her repeatedly, but she isn't answering her cell phone. Neither is Ole.

"Have you any idea where your daughter and son-in-law might be?"

"No." Stefan is wearing work clothes—blue dungarees over a checked flannel shirt.

"When was the last time you spoke to Rebecka?"

"When was it . . . Friday, maybe?"

"Is that normal?" Hanna chips in, looking at Ann-Sofie. "How often do you usually speak to her?"

Again, it is Stefan who answers, even though Hanna addressed her question to Rebecka's mother.

"Once a week, perhaps. At least once every two weeks." His voice has a deep bass tone.

"Do you have any idea if Rebecka and Ole might have gone away?" Daniel asks. "Could they be visiting friends?"

"Not that we know of, but then we don't have that kind of insight into their daily lives. Rebecka is a grown woman."

"Wouldn't they tell you if they were going away?" Hanna persists.

Ann-Sofie is nervously fiddling with the cross around her neck. "Do you think something's happened?" she bursts out. "Is Rebecka in danger?"

"We can't answer that," Daniel says. "But it's very important that we get a hold of her and her husband."

"Why?" There is a hint of unease in Stefan's eyes. Some form of reaction at last. The man must have a heart of stone if he's not concerned when two police officers show up and start asking questions about his daughter.

"We'll get to that," Daniel says. "When did you last see Ole?"

"It would have been at church on Sunday, at the service."

"Was Rebecka there too?"

"No, Ole came alone. He said Rebecka had a bad cold and needed to stay home."

"How did you react to that?"

"I didn't give it much thought."

Hanna clasps her hands in her lap and takes over.

"What was the relationship between your daughter and her husband like?"

"Ole is a good person and an excellent pastor. He is highly valued within the church and puts a great deal of effort into spreading God's word. His sermons are very popular among our members."

Stefan has chosen to praise Ole rather than answering the question. Hanna tries to suppress her irritation. "Would you say that Ole and Rebecka are happy together?"

Ann-Sofie leaps up and fetches the coffeepot.

"Our daughter was lucky to marry such a fine man," Stefan says firmly.

Personally, Hanna doubts that very much, but the pride in Stefan's voice is genuine and unmistakable. There is no doubt about whose side he is on.

"Ole will eventually succeed Jan-Peter Jonsäter, our current leader."

Rebecka's father doesn't seem to have a clue about how serious her situation might be. Or he doesn't want to know. Hanna looks at Ann-Sofie, who is fully focused on refilling her husband's cup. So far, she hasn't said a word about Ole and Rebecka's relationship.

Might as well take the bull by the horns. Hanna tries to catch Daniel's eye to make sure that he is on board, but without success. She decides to go for it anyway.

"We have reason to believe that your daughter has been subjected to domestic violence. Are you aware of this?"

Stefan has just reached out to pick up his coffee cup, but he allows his hand to drop. He looks incredulous.

"What has she done?"

His assumption that Rebecka is the cause of any violence infuriates Hanna. Why is the woman always blamed in circumstances like this? The injustice fills her mouth with a bitter taste.

"Are you saying that a woman must have *done* something to provoke domestic abuse?"

She is fully aware that she is skewing his response, but still allows herself the sharp retort.

"You are misinterpreting my words," Stefan says.

"In that case perhaps you would like to explain how your comment should be interpreted."

Daniel clears his throat—a discreet but definite signal that she needs to back off.

"Are you aware of any violent incidents within your daughter's marriage?" he says before Hanna can open her mouth again.

"I can't imagine such a thing." Stefan's tone brooks no contradiction. "As I said, Ole is one of our pastors. He is deeply committed to the church and is a much-loved member of our community."

As if that would stop him from beating his wife in the privacy of his own home. Maria Törnlund had seen the bruises on Rebecka's arms. Hanna has to bite her tongue to stop herself from making another sarcastic remark.

"Rebecka has never mentioned any violence on the part of her husband?"

"Absolutely not."

295

Hanna ignores Stefan and turns her attention to Ann-Sofie instead. She is sitting with her hands on her lap, rubbing one thumb with the other. The skin is getting redder and redder, but she doesn't stop.

"How about you, Ann-Sofie?" Hanna deliberately uses her name in order to force her to speak. "You're her mother—hasn't Rebecka told you about the way things are at home?"

It's a leading question, but that can't be helped. Not when Stefan is so domineering.

Ann-Sofie looks away. Hanna could swear that she is fighting back tears.

"We've never discussed it," Ann-Sofie says with a pleading look at her husband. "Rebecka has always been happy with Ole. Hasn't she?"

"I'm not listening to this nonsense any longer," Stefan says. He is about to stand up when Hanna throws a new question at him.

"What is the church's view on divorce?"

Stefan's expression is blank, as if he doesn't understand what she means.

"Is it possible to divorce and remain a member of the Light of Life?" Hanna clarifies. "Or would those concerned have to leave?"

For the first time, Rebecka's father gives a faint smile.

"'What God has joined, let no man put asunder.' Matthew nineteen, verse six. It's not a matter of the church's view. Jesus has already spoken on the matter."

Daniel steps in again.

"Do you know if your daughter had a relationship with a man called Johan Andersson?"

Ann-Sofie inhales audibly. Hanna waits for Stefan's reaction. Daniel has asked a risky question; if the parents tell their son-in-law, Rebecka's safety could be jeopardized.

"I can't imagine that," Stefan snaps. "Our daughter is a decent woman." He pushes away his coffee cup with ill-concealed irritation. The unused spoon clinks against the saucer. "Who is this man anyway?"

"Johan Andersson was a well-known skier from Duved," Daniel explains. "When his career ended, he became a plumber and carried out several jobs at the preschool in Ånn where your daughter works. We have reason to believe that they knew each other well. Unfortunately, Johan was found murdered last Saturday in Tängböle—you might have read about the case?"

"Murdered . . . ?" Ann-Sofie grips the edge of the table so hard that the thin skin covering her knuckles turns white, the blue veins crisscrossing the tensed sinews like snakes.

"Our daughter would never be involved in such a thing!" Stefan is outraged.

"Is Rebecka in danger?" Ann-Sofie whispers.

"She is under God's protection," her husband informs her. "Nothing is going to happen to her."

The way Stefan dismisses his wife's concerns suggests that this isn't the first time. Ann-Sofie doesn't protest; she simply slumps a little lower on her chair. Hanna is tired of this. She has to get something out of this conversation that might help them find Rebecka.

Time is short, she can feel it in her bones.

She looks at Ann-Sofie again, wonders if she can get a few moments alone with her.

"Could I possibly use your bathroom?" she says.

"Of course."

"Can you show me where it is?"

Hanna gets to her feet, leaving Ann-Sofie no choice but to do the same thing. Rebecka's mother leads the way out of the kitchen and points to a door in the hallway. Hanna hesitates; she needs Ann-Sofie to move farther away from the kitchen so that Stefan won't overhear their discussion.

Ann-Sofie edges closer.

"We really do need to contact Rebecka," Hanna says quietly.

"Do you think Ole has hurt her?" Ann-Sofie's words are barely audible.

At last.

"That's what we suspect—our priority is to find them. If you know where Ole and Rebecka might be, then you have to tell me. For Rebecka's sake."

Ann-Sofie glances around, making sure that she can't be overheard.

"Speak to Pastor Jonsäter. If anyone knows where Ole is, it's him."

59

As soon as Daniel gets in the car, Hanna starts telling him about her conversation in the hallway.

"She said we ought to speak to Pastor Jonsäter," she says, fastening her seat belt. "The question is, where do we find him?"

She googles his name as Daniel backs the car around and drives away. From the corner of his eye, he sees Ann-Sofie watching from the kitchen window, her arms wrapped tightly around her body. There is no sign of her husband. Stefan Ekvall couldn't get rid of them fast enough.

Daniel groans to himself. He is very pleased that Hanna managed to get something out of the mother, but she was noticeably sharp with Rebecka's father, creating friction and putting him on the defensive.

They have reached the junction with the E14. Daniel stops to allow a truck with a trailer and Norwegian license plates to pass.

Hanna clears her throat, as if she has read his mind.

"Sorry if I went in a bit too hard back there. I just got so frustrated when that arrogant bastard refused to acknowledge the seriousness of the situation." She exhales loudly through her nose. "Rebecka 'is under God's protection,'" she intones, producing a surprisingly good imitation of Stefan Ekvall's voice and pronunciation. She even manages to frown in exactly the same way.

Daniel can't help smiling.

"As if that's any use," Hanna says in her normal voice. "I don't understand how he can fool himself. No one has seen or spoken to

Rebecka since Friday afternoon. It's Wednesday now, which means she's been missing for five days."

She slams her clenched fist on the seat. Her frustration is obvious, but it is hiding something else: a deep concern for a vulnerable woman. Right now, Rebecka's well-being takes precedence over everything else in Hanna's mind.

Daniel knows how easy it is to be completely swallowed up by a case; the same thing has happened to him. She shouldn't really let herself become involved on such a personal level, but then that's why she's a good cop. Hanna cares.

"If my daughter was missing, I wouldn't sit there rattling off prayers!"

Me neither, Daniel thinks. He sees Alice's chubby little face in his mind's eye. Her blue, blue eyes. An intense longing comes over him. He wants to shut out the world and hold her. He promises himself that he will leave on time today. He will give Alice her bath and put her to bed, rather than spending all evening at the station caught up in endless police work.

"So, what are we going to do about Pastor Jonsäter?" he says.

Hanna holds up her phone.

"Found him. Jan-Peter Jonsäter, married to Karin. They live in Handöl—I should have guessed. The movement was founded in Snasadalen, and that's where the church and the community center are."

Daniel looks out the window. In the distance he can just see the impressive mountain known as Snasahögarna. It lies to the south, a wide mountain range consisting of four peaks, on the other side of the lake from Åreskutan. Storsnasen, the highest point, measures forty-eight hundred feet above sea level.

Snasadalen lies at the foot of the mountain. That's where the Light of Life was founded in the thirties by a few dozen devout families.

He begins to drive eastward, toward Enafors and Handöl. According to Rebecka's mother, Pastor Jonsäter is the person who should know where Ole is.

For Rebecka's sake, Daniel hopes that is true.

He agrees with Hanna; this is beginning to feel urgent.

60

An elegant avenue of tall, downy birch trees leads to Jan-Peter and Karin Jonsäter's home in Handöl. The mustard-yellow wooden house is adorned with beautiful carved features and paned windows with neat white lace curtains.

Hanna looks up. Smoke is rising from one of the chimneys, which means someone should be in. Daniel catches up with her by the front door, which forms part of a glass veranda. He places a hand on her shoulder.

"Take it easy this time, okay?"

He doesn't need to say any more; Hanna nods immediately.

"Don't worry."

She has no intention of allowing the pastor's views to get under her skin. She is prepared.

They knock, and the door is opened by a strikingly stylish woman in her sixties. She is wearing a pleated skirt and a lamb's wool sweater, and her silver-white hair is tied back in a low ponytail. This must be Karin.

"We'd like to speak to Pastor Jonsäter," Daniel says, showing his police ID.

"Come in. My husband is in his study."

A large black dog is lying on the kitchen floor. It looks like the one that chased Hanna the previous evening. It half rises and growls threateningly; she finds it hard to suppress a shudder.

Karin shows them into a study with dark wooden paneling and a broad desk in the English style. A tall man wearing glasses and a tweed jacket is sitting behind the desk. He looks up when they appear in the doorway.

"Two police officers to see you," Karin informs him before turning to Hanna and Daniel. "Can I get you a coffee? Or a glass of ice water?"

"I'm good, thanks," Daniel says, and Hanna murmurs her agreement.

Karin leaves the room, closing the door carefully behind her.

Pastor Jonsäter puts down his pen, an elegant model in black with two gold bands around the shaft. It looks as expensive as the rest of the decor. After the visit to the Nordhammars' house and the farm where Rebecka's parents live, Hanna hadn't expected such a well-appointed home. It's more like a lavish summer villa in the Stockholm area than a permanent residence way up north in Jämtland.

A stately Mora clock decorated with folk art details is ticking away in the corner. The hands are showing eleven thirty.

"What can I do for you?" the pastor asks politely, but without the curiosity the situation ought to evoke.

"We're trying to contact Ole and Rebecka Nordhammar," Daniel explains. "We're wondering if you might know where they are."

Jonsäter rests his elbows on the desk as he considers the question. "Why do you want to speak to Ole and Rebecka?"

His voice is deep and reassuring, with the authoritative note that comes from many years of leadership. Hanna has no difficulty imagining him in the pulpit. The steel-gray hair is still thick, and he radiates power and confidence. She feels as if they have been granted an audience, even though they've come here on police business.

"We're in the middle of an ongoing homicide inquiry, and we need to ask Ole and Rebecka a few questions. We've been trying to get a hold of them for several days, but we haven't managed to reach them. Their house appears to be empty."

Daniel adds that the case they are working on is the murder of Johan Andersson, but he doesn't mention any possible connection between Rebecka and Johan.

Hanna thinks that's very wise. She's not sure that kind of information would go down well with the man in front of them.

"Sounds serious," Jonsäter says. "I'd like to help, but I haven't spoken to Ole since Sunday, when we saw each other in church."

He turns the pages of a diary on the desk; it seems to be full of meetings and appointments. "Have you tried his cell phone?" he suggests in a pleasant tone of voice.

"We have," Hanna says in an equally pleasant tone. "We've called both Ole and Rebecka repeatedly, without success."

"Let me think." Jonsäter rubs his forehead. "Ole came to church alone on Sunday. I think he said Rebecka was sick—a bad cold, maybe?" He takes off his glasses, weighs them in one hand. "Perhaps they were out on a short errand when you stopped by? You should try again."

Hanna can feel her patience disappearing fast.

"I don't think you understand the seriousness of the situation," she says, making a huge effort to remain calm. "Rebecka hasn't been seen since Friday. No one has had any contact with her for five days. We have reason to believe that she might be in danger, and the fact that we can't get a hold of her husband either is very worrying."

Jonsäter has his back to a bookcase that covers the entire wall—row upon row of thick theology tomes. The titles reveal the contents; many are in English.

Hanna wonders if he believes he has a direct connection with God. Presumably that's what it means to be a pastor in the Light of Life.

"I'm very sorry," Jonsäter says, shaking his head. "Unfortunately, I don't know how I can help you."

REBECKA

2020

MONDAY, FEBRUARY 24

Rebecka's hands are aching after spending several hours trying to pick the lock. Her skin is red where the crochet hook dug in; her knees are aching from the uncomfortable position she was in. Now she is lying on the bed, resigned to failure.

She has tried and tried without success, turning and twisting the hook in every way imaginable.

Nothing worked, and now dusk is falling outside. The light in the little room is fading. The day is coming to an end. Soon she will be alone in the darkness once more.

Ole could come back at any moment.

She rolls over onto her side and feels her belly protruding, as if the little one inside is reminding her not to give up.

But what can she do? The doctor she saw the last time she visited the health center was worried. He was going to contact her this week about her test results; her blood pressure didn't look good. He specifically told her to avoid stress.

And now she is lying here, imprisoned by her own husband.

Fresh tears fill her eyes. Rebecka curls up on the lumpy mattress and tries to keep up her spirits. Surely Maria will be wondering where she is. Johan too—he knows how scared of Ole she is. But it's no good, the black thoughts come creeping in. She and her baby are going to die here.

What's the point of even attempting to escape?

She is thirsty and reaches for the water bottle, but after a few sips she stops herself and puts it back on the nightstand. This might be the only thing she has to drink for a long time. What if Ole doesn't bring more?

She pushes her hands between her thighs. He couldn't bring himself to kill her when he found out about the pregnancy—but maybe he's prepared to let her die of hunger and thirst instead?

But if that were the case, why had he left the bag of food and water?

Her inner voice has an answer to that too.

Because then Ole wouldn't be directly responsible. That might have been his final Christian act before leaving her to the forces of nature. His conscience is clear. He cannot be held to account for what happens when the food and water run out.

Rebecka does her best to fight the growing sense of hopelessness, but she is so tired that she can't think straight. She sinks back onto the pillow and closes her eyes. Time passes. When she opens her eyes again, it is dark.

The world is a black wall outside the window.

She closes her eyes once more, tries to imagine that everything is warm and welcoming, with soft lights glowing. She is with Johan, in his arms. She recalls the little borrowed cabin, the fire crackling cheerfully as they lay in bed together, the beautiful dancing orange-yellow flames.

It doesn't work.

With a sigh of disappointment, she curls up on her side again. When her weight shifts onto her injured hip, a stab of pain shoots through her body. It hurts so much that she doubles over.

The tears begin to flow again, even though she knows that crying doesn't help. She has already done enough crying.

The walls creak, a desolate noise that heightens her feeling of vulnerability and isolation.

She clasps her hands in prayer, as she has done so many times in her life. Her lips form the familiar words:

"'Our father, who art in heaven . . .'"

She wants to believe that the Lord will help her, but in her heart she is beginning to grasp the truth.

She is not worth helping. She has lied and betrayed and sinned. Offended against both her husband and God.

She deserves to die here in the darkness.

61

Anton is in his office, reading through Carina's preliminary report on the van. His desk is full, but all the papers are sorted into neat piles. He doesn't like to be surrounded by mess.

The report contains reams of technical facts. In spite of the tragic circumstances, Carina uses expressive, almost poetic language to describe the examination. She talks about widespread spatter patterns and the silhouette of the deceased in the dried blood on the floor. About how Johan's cheek was pressed against the rubber mat, leaving a unique impression on the grooves.

The team has meticulously searched the van for fingerprints, DNA, and other biological traces, as well as anything else the perpetrator might have left behind, such as clothing fibers or shoe marks.

Carina states that the van was not broken into from the outside; therefore the perpetrator must have had access to the keys. This fits with the hypothesis on how Johan Andersson's murder happened.

A considerable amount of material has been sent to the National Forensic Center in Umeå for further analysis, but Anton notes that Linus's fingerprints are all over the inside of the back of the van. He has definitely been in there at some point.

Of course, that can be explained by the fact that Linus worked with Johan, but Anton still finds it interesting. Once again, it supports their suspicion that Linus is the killer.

He carries on reading. His phone buzzes in his back pocket; he takes it out and sees that he has a text message from Carl.

Can I call you?

His stomach does a little flip. He'd thought it was all over after his clumsy behavior yesterday evening.

He looks around. Daniel and Hanna are still out, trying to track down Ole and Rebecka Nordhammar. Raffe is in his office down the corridor; he seems to be busy on the phone.

Just to be on the safe side, Anton closes his door before replying to the text.

Carl calls right away. "Sorry to disturb you."

"No problem. How are you?"

"Er . . . this isn't . . . about us," Carl says.

Anton didn't know there was an *us*; this cheers him up enormously.

"Sandra Sundin called me a few minutes ago," Carl goes on. "She wondered if I knew where Linus was."

"Oh?"

Carl makes a sound that is somewhere between clearing his throat and a cough. "She sounded worried."

"Why?"

"Apparently he didn't come home last night, and he's not answering his phone."

"You mean he's disappeared?"

"It sounds that way. She's made some calls, but no one has seen him. I told her I'd contact you."

The conversation isn't exactly developing as Anton had expected, and of course he can't tell Carl anything about the investigation, even if he wanted to.

"I thought maybe you'd . . . arrested him without telling Sandra?"

"That's not the way it works," Anton says quickly. "But I can certainly give her a call."

"Thank you."

It's time to hang up, but Anton can't bring himself to say goodbye when he's been given another chance. He spent half the night lying awake, worrying about how he'd treated Carl. He pictures Carl in his mind's eye again, sleeping in the moonlight.

"You mentioned dinner . . ."

"Yes?"

There's a hint of eagerness in Carl's voice, isn't there? Or maybe it's Anton's imagination. He doesn't know whether there is any hope, but he decides to go for broke. He is about to suggest meeting up on Friday when the door of his office flies open.

Raffe is standing there holding his phone.

"We've just had a call from the regional dispatch in Umeå about a death that's connected to our investigation—we need to get over there right away."

Another opportunity lost. Anton sits there as if he has been turned to stone.

Raffe is already on his way. "Are you coming?" he calls over his shoulder.

"I have to go," Anton says much too curtly, and hangs up.

62

It takes half an hour to travel from Handöl to Duved, even though Daniel is driving as fast as he can.

"Take it easy!" Hanna shouts as he performs a risky maneuver to overtake another car on the E14.

Anton passed on the emergency alert from the regional dispatch just as they took their leave of Pastor Jonsäter. A car has crashed into a rock face outside Duved, with fatal consequences. It is not possible to say at the moment whether it was an accident or the vehicle was forced off the road.

It is five past one when they reach the scene, which has already been cordoned off with blue-and-white tape. Several police cars are lined up there, and uniformed officers are redirecting traffic.

Daniel notices several curious teenage boys on the edge of the area. One is filming, holding his phone high in the air and sweeping it from side to side to capture as much as possible.

"Can't someone stop that idiot?" he mutters, hurrying forward with Hanna.

A white van is standing a short distance from the road, with the entire front section crushed against a rock face. The wheels are dirty, the flaps spattered with mud. The passenger door has flown open due to the impact, and blood is visible on the window.

Daniel recognizes the company name on the side. He has a sudden flashback to another white van standing by the side of a road on Sunday. Only three days have passed since then.

Today there is no doubt about what has happened. The van has come off the road and smashed into the rock face.

He takes in the scene, the gray-white cheek resting against the window on the driver's side, the dead man's wide-open eyes.

His head appears to have slammed into the glass. The body is slumped, the chest covered by the airbag.

"What the fuck?" Hanna exclaims. "That's Linus Sundin!"

63

It is three o'clock in the afternoon by the time the team gathers back at the police station to go over the details.

The smell of damp wool and freshly brewed coffee hangs in the air in the conference room. Carina Grankvist has joined them; she is sitting opposite Hanna and going over her notes.

When she notices Hanna looking at her, she gives a weary smile. There are fine lines around her mouth, and her lips are chapped from the cold.

"It's a lot right now," she murmurs.

Hanna reaches for the open packet of Ballerina cookies on the table. There was no time for lunch. Having to shift focus so quickly is tiring, but it can't be helped.

Birgitta Grip appears on the screen; she doesn't bother saying hello. "What's happened? Daniel?"

"We have another death, and it has a bearing on the ongoing homicide investigation." He scratches the back of his neck. "Johan Andersson's business partner, Linus Sundin, was found dead in his van outside Duved a few hours ago. It looks as if only one vehicle was involved, and death appears to have been instantaneous. He drove off a straight section of road and smashed head-on into a rock face."

"Was it definitely an accident?" Grip asks.

The question brings back the macabre scene. Linus's neck was broken. His seat belt, covered in blood, wasn't fastened.

"Any indication that the vehicle was forced off the road?" Grip continues.

"There were scratches in the paint on the left-hand side," Carina says. "At the moment I can't tell you if they were fresh or if they've been there for some time."

"The road was covered in snow, and it's a busy route," Daniel adds. "We didn't find any sign of braking."

"So what are we looking at here?" There is more than a hint of impatience in Grip's voice. "Could it be suicide?"

"It's possible, given the circumstances," Anton says. "Linus's financial difficulties, the investigation into Johan's murder."

He had a wife and a young son, Hanna wants to say. *Does someone take their own life when that's the case?*

Maybe the pressure on Linus Sundin became too much. They had deliberately pushed him hard, hoping for a confession.

Is it their fault that a little boy has lost his daddy?

She helps herself to another cookie. The chocolate paste sticks to her palate, and she spits the last bit into her hand. She grabs a napkin and hides the gooey mess.

"According to our preliminary information, Linus hadn't been seen since yesterday evening," Anton says. "His wife has stated he was gone all night."

"Did he leave a suicide note?" Grip says.

Carina shakes her head. "We didn't find anything in the van."

Most people who take their own lives leave an explanation.

But not all of them.

"Is there any reason to think that a crime has been committed? Do we have anyone who might have wanted to get rid of him?" Grip asks.

Hanna glances at Daniel. They practically shouted from the rooftops that Linus was suspected of murdering Marion's husband.

Could she have decided to take matters into her own hands?

REBECKA

2020

It is snowing, and the food is running out. Rebecka is sitting on the floor with her back against the wall. She has wrapped her arms around her legs and is resting her head on her knees.

According to her wristwatch, it is almost six o'clock. The daylight is fading, so it must be Tuesday evening. That means she has been locked up for three long days.

She turns her face toward the small square window. The view is unchanged, endless rows of birch and fir, snow-covered ground stretching into the distance. Nothing is moving in the deserted landscape where she is a prisoner.

She will never be able to get away from here.

The stench from the bucket reaches her nostrils. It makes her retch and want to throw up, but the acrid ammonia smell overcomes the hopelessness.

Her body feels more alert.

I have to escape.

The thought takes root. Yesterday she was beginning to accept her fate, she had almost convinced herself that she deserved her punishment—and yet there is something deep inside her that refuses to give up.

She owes it to her child to fight.

She glances over at the locked door. She hasn't managed to open it so far, but maybe she should make a fresh attempt? She reaches into the pocket of her jeans, finds the crochet hook. It could still help her.

A few hours ago she was ready to lie down and die. That seemed like the best option, to slip into that final sleep and give herself up to God's mercy.

But no doubt that is exactly what Ole is hoping for. He would like her to make it easy for him so that he doesn't have to get his own hands dirty.

If she disappears, he can build a new life with a new woman. A woman who can bear his children and listen to his pontificating. Admire him just like Rebecka did in the beginning before he showed his true colors.

She holds up the crochet hook, sees the silvery metal glinting in the last of the daylight.

She has been meek and accommodating for almost eight long years. Ole has gotten used to her obeying his slightest whim, and yet he has always been dissatisfied and accused her of being a bad wife. He has humiliated her in the name of God, called her ugly and worthless, impossible to love. Not a real woman.

He has made her believe that it is the Lord who has forced him to beat her, for her own good.

A new resolve is growing within her, pushing against her fear of Ole and giving her the strength to act.

She's not going to do it.

She's not going to die so that Ole can move on and subject another woman to the same abuse in the name of Jesus. The God Rebecka believes in would never allow a man to torture her as Ole has done.

This suffering comes from Ole's twisted psyche—it has nothing to do with the Lord.

She will fight to the last drop of her blood, even if it means he has to strangle her with his bare hands.

She and her child *will* live.

64

The briefing is over, and Daniel and Hanna are still sitting in the conference room.

Anton and Raffe have gone to tell Sandra Sundin what has happened. Hanna is grateful she doesn't have to deliver the news this time. She gazes at the blank screen from which Birgitta Grip chaired the meeting.

The table is littered with empty coffee cups. She still feels slightly sick from the cookies. She probably needs to eat some decent food, but that will have to wait.

"We ought to speak to Marion Andersson," she says. "There's no one else with such a strong motive to want Linus Sundin dead."

"You really think she could be involved in this?" Daniel sounds far from convinced.

"Hard to say, but if we're looking for someone who had a good reason to hate a person suspected of murdering Johan . . . then we can't ignore Marion."

Daniel gazes thoughtfully at his colleague.

"Does she seem like the archetypal female avenger to you?"

"Not exactly, but people do strange things when they're traumatized. Marion's husband was brutally beaten to death only a few days ago. We don't even know if she has a weapon at home."

From Marion's perspective, her entire life has collapsed. She doesn't seem to have been aware that Johan was about to leave her for Rebecka.

She has been hit very hard. On top of that, she is childless; she had only Johan.

"There's a lot to suggest that Linus took his own life," Daniel says. "The place where he came off the road is lined with rock faces. It's an easy way to kill yourself if you're feeling suicidal."

"True, but isn't it slightly too neat a solution to this story? On Saturday Johan was found murdered. Only five days later, the person who had the clearest motive kills himself."

Daniel rubs his eyes. "You're probably right. We should go and see Marion. If nothing else, she deserves to hear about Linus's death from us rather than reading it online or in the papers."

He takes out his phone. "I'll just text Ida. She'll be furious when I tell her I won't be home on time tonight either."

As he begins to type a message, Hanna's phone buzzes. A text from an unknown number. She reads it with mounting surprise.

She turns the screen to show Daniel. "Look what Maria Törnlund has written. She's had a text from Rebecka saying that everything is fine, and she'll be back at work soon."

"Excellent." Daniel pushes back his chair. "Shall we go and see Marion Andersson now so that it doesn't get too late?"

Hanna is trying to digest this new information. They still need to speak to Rebecka, investigate her role in what happened to Johan, but that can wait a few hours. Right now, other matters are more urgent.

This doesn't mean that Hanna has any intention of dropping the issue of Rebecka's situation at home, but if it turns out that Linus Sundin really did commit suicide, and that he is guilty of Johan's murder, then Ole Nordhammar is no longer a suspect.

They still have to complete the homicide investigation, but there is less urgency now. The important thing will be to clarify the course of events so that the prosecutor can establish that the perpetrator is dead and cannot be charged.

Daniel has gone to fetch his jacket. "Are you coming?" he calls out from the corridor.

Hanna puts away her phone. The main thing is that Rebecka is okay.

65

"Shall we pick up something to eat on the way?" Hanna suggests.

They are about to set off for Marion Andersson's house. How many miles have they covered today? Far too many; her back is already complaining. Her former colleagues in Stockholm wouldn't be able to get their heads around the distances up here.

"Good idea. Where do you think will be the quickest, given the number of tourists?"

"It'll probably be just as bad wherever we go."

Hanna would have liked to stop for a megaburger at Broken, but it would take an hour to drive into the village, find a parking space, then stand in line to order.

"How about a hot dog and a Coke from the kiosk by the VM6 chair lift?"

"Okay."

They devour the food, sitting in the car. When Hanna takes the first bite, she realizes how hungry she is. She eats way too fast and gets stomach cramps. It's better than the cookie-induced nausea, but her stomach feels unpleasantly bloated. The fizzy soda doesn't help.

As soon as they've finished, Daniel starts the car and heads for Duved.

Hanna glances over at the lake, where two Ski-Doo riders are whizzing across the ice, following a parallel course toward Duved. She likes driving snowmobiles but prefers to be on a mountain or in the forest. She was only thirteen when she tried it for the first time—much too young according to the law, but she was immediately hooked.

It was her father who took her out, one of the few precious times they spent together without her mother. Lydia and Richard have an Arctic Cat that she borrows when she wants to get away for a few hours. There are plenty of lovely and inviting snowmobile trails around Åre.

All at once she longs for a day off, far away from police investigations and abused women. A few hours surrounded by nature, all on her own.

It is a special feeling, driving in thick snow among the trees. The challenge of guiding the machine around a big tree trunk without tipping over or getting stuck. And then the burst of light when you emerge from the forest onto a marsh or a frozen lake, with the endless blue sky up above.

She loves to stop and have a cup of coffee on the mountain, to feel the peace when everything falls silent and there isn't a soul in sight.

"Are you falling asleep?" Daniel turns down the heat.

"No."

Hanna stretches to give herself fresh energy. Her thoughts return to Rebecka, as they have done so often over the past few days. She is still wondering about the message from Maria.

"Don't you think it's strange that Rebecka contacted her colleague, just like that?"

"She's probably been away and hasn't checked her phone." Daniel grabs a paper napkin and wipes his mouth; a small amount of ketchup has gotten stuck next to his beard. "I'm guessing she wasn't sick at all; then she got cold feet when you started calling."

"So why didn't she call me instead of texting Maria?"

"Are you sure that all citizens enjoy talking to the police?"

Hanna chooses to ignore the gentle sarcasm. "I must have left a dozen messages on her voicemail."

"Exactly. You frightened the life out of her."

Hanna can't let it go. Something doesn't feel right.

"Do you honestly think she's gone away with her husband? If that is the case, how do we explain her involvement in Johan's life?" She gathers up the rubbish and puts it in the paper bag the food came in. "If Rebecka wasn't the mysterious person he was taking to Strömsund, then who was it?"

Daniel takes some time to consider the question. "She could still have been intending to leave with Johan on Saturday night," he says eventually. "When she found out he was dead, obviously the plan fell through. It doesn't have to be any more complicated than that."

Hanna thinks back—when did they release Johan's name? Could Rebecka have known that he was dead on Saturday? The information had definitely been released to the public by Sunday evening; the press conference had already taken place, and Johan's death was all over the news.

"Am I overreacting?"

"Not at all. I just mean there could be a perfectly reasonable explanation for why she's kept a low profile."

Hanna tries to see it from Rebecka's perspective. If she'd decided to run away with Johan on Saturday and he didn't show up, then she would have found herself in a very difficult situation. If she then heard the tragic news on Sunday, she must have been devastated.

Maybe it's not so strange that she couldn't face going to work.

Or that she didn't feel like talking to the police.

If her lover was dead, she would hardly want to be dragged into a homicide investigation, running the risk of her husband finding out the truth.

That would bring a new personal disaster.

"I'm sure you're right," she says, settling back in her seat. "Let's not look for complications."

66

The sound of a car pulling onto the drive makes Marion look out the window. She immediately recognizes the two police officers; they're the same ones who came to tell her about Johan.

The grief hits her like a hammer blow.

Will it never end?

She hurries into the bathroom to splash her face with cold water. She hardly got any sleep last night. Florian arrived yesterday evening, and they sat up talking until long after midnight. She woke at dawn and couldn't get back to sleep.

"Sorry to bother you," the officer called Daniel says. "Could we have a little chat?"

Marion shows them into the living room.

"How are you?" the female officer asks. Hanna? Just like last time she has her hair in a ponytail, but today there are loose strands around her face.

Marion hesitates. She doesn't want to tell them about her inconsolable weeping night after night, about the tears that keep on coming.

"Not too bad," she says instead.

"We're here to inform you that your husband's business partner, Linus Sundin, has been found dead in Duved," Daniel says.

Marion's hand flies to her mouth. She can't hide her reaction, not after everything that's happened.

"Linus?"

Hanna's expression is sympathetic. "It seems as if he died early this morning."

He deserved to die after all the trouble he caused. Marion can't pretend she's sorry; she just wishes that Johan were still here.

Her beloved Johan.

The kitchen clock ticks behind her like a perpetual motion machine.

"How did he die?" she asks through stiff lips.

"His car crashed into a rock face. We believe his death was instantaneous."

A sound makes Marion look up; Florian is standing in the doorway. He had gone for an afternoon nap in the guest room, but their voices must have woken him. He still looks half-asleep, his dark hair pressed flat to his scalp on one side.

"This is my older brother, who arrived yesterday evening," Marion says quickly. She turns to Florian and explains in German, "They're from the police, about Linus. He's dead."

Florian frowns, then holds out his hand and greets them in English.

"Wir können gerne Deutsch sprechen," Hanna says. *"Wenn das besser ist?"*

The fact that she can speak fluent German takes Marion by surprise. Her pronunciation is perfect. It's fortunate that this came out before Marion said anything else to Florian in their mother tongue.

"You speak German?"

"I worked in Berlin for a while," Hanna replies with a dismissive gesture. "A long time ago."

Florian assures her that English is fine.

"You're very much alike," Hanna says. "There's a strong family resemblance."

Marion is used to hearing this. She and Florian have the same-shaped face, with strong eyebrows and a firm chin. Her coloring is paler, but otherwise there isn't much to separate them.

She is so relieved to have him here. It's nice not to be alone in the house.

"There are only seventeen months between us," she explains. "It's known as pseudotwins."

"Should I leave you alone?" Florian wonders.

Daniel gestures to one of the armchairs. "You're welcome to join us."

"Do you often come to visit?" Hanna asks.

"A couple of times a year," Marion answers on his behalf. She almost wishes that he hadn't appeared—now the police know he's in the country. She's told them everything she can, she doesn't want her brother dragged into her terrible life.

Florian tries to catch her eye, but she avoids looking at him. She just wants the police to leave.

Hanna turns to Florian.

"Did you know Linus Sundin, Johan's business partner?"

"We met a few times when I was visiting my sister."

"I see. We're here because he died in a traffic accident earlier today."

"I'm sorry to hear that." Florian pulls down his dark-green fleece top, which has ridden up a little.

"We need to ask you where you've been for the last twelve hours, Marion."

"Me?"

Marion's stomach contracts. Do they suspect her of some involvement in Linus's death? If she closes her eyes, she can see his face when he forced his way into the house the other night. The red-rimmed eyes, the raised fists.

"I've been here ever since we got back from the airport in Östersund."

Her mouth feels weird, it's hard to speak normally.

"When was that?"

Marion's mind goes blank. She can't remember, everything is a blur.

"My plane landed shortly after eight. We came straight here and arrived shortly before ten," Florian clarifies.

"And what did you do then?"

Marion is incapable of speech. Florian will have to supply the details.

"We had something to eat; then we sat up talking half the night."

"And what have you done today?"

"Nothing, we just decided to take it easy." Florian places his hand on Marion's, as if to give her strength. His voice is perfectly calm. "We haven't left the house. Why do you ask?"

The two officers exchange a glance; then Hanna nods, as if she is happy with Florian's answers. Does that mean they will be going soon?

Marion doesn't know how long she can sit here; she can't cope with any more questions. She feels as if she is about to faint. Everything seems to be receding; she is finding it hard to hold it together. She closes her eyes, hopes they will leave her in peace.

"On another matter entirely," Daniel says. "Are there any guns in the house?"

The unexpected question makes Marion open her eyes. But she has nothing to hide; Johan had both a hunting license and a gun license, all the paperwork is in order. Sometimes Florian would join him on the annual moose hunt.

And Linus, although he couldn't even stay sober then.

According to Johan, the hunting club had threatened to throw him out if he didn't pull himself together. A drunken hunter is a danger to everyone present.

"Johan used to hunt. He owned several rifles."

"How about you?"

Marion shakes her head. "No."

"Where are the rifles now?"

"In the gun cupboard. Johan always kept them locked away."

He was careful to follow the rules; it was part of his nature. Marion tries to hold back a sob, but without success. Florian squeezes her hand.

"Could you show us Johan's guns?"

Marion fetches the keys and leads the way to the storeroom, where the tall, pale-gray gun cupboard is located. It is made of steel and is bolted to the floor.

Daniel and Hanna wait while she unlocks the door.

There are three rifles and several boxes of ammunition.

"You know you have to hand them in now that your husband is dead?" Hanna says.

"Feel free to take them with you." Somehow Marion manages to force the words out. She can barely stand up, everything is spinning.

Daniel holds up his hand. "We don't need to worry about that now. There are forms to fill in." He looks at Florian. "The two of you can bring the guns into the station later in the week."

A wave of exhaustion washes over Hanna as they leave Marion Andersson's house. The sun has gone down, and the sky in the west is covered with dark clouds. The forecast on the radio has just issued a warning about a storm approaching from Norway.

Daniel is driving. "So, what did you think?"

Hanna considers her answer. Marion had sat there stupefied when they told her about the accident. It seemed as if Linus's death was a real surprise; her face lost all its color.

"She sounded very shocked at the news." Both Marion and the German brother. Who popped up out of nowhere. "Don't you think it's a bit strange that her brother turned up, just like that?"

Daniel shrugs. "Her parents are dead and her husband was murdered this weekend. Wouldn't you want your only sibling to come over to Sweden?"

"I suppose so."

"By the way, there are no scrape marks on Marion's Volkswagen. I checked before we left."

They will have to wait for the forensic examination of Linus's van. Maybe it was just an accident on a treacherous road surface. Or a drastic measure for Linus to solve his problems. He was a man in crisis, in many ways.

Hanna rests her weary head on the window; the glass is cool against her skin. She closes her eyes, and when she opens them again, they are passing the recycling center in Staa. The barred gates flash by. Someone couldn't be bothered to take their trash inside and has simply dumped the bags outside the gray steel fencing.

Why do these places always have to look so depressing?

She automatically takes out her phone and checks her messages. Nothing new; the top of the list is still the text from Maria, sent a few hours ago. Hanna reads it again.

> Rebecka has been in touch. She says she's fine and will be back at work soon. PS: Just wanted you to know.

On an impulse Hanna allows her thumb to touch the number and call Maria.

When she answers, Hanna thanks her for the message. "Actually, I was wondering if you could forward Rebecka's original message so that I can see exactly what she wrote."

"No problem—I should have thought of that myself. I was just so relieved to hear from her that I contacted you right away. Hang on a minute."

Hanna's phone pings, and she reads the words carefully while Maria is still on the line.

> Hi Maria, excuse the radio silence. I'm feeling much better but have had to go away for a few days. I'll be back at work soon. Best wishes, Rebecka.

It looks perfectly normal.

"Oh, there was a PS too," Maria says. "I'll send it over."

The new message arrives in seconds, and Hanna opens it up.

> PS: Am using Ole's phone because I've lost mine.

"She didn't send it from her usual number?" Hanna wants to be absolutely certain that she hasn't misunderstood.

"No, it seems she used her husband's phone—but I don't have his number, so I can't swear to that."

Hanna has Ole Nordhammar's number in her notebook. She flicks through the pages—it's a match. Rebecka's message was sent from his phone. If Rebecka has lost hers, then that explains why she hasn't responded to Hanna's efforts to contact her.

It still doesn't feel right.

Was it really Rebecka who wrote the message? It's hard not to speculate. And even if her phone is missing, Ole's is clearly working— so why didn't he answer when Hanna called? She's left him several voicemails too.

"Maria, can I ask you something? Does this message sound like Rebecka?"

"You mean . . . she might not have written it?"

"I don't know," Hanna says honestly. "That's why I'm asking."

Maria hesitates. When Daniel changes gear, Hanna becomes aware of the engine's low hum.

"I assumed it was from her," Maria says in a subdued voice.

"Could you take another look?"

Hanna waits as Maria rereads the message, murmuring the words to herself.

"That last bit, right at the end . . ." Fear colors Maria's tone. "Where it says 'Best wishes, Rebecka.' It sounds kind of stiff and formal, not like her. She usually ends with 'love Rebecka.'"

Hanna needs something to compare it with.

"Have you saved any old messages?"

"I'm sure I have. Wait a minute . . . I've got three. She's signed off each one with 'love Rebecka.'"

"That's very helpful. Thank you."

Hanna ends the call. Her tiredness has gone, replaced by a surge of adrenaline. It seems more than likely that Ole has faked the text from his wife. Why would he do that unless something was wrong?

Hanna's suspicions are back in full force.

Daniel has heard the whole conversation. "It sounds as if Rebecka is still in danger," he says grimly.

Hanna is thinking along the same lines. They have talked about Marion and about Linus's accident, but now they must focus on Rebecka again. Linus is already dead, but hopefully she is still alive.

"I think we need to put out a call for both of them," she says. "This can't wait."

A sense of impending doom is growing within her. Five days have passed since Rebecka was seen. Anything can have happened during that time. Fear stabs through her body. They need to get a hold of Rebecka's husband. He can't have gone up in smoke; it must be possible to find him.

"We should put a trace on Ole Nordhammar's phone," she says. "See if we can pinpoint his location."

It is dark now, the landscape blending into shades of black and gray. The wind has already picked up ahead of the incoming storm.

"Good idea. Contact Anton and see if he can run it immediately. Ask him to put out the call as well."

Hanna sends a quick text to Anton.

"What do you think about going back to see Pastor Jonsäter again?" she says.

"Jonsäter?"

"Someone must have told Ole that we're trying to track down Rebecka—otherwise why would he have bothered to send a message in her name? The only people who know we're looking for them, apart from Maria Törnlund, are Rebecka's parents and Jan-Peter Jonsäter."

"If that's the case, then Jonsäter must know where he is," Daniel agrees. "Or at least they must be in touch."

Hanna takes a deep breath. "This could be our only chance to get a hold of Ole before it's too late."

She can see her own anxiety reflected in Daniel's eyes.

"Let's do it," he says, turning the steering wheel with one powerful movement.

68

Alice has finally fallen asleep in her stroller, and Ida sinks down on the sofa in the living room.

She wants to be a good mom, but never having any time to herself is driving her crazy. The days blur into one another; the apartment is a complete mess. Sometimes she could scream when Alice whines for attention, although of course she adores her daughter.

All she longs for is a few hours alone. She is desperate to head out onto the slopes, the way she used to do back in the day. Fly downhill until she's breathless with the wind in her face. She used to stay on her skis until the lifts closed, never too tired for one last run. Now she stares at the wall. She doesn't even have the energy to clean up or take a shower when Alice is asleep. She was exhausted after yesterday's brief outing, and Daniel has barely been around since Saturday. He leaves for work before she wakes up and comes home after she's fallen asleep.

If he really loved her, surely he would want to be with her instead of working nonstop?

What if . . . What if he doesn't love her anymore?

She can't bear the thought of losing him.

Ida gets up and goes into the hallway. She examines her reflection in the mirror, which depresses her even more. Her face is sallow, exhausted. Her hair needs washing.

At the same time, she hates her own constant complaining. She doesn't recognize herself; she doesn't normally sound like this, especially when her partner is struggling with a serious crime investigation.

And on top of everything else, Tove saw Daniel having lunch with an attractive brown-haired girl. Judging by the description, Ida thinks it must have been Hanna, his new colleague.

Her stomach contracts at the thought that he would rather spend time with her than with Ida.

The phone rings; it's her mother, Elisabeth. Ida starts crying the second she answers. Suddenly she feels totally inadequate, both as a mother and a partner.

"Sweetheart, whatever's wrong?"

Ida goes into the kitchen and closes the door so that she won't disturb Alice.

"I'm so tired," she sobs. "Looking after Alice is too much. I can't do this."

"Where's Daniel?"

"He's at work. He's never home!"

"Men don't understand what it's like to look after a tiny baby. They never have. It's always the mother who bears the brunt."

"I can't do this anymore," Ida weeps.

"There, there," her mother tries to console her. "It'll get better. Alice is still so little. You must tell Daniel that he needs to be around more, face up to his responsibility as a father."

Ida has already tried that. It ended with a huge outburst of rage on his part; she doesn't dare confront him again. She wishes she could be a little girl again, hide in her mommy's arms. Ditch the responsibility.

Rewind the tape.

Every scrap of frustration that has built up inside her comes pouring out. She can't stop moaning about Daniel and how much he is away from home. She tells Elisabeth how frightened she is that something will happen to him at work. Finally, she confesses to the jealousy that hit her when Tove mentioned that she'd seen Daniel at Werséns with Hanna, the fantastic colleague whose praises he is forever singing.

Her mother listens, makes sympathetic noises while Ida unburdens herself.

"Listen to me," Elisabeth says when Ida has run out of steam. "You can't go on like this. You need to put your foot down, make Daniel understand that you're serious."

69

The mighty peaks known as Snasahögarna are concealed by darkness when Daniel heads for Handöl and Pastor Jonsäter's house for the second time today.

Hanna has just tried Ole again—still no answer.

The headlights illuminate the white road ahead. There are no streetlamps; it is impossible to see anything beyond the beam, which provides visibility only a few yards at a time.

Daniel is driving as fast as he dares.

Hanna's phone rings as they are passing Oppdalsvallen. From her responses he realizes it must be Maria again. It's not long since they spoke—what's happened now? Hanna asks a couple of questions before hanging up.

"You heard who that was?"

"I did."

"A doctor from the health center in Åre has been trying to contact Rebecka. She gave the Little Snowdrops number instead of her cell phone. The doctor had called several times, and now he's left a message on the school's answering machine, saying that she needs to call him as soon as possible."

"That means it must be urgent," Daniel says. "But why wouldn't Rebecka have given her own number?" He drums his fingers on the steering wheel, well aware that things could turn out to be even worse if Rebecka is suffering from a serious illness. "We need to speak to the doctor."

Hanna glances at her watch.

"The center is open till seven, isn't it? It's only ten to—maybe I can get a hold of him now."

She makes the call, waits while she is put through to the right person. Daniel listens as she tries to convince the doctor that the urgency of Rebecka's situation overrides patient confidentiality. He doesn't seem to agree, but Hanna refuses to give in, and eventually she prevails.

"How far along did you say she was?"

Daniel begins to understand what this is about. They're not just looking for a vulnerable woman; it's much worse than that.

Rebecka is pregnant.

He remembers the ultrasound image of Alice in Ida's womb, the overwhelming realization that there was a tiny baby in there. For the first time the pregnancy felt real, and all his protective instincts kicked in.

Rebecka's child must also be protected.

"How dangerous is it?" Hanna asks. After a few more questions, she ends the call.

"Rebecka is in the fourth month. Her doctor is worried about some of her test results; she needs to see a specialist as soon as possible. Her blood pressure is way too high."

That doesn't sound good.

"One more thing. Apparently, Rebecka refused to say who the father was. She insisted that all contact had to go through her."

The implications are clear to both of them.

"Do you think she could be pregnant by Johan?"

Hanna nods, her expression grim.

"God help Rebecka if her husband has found out."

REBECKA

2020

WEDNESDAY, FEBRUARY 26

When morning breaks on the fifth day, Rebecka can barely move her fingers after all her efforts to pick the lock.

She has almost run out of water. She is desperately thirsty but dares not drink more than a few sips. She has already eaten the sausage and bread that was in the bag. The lack of food and drink is making her weak; her strength is almost gone. She can't bear to think about how this is affecting the little life in her belly.

Nor about the doctor's exhortation to avoid stress and stay calm.

The revolting stench from the bucket in the corner is mixed with the odor from her own body. If only she could have a shower, or at least brush her teeth. There is a horrible coating on her tongue, and she has been wearing the same clothes for five days.

A gust of wind rattles the windowpanes and howls around the house. Snow has begun to fall with big, hopeless flakes covering the desolate wilderness where she is a prisoner.

If it blows up into a storm, she will never be able to get away, even if she manages to escape from the house.

Somewhere deep inside she still hopes that Ole will come back and take pity on her, but that hardly seems likely after such a long time.

She wonders where he is right now. Presumably he has gone home to Enafors. Maybe he is having breakfast among all the ugly furniture he likes so much. Or maybe he is preaching to an admiring congregation. They listen to every word he utters and shout, "Amen," on his command. In their eyes Ole can do no wrong. They would never believe the truth about their revered pastor.

He has probably suppressed the knowledge that he has left her here. Ole is good at that, creating his own version of reality. Anything he doesn't like—weaknesses, deviations—he simply removes from his world.

He has always divided life into black and white. People who fail to live up to his demands cease to exist. No doubt Rebecka falls into that category from now on.

She no longer exists, as far as he is concerned.

70

There is a warm, welcoming glow from the ground floor windows of Pastor Jonsäter's home. The beautiful turn-of-the-century house is an idyll, but the memory of the smiling pastor flatly refusing to recognize Rebecka's vulnerability makes Hanna shudder. This time they have to make him see the seriousness of the situation.

Once again it is Karin who answers the door. She is clearly surprised to see them.

"You're back!" she exclaims. "Sorry, I mean . . . are you looking for Jan-Peter?"

"We are."

"I'm afraid he's not here at the moment."

"Where can we find him?"

Karin hesitates. She fingers a gold cross at her throat; it is similar to the one Ann-Sofie Ekvall was wearing, although this one is more elegant.

"We really do need to speak to your husband," Hanna says firmly.

"He's at the community center—it's the Wednesday service. I stayed in to look after our grandchild."

Hanna waits impatiently while Karin explains how to get there. It's not far, only five minutes by car.

"Can I ask you something?" Hanna says as they are about to leave. "When did you last see Ole Nordhammar?"

Karin smooths down her already perfect hair. Then she adjusts her brown leather belt. Her eyes dart from side to side. "Why do you ask?"

"Because we need to get a hold of him too. And his wife, Rebecka."

"I haven't seen Rebecka in over a week." She refuses to look either Daniel or Hanna in the eye. It's obvious that she knows more than she is saying; Hanna would like to grab her by the shoulders and shake her.

"It's extremely important that we find Ole and Rebecka," she says. "If you have any idea where they might be, please tell us."

"I'm afraid I can't help you."

"Let's go," Daniel says, setting off toward the car. Hanna follows him; then she stops and runs back to the glass veranda. Karin is about to close the door.

"We think Rebecka is in danger of being badly hurt by her husband. For God's sake, if you know where he is, you have to tell us!"

Karin still won't look her in the eye. Loyalty within the church seems to be incomprehensibly strong; Hanna has no idea how it can hold both Rebecka's mother and Karin in such an iron grip.

Not when a woman's life is on the line.

She takes out her card and presses it into Karin's hand.

"Here. If you change your mind, you can call me anytime."

71

The community center is on a hill right at the beginning of the narrow Snasa valley. Beyond the building the mountains open up on either side of the barren white landscape, with Snasahögarna towering in the background like nature's silent guardians.

Daniel pulls in beside a wide white wooden building with wings to the right and left. The church itself seems to be in the central section; there is a large cross above the door.

The parking lot is full.

"It seems as if we've arrived slap bang in the middle of the action," he says drily.

"Does it matter?"

"Not at all."

Daniel has never been particularly religious. His mother was raised a Catholic but distanced herself from both the church and her family when they couldn't forgive her for getting pregnant when she wasn't married.

This wouldn't have been regarded as a scandal in Sweden, where half of all children are born into relationships where the parents are unmarried, but Daniel's mother paid a high price. When she left Ravenna to be with his father in Sweden, she lost all contact with her relatives.

"In we go," he says, getting out of the car.

His phone pings, and he glances at the screen. Several angry messages from Ida come pouring in. She didn't take the news that he was going to be late very well. He knew she wouldn't be happy, but she sounds furious.

She's never been like this before, and it stresses him out. It's hard being caught between his partner and his job. He would do anything for Ida and Alice, but being a police officer is more than an ordinary profession; it's who he is.

The core of his being.

He thinks he's a good cop, but more and more often he is wondering how to be a good partner and father as well. Right now, he can't get back in the car and go home—there is too much at risk. He already feels guilty for not working longer hours over the past few days.

This isn't only about duty or what he wants. Rebecka and her unborn child could be in mortal danger.

Daniel hesitates—should he call Ida, try to explain? Promise to prioritize her and Alice as soon as the case is over, but at the moment he is trying to save a pregnant woman.

He glances over at the church. Hanna is already standing by the door, beckoning him impatiently.

With a sigh he puts his phone away. It will have to wait. He will call Ida after they've spoken to Pastor Jonsäter; it can't be helped.

72

As soon as Daniel and Hanna step inside, they are met with the sight of a large, brightly lit space with a golden cross facing them.

There are several dozen people seated in the front rows, and Hanna can see that they are all totally focused on the man leading the service.

It is Jan-Peter Jonsäter, of course. His eyes are shining with happiness.

"Our church has a unique task," he informs the congregation. "God has made us intercessors for the whole world. But the Lord expects more than that. He has also chosen us to be the answer to the prayers of others."

He pauses deliberately, holds up his hands.

"Think of all those who pray for things they do not receive. What if the power of your prayers could fulfill their innermost wishes? When our fellow human beings kneel and pray, when they pray to God and ask him to solve their problems—the answer can come through us."

Hanna listens in fascination. Does Jonsäter really believe what he's saying, or is it merely a well-rehearsed act?

Another pause. The pastor allows his gaze to travel across each row in turn, as if he wants to acknowledge and validate every single person.

"What joy to be able to fill someone else's innermost wishes!" he exclaims. "What joy to be chosen by the Lord to pass on his great love! Because he wants to answer our prayers, and through the love we can pass on, we have the privilege of helping God to do exactly that!"

"Amen!" everyone responds.

"Thank you!" Jonsäter shouts, turning his face up to the ceiling. "Thank you, God, for allowing us to become your helpers. Thank you for allowing us to be at your disposal. Thank you for allowing us to pass on your grace to our fellow human beings!"

Hanna is reluctantly impressed. The pastor is completely taken up by his message; his conviction is palpable. He evokes an intense feeling of community with great skill and effectiveness, a feeling so powerful that it is almost irresistible.

"Thank you, God!" he concludes with pure happiness in his voice. "In the name of Jesus. Thank you."

When he holds out his hands, everyone rushes toward him to receive his blessing.

Hanna contemplates the scene that is playing out before them. Daniel shakes his head.

She can see that the members of the congregation are smiling—no, beaming—at Jonsäter. It must be fantastic to be a part of this kind of fellowship, to share this love with family and friends.

Equally, it must be horrific to be excluded from it.

What happens when the group closes ranks and freezes out a member of the church?

Where does that person go then?

73

As soon as the service is over, the pastor disappears through a side door next to the pulpit.

Daniel quickly strides after him, gesturing to Hanna to follow. He is uncomfortable, despite his determination not to let the service get to him. The message of love in Pastor Jonsäter's sermon doesn't sit well with their errand this evening, the suspicion that another pastor has abducted his wife against her will.

He opens the side door, which leads to a dark corridor with no overhead lighting.

"Where the hell has he gone?" Daniel whispers to Hanna. She points to a gray door with light seeping out from underneath. Daniel marches over and knocks, then opens the door without waiting for a response.

Jan-Peter Jonsäter is sitting behind a large desk, just as he was when they visited him at home. This one is a simpler piece, however; although it is cluttered with just as many piles of papers.

His expression darkens when he sees Hanna and Daniel. Then he removes his square-framed glasses, places them on the desk, and smiles as warmly as before.

"You two again. How can I be of assistance this time?"

Daniel doesn't bother returning the smile.

"We have reason to believe that you are in contact with Ole Nordhammar. You must help us to track him down."

Hanna adds, "Rebecka could be in real danger, and Ole is the only person who knows where she is. If you meant what you said in your sermon just now, that you want to pass on God's love, then you must ensure that we find Ole right away. Before he hurts Rebecka."

Jonsäter doesn't answer, but Daniel can see from the movement of his chest that he is breathing more heavily. Doesn't he realize the gravity of the situation, or is he so caught up in his own way of thinking that he can't accept the truth about a fellow pastor?

"Help us, please," Hanna begs. "Where is Ole?"

Still no answer.

"There's an offense known as protecting a criminal." Daniel's tone is harsher now. "Anyone who knowingly assists a criminal can be sent to jail."

He takes a step forward. They don't have time for this; he is getting very tired of Jonsäter's attitude.

"Ole isn't a criminal," Jonsäter protests. "He's one of our pastors."

"We already know that he's beaten his wife," Hanna informs him.

"We don't have people like that in our church." The pastor's expression doesn't change; his face looks as if it is carved in stone. "That kind of thing doesn't happen here."

Daniel is on the verge of losing control.

"We suspect he's abducted his wife—is that criminal enough for you?"

"I can't believe that of Ole," Jonsäter insists. "He would never raise a hand to his wife, not in that way. He might have needed to discipline her, but no more than that."

The choice of word makes Daniel see red. *Discipline*, that's not what you do to the person you married. This is a young woman whom Jonsäter must have known for many years. He can't even use her own name—in his eyes she is simply Ole's wife.

Her name is Rebecka, Daniel wants to yell. *She's pregnant and she needs medical attention.*

"I'm not going to sit here listening to your ridiculous accusations," the pastor continues. "I have known and worked with Ole for a very long time. He is a conscientious and God-fearing man who wants nothing but the best for his wife."

Daniel stares at him, but Jonsäter refuses to be intimidated.

"You can't come here and slander members of our church." He stands up. He may be around sixty, but he is still a tall and well-built man, several inches taller than Daniel. He has a strong presence. "I won't tolerate it."

Daniel is trembling with frustration. He is about to explode, although he knows he mustn't do that. He must behave professionally; he is well aware that he can't lose his temper the way he did when he and Ida quarreled.

That would destroy their only chance of finding Rebecka. He has to get Jonsäter to cooperate.

At that moment the pastor looks at him with utter contempt, and Daniel realizes that he doesn't give a damn about Rebecka. All that matters to him is the church, and its precious reputation.

If Rebecka has to be sacrificed in order to preserve that reputation, then so be it.

All that talk about God's love is nothing more than empty words.

The knowledge hits him like a physical blow.

"How do we get in touch with Ole Nordhammar?" he says in a flat voice.

"Surely it's your job to find out?" Jonsäter sits down again. He reaches for a document from one of the piles on his desk and demonstratively begins to read, as if he were alone in the room.

It is impossible for Daniel to ignore this provocation. "Where is Ole Nordhammar?"

Jonsäter doesn't even bother to reply.

The blood is pounding in Daniel's temples, and suddenly he doesn't care if he behaves like his bad-tempered maternal grandfather.

He could kill Jonsäter right now.

Self-control gone, he takes a step toward the desk. With one hand he sweeps the nearest piles of papers to the floor. They take a paperweight and a hole punch with them. The pastor looks up.

Hanna grabs a hold of Daniel's arm, but he shakes her off.

"Where is Ole?" he yells.

Hanna tries to pull him back.

"Rebecka is pregnant," he goes on, still shouting. "If Ole harms her, then you will have the lives of two people on your conscience."

Pastor Jonsäter walks over to the door and opens it wide. There is no trace of the warmth and love that filled his sermon.

In fact, God's love is notable by its absence.

"Get out of here," he says with ice in his voice. "Before I contact your superiors."

Daniel marches straight out into the parking lot and kicks the first tree he comes to, a birch by the entrance.

It hurts his foot, but it doesn't make him feel any better. He could tear that pastor to pieces. He talks about God's love, but his only concern is to protect the good name of the church. No doubt he has already called Ole to warn him about the police's interest.

At the same time, Daniel is furious with himself for so obviously losing control in there. He kicks the tree again. It hurts just as much as before, but he doesn't care. He ought to know better.

How many times has he promised himself that he won't lose his temper at work? It's unprofessional, plus he hates not being in control. It's only a couple of months since he frightened the life out of Ida with his outburst in the kitchen. He's got to learn how to handle a few days of intense stress without getting into this state.

Hanna comes running toward him. He left so fast that she couldn't keep up. She places a hand on his arm. "Are you okay?" Her tone is calming, as if she intuitively understands how much he hates his own reaction.

Daniel shakes his head. He can't talk about it; it's too hard. He isn't going to be like the men in his family.

He is not his grandfather.

"Give me a minute," he manages to say. He would rather just go home and give Alice a big hug.

"No problem."

Hanna turns and moves away, leaves him in peace. She takes out her phone and checks her messages, giving him the space to compose himself.

He clenches and opens his fists several times, forcing himself to take deep breaths. It's a long time since he lost it at work, but that hypocritical bastard's behavior pushed him over the edge. They are talking about a pregnant woman who might have been abducted, and all Jonsäter could think about was defending his male colleague.

But that still doesn't justify his own conduct. He needs to pull himself together.

"Excuse me," says a timid voice a few yards away.

A short figure in a thick padded jacket emerges from the shadow. A woolen hat is pulled down over the forehead; the eyes are barely visible. Daniel turns his head, and Hanna comes over.

"You came to see us this morning," the woman says. "I'm Ann-Sofie—Rebecka's mother."

"Of course," Daniel says, doing his best to sound like a normal person rather than someone who has just taken leave of his senses. "I'm sorry, I didn't recognize you."

"Have you heard any more about Rebecka?"

The voice is thin, at breaking point. Ann-Sofie sounds weak and fragile.

Daniel has to move closer in order to hear her properly.

"Do you know where she is?"

"We're still looking for her and Ole," Hanna explains. She points to the church. "We tried to talk to Pastor Jonsäter, but he wasn't very . . . helpful."

Ann-Sofie bites her lip.

"If you have any idea where Ole might be, please tell us," Daniel says.

Rebecka's mother pushes her hands deep in her pockets. She glances toward the parked cars, as if she is afraid that someone is sitting there watching them.

"Rebecka is pregnant," Hanna tells her.

Ann-Sofie stares at her, eyes wide with shock. "That's impossible," she whispers. "It can't be true!"

"I can assure you it is. I've spoken to her doctor at the health center."

"But she and Ole can't have children. They've been trying for years."

"Your daughter is pregnant," Daniel assures her. "There's no doubt."

Telling Rebecka's mother might be risky, but right now they have to use every means at their disposal to find her.

Hanna takes over. "Unfortunately, there are one or two complications with the pregnancy. Now do you understand why it's so urgent that we find Rebecka and Ole?"

Ann-Sofie looks panic stricken.

"Do you really have no idea where your son-in-law might have gone?" Daniel hears the pleading note in his voice.

"Ole has a big family in Norway," Ann-Sofie replies after a long silence. "His mother was Norwegian."

"Where in Norway?"

"Trondheim. There's a Norwegian branch of the Light of Life that is active there."

A middle-aged couple appear, walking toward the community center. Rebecka's mother falls silent and turns away. She doesn't speak again until they are out of earshot.

"Ole's maternal grandparents owned a cottage in Meråker, just across the border."

Hanna is making notes. "Do you think that's where Ole could be hiding?"

"Possibly. His grandfather died a few years ago, and I think he inherited the property because his mother was already dead. He often spends time in Norway."

"Do you have an address?"

Ann-Sofie shakes her head.

"What was the grandparents' surname?"

"I don't know."

The door of the center opens again, and a young woman emerges, walking quickly toward the parking lot. She gives them a curious look, and once again Ann-Sofie turns away.

"I have to go," she mumbles.

"Thank you so much," Daniel says. "Please get in touch if you find out anything else."

Ann-Sofie nods. She takes one step, then stops.

"Ole wasn't . . . very nice to Rebecka," she whispers. She is clearly afraid.

"Are you sure?" Hanna says gently.

"They weren't happy together. Rebecka tried to talk to me about it more than once, but I wouldn't listen . . . I couldn't believe that Ole was the kind of man who . . . who hit his own wife." She makes a despairing, whimpering sound. "I think it's been going on for a long time, but I did nothing. I didn't help her. I told my daughter to pray to God for guidance."

The glow of the streetlamp falls on Ann-Sofie's face. It is haggard with guilt; her eyes are like two wells filled with pain and sorrow.

"I was too much of a coward to help her when she came to me, even though I'm her mom."

She lets out a sob, then grabs Hanna's hands. Daniel can see how tightly she is squeezing them. The tears begin to flow.

"You have to find her—before Ole does something terrible."

REBECKA

2020

WEDNESDAY, FEBRUARY 26

Rebecka is in a kind of daze, slipping in and out of sleep. She drank the last of the water in the middle of the day, and there is nothing left to eat.

The fear is constantly growing; soon her body will not be able to nourish the little life in her belly. If he or she is still alive . . .

She doesn't want to think that way, although she can't stop herself. And even though she has promised herself that she won't give up, her body is getting so weak.

It is dark outside; time is running out.

A humming sound makes her open her eyes. It sounds like a car. She forces herself to raise her head and look out of the window. The beam of two headlights illuminates the roadway. A vehicle stops outside the cottage. The engine gives a little cough as it is switched off.

Her heart is pounding.

Has Ole come back? Or is it someone else, someone who is here to save her?

She feels a little spark of hope.

Could Johan have found his way here?

Rebecka drags herself to her feet and leans toward the window to see better. The car door opens, and a man gets out of the driver's seat. She peers through the heavy snowfall; the flakes are whirling, giving the scene an air of unreality. They create a white mist that envelops the stranger, distorts all proportions.

He looks like Ole, not Johan.

Rebecka whimpers. Her hands begin to shake, her pulse quickens. She breaks out into a cold sweat.

Ole walks over to the front door and unlocks it. Rebecka snaps out of her trance. Where is the crochet hook? She reaches into her pockets, but it's not there. Did she put it down on the nightstand yesterday?

It's nowhere to be seen.

She feels around in the bed, under the stained pillow. She has to find it, it's her only defense.

Finally, her fingers close around hard metal. It had fallen out of her pocket and gotten wedged between the mattress and the wall.

Rebecka weeps with relief. Then she hears the heavy footsteps on the stairs.

He is coming.

75

Hanna has taken over the driving. She leaves the community center and Snasadalen behind her and heads for a small parking area a mile or so along Handölsvägen. She stops, unfastens her seatbelt, and turns to Daniel.

"Thank goodness Rebecka's mom came to find us. Now we have confirmation that Ole has been abusing his wife for a long time. If he's found out about the affair with Johan or the child she's expecting, things are very serious."

She can see that Daniel is equally worried. There are complications with Rebecka's pregnancy; every hour could be vital.

"Do you think she's in Meråker?" he says.

Hanna closes her eyes, tries to get her weary brain to function. Meråker is only about forty-five minutes from Handöl. The border between Sweden and Norway is open; anyone can simply cross from one country to the other.

"We should go there."

Daniel nods. "We'll have to call the on-duty officer in Trondheim and ask for assistance."

"Rebecka has been missing for five days. We can't wait for the Norwegian police to get their act together."

Daniel runs his fingers through his hair. "I know. I'll attend to it while you drive."

It has started to snow. Heavy flakes are falling from the dark, low clouds, and the wind is picking up, whirling along the shoulder and pushing the snow in front of it. The birches lining the road are bending and swaying; the branches look as if they might be ripped off at any moment. The weather forecast is dire—storms and winds of up to forty-five miles per hour.

Hanna fastens her seatbelt.

"Okay, let's go. How are we going to get the address?"

"We could look up Ole's parents in the electoral register; that should tell us his mother's maiden name."

"If Anton is still at the station, maybe he could help us."

Hanna's phone rings, and she switches it to speaker.

"This is Karin Jonsäter."

Hanna is shocked. She was desperate when she gave Karin her card, and thankfully it seems as if the woman has changed her mind. Or Ann-Sofie has persuaded her to talk to the police, despite the oppression within the church.

Perhaps there is a form of female solidarity that exists beneath the radar of the patriarchal organization?

"You asked me to call if I knew where Ole might be . . ." Karin takes a deep breath. There is fear and anxiety in her voice. "You can't tell my husband that I've spoken to you."

"You have my word."

"I think Ole is in Norway. I heard Jan-Peter on the phone to him after your first visit, this morning. It sounded as if he was trying to persuade Ole to come back to Sweden—along with Rebecka." Karin takes another deep, trembling breath. "Which must mean that Ole . . . is holding Rebecka there against her will."

76

Anton is still at the station even though it's late. He can't face going home to an empty apartment; he'd rather stay and work for a while.

It has been a long and difficult day. There is now an official call out for Rebecka and Ole Nordhammar. Linus Sundin is dead, and his name has been released.

Giving the news to his family was tough. He can't get the image of Sandra's shocked face out of his mind. She couldn't take it in, couldn't grasp the fact that her husband was dead. She clung to her young son, who wept loudly and inconsolably.

She was adamant that Linus would never have taken his own life. She dismissed the suggestion immediately. Linus would never do that to his family, she sobbed.

And they still haven't found a suicide note.

If Sandra is right, that leaves two alternatives. Either it was a genuine accident, or Linus was forced off the road, which means they are looking at premeditated homicide.

Anton isn't sure how much weight to give Sandra's opinion. It could easily be wishful thinking on the part of a woman in despair. Carina's initial report on Linus's van has just come through: the scrape marks on the side are relatively recent, but it's impossible to say whether they are brand new.

There is still a lot to suggest that Linus murdered Johan.

He should probably tell Daniel what Sandra said, but Anton decides to wait until tomorrow. No doubt Daniel has finished for the day; it's after eight, and Anton knows things have been tricky at home lately.

He has met Ida a few times—she's a nice girl. At the same time, it's not easy being in a relationship with a cop; the high level of divorces within the police force is no coincidence. It takes a toll on the relationship to have a partner who must constantly respond to calls and often works irregular hours.

It's no fun having dinner with someone who is mentally fixated on a corpse that's just been discovered.

It's hardly surprising that couples split.

He can't help thinking about Carl and how he would cope with a partner who was a police officer.

Stop dreaming. It's not going to happen.

However, when the phone rings he hopes it might be Carl—but no, it's Daniel. He's in the car with Hanna, so he is obviously still working.

"Can you help me find an address in Meråker, Norway?" he says without any preamble. Daniel explains that the property belongs to Ole Nordhammar, who has inherited it from his mother's side of the family. He also wants Anton to dig out Ole's mother's Norwegian maiden name. "As quick as you can."

"Why do you want the address? We've already put out a call for him."

So far no new information has come in—although Anton realizes that the call applies only to Sweden, not Norway. To cover the whole of Scandinavia, an arrest warrant must be issued, but the suspicions so far directed at Ole Nordhammar would not justify such a measure.

"Why is it so urgent?" Anton adds.

He can hear Hanna talking in the background.

"We think Rebecka Nordhammar is being held against her will in Meråker," Daniel explains. He is obviously worried; his voice is raw and stressed.

"So are we talking about abduction?" Anton wonders.

"It seems that way. And Rebecka is pregnant, probably by Johan rather than her husband. Her mother has just confirmed that

Nordhammar has been subjecting Rebecka to domestic violence for years."

Anton realizes how serious the situation is. Hanna was right all along—this is much worse than he'd thought.

"I'll see what I can do," he says. "Although you should probably update Grip."

"Later. First, I have to contact the on-duty officer in Trondheim and ask for assistance."

REBECKA

2020

WEDNESDAY, FEBRUARY 26

Rebecka curls up on the bed with her back to the wall. Ole's footsteps have stopped outside the door.

Her breathing is so rapid and shallow that she's not taking in enough oxygen. It feels like holding her breath underwater. So far, she has sufficient air, but her body knows that it will soon run out.

Every muscle is strained to the breaking point.

For a second she considers hiding behind the door, attacking him as soon as he comes in. She pictures herself flying at him with the slender crochet hook in her hand, stabbing him in the eye so that he falls to the floor. Then she runs downstairs to the car and drives away.

But fear makes her abandon that idea. He is too strong—she will only get one chance. If she misses, things will be much worse.

Besides, she doesn't know if she is capable of deliberately injuring another human being. Not even Ole, despite everything he has done to her. If she pretends to be crushed and submissive, then maybe she can persuade him to let her go.

The odds on that happening aren't great, but she is clinging to the possibility. Ole is a servant of God, a pastor in their church. She has heard him preach his message of love on many occasions.

Surely, he wouldn't kill a pregnant woman?

Rebecka runs a hand over her belly, tries to find strength in knowing that a life is growing inside her.

She hears him take hold of the key in the lock. It is stiff and makes a grinding noise when he tries to turn it. Eventually he has to remove the key and insert it again.

Rebecka stares at the door as if she is hypnotized. Maybe her efforts with the crochet hook have broken the lock. He might be shut out, just as she is shut in.

Another grinding noise.

Her lips move in prayer, the same words she has repeated ever since she was a little girl.

"God, who holds the children dear . . ."

77

When Hanna reaches Storlien, she sees an illuminated sign with the words TULLGRÄNS—CUSTOMS BORDER, marking the boundary between Sweden and Norway.

Daniel has just ended his conversation with the Norwegian police in Trondheim. He puts away his phone, looking worried.

"They'll send a patrol as soon as they can, but right now everyone in Meråker is out on another call."

Hanna presses her lips together. Not much seems to be going their way this evening. She increases her speed as much as she dares and heads for the lane marked green. They pass a wooden building with the emblems of both the Norwegian and Swedish customs above the door. The place is in darkness, no customs officers present.

The flagpoles are rattling in the strong wind as Hanna drives into their neighboring country.

Now they are in Norway. They have no authority here.

A blue sign informs them that they are in the county of Nord-Trøndelag and the village of Meråker. They continue along Mellomriksveien, as the E14 is called in Norwegian.

Daniel remains silent and tense in the passenger seat.

The weather has deteriorated. The snow is whirling in the beam of the headlights; driving in these conditions demands Hanna's full concentration. She hopes the cottage isn't too remote and isolated; if it is, they might not be able to get through. The car is a four-wheel drive, but in a storm like this, the roads can become impassable in a few hours.

It is almost nine o'clock, half an hour since they spoke to Anton. They still don't know where they're going.

At last Daniel's phone rings. He switches it to speaker.

"I've got the address," says Anton. Hanna lets out a long breath.

"It's northeast of the E14." Anton explains that they must take a right after a gas station and follow the road for some distance, until they reach a narrow bridge that crosses a tributary of the Stjördal River. The cottage is at the end of that road.

"Ole Nordhammar's mother's maiden name was Hauge," he goes on. "His maternal grandparents were Ruth and Sigurd Hauge, in case you need to ask for directions."

"Thank you," Daniel says.

"By the way, do you want the details of Nordhammar's car? He drives a white Nissan Qashqai, it's a small SUV, and the license plate number is NQX 026."

Well done, Anton, Hanna thinks. In their haste they'd forgotten to ask about the car.

"Remember this guy could be dangerous," Anton adds. "You might need backup."

The darkness is growing dense outside the windshield. The wipers are swishing frantically back and forth before Hanna's eyes.

"The Norwegian police have confirmed that they're on the way," Daniel says. "Don't worry—we're not going to do anything stupid."

REBECKA

2020

WEDNESDAY, FEBRUARY 26

When the bedroom door opens, Rebecka sees a dark silhouette surrounded by a bright light. It is impossible to make out the facial features, and for a second she actually believes it's an angel who has come to save her.

Then her eyes adjust, her vision clears, and she sees that it is Ole standing in the doorway. She presses herself against the wall; there is nowhere to go.

Ole doesn't say a word, he simply steps forward, grabs her arm, and drags her to her feet.

"What . . . what are you doing?"

Still he doesn't speak. He pushes her in front of him, out of the little room, and down the steep wooden staircase. She has neither her boots nor her bag, just the clothes on her body.

Through the hall window she sees the storm that has taken hold. The snow is lashing against the glass; the wind is howling down the chimney in the kitchen. The sudden gusts bend everything in their path.

When Ole opens the front door and shoves her outside, the cold hits her skin like the crack of a whip. She cowers in the gale; the snowflakes are like sharp needles on her skin.

"Where are we going?" she shouts. No response. She is in her stocking feet and isn't wearing a jacket, but Ole doesn't care. He pushes her toward the car.

The snow instantly freezes the soles of her feet. Her hair and the back of her neck are already soaking wet. She is so cold she is shaking.

"Let me go!" She does her best to resist. A few minutes ago she was prepared to do anything to get out of the cottage, but now that dirty little room represents her only refuge.

"Silence, woman!" Ole roars.

He is too strong; she has no chance against him.

She never did have.

He opens the back door and practically throws her into the car. She loses her balance and hits her head on the door on the other side; the pain makes her see stars. By the time she manages to sit up, he has already started the engine.

"Where are we going?" she shouts again.

Ole drives out into the darkness.

"You are going to meet God."

78

Hanna is driving as fast as she dares on the snow-covered road. It runs parallel with a small riverbed for some distance, then continues in a northerly direction.

Two headlights on full beam are coming toward her. She is dazzled, but the driver makes no attempt to adjust them, even though Hanna flashes her own headlights angrily.

The other car is moving so fast that she is afraid they're going to collide. She is forced to jerk the wheel violently to one side. She only just manages to avoid getting the fender stuck in a snowdrift.

The SUV whizzes past, oblivious to what has happened.

"Shit!" Daniel exclaims. "That was him!"

Hanna looks in the mirror to see the white car disappearing from view. "Are you sure?"

"It was a Nissan Qashqai—I recognize the model."

Hanna wrestles with the wheel and turns the car around. "I hope you're right," she mutters, putting her foot down.

No sign of any red rear lights as she chases the white SUV. She has to catch up before Ole reaches the E14; otherwise he could simply vanish.

"Did he have Rebecka with him?"

"I couldn't see. There might have been someone in the back seat, but I can't swear to it."

As Hanna drives past the last side road, Daniel yells, "Stop!"

She slams her foot on the brake, narrowly avoiding another skid off the road.

"I thought I saw tire tracks back there."

Hanna backs up and turns where Daniel is pointing. The snow hasn't been cleared, and the headlights pick out the marks left by another vehicle.

Please let it be Ole Nordhammar's car, Hanna prays silently.

She keeps going, following the tracks. The forest is even denser here; it's impossible to see anything beyond the beam of the headlights. The wind is so strong that she can feel the car being pushed sideways, which frightens her. She doesn't want to get stuck in a snowdrift, at the mercy of the power of nature.

"Can you see anything?" Daniel says, a note of desperation in his voice.

Hanna is doing her best. There is no sign of Ole. The windshield wipers are operating at full speed as she peers ahead, but all she can see is darkness and huge amounts of snow falling from the sky. You could freeze to death out here in just a few hours.

Her stomach contracts at the thought.

They have to find Rebecka—before it's too late.

REBECKA

2020

WEDNESDAY, FEBRUARY 26

Ole is driving so fast along the narrow road that Rebecka closes her eyes and clutches her belly. All three of them are going to die if he doesn't slow down. It's only a matter of time before they crash into a tree or another car.

She is crying with her mouth open.

The car jolts as Ole lurches onto an even narrower track, and Rebecka is thrown to the other side of the back seat. She manages to brace herself with one hand at the last second to protect her belly, but her shoulder receives a hard blow.

He keeps going straight on, still at a dizzying speed. There is no sign of buildings or lights anywhere around them; they are in the middle of nowhere.

"Please stop," Rebecka whispers, even though she knows he can't hear her.

She has no idea where they are going.

Suddenly Ole slams on the brakes. He doesn't bother switching off the engine as he opens the back door and drags her out.

One last time she begs for the life of her unborn child.

"I'm pregnant," she sobs.

For a second she thinks Ole is going to spit on her.

"It's not my fucking baby."

"Please, Ole—don't do this."

But Ole ignores her pleas. "You and your bastard kid will answer to God!"

He drags her over to the nearest tree and throws her onto the ground, facedown. Rebecka can't see anything; the icy snow scrapes her cheeks.

As she struggles to sit up, she hears the car doors bang shut. The engine roars, and Ole drives away.

She raises her arm to try and stop him, and the cold air hits her palm.

The car disappears from view.

He's gone.

Rebecka blinks, tries to understand what has happened. Then it sinks in. Ole has left her in the middle of the forest. She has no outdoor clothes, no phone. She doesn't even have shoes on her feet.

No one knows where she is. Johan will never be able to find her.

She and her child will freeze to death out here, buried beneath the snow that is falling more and more heavily.

The world tilts. The landscape turns blue in the dark night. The bare black branches of the trees reach for her frozen body.

Something breaks inside her.

Ole really does want her to die.

Surely God would not forgive such wickedness—but no one would accuse her husband when she was eventually found. Everyone would assume she'd lost her way when the storm came.

Poor Rebecka, who accidentally froze to death.

"No," she whispers into the blackness. "No!"

She gets to her knees and manages to stand up; it's hard to maintain her balance. Every step is like walking on nails.

She is so cold that her body is jerking spasmodically.

One single thought keeps her moving forward.

If she doesn't get help, her child will die tonight.

79

The snow is freezing as it hits the windshield now. Hanna is crawling along; she feels as if she is in a lunar landscape; there are no contours, no fixed points with which to orient herself. Her fingers are clamped around the steering wheel; she has to summon every scrap of concentration in order to stay on the road.

Suddenly a bright light appears up ahead, and once again Hanna is almost pushed into the ditch.

"It's him—turn around!" Daniel yells.

She mustn't lose Ole this time. She mumbles to herself; the seconds tick by as she reverses, turns, reverses, turns. At last, they are facing the opposite way and can follow the white SUV.

She is driving much too fast on the treacherous surface. It reminds her of the accident back in December, when she lost control of the car. That can't happen this time. Today she is not alone; Daniel is beside her. He has a family, a baby daughter. She has to slow down, for his sake if not her own.

The red rear lights have disappeared around a bend. Hanna keeps going. Suddenly they have reached the E14. It is deserted in both directions.

Oh no.

"Can you see him?" Hanna asks, although she knows what the answer will be.

"He's gone."

Daniel sounds as defeated as she feels.

She peers both ways; nothing.

"Shit! We were so close. *So* close."

"I know."

Hanna rests her head on the wheel, then swears vociferously.

"What do we do now?"

"We go back, carry on looking for his grandfather's house," Daniel decides. "We don't know for certain that Rebecka was in the car; there's a chance that she's still locked in the cottage."

He's right; they mustn't give up hope of finding Rebecka, but Hanna is furious that Ole Nordhammar got away.

She turns around and sets off again, heading for the address Anton gave them. When they reach the turnoff where Ole's car vanished, Daniel stops her.

"Wait."

Hanna brakes. Daniel stares at the entrance. The thick fir trees swallow the road after only a hundred yards or so. The headlights provide a tiny strip of brightness in the heavy darkness.

"Why did he turn in there?" Daniel wonders.

Hanna shrugs. "Maybe he was trying to hide from us? It worked— we lost him."

"But we would probably have lost him sooner if he went straight to the E14. There has to be a reason," Daniel insists. "What do you think?"

With her hands resting on the wheel, Hanna tries to imagine Ole's thought process.

If he knows that Rebecka is pregnant by another man, then he would want to be the one who punishes her. It is a huge insult to him, as both a husband and a pastor. A man with his psychological profile must be furious by now.

At the same time, he knows that the police are after him. That might make him desperate, even if he blames God for his actions.

Maybe he's moved Rebecka so that she won't be found before he has carried out her punishment.

"Could there be another cottage down there?" she suggests tentatively. "One we don't know about?"

Daniel's gaze is fixed on the tire tracks in the snow.

"I think we should go and take a look," he says.

REBECKA

2020

Rebecka staggers toward the place where Ole stopped the car. Every step is an effort; several times she is close to collapsing, but the thought of the child keeps her on her feet.

She can't let it die.

Her cheeks are frozen, her lips stiff with cold. She can't cry; she certainly can't call for help.

How can a stretch of twenty yards be such a long way?

At last, she reaches the spot and begins to drag herself in the direction of the wider road. She follows the tracks of Ole's car, peers into the darkness. She mustn't get lost. The wheels have plowed deep tracks in the thick snow, making it easier to walk.

She has no feeling left in her legs, but she forces herself to lift her feet, one at a time. One foot in front of the other. One step, then another.

There is no end to the swirling snow. The sky is laughing at her.

She has prayed to God so often, begged him to save her, but he has never come to her rescue. He has never had any time for her, only for his pastor. His chosen servant, Ole. The man who left his own wife to die out here in the snowstorm.

Rebecka wants to spit on both him and God. Rage and shake her clenched fist at the sky.

She doesn't have the strength.

All her life she has been told that she and the members of the church have walked through the valley of the Lord. The place for the chosen, where God gave them the Light of Life, the light that they must take to the people of the world.

But she has met with nothing but darkness.

If she survives, she is going to leave the church. Her child will not be exposed to the faith that has caused her such pain.

Is the little one still alive?

Rebecka whimpers at the thought that the opposite may be true.

She becomes aware of a faint glow among the trees; it seems to be getting closer. Is it a car or simply an illusion, a fantasy that her confused brain is evoking in order to ease her pain?

Has Ole changed his mind?

Rebecka tries to make out what is causing the glow, but everything flickers before her eyes. She is too exhausted. She wants to wave, shout out that she's here, that she needs help, but she can't even manage to raise her arm.

Her body is weak; it will no longer obey her. She can do no more.

Rebecka drops to her knees and collapses in the snow. It is too late. She and her child are going to die here, in the darkness and the shadows.

Just as she has lived her entire life in darkness and shadow.

80

The narrow track leads nowhere. All Hanna can see is a black-and-white shadow landscape; there doesn't seem to be a single building out here, deep in the forest.

She is beginning to lose heart. It would probably be better to turn back.

"It looks pretty desolate," she says to Daniel.

"You might as well carry on—it must end soon."

Hanna's anxiety is growing by the minute. She wants to get to Ole Nordhammar's cottage as soon as possible. Rebecka could still be locked up; it's their last hope.

"Ole must have driven all the way—you can still see the tire tracks," Daniel points out.

This is true. Hanna slows right down. The track is winding, and in places the wind has formed tall drifts that obscure her view. She is still afraid of skidding and getting stuck in the middle of this wilderness.

They reach a short straight section that seems to lead to a turning area, much to Hanna's relief. Now they can head for the cottage and hopefully find Rebecka.

"Stop!" Daniel yells. "There's something on the ground up ahead!"

Hanna brakes sharply. She is traveling at less than twenty miles per hour, but the back of the car skids alarmingly.

On the very edge of the headlights' beam, she sees a figure lying in the middle of the track. They both leap out of the car, but Daniel gets there first. He grabs the limp body by the shoulders, turns it so that the face is visible.

The woman's eyes are closed; her skin is chalk white, but Hanna recognizes her immediately.

"It's her!"

Rebecka looks more dead than alive. There is no color in her lips; her long, wet hair is stiff with the cold, plastered to her head.

Hanna pulls off her glove and checks the slender throat for a pulse.

"She's alive!"

"Good—but she's ice cold."

Hanna looks down and sees that Rebecka's feet are protected by only a pair of tattered socks.

"She's not wearing any shoes!"

The anger surges up like boiling lava. She has encountered many violent men, but it is difficult to comprehend this level of cruelty. Ole has deliberately left his wife in the snow to freeze to death.

"We need to get her into the warmth right away," Daniel says. He lifts Rebecka up in his arms and carries her over to the car.

"If you drive, I'll sit in the back with her," Hanna says, unbuttoning her jacket. "I'll try and warm her up as best I can in the meantime."

They exchange a glance. Rebecka needs urgent medical attention.

"We'll drive to Sweden," Daniel decides. "The air ambulance can pick her up in Storlien."

81

By the time Daniel gets back to the apartment at two in the morning, almost twenty-four hours have passed since he was home. Somehow, he is going to have to make it up to Ida, but right now he doesn't regret what he did.

Rebecka is safe; that's the most important thing.

Ida will understand, if only she gives him the chance to explain in the morning.

He creeps into the hallway and peels off his outdoor clothes, careful not to wake anyone. Then he goes into the kitchen, pours himself a glass of water, and drinks it in one go. After a brief hesitation, he takes out the bottle of cognac from the back of one of the cupboards. The liquor sears his throat, but his tense muscles relax a fraction.

His hands are trembling with exhaustion as he replaces the bottle.

By now the air ambulance should have landed at the hospital in Östersund. Despite the high winds, it managed to land and pick up Rebecka in Storlien. She had regained consciousness in the car. Her cries of pain as the feeling gradually returned and her skin reddened and swelled were agonizing to hear.

Severe frostbite is caused by ice crystals forming in the cells; they burst the blood vessels. It is extremely painful when the crystals dissolve and the capillaries begin to function once more.

He hopes that the doctors will be able to save Rebecka's hands and feet from permanent damage; they had a horrible waxy pallor when she was found. He knows from experience how quickly frostbite can occur.

The same thing happened to Hanna last year.

Rebecka wasn't outdoors for very long, but damage can occur within ten minutes in severe conditions. He dares not speculate about the welfare of the baby, but presumably the odds aren't great. If the cold hasn't taken the child's life, there is a considerable risk that the shock will have done so.

Ole Nordhammar is a bastard.

What kind of man—a Christian pastor—leaves a pregnant woman to freeze to death like that?

Daniel wonders how much Jan-Peter Jonsäter knows about Ole's violent behavior. Or how he will react when he finds out what his valued colleague has done. Daniel is determined that Jonsäter will also answer for his actions.

He finishes off the last of his cognac and puts down the glass, then creeps into the bedroom. He feels completely washed out; all he wants to do is crawl into bed next to Ida and fall asleep as quickly as possible.

It takes a moment for his eyes to get used to the darkness—then he sees that the double bed is empty.

So is the little crib beside it. Ida and Alice are not there.

He looks around in confusion. When he switches on his bedside lamp, he finds a note on the pillow. He recognizes Ida's handwriting.

I can't do this anymore. I've moved back home to Mom's place. / I.

THURSDAY, FEBRUARY 27

82

Hanna's body is aching with tiredness when she drags herself to the station at seven o'clock on Thursday morning. Less than four hours' sleep is nowhere near enough, but it can't be helped.

The main thing is that they managed to find Rebecka in time.

She swipes her pass card and opens the door as Daniel appears behind her. He stamps the snow off his boots and joins her in the corridor. He has dark circles beneath his eyes, and his complexion has a grayish tinge. Neither of them has slept much, but Daniel looks absolutely terrible.

"How are you?" Hanna asks.

"Didn't get much sleep."

He heads toward his office, but Hanna follows him.

"Are you okay?" she says quietly. It's only a few hours since they got back from Storlien, but something isn't right—she can feel it. "You can tell me."

Daniel grimaces. "It seems as if my partner doesn't want to be with me anymore."

"What?" This is not at all what she'd expected.

"Ida has gone home to her mom. There was a note in the bedroom last night."

Hanna doesn't know what to say. Ida and Daniel have a baby daughter, and last night Daniel made a real difference. If he hadn't insisted that Hanna should drive along that track in Meråker, it would have been too late for Rebecka.

Daniel's instincts saved her life. In Hanna's eyes, he is a hero. She places a sympathetic hand on his shoulder.

"I guess Ida needs some space to work things through," she says. "It's not easy, being a mom for the first time. She's overreacting." She can hear how trite it sounds. "I'm sure it'll be fine," she murmurs, doing her best to sound encouraging.

Daniel takes off his jacket and hangs it up, then nods in the direction of the conference room, where Anton and Raffe are already waiting. "We need to get started."

It is a clear indication that he doesn't want to discuss his home situation anymore.

"Okay." Hanna turns to leave but pauses in the doorway. "Listen, I'm here if you want to talk. You only have to say the word."

Daniel gives her a weary smile. "I need a coffee before we start."

83

As soon as the briefing began, Grip handed over to Daniel. He has outlined the previous day's developments in Norway, with Hanna filling in where necessary.

The lack of sleep is making him feel nauseous; he is struggling to maintain focus.

"We put a call out for Ole Nordhammar across Scandinavia last night," he concludes. "We're going to need the assistance of the Norwegian police to preserve the cottage in Meråker as a crime scene and carry out a forensic examination."

Grip makes a note. "Have we heard from the hospital? How are Rebecka and the child she's expecting?"

"I was going to check when we're done here," Hanna replies.

"Okay." Grip raps her knuckles on the table, as if to remind them that the investigation into Johan's murder is far from over. Daniel is well aware of that. They were sidetracked by Rebecka's abduction, which demanded most of their attention yesterday.

Or is there a connection?

He tries to get his tired brain to function while Anton summarizes the latest information on Linus Sundin's death. He places particular emphasis on the fact that Linus's wife refuses to accept the idea of suicide.

The investigation into a possible crime behind the incident is in its very early stages.

"Bearing in mind what Ole Nordhammar did to his wife," Grip says, "surely we need to revise our original theory that Linus Sundin was the perpetrator?"

Most of those around the table nod. Grip taps her keyboard, and an enlarged image of Ole's passport photo appears.

Daniel contemplates the forty-one-year-old on the screen. The first impression is positive; he looks like a man of the church, charismatic and convincing, not unlike a younger version of Jan-Peter Jonsäter. However, on closer scrutiny the features become sharper, the gaze has a cold undertone.

He thinks about Rebecka lying in the snow, on the point of freezing to death. She was barely able to speak when they reached Storlien, but Hanna managed to get a few words out of her before the air ambulance took her to the hospital.

The young woman whispered that it was her husband who had kept her locked up, then dragged her out of the car and left her to die in the storm. She also confirmed her relationship with Johan.

Which gives Ole Nordhammar a motive for Johan's murder.

That man has a great deal on his conscience.

The question is how to proceed. He draws a circle with his index finger while he thinks. There is still no forensic evidence against Ole. His fingerprints might be in Johan's van, but they are still waiting for the results from the National Forensic Center in Umeå. They ought to take a look at the house in Enafors, see if there's anything to support the idea of his involvement.

"We need to carry out a search of the Nordhammars' house in Enafors," he says. "As soon as possible."

This time Grip has no objections.

"We should also ask Carina to take another look at everything that was found in the van—check for anything that could be linked to Ole."

Carina isn't in attendance today; she excused herself from the briefing so that she could finish examining the van. Yesterday's report included only her preliminary findings.

"What about Marion Andersson?" Hanna says. "She might recognize Ole. If she's seen him around Johan, we could be a step closer to regarding him as the perpetrator."

Daniel agrees.

Tasks are allocated, and Grip draws the meeting to a close. Anton will organize the house search and contact Carina. Daniel and Hanna will go and see Marion, since they have already spoken to her.

"Find out if anyone else saw Nordhammar anywhere near Johan on Friday," Grip says. "We know where Johan was—at Linus's house, at Pigo, and at the preschool. He might have been picked up by CCTV cameras somewhere along the way."

84

Anton gets himself another cup of coffee before returning to his office. The last few days have been overwhelming, on both a personal and a professional level. Born and raised in Duved, he has always thought of Åre as a safe place, but now several serious crimes have taken place in a matter of weeks.

He sits down at his desk and tentatively sips his hot coffee.

He really wants to think about Carl, all the things he should have said instead of what he actually said, but he forces himself to switch on the computer and focus. He needs to plan a house search rather than brood over his inability to handle relationships. He is well aware that he has messed up, even though it's the first time in forever that he's had genuine feelings for another person.

He brings up a blank document. Grip's final comment about CCTV cameras has given him an idea. The witness who called about Johan's van said that it had been parked on Klubbvägen for a while—that was before it was driven to Tångböle, then hidden by the lake.

Anton has a vague memory that there are cameras at the recycling center in Staa. He thinks he saw them the last time he went there with a load of electronic scrap. The van should have passed along that road.

So far they have only discussed gas stations—there aren't many other places with CCTV, but he doesn't think his colleagues have checked the recycling center.

It's worth a shot.

His phone buzzes—a text from Carina.

Can you and the team fit in a short video meeting?

Anton thinks for a moment. Daniel and Hanna have already gone to see Marion, but Raffe is still around. He messages back:

No problem.

Then he goes along to Raffe's office before heading back to the conference room.

Carina's face appears on the screen. Judging by the background, he gathers that she is in Östersund, in the building that houses the police and other emergency services. She looks very pleased with herself.

"We've got the data from the electronic logbook."

Raffe whistles appreciatively.

"It tells us exactly where the vehicle traveled," Carina continues. "I can show you with the help of a piece of software that plots its route on a map."

"Brilliant," Anton says. They couldn't have hoped for better news right now. "So you can see where the van was between Friday afternoon and Saturday morning? Where Johan went after he left the restaurant?"

"Exactly." Carina splits the screen, and a map appears. "So, you can see Johan's complete journey log—or at least the van's log, since we have reason to believe he wasn't driving on Friday night, Saturday morning."

Anton recognizes the area between Åre and Tångböle. There are a number of red markings.

"The red dots show where the vehicle stopped during Johan's final twenty-four hours," Carina explains. She uses the cursor to trace the van's movements on Friday, and goes through each stop.

Johan leaves home at about seven in the morning. He drives to the construction site in Sadeln and stays there until lunchtime. Then he goes to a restaurant in Björnänge, where he spends forty-five minutes before returning to the site. At three thirty he drives to the preschool in

Ånn. After slightly less than fifty minutes, he drives home to Staa. He sets off again two hours later and drives to Pigo, where Carl Willner is waiting.

"Look," Carina says, placing the cursor in the center of Duved, where the restaurant is located. "The van was parked here from ten past seven on Friday evening until seven thirty."

This matches the information Carl gave them about the time Johan left the restaurant.

Anton leans forward. "Where does he go then?"

"He arrives at Linus's house at seven forty and stays for twenty-four minutes. He leaves at about five past eight."

Again, this matches what they've already been told. Carina indicates the next red dot.

"And then the van continues to Klubbvägen?" Anton says before she can speak, but then he realizes that the cursor is resting on a completely different red dot.

"That's the thing . . . ," Carina says.

85

The heated seat in the car is turned up to maximum, but Daniel can't shake off the chill in his body.

It is probably a combination of exhaustion and shock. After finding the note from Ida, he'd lain awake for a long time. He might have dozed off for an hour or two in total, and now he has to get through the day somehow.

He and Hanna are on their way to see Marion in Staa.

A part of him wants to leave the investigation to its fate and rush over to Järpen, where Ida is. Get down on his knees and apologize, bring her and Alice home.

Another part of him is furious. How can she do this to him? He wants to yell at her, tell her she's behaving like a spoiled child. If he hadn't acted as he did last night, then Rebecka would almost certainly be dead by now.

It's like being torn apart.

Hanna is leaving him in peace, making no attempt to chat, and he is grateful for that. At the same time, he can feel her wordless sympathy flowing in his direction.

She understands him.

They arrive shortly after nine. This time it is Marion's brother, Florian, who opens the door. He is unshaven and barefoot and looks worn out.

"Marion is in the kitchen," he says in English.

She barely glances up when they walk in. Her hair is tied back in a greasy ponytail; her face is gray and haggard.

"Back again?" she says wearily. "What is it this time?"

Hanna takes out the photograph of Ole Nordhammar and holds it up.

"Do you recognize this man?"

"No. Who is he?"

Hanna hesitates before answering, and Daniel understands why. Marion doesn't seem to be aware that her husband had been having an affair with Rebecka, or that he was expecting a child with her. Up to this point she has been mourning the loss of Johan without the knowledge of his infidelity. Marion is already at rock bottom. If they tell her about the secret relationship, her image of Johan will be forever tarnished.

It's a difficult balancing act.

Daniel sees Hanna take a deep breath as she prepares to reveal the truth.

It's the right decision. They have no right to withhold this kind of information, even if Marion will be deeply hurt.

In order to track down Johan Andersson's murderer, they need to explain who Ole Nordhammar is.

And why he is involved.

86

Hanna has placed the photograph of Ole in the middle of the table in front of Marion. Daniel has just gone into the hallway to take a call from Anton.

She hates the thought of what she is about to reveal to this poor widow. It is a terrible shock for anyone to learn that they have been betrayed, and under these circumstances it is even worse.

"Who is he?" Marion says again, giving the photo a little push. "Why are you asking if I recognize him?"

Hanna hears Daniel talking; she would prefer to wait until he's back, but she can't really put this off any longer.

Florian has joined them in the kitchen. He is leaning against the counter with his arms folded, all his attention focused on his sister.

Hanna steels herself. "His name is Ole Nordhammar."

Marion still looks at a total loss. Hanna takes out her phone and shows her a picture of Rebecka. "Do you know who this is?"

Marion stares at the photo without the slightest sign of recognition.

"This is Rebecka, Ole's wife. She works at a preschool called Little Snowdrops in Ånn. Johan did several plumbing jobs for them."

Marion rubs her forehead. "Oh yes, I remember the name from the invoices we sent."

Hanna is trying to find a gentle way of putting what she has to say, although that's hardly going to help Marion when she finds out the painful truth.

"We have reason to believe that Rebecka and Johan were having an affair," she says eventually.

Marion stiffens. Her body becomes so rigid that the veins in her neck look like two tightly stretched wires. Her brother realizes that something is wrong, even though Hanna is speaking Swedish. He takes a step forward, places a hand on his sister's shoulder. She shakes it off, as if she can't bear anyone touching her.

"Were you aware of their relationship?" Hanna asks tentatively.

"Johan and I were happy together." Marion is breathing heavily through her nose. Hanna feels desperately sorry for her.

"We think that Rebecka's husband found out what was going on and attacked Johan on Friday evening. We suspect Ole Nordhammar of murdering your husband. Ole also tried to kill his wife last night."

Marion wipes her nose with the back of her hand. She is clearly struggling to maintain her self-control. "We were happy," she repeats, her voice breaking.

Daniel walks in, still holding his phone. He has an odd expression on his face.

"I need to ask you a question about your husband," he says to Marion, even though Hanna is in the middle of breaking the news. She gives him a look, but he takes no notice.

"You told us earlier that you didn't see Johan after seven o'clock on Friday evening," he goes on. "That was when he went off in the van to meet his friends at the restaurant. You called him several times, but he never came back. Is that correct?"

Marion nods.

Hanna doesn't understand where Daniel is going with this.

"Then we have a problem. I've just been informed that the electronic log in Johan's van shows that he returned home after visiting Linus. He was back here at eight thirty on Friday evening."

An oppressive silence fills the room. Hanna looks at Daniel, then at Marion, but before she can say anything, Daniel continues.

"Is it possible that Ole Nordhammar came here on Friday evening?"

87

Hanna is about to interrupt Daniel and reclaim control of the interview when she realizes the significance of what he has just said.

Johan came back home *after* his visit to Linus Sundin—in other words, he was still alive when he left Linus. There can be only one explanation. Ole must have waited for his victim and struck when Johan returned home. Which means that Johan was murdered outside his own house.

Shouldn't Marion have noticed that?

Hanna turns her head, looks around. The kitchen window overlooks the parking area, but the living room, where the television is, faces in the opposite direction. If Marion was in there, she wouldn't have had a view of the road, and if the TV was on, she probably wouldn't have heard Johan's van.

Or Ole's car.

Daniel's question is still hanging in the air.

Marion's face is chalk white. "He didn't come in," she whispers.

"Into the house?" Hanna says, seeking clarification.

Marion blinks.

"Did you see anyone moving around outside on Friday evening? I'm wondering if Ole Nordhammar could have been lying in wait for Johan?"

Marion begins to rock back and forth on her chair. She looks like a woman in a trance; her eyes are wide open; her bloodless lips are moving, but without forming words.

Hanna tries to interpret her expression. She seems to be afraid. She must have seen something terrible to react like this. What if she came across Ole Nordhammar and he threatened her? If she didn't keep her mouth shut, she would meet the same fate as her husband.

Florian crouches down in front of his sister.

"Was passiert?" he asks anxiously. *"Ist alles in Ordnung?"*

He is wondering what is going on. So is Hanna.

"Marion?" she says gently. "Can you tell us what happened when Johan came back on Friday evening?"

Marion stands up. "Excuse me," she mutters, covering her mouth with one hand. She hurries out of the kitchen and into the small guest bathroom in the hallway. They hear the sound of vomiting, followed by the toilet flushing, then water running into the handbasin.

"Could she have witnessed her husband's murder?" Hanna says quietly to Daniel.

The bathroom door opens; then Marion's footsteps disappear up the stairs.

Several minutes pass.

"Where's she gone?" Hanna says. She gets up and goes over to the doorway to see if Marion is on her way back, but there is no sign of her.

She turns to Florian. *"Wo ist denn Ihre Schwester hingegangen?"*

Where has your sister gone?

"Keine Ahnung."

I've no idea.

Hanna turns to Daniel. "I'll go and check, just to be on the safe side."

She heads quietly up the stairs. At the far end of the landing is what ought to be Marion and Johan's bedroom. The door is closed. She is about to go along there and knock when Florian comes running upstairs and grabs her by the arm.

"Kommen Sie!"

He wants her to go with him.

They go back downstairs. Florian passes the kitchen and continues to the storeroom, where the gun cupboard is.

The metal door is wide open.

Yesterday there were three rifles side by side. Now there are only two.

88

Everything is in place for the search of the Nordhammars' house in Enafors.

Anton is on his way over with Raffe; a patrol car will meet them there. They are discussing the electronic logbook that Carina found, which unexpectedly showed that Johan went back home after visiting Linus.

They have just passed Duved, and Anton automatically thinks of Carl. He would like to show him the photograph of Ole Nordhammar—maybe Carl saw him hanging around near Pigo on Friday evening?

But Carl had talked about his work with the church; he too could be a member of the Light of Life. He might know Ole, be involved somehow. Anton noticed the hymn book on the nightstand in Carl's bedroom.

He is also hesitant to initiate fresh contact, even if Carl is totally innocent. There have already been so many ups and downs. Yesterday Anton virtually slammed the phone down on him, and the other day he was cold and dismissive.

What if Carl hangs up when Anton calls or—worse still—makes it clear that he no longer wants anything to do with him? Anton sighs. He's not sure if he can handle being openly rejected.

He has never hated his professional role more than he does now.

They have reached Staa; a sign informs them that the recycling center is to the left. Before they left the station, Anton tried calling about the CCTV cameras, but no one answered.

He has an idea and takes the left turn.

"Where are you going?" Raffe asks.

"I just want to check on something."

He drives up to the metal gates marking the entrance to the recycling center. Just as he thought, there is a big sign that proclaims, **BEWARE—CCTV Cameras in Operation.**

Why hasn't it occurred to anyone that there might be cameras here, given that Johan's van was parked on Klubbvägen?

He drives past the various dumpsters to the little office, which resembles a hut on a construction site.

Raffe isn't happy. "What are we doing here? The patrol car and the CSIs are already on their way to Enafors. We'll be too late if we don't go straight there."

Anton holds up one hand, fingers spread. "Five minutes max—I promise."

He and Raffe get out of the car and go into the office. It's a narrow space, with two desks opposite each other. A woman in her thirties, with short bright-red hair, is sitting at a computer.

Anton introduces himself, shows his police ID, and explains why they're there.

"Would it be possible to look at the CCTV footage from last Friday?"

"Let me see."

The woman types in various commands, her fingertips flying rapidly and professionally across the keyboard. She has the outlines of a moon and a star tattooed on the back of her left hand.

"Found it," she says after a moment. "What time are you interested in?"

"Hang on." Anton goes outside to call Carina, and when she answers, he asks, "When did you say the van left Johan's home for the last time, according to the new information?"

"So . . . it left Linus's house at five past eight and reached Dalövägen at eight thirty. Then it arrived on Klubbvägen just over half an hour after that," Carina says.

Anton returns to the office and says, "Can you fast forward the footage starting at ten to nine?"

The red-haired woman turns the screen toward Anton and Raffe so that they can see more clearly.

One camera is mounted on the fence by the entrance. It is focused on the gates, but also captures a decent amount of the road. The image is grainy, the light poor, and there is no street lighting outside the center, but it is still possible to see quite a lot. The fact that the footage is in black and white helps; the contours are sharper, the contrasts more marked.

The digital timer ticks away in the bottom corner.

Five to nine, and no car passes by. Nine o'clock. A dark Toyota drives past, then a red Volkswagen with a thick layer of snow on the roof.

"There!" Raffe shouts as a white silhouette approaches.

It is definitely Johan Andersson's van; they can just make out the name of the firm on the side. Before Anton has time to react, it has disappeared.

"Can you rewind, just a few seconds? Then go to slow motion so we can get a good look at the van."

The woman does as he asks, and the white van fills the screen. When it reaches the middle of the screen, she presses pause. A couple of clicks and the image becomes brighter, the sharpness improves.

"What the . . . ," Anton says.

He leans forward. The face of the person at the wheel is partially hidden by a pulled-down woolen hat, but the profile is clear enough to make out the features.

The driver of the van is neither Linus Sundin nor Ole Nordhammar. It is Marion Andersson.

89

Hanna stares at the open gun cupboard. The place where the third rifle stood is empty. A box of ammunition is also missing.

Judging by Florian's panic-stricken expression, it is Marion who has taken the gun. In which case she might well have it with her in the bedroom.

Let's hope she's not suicidal.

Daniel has followed them into the storeroom. He looks from Hanna to Florian.

"Is your sister armed?" he asks in English.

"I suspect so," Florian replies, in heavily accented English. "I think she took the gun last night after I had gone to bed. She lied to you when she said she didn't hunt. She has her certificate—she's a very good shot."

Hanna had no idea that Marion could handle guns.

"We sat up talking for a long time. I tried to persuade her to . . ."

Florian sinks down on a chair and buries his face in his hands.

Hanna's mind is whirling. If Marion was feeling suicidal after the tragic events of the past few days, then the information about Johan's affair with Rebecka must have come as the worst imaginable news. And it was Hanna who told her. She might as well have handed the gun to the poor woman herself.

Why didn't she realize before she started talking? Why hadn't she been more perceptive? They should have taken the guns and the ammunition with them the last time they were here. She could kick herself.

There is still a deathly silence from upstairs, where Marion has shut herself in the bedroom. *At least she's still alive,* Hanna thinks. *Otherwise, we would have heard the shot.*

A dull headache is beginning to throb at her temples. She must try to rescue this situation. This case has already claimed too many victims. She can't cope with another death.

"I'm going upstairs," she says to Daniel. "We need to get Marion out of the bedroom before she does something stupid. We can't let her take her own life right in front of us."

"Wait," Daniel says. He goes over to Florian, who is sitting there in a kind of trance, his forehead shiny with sweat.

"What were you about to say?"

Florian straightens up and looks at Daniel. His face is ashen, and it crumples in despair.

"I tried to persuade Marion to tell you the truth."

90

There is silence in the bedroom where Marion has sought refuge. She is sitting on the floor in the corner beside the unmade bed.

The butt of the rifle rests between her feet.

Her eyes are fixed on the door handle.

They could come in at any moment. There is no lock on the door; they never needed one. Only she and Johan lived here.

And now Johan is dead.

It's her fault.

She has loved him ever since the first time she saw him in the après-ski bar in Kitzbühel.

That was twelve years ago.

His warm smile made her fall deeply in love. For Johan's sake she gave up her country and her family; she followed him to Sweden and started a new life with a new language.

She could never have imagined that he would leave her. They were meant to be together forever.

Until last Friday, when he came home and told her that he was in love with someone else. And not only that—he was going away with her the very next day.

He had just been to see Linus to let him know that he would be away for a while so that his partner could take care of the jobs that were already booked.

Linus, whom Marion loathes, had found out the truth before her.

The scene comes back to her with terrifying clarity. The same scene that has haunted her night and day for almost a week.

She was in the kitchen, clearing up after dinner. She was about to wash the cast-iron griddle and the meat hammer she had used to tenderize the moose fillet. She had treated herself, because Johan was meeting up with the boys. She was so happy when she saw the van pull up outside. She thought he'd come home early because he missed her. She'd had a couple of glasses of wine, but there was enough left in the bottle for them to have a drink together.

How naive was she?

Instead, Johan said they needed to talk.

Something was wrong, she could tell from his serious expression.

He stood there by the kitchen table and told her about the other woman. Said he wanted to spend the rest of his life with her. Begged for Marion's forgiveness, explained that he had tried to resist, but it was impossible.

His voice came from a long, long way off.

They had become like brother and sister, he said. It was better this way—to part as friends. He was still fond of her, but he wasn't in love with her.

Their marriage was over—surely, she must have realized the same thing?

No.

She loved him, she would love him forever.

Didn't that matter to him?

At first, she was struck dumb; then the words came pouring out. She pleaded with him not to leave her. If he went, she would be all alone. Everything would be taken away from her.

When he refused to change his mind, shock and grief gave way to panic. He couldn't do this to her. She shouted and swore, yelled insults about Johan and his whore, words she never thought she would utter.

Johan simply stood there. He didn't argue, didn't contradict her. When she ran out of steam, he opened his mouth and said, "We're having a baby. I'm sorry."

When he turned to walk away, everything went black. Marion closes her eyes, tries to shake off the memory, but without success.

Afterward, when she came to her senses, Johan was lying on the kitchen floor. His face was bloodied, his nose broken where it had hit the step.

The back of his head was covered in blood.

When she looked down, she saw the meat hammer in her hand.

It was also covered in blood, dripping slowly onto the floor. There were splashes of red everywhere, including on her clothes.

Somehow, she managed to drag Johan out of the house and heave him into the back of the van. She thought he was dead, although he was still bleeding heavily. To be on the safe side, she bound his wrists with some cable ties she found among his plumbing supplies.

She has always been fit and strong, but her muscles were trembling with exhaustion by the time she finished.

Then she drove the van to Klubbvägen and parked it there.

When she got home, she cleaned the kitchen, scrubbed and scrubbed until every trace was gone. Until it looked exactly like it always did.

It was midnight before she was done. She realized that she couldn't leave the van on Klubbvägen; there was a risk that someone would wonder what it was doing there.

She put on her outdoor clothes. It had started snowing; thick flakes filled the air.

Marion knew what to do. She took out her cross-country skis and skied back to the van. She got in and drove to Tångböle, a remote and sparsely populated area. She stopped by some low-growing bushes, dragged Johan out, and hid him among the branches in the snow. The snow was falling more heavily now, his body would soon be completely covered. No one would find him for months.

And no one would suspect her.

It was just so hard to say goodbye.

She crouched down, took off her glove, and stroked Johan's forehead with her fingertips. His skin was already cold, his body unnaturally still. She tried not to look at all the blood.

The thought that he would no longer be around seemed unreal.

"Goodbye, my darling," she whispered. Her words drowned in the wind. Her tears almost froze in the cold.

"I love you. So much. I always will."

She sat there until her legs went numb, until she was so cold that she could barely get to her feet. Then she drove the van to a spot by Lake Gev, where she knew there was an abandoned barn. She hid the vehicle as best she could, then skied home through the whirling snow, weeping inconsolably every step of the way.

She had thrown Johan's phone out into the snow but decided to call it a few times during the night so that it would look as if she'd been worried.

She had no intention of acknowledging the existence of the other woman. Marion was determined to erase her from her mind. No one would find out that Johan had been having an affair.

Or that she had known about it.

A gentle tap on the door brings her back to reality. Back to the bedroom, with the rifle between her feet.

"Marion?" Hanna calls out. "Can I come in? Can we talk?"

Marion's eyes fill with fresh tears.

"Listen, we can sort this out. I promise—if I can just talk to you."

Marion looks around. Her gaze falls on the wedding photograph on the chest of drawers, she and Johan standing together on the mountain, immediately after the ceremony. The white snow is sparkling in the afternoon sun, the tall Alpine peaks form a dramatic background against a clear blue sky.

Johan has his arms around her waist, and she is leaning into him, wanting to be as close to him as possible.

He is looking at her with endless love.

They were so happy together.

Marion opens her mouth, closes her lips around the barrel of the gun. The metal is cold against her teeth; it has a slightly salty taste on her palate.

She releases the safety catch, prepares herself. It is an ironic twist of fate that she is going to die now.

Just like Johan.

And poor Linus.

Maybe it is an appropriate punishment, given that she tried to direct the police's suspicions toward him in order to avoid scrutiny herself.

"I'm coming in now," Hanna says from the other side of the door. "I just want a little chat, that's all."

Marion sees the door handle gradually being pushed down.

"Forgive me," she whispers to the photograph of Johan.

It wasn't supposed to end like this.

Then she pulls the trigger.

91

The sound of a cheerful gang of teenagers on their way to an après-ski celebration can be heard as Daniel and Hanna get out of the car at the police station.

The air is cold and misty. Yesterday's wind has dropped; the temperature is around freezing, and a change in the weather is on the way.

Daniel goes on ahead and unlocks the door. He glances over his shoulder; Hanna is moving like a robot behind him. It is almost three o'clock. It took an eternity to preserve the scene and arrange for Marion's body to be collected.

"Come on," he says, leading her into the employee break room, where there are two armchairs. "Let's sit down here and have a chat."

He fetches two mugs of hot chocolate and gives one to Hanna. "How are you feeling?"

She is sitting there like a rag doll. Her eyes are glassy, as if she can't shake off the gory sight. If people realized how horrific the aftermath is when someone shoots themselves in the mouth, no one would commit suicide that way.

"Terrible, to be honest." She is clutching the mug with both hands. "If only I'd gone into the room a few seconds earlier . . . Why wouldn't she listen to me? We could have sorted it out. She didn't have to die."

If only . . . Daniel had thought the same on many occasions, lying awake at night after a call had gone wrong.

"You can't blame yourself," he says gently. "It was her decision. Nobody forced her to pull the trigger."

"I know . . . but it doesn't feel that way. I should have grasped the true situation much earlier. I never suspected that she was involved in Johan's murder."

"Me neither." Daniel sharpens his tone, determined to drive his message home. "It was *not* your fault. And even if it had been, then we are both equally responsible. I was there too. I didn't manage to stop her either. Neither of us knew she was suicidal, or that she was behind Johan's death."

Hanna closes her eyes tightly, but the tears spill over anyway.

Daniel goes over to her. He kneels down in front of her chair, gently removes the mug from her hands and takes her in his arms.

"Hanna . . ."

She weeps silently into his shoulder as he holds her.

"It's okay," he says, rocking her back and forth. "Everything will be fine, I promise."

Her brown hair is tickling his nose; her body is warm against his. Suddenly he doesn't want to let go.

Eventually Hanna lets out a long, shuddering sigh and straightens up. She manages a shaky smile, wipes beneath her eyes with her index fingers. Her mascara has run.

"I'm sorry. I don't usually break down like this."

Daniel is still kneeling before her. Their faces are only inches apart. Her mouth is trembling with suppressed emotion.

With a huge effort of will, he gets to his feet and goes back to his chair.

"We both need a few days off. Above all we need to get some sleep." He looks at his watch. They are due to have a debrief with Grip shortly.

"I'll take the meeting with Grip," he says firmly. "You go home and rest."

"Are you sure?"

"Absolutely."

Hanna stands up. Her face is gray with tiredness, her eyes red rimmed. "Thank you. I'll speak to you tomorrow."

409

92

Anton is already waiting in the conference room. Raffe is busy setting up the connection with Östersund.

"Where's Hanna?" Anton asks.

"I sent her home to rest." Daniel grimaces. "She was in the room when Marion Andersson shot herself."

He doesn't need to add any further explanation; Anton understands. The sight of a person who commits suicide is hard to escape. It eats you up from the inside.

Daniel notices that Anton looks as exhausted as him. His movements are sluggish; he lacks energy. He has spent the day in Enafors with the CSIs, searching the Nordhammars' house for evidence of the long-term domestic abuse that has gone on within the marriage.

Neither of them is in top form, but it can't be helped. They are about to go through the events of the day and plan the continued search for Ole. He is innocent of Johan's murder, but an arrest warrant has been issued for the attempted murder of Rebecka. She was able to manage a short interview in the hospital in Östersund and gave valuable information.

Anton pushes a sheet of paper over to Daniel. It is a copy of a handwritten note.

A suicide note.

"Sandra Sundin found a note from Linus a few hours ago. Apparently, it had fallen down behind a chest of drawers in the hallway where he'd left it. There's no doubt that he deliberately drove into the rock face."

"Poor bastard."

Daniel begins to read. His eyes are gritty; he has to blink several times to see properly. The few lines bear tragic witness to a man who had reached the end of the road.

Linus apologizes for all the debts he has left behind and all the trouble he has caused. He also swears that he had nothing to do with Johan's death.

Which he didn't.

If only Linus had waited a few days, he would have found out the truth, then perhaps he wouldn't have felt so desperate that he took his own life. It might have been possible to sort out his financial problems.

Daniel is overcome with sorrow. With hindsight they should never have pushed Linus so hard, but there was a great deal pointing in his direction. There was evidence and motive. Daniel himself had believed that Linus was the perpetrator.

Now Sandra has lost her husband.

And a little boy no longer has his daddy.

The consequences are devastating, even if the police acted in good faith at the time.

Grip's face appears on the screen and her voice brings him back to reality.

Time to start the meeting.

93

Daniel's phone is ringing when he gets back to his office after the thirty-minute video conference. Much of the time was spent discussing how to allocate resources now that they are dealing with both Johan's murder and Ole's attempt on Rebecka's life.

He doesn't recognize the number on the display but answers as he pulls out his chair and sits down.

"This is Jan-Peter Jonsäter," says a deep voice. The hypocritical pastor doesn't sound quite so arrogant now.

"Yes?" Daniel snaps. He is too tired to pretend to be polite.

"The thing is . . . I've been in touch with Ole Nordhammar."

Daniel exhales through his nose.

"You do realize that your pastor is wanted throughout Scandinavia for the attempted murder of his wife?" He doesn't even try to hide his accusatory tone. After what has happened, he has no intention of making the conversation easier for Jonsäter.

"I am aware of that, yes. The situation is most . . . unfortunate." Jonsäter clears his throat. "Ole has decided that he would like to hand himself in to the police."

Daniel wonders how that came about. Has Jonsäter put pressure on Ole? Presumably the older man had grasped that it was better to cooperate with the police and sacrifice his colleague to save the reputation of the church.

If that's possible at this stage.

"Where is he?"

Jonsäter hesitated.

"Tell me where he is, and I'll send a patrol car to pick him up."

"He's here with me. At my house in Handöl."

"Okay. Make sure he stays there. Someone will be with you within half an hour."

"Ole deeply regrets his actions," the pastor adds. "He doesn't know what came over him."

Daniel doesn't believe a word of it. Ole has abused Rebecka for years. He took her to an isolated cottage in Norway, then left her to freeze to death in the snow, even though she was pregnant.

To claim that he now regrets what he did and feels ashamed is a blatant lie. Jonsäter's remarks are more about his own need to justify his former belief in Nordhammar's innocence.

And to escape censure.

"I think it's too late for that," Daniel says, ending the call.

He remains seated, the phone in his hand.

Ole Nordhammar will be remanded in custody as soon as he is brought in. With the evidence they have, the prosecutor should be able to ask for a life sentence for attempted murder. The course of events was both cruel and long drawn out; Rebecka feared for her own life and that of her unborn child.

When the patrol arrives at Jonsäter's home, he will also be arrested for aiding and abetting a criminal.

Daniel refrained from pointing that out during their conversation, but Rebecka has said that the pastor was present when she was abducted on Saturday. Jonsäter has known the truth all along.

He slips his phone into his back pocket. That man makes his skin crawl. Maybe that's why he lost his temper at the church, despite his resolve never to flare up like that again.

The shame over his volatile temperament washes over him yet again, stronger than before. Why can't he keep the most important promise of all?

The promise he made to himself.

Daniel grips the edge of the desk and takes deep breaths. He doesn't want to be a man who loses control. If he carries on like this, both his relationship and his career are at risk. And above all, he hates himself afterward.

He can't live like this.

Soon he will get in the car and drive the fifteen miles to his mother-in-law in Järpen. He has to try and fix things with Ida, create some kind of harmony at home—for their daughter's sake, if nothing else.

This can't go on.

He misses Alice so much.

It's time to leave, but instead he reaches for the mouse. He adjusts the screen so it can't be seen from the corridor and clicks on Google.

His fingers are shaking as he types in the search word.

"Psychotherapy."

94

Veranda is packed. Hanna is sitting in a dark corner.

Everyone flocks to one of Åre's most popular après-ski bars. It is crowded, hot, and sweaty. A perfect place to spread the coronavirus that everyone is talking about, but right now she doesn't care if one of the revelers around her is carrying it.

She takes a swig of vodka from her glass. The DJ is playing loud, throbbing music. Hanna was on her way back to Sadeln when she changed her mind and drove back to the parking lot by the station, where she left her car. The thought of going home to Lydia and the family was impossible. She can't pretend that everything is okay, nor can she tell them about the day's events, tell them that her clumsy words and lack of perception have contributed to a woman's death.

She would like to obliterate forever the sight that met her eyes when the shot was fired, just as she opened the door of Marion's bedroom.

Marion was sitting on the floor. A second later her face was . . . gone.

There was nothing left except blood and scraps of red flesh, a lifeless body that slumped to the side.

While Hanna screamed.

She has seen dead bodies before; she has been involved in cases of tragic domestic violence. But it has never happened right in front of her.

The vodka glass seems to be empty. She grabs a harassed waitress who is hurrying past, and orders another.

Alcohol is not the answer, but she can't think of a better way to anesthetize her brain. She must make those horrible images disappear.

Her phone buzzes, and she takes it out of her pocket. It's a short text from Daniel.

How are you feeling?

Like shit.

But she doesn't say that.

She wishes desperately that he were here, holding her. She wants to ask him to come over and whisper in her ear that this will pass, that everything will be all right, that she doesn't need to be afraid.

She wants to be in his arms.

It is a forbidden desire that she has barely acknowledged to herself. But here in the dimly lit bar, she knows it's true, although there can never be anything between them.

They are colleagues, they work together. He is probably on his way to Järpen right now to make up with Ida.

That's good; that's the way it has to be.

When the waitress arrives with her vodka, Hanna knocks it straight back and asks for another. A big group of twentysomethings has just arrived in their ski suits and thick padded jackets. They sit down a few yards away from Hanna. One of the guys, his tousled brown hair flattened by his helmet, leans forward and kisses a girl on the lips. Then he heads for the bar.

The DJ turns the volume up even more, and Avicii's last track, "SOS," comes pouring out of the speakers.

Hanna blinks back the tears.

Tomorrow, she will pull herself together, be back to normal. In a little while she will order a cab, go home, and tell the family she has a headache. She will go straight to bed and try to sleep away the angst.

But she can spend a few more minutes dreaming of Daniel.

95

Ida is watching TV in the living room when the doorbell of her mother's apartment rings.

It must be Daniel; she can feel it in her bones.

She had spent all day wondering whether she'd done the right thing in coming here when Daniel was in the middle of a challenging investigation—but she was so upset and frustrated. When her mother suggested she should come straight over with Alice, it seemed like a good idea.

It is a quarter to eight; she has just put Alice to bed. There was a piece on the news about the Åre police and their intervention in the case of the pastor who tried to murder his wife in Norway. Johan Andersson's homicide has also been cleared up. It turned out to be a terrible family tragedy.

"Coming," she calls out, hurrying into the hallway.

Daniel is pale, his expression grim. He has dark circles beneath his eyes.

"We need to talk."

Ida swallows. "Come in."

He steps into the hallway and looks around, presumably to check where Elisabeth is.

"Mom's watching TV. We can go into the kitchen."

Daniel follows her and sits down at the table.

"Can I get you anything? Coffee?"

"No, thanks."

Silence. Daniel looks utterly exhausted. Ida is seized by the urge to throw her arms around him, make everything all right again.

"Where's Alice?"

"I've just put her down. Do you want to see her?"

"Later."

Ida sits down opposite him. She can hear the sound of the TV program her mom is watching in the living room.

"I heard about the pastor," she says, fiddling with the braid hanging over her shoulder. "The guy who tried to kill his wife. Was it you who . . . intervened?"

Daniel nods.

Ida's guilty conscience kicks in with full force. Yesterday he saved a woman's life, while she issued an ultimatum because he didn't get home in time. She is just about to apologize, tell him she hadn't been thinking straight, when he goes on.

"It was me and Hanna. She was fantastic."

Hanna.

Ida doesn't want to hear about Hanna. Especially now.

"Great," she says in a thin voice.

The prickliness between them is back—she can't help it. The feeling of being inferior to Hanna, of being a less-than-satisfactory girlfriend and mother, is inescapable.

She's not good enough.

Daniel reaches out and takes her hand. She has longed for this moment, she knows exactly how his skin feels against hers, and yet she pulls away, hides her hands beneath the table.

"Can't we go home?" he pleads. "You, me, and Alice?"

Ida doesn't know what to say.

Daniel continues, without looking at her.

"I've made an appointment with a psychotherapist. To talk about my . . . outbursts. I'm determined to change."

Ida suddenly has a lump in her throat. She loves Daniel, and he's Alice's daddy. However, she is torn. She wants to believe him, but she's afraid of ending up in the same predicament as before. She is so sick of whining all the time, feeling as if she's totally inadequate.

He looks her in the eye, and she can't help seeing the exhaustion and the sorrow deep inside him.

"I try to be a good man and a good dad," he says quietly. "Honestly, I do try."

She wants them to live together, she really does.

"For my sake?" she says, placing her hand on his.

"For our sake."

MONDAY, MARCH 2

REBECKA

Rebecka has been given her own room at the hospital to protect her from curious eyes.

The story of the pastor who tried to murder his pregnant wife by forcing her out into a snowstorm is all over the papers and the TV news reports.

She is lying on her back, just as she has done for the past few days. Her hands and feet are covered in blisters due to the damage caused by the cold; those on the soles of her feet are dark colored and filled with blood. They look terrible, but the doctors say that this is a good sign.

The blisters are a sign of deep dermal trauma, but not of widespread necrosis. If that were the case, then the skin would be waxy and leathery. In the worst cases it can lead to amputation.

It's early days, but the last doctor she saw said things were looking positive—but they would have to wait and see.

Frostbite in January, amputation in June—isn't that what they used to say?

Rebecka wishes she'd never heard those words.

The television is on, some family sitcom, but she doesn't have the energy to follow the storyline. She spends most of her time just lying here, half dozing, with one hand resting on her belly. Miraculously, her baby has survived. She has had several ultrasound scans and lots of tests. Everything seems fine, although she will need to be closely monitored for the rest of her pregnancy.

In her former life she would have thanked God for that.

Now she knows she will never turn to him again.

If anyone is responsible for the fact that she is still alive, it is Johan. He is the one who gave her the most precious gift of all. Without the child growing within her, she would not have found the strength to survive.

Darling Johan, who will never meet their love child.

Hot tears trickle down Rebecka's cheeks. He hadn't abandoned her as she feared. On the contrary, he died for her sake.

He sacrificed everything.

Now there are only the two of them left—Rebecka and their baby. She will have to be both mother and father to the little one; there's no one else. Her own parents haven't been to visit her in the hospital. No one else from the church has contacted her, not even Lisen.

The only person who has been to see her is Maria.

Rebecka will owe her a debt of gratitude for the rest of her life. If her colleague hadn't told the police about her suspicions, she would probably be dead now.

A sound from the doorway makes her turn her head.

She sees a man and a woman in their late sixties. The woman steps into the room, and as soon as they make eye contact, she begins to cry.

Rebecka has never seen them before, but she instantly knows who they are. Johan's father, Torsten, is an older version of his son.

Tarja comes over to the bed and introduces herself, then sinks down on a chair.

"Dear Rebecka," she says in a shaky voice. "The police have explained everything to us. What you've had to go through. The cruelty . . . It's dreadful . . ."

She manages a sad smile.

"They told us about the baby. That you're pregnant with Johan's child."

Rebecka nods.

"We just wanted to say . . ." Tarja exchanges a glance with her husband, who gives her an encouraging nod. "That we . . . we're here for you, if you will allow us to be a part of your life?"

Johan's mother reaches out to take Rebecka's hand, but the blisters make this impossible, and she has to settle for a clumsy pat on the arm. "We will never get our son back, but if we can help you, if you will let us support you through your pregnancy, we would be eternally grateful."

"We want to be your family, if that's possible," Torsten says. "We wondered if you might like to come and live with us until you sort things out?"

Tarja is weeping now, and Rebecka can't hold back the tears either. She had thought that she would be alone for a long, long time. Her own mother and father want nothing to do with her, and the church has closed ranks.

Now Johan's parents have opened their arms.

She has a new family.

"Thank you," Rebecka says, smiling through her tears. "Thank you so much."

It is so dark in Anton's living room that he can barely see the saxophone, but it doesn't matter. He knows the melody by heart; he can play "If I Should Lose You" by ear.

There are many different versions, but Nina Simone's is the one he likes best.

The melancholy notes echo through the silence. His fingers move over the keys. He blows into the mouthpiece and is astonished, as so often in the past, that his own breath can be transformed into such beautiful tones.

He sees Carl's face in his mind's eye. He has made no attempt to contact him again, no phone calls, no text messages. He did, however, check out Carl's connection with the church; it turns out that he runs a perfectly ordinary choir in the parish of Åre.

That's all.

Last night Anton once again walked past the red-painted building where Carl lives. He stood there in the cold for a long time, gazing up at the apartment's windows. The lights were on. If he'd caught a glimpse of Carl, he might have found the courage to take out his phone, but it didn't happen.

It was probably a sign.

Carl isn't interested anymore, and why should he be? Anton has done his best to put him off. He has been brusque and dismissive.

Now it's too late.

No doubt it's just as well, he tells himself. A serious relationship would never work. He doesn't know how he would handle the consequences of that particular choice, on a personal or professional level.

He's not ready.

Anton closes his eyes and tries to get rid of the leaden lump in his chest. His fingertips caress the instrument, evoking his own version of the song's lyrics:

If I should lose you, my friend,
The stars would fall one by one
If I should lose you, my friend,
I would never find my way home

With you by my side,
No cold wind would blow
With you by my side,
I feel at home everywhere . . .

ACKNOWLEDGMENTS

It is impossible to write a book alone, and I am very fortunate to have had the help of so many generous individuals. As I am relatively new to the Åre area, it has been particularly important to be able to rely on those with local knowledge.

However, I have taken certain liberties and made changes here and there:

Snasadalen is a fictional place, invented to fit the narrative. However, the mountain known as Snasahögarna does exist, and is well worth a visit.

Most of the street names do not exist. I have invented them in order to avoid picking out specific locations.

Ånn is very small—even smaller in reality than in the novel. At the time of publication, it has neither a preschool nor a café.

The assertion that Johan Andersson won the bronze medal in super-G in 2009 is pure fiction. The medal in Val d'Isère was quite rightly won by Aksel Lund Svindal from Norway. Credit where credit is due!

There is no free church called the Light of Life, at least not as far as I am aware at the time of writing.

I have provided the recycling center in Staa with both an office and CCTV cameras.

I take full responsibility for any errors in the narrative.

Åre residents Ulrika Bauman Edblad and Anders Edblad have been extremely helpful during my journey. A big thank-you to both of you. I would also like to thank District Police Officer Victoria Norman, who generously shared her expertise and knowledge, as well as Mikael Nordqvist at Ocke Trädgård, who told me about the flora and fauna of Jämtland.

Thanks also to Detective Inspector Rolf Hansson, who has once again answered countless questions on police work. My dear friends Anette Brifalk, Helen Duphorn, and Madeleine Lyrvall, as well as Gunilla Petersson, have all read and commented on the manuscript during the writing process. Thank you so much!

Hidden in Shadows is without doubt the result of superb teamwork. Warm thanks to my fantastic publisher, Ebba Östberg, and to my good friend and development editor, John Häggblom. Without my incredibly committed editor, Lisa Jonasdotter Nilsson, this book would have been nowhere near as good. Many, many thanks, Lisa!

I also love working with the superprofessional Sofia Heurlin and everyone else at Forum.

Anna Frankl, you are a wonderful agent who is always there for me!

I also want to thank my loyal naprapathic therapist, Tommy Lundqvist, who took care of me in Sandhamn all summer when I was editing around the clock to meet my deadline. My shoulders and neck would have collapsed long ago without your skills.

Jens Rennstam's book *Sexuality in the Swedish Police: From Gay Jokes to Pride Parades* was extremely useful for my portrayal of Anton.

The lines at the end of the novel are my own free interpretation of Leo Robin's wonderful lyrics to "If I Should Lose You."

Finally—thank you to my darling Lennart for reading the manuscript so meticulously and boosting my self-esteem when I was beset by severe doubts toward the end of the editing process.

Camilla, Alexander, and Leo—you are the light of my life.

Åre, September 1, 2021
Viveca Sten

ABOUT THE AUTHOR

Photo © 2021 Niclas Vestefjell

Viveca Sten is the author of *Hidden in Snow* and *Hidden in Shadows* in the Åre Murders series and the #1 internationally bestselling Sandhamn Murders series, which includes *Buried in Secret, In Bad Company, In the Name of Truth, In the Shadow of Power, In Harm's Way, In the Heat of the Moment, Tonight You're Dead, Guiltless, Closed Circles*, and *Still Waters*. Since 2008, the series has sold close to eight million copies, establishing her as one of Scandinavia's most popular authors. Set on the island of Sandhamn, the novels have been adapted into a Swedish-language TV series shot on location and seen by almost one hundred million viewers around the world. Viveca lives in Stockholm with her husband and three children, but she alternates between Sandhamn in the summer and Åre in the winter, where she writes and vacations with her family. For more information, visit www.vivecasten.com.

ABOUT THE TRANSLATOR

Marlaine Delargy lives in Shropshire in the United Kingdom. She studied Swedish and German at the University of Wales, Aberystwyth, and taught German for almost twenty years. She has translated novels by many authors, including Kristina Ohlsson; Helene Tursten; John Ajvide Lindqvist; Therese Bohman; Theodor Kallifatides; Johan Theorin, with whom she won the Crime Writers' Association International Dagger in 2010; and Henning Mankell, with whom she won the Crime Writers' Association International Dagger in 2018. Marlaine has also translated nine books in Viveca Sten's Sandhamn Murders series and *Hidden in Snow*, the first book in the Åre Murders series.